SHAMROCK ALLEY

A NOVEL

RONALD DAMIEN MALFI

Medallion Press, Inc.
Printed in USA

SHAMROCK ALLEY

A NOVEL

RONALD DAMIEN MALFI

DEDICATION:

For Dad, who attended every basketball game,
swim meet, and karate tournament . . .
and still found time to save the world.

Published 2009 by Medallion Press, Inc.

The MEDALLION PRESS LOGO
is a registered trademark of Medallion Press, Inc.

Cover Design by Michael Kellner
Book Design by James Tampa

Printed in the United States of America
Typeset in Baskerville

Library of Congress Cataloging-in-Publication Data

Malfi, Ronald Damien.
Shamrock Alley / Ronald Damien Malfi.
p. cm.
ISBN 978-1-933836-94-2
I. Title.
PS3613.A4355S53 2009
813'.6--dc22

2009005944

10 9 8 7 6 5 4 3 2 1
First Edition

ACKNOWLEDGMENTS:

The following is based on a true story. Though I have taken some liberty with certain names and events herein, the characters of Mickey O'Shay and Jimmy Kahn are quite real. The Irish gang of which they were the ringleaders terrorized Hell's Kitchen for many years, to the point where even the sheer mention of their names caused doors to be bolted and prayers to be prayed. The following is the story of the young Secret Service agent who managed to infiltrate their organization in hopes of putting an end to their ghastly reign of terror.

That agent was my father.

NOVEMBER

CHAPTER ONE

BENEATH A SWELL OF DANCE-FLOOR LIGHTS, John Mavio dropped the zipper of his leather jacket and shook his greasy hair down over his eyes. Industrial music shook the walls. Before him, a mob of dancers jerked and flailed like corks tied to elastic strings, their bodies intermittently bleached by harsh neon lights and shrouded by dense smoke. His mouth was dry, tasted sour.

To his left, Jeffrey Clay snorted and offered him a cigarette.

"No, thanks."

"You see some of these bitches?" Clay was young, maybe in his early twenties, but his creased face and nicotine complexion made him appear ageless. A wedge of wriggling, leather-clad women by the bar had collected his attention; Clay eyed them now like a hungry wolf. "Every goddamn weekend. You been to the Lavender Room? Just like this, only better." Clay whistled. "I mean, you see these women or what?"

John pitched forward off the wall and caught a glimpse of Tressa Walker over Clay's shoulder. Amphetamine-thin, her skin ghostly white, Tressa Walker caught his eyes and immediately looked away. On a riser above her head and sealed in a glass booth, a disc jockey wearing a wool cap spun records. Studio lights reflected off the glass.

John shifted his weight. He was of average height, well-built, his features predominantly Mediterranean. He felt out of place in the club. "What's taking so long? Where's your boy?"

Clay lit his cigarette, inhaled. As if tasting something bitter, his lips drew into a frown. Still watching the girls, Clay said, "Chill out. It's all about good times—live in the moment. This is all for the fuckin' moment, you know what I mean? No rush."

"There's people I need to get back to."

"It's all right, man."

"This guy, he's good?"

"We go back a long time, me and Frankie. Grew up in the same neighborhood, smelled the same shit."

"I hate these places."

"So drink something, screw somebody," Clay said.

"Christ, no more beer."

"Cigarette?"

"Give it to me."

Clay took one last drag and passed the cigarette to John. Behind Clay, Tressa Walker looked desperate to disappear. She was twenty-two and had a kid but didn't look like anybody's mother. Her eyes narrowed and her lips pressed tightly together, she stared into the sea of dancers, her thoughts nearly as loud as the music. She appeared to recognize someone in the crowd and brought her head up. She touched Clay on the shoulder. "Jeffrey," she said.

Jeffrey Clay rolled his head, tendons popping in his neck, and grinned. Two men wove their way through the crowd. The lead man, dressed in a tight-fitting Italian shirt and pressed slacks, clapped Clay on the shoulder, whispered something into the crook of his neck. They both laughed. John recognized him as Francis Deveneau. Deveneau's taller companion, decked in leather pants and silver contact lenses, his face a festival of complex piercing, stood off to one side, eyeing John with obvious disapproval. His skin was pale enough to look translucent beneath the club's lights.

"This is Johnny," Clay told Deveneau.

"Bonsoir, Johnny," Deveneau said and saluted. His eyes were bloodshot and sloppy. "Francis Deveneau."

John nodded. "This your place?"

Deveneau bobbed his head, struggled with a lopsided grin. He was tapping one foot to the music. "Some of it. Just the good parts. You like it?"

"Some of it," John said. "The good parts."

Deveneau laughed. "You ate?"

"I'm good."

"Jeffrey's been picking up the tab?"

"He's a cheap bastard," John said, and Francis Deveneau laughed again. Behind him, his paleface companion shifted impatiently.

"Come on," Deveneau said, "it's all good tonight. Whatever you want on the house." He turned his attention to Tressa Walker, who offered him a nervous smile, which Deveneau returned. His teeth looked dry and lackluster. "How you doing, babe?" He was a slender guy with hands as bony as hooves. "You been all right?"

"Yes." It was the most she'd said all evening.

"You've eaten?"

"I'm hungry."

"This place," Francis said, "has terrible food. I'm not kidding. Can't help it." He glanced at John. Winked. "Horrendous, *sans doute.* After," he told the girl. "After. Someplace nice downtown. Guspacco's, maybe." He looked back at John. "So you went to school with my girl?"

"For a little while. Before I dropped out."

"You two dated?"

John smirked. "Nope."

"She's a good one," Deveneau said.

Tressa took Deveneau's arm. "He was older," she said.

"Different grade."

Deveneau smiled. Clapped his hands together. "Big man on campus."

"Not exactly," John said. "More like no man on campus."

Clay pushed his way between them. "Come on," he said, and wrapped his fingers around John's forearm.

They maneuvered through a maze of grinding hips and swinging arms. The albino stuck to John like a dog, never saying a word, his eyes viciously sober. Only occasionally did he glance at Tressa, though never when the girl was looking in his direction. He looked at John, too, and with evident distrust. The music drummed on, programmed as one continuous loop. John spat on the floor and tossed his cigarette just as he and Clay followed Francis Deveneau, Tressa, and the albino down a flight of iron stairs. A corrugated concrete hallway closed around them. Metal creels hung from chains in the ceiling, adorned with flickering candles. As they sank deeper into the ground, the odor of sweat and mildew and incense grew strong.

"Frankenstein's castle," John muttered, and Clay snickered.

The stairwell emptied into a dimly lit corridor that seemed to lead everywhere and nowhere at the same time. They moved across the corridor and entered a large barroom. Red velvet couches, damp with rot and threadbare with age, were staggered like grazing cattle. A zinc bar clung to the far wall, collecting drinkers like fruit flies. Their shadows loomed large and distorted against every wall. A string of Christmas lights sagged against the wall behind the bar, most likely a year-round staple.

"They did a hell of a job down here," Deveneau said. "Whole place was filled with sewage, maybe—what? Ten months ago, Jeffrey? Busted lines, rotted pipes. Christ knows. Rats the size of Thanksgiving turkeys watching you from every corner, hearing their little feet shifting through the muck. I been trying to talk Eddie into turning this place into some sort of underground casino. Like you see in the movies. Some fuckin' tables, wheels, dice—the whole nine."

"And when the cops come, he's gonna spin the tables around and they'll disappear behind the walls like in them gangster movies," Jeffrey Clay said, chuckling.

Deveneau shook his head and glanced at his friend from over his shoulder. "You always gotta be a wise guy?"

But Clay was on a roll. "There'll be a full bar on the other side, and some hot barmaid mixin' drinks, real James Bond shit . . ."

John managed a grin. He was becoming more and more restless, charged by the stress of inactivity. The few drinks he'd had earlier were hitting him hard, and he suddenly felt as though he were moving two steps behind himself.

"You can see it though, can't you?" Deveneau paused suddenly, causing the rest of them to catch their feet. He looked up, looked around. His left eyelid twitched. Some of the people at the bar glanced in his direction. "Lights and buzzers, heavy in cigar smoke. Air stinking of alcohol and cheap perfume. Breathe it in, man. All of it. All of it." Deveneau shook his head. "Better than the goddamn swingers club Eddie wants to stick down here." He jerked a finger in John's direction. "You got your money?"

"You got my end?"

"Goddamn," Deveneau said, grinning. From behind him, a number of middle-aged, overweight men pushed out of the darkness surrounded by a group of young girls carrying tropical drinks. A door must have opened somewhere; music was suddenly audible. Someone at the bar laughed too loudly. As the men and women passed, the vague, intermingled aroma of sweat and marijuana followed them. Deveneau's albino companion shifted to let them pass, bumping John in the process. John felt the man's hand brush against his hip.

"You curious about something, powder?"

The albino said nothing. At this proximity, John could smell him: a conglomeration of hair grease, fluoride, and ammonia. There was a faint scar the shape of a comma at the corner of his mouth, pink and raw-looking.

The passing wave of tension did not vex Francis Deveneau. "Should we get a drink? Let's get a drink."

"I've got some other business to take care of," John said. "Besides, one more drink and I'll never find my car."

"Yeah, Frank," Clay intervened, "let's just do it. Johnny-cakes don't seem too social tonight."

Deveneau kissed Tressa on the cheek and ushered her toward a small doorway beside the bar. John followed, aware that the albino was directly behind him; he could feel his shadow pressing heavy against his back.

Francis Deveneau laughed at something the bartender said while absently swatting away a fly with his right hand. Tressa shifted within the fold of Deveneau's arm, caught John's eyes, and quickly looked away.

Someone screamed. And then there was the sound of a dozen muted reports going off at once: rushing feet. Or maybe it all happened at the same time—the scream, the footfalls, the breaking of glass behind the bar, the swarming of indecipherable shadows: coming together, dispersing, coming together, dispersing. There was too much noise for him to pick out distinct, individual sounds—words; commands—but his eyes assessed the room quickly, processed the information, told him something had gone terribly wrong.

"Police!" A flood of blue nylon jackets spilled into the room, fanned out along the walls, dipping into the nooks and shadows. A table was quickly overturned. Then another. Then one of the mildewed sofas. People scattered. "Freeze! Freeze! Police!" They struck like insects in a swarm, immediate and unified, only to disperse at the last moment and scatter like fractured light.

"Freeze, goddamn it!"

"Police! Nobody move!"

John hit the wall as if struck by a passing locomotive and wasted no time gathering his legs up around his body and rolling behind the corner edge of the bar. His head struck the side of the bar and bright, oily spirals exploded behind his eyelids. Legs flitted past him; a barstool crashed to the floor. Breathing heavy, his throat suddenly burned. Something flailed beside him. It was Jeffrey Clay, the color abruptly drained from his face, his eyes bugging out to the size of chicken eggs. Clay fumbled with a .38, juggled it as if unaccustomed to its weight and texture.

He waved a hand at Clay. "Shit," he hissed through clenched teeth. "Shit, Jeffrey!"

Jeffrey Clay did not hear him.

They were pegged behind the bar and against the wall. One of the officers shouted for them to stand, and no one moved. The room thundered like a series of amplified heartbeats. Frantically, John surveyed his immediate area for any sign of Francis Deveneau. At first he didn't see him, but then caught a glimpse of the man edging back across the floor on his hands and knees, his face twisted, his eyes darting. He was crawling backward toward a darkened room. Their eyes met briefly and locked.

Tressa Walker had pressed herself against the doorframe behind the bar, her pale, slender arms wrapped tight around her knees. She was visibly shaking; John thought he could almost hear the sound of her head thudding against the wall, her teeth rattling in her skull . . .

"Stand up!" one of the cops shouted. The voice was too close. John could sense their presence all around him, thick like humidity. The walls vibrated. "Stand up *slow!*"

John slid himself against the wall beside Clay. The guy was shaking. He pushed his hand against Clay's gun. "Chill out," he half-whispered. "Chill out. You're gonna blow your own goddamn foot off. Give me the gun."

Clay didn't respond.

"Jeffrey . . ." He closed his fingers around the grip of Clay's gun, slid his index finger behind the trigger. "Give it to me . . ."

Clay snapped from his stupor and jerked the gun away. He was struggling with quick, gasping breaths.

"This is bullshit." The voice sounded oddly composed. John turned and saw the albino creeping along the floor behind the bar. "This is some shit." The albino pushed his way in front of Francis Deveneau, his knee striking a bottle of whiskey and sending it in revolutions across the floor. Beside John, Clay leaned his head against the wall and squeezed his eyes shut.

"We got guns!" Clay shouted, his voice breaking.

"Put them down, and stand up!" one of the cops responded.

Clay shook his head, eyes still shut. He chewed at his lower lip. Opened his eyes. "Don't fucking move!" he shouted, more forceful this time. "None of you fucking move! Just stay the hell where you are!"

The albino's face was inches from Deveneau's. He was irate. A purple vein throbbed at his temple; cords stood out in his neck, thick as elevator cables. One white hand shot out and grabbed Deveneau's collar, shook him, slammed his head against the wall.

"You see this? This fucking *mess?*" He relinquished Deveneau with a single shove and Deveneau's head rebounded off the wall. "What did I tell you? What did I say from the beginning? What—" And his hand shot out again, this time grabbing Tressa by the hair, yanking her across the floor. "You see this? You see it?"

From the other side of the bar: a smattering of footsteps. In an apprehensive burst, Jeffrey Clay shouted at the cops to stop moving, stop moving, stop goddamn moving, couldn't they understand English?

The albino gave Tressa's hair another yank, and the girl shrieked. John heard Clay curse under his breath. The albino righted the girl against his chest, wrapped a pale arm around her neck. Tressa groaned.

"I'm on fucking *probation,*" he said to Deveneau. "You insist on dragging this bitch around and you don't know who she tips off, where she goes shootin' her mouth off! *And now this?*" He drove a fist into Deveneau's face. *"What did I tell you about her?* What did I say? Son of a bitch, we've been *through* this! Didn't I say she's been talkin' to the cops? Didn't I say she was trash, she was goddamn—"

In one fluid motion, the albino withdrew a handgun from the waistband of his pants, swung it around, and pressed the barrel to Tressa's head. His elbow struck a broom that, in turn, struck a tortoiseshell mirror above the bar. The mirror swiveled and repositioned itself, and in an instant John could see a number of police officers, guns drawn, legs spread, hovering just a few feet beyond the bar in its reflection. They were crude renditions of people: no faces, no details. Just guns with legs.

The albino squeezed the girl's neck, pushed the gun hard against her temple. His face had flushed red, had erupted into colorful magnolia blossoms.

It was as if some merciful and divine being suddenly reached out and turned the dial to slow. The albino—the gun—the entire room—became suddenly magnified. And in his mind's eye, John could see the hammer being pulled back, could see that pale, slender finger press back on the trigger, could see the slow revolution of the chamber as a fresh round positioned itself . . .

John fired two shots from his own gun buried deep within the pocket of his leather coat. The first shot hit the albino in the forehead, killing him with an almost bloodless vigilance. The albino's face remained expressionless. Only his right arm jerked, the fingers tensing on the trigger of his weapon. An arbitrary shot exploded and ricocheted off the ceiling. The albino fell backward like a piece of driftwood. John's second shot missed completely and shattered a collection of half-empty liquor bottles beneath the bar.

The police began shooting, returning the fire. John flinched, ducked, grabbed Tressa, and pushed her face against the dirty floor. Above their heads, slugs slammed into the wall, bursting bottles and splintering wood. The enormous wall mirror that ran the length of the bar shattered into a blizzard of knifelike shards of glass. Beneath him, the girl struggled to free herself and sit up. He kept one hand against the top of her head, restricting her movement. One of her arms swung up and cracked him against the side of the face, blurring his vision.

"Here, here!" Deveneau shouted at him, motioning for them to take cover behind him in the darkened room. He, too, was now fumbling with a handgun, sliding rounds into the chamber. "Move it!"

Jeffrey Clay, his face now pinched down the middle, his eyes exaggerated a dozen times over, pushed himself from the wall and staggered to his feet. He held his .38 out with a straight arm, his body half-bent at the shoulders, and screamed loud enough to rupture his throat. In constant motion, like a carnival target on a moving track, Clay stumbled the length of the bar and unloaded his gun in a series of sharp cracks. Flame licked from the muzzle. He fired quickly and perhaps even managed to empty the gun before he was hit. The first slug took him in the shoulder, two more in the chest, one clipped his right cheek . . . then it all went down too quickly for John to make heads or tails. Jeffrey Clay jerked spastically, pitched forward, and struck the top of the bar like a wet sack of flour. He slid and dropped, staggered, collapsed to the floor. His face had gone powder-white, speckled with the brilliant red of blood, like some piece of postmodern art, and he coughed wetly deep in his throat. Blood frothed from his lips.

From there, everything exploded. There was no order, only chaos . . . like so many pieces of a great jigsaw puzzle arbitrarily scattered across the floor of an otherwise empty room.

He heard sudden movement from across the room, followed by the unmistakable *chuck-chuck-chuck!* of spent cartridges being discarded. Someone was shrieking. John felt a hand grab his shirt collar. He turned and faced Deveneau, who exhaled sour breath into his face. John withdrew his own gun from his leather jacket, the barrel still smoking.

"You said this shit hole was safe," he breathed. "What happened?"

"Stick close to me," Deveneau said. "Come on. Quick." And he was already up on his feet and crouch-walking through the darkness of the adjoining room. John caught the feeble outline of Tressa being raised and pushed forward.

He followed them into the darkness, his heart rattling in his chest. In the room, their breathing was amplified. Their footfalls echoed. John whispered to Deveneau, and the sound of his voice sustained for several seconds. The room was bigger than he'd initially thought. No, not a room—the back opened up and split off into a series of narrow, cylindrical tunnels.

"This way," he heard Deveneau mutter.

Behind him, he could hear the distant but fast approaching sounds of the police—their voices and heavy feet. The only other sounds audible were the crunch of his own shoes on the crumbling cement floor, Tressa's soft moaning, and the almost meditative hiss of running water whispering through the walls all around them.

"Where are we going?" he half-whispered. Deveneau and the girl were some distance ahead of him.

"Out," Deveneau's voice floated back to him.

He heard Tressa groan louder. Something wet fell into his face, his eyes, and he stumbled and ran himself along the cold, cinderblock wall. His feet splashed through icy puddles.

"Can't see—"

They rounded a turn and paused, catching their breath beneath grated light. John looked up and saw what appeared to be a rectangular iron sewer grate roughly fifteen feet above their heads. Water splashed down from it and collected in pools at their feet. Curved metal rungs rose up the side of the wall and led to the surface.

"That the street?"

Deveneau gripped one of the rungs. Runoff splashed across his face and down his back, soaking his shirt. His skin showed through. "Yeah," Deveneau said, nearly out of breath. "Back alley. I'll go first and remove the grate. Send her up next; then you go."

"Move it." He could hear muffled sounds echoing through the tunnels now. "They're coming."

Deveneau climbed the rungs quickly. It took him only a few seconds to reach the top. Water from the street above pattered against his face, his hands, his shoulders. He reached out with one hand and grabbed one of the grate's bars. His hand shook and he muttered something to himself, slid the palm of his hand down his right pant leg, and grabbed the bar again. After a few forceful pushes, the grate came loose, scraping along the rectangular concrete rim.

John grabbed Tressa's arm, urged her toward the iron rungs. She looked at him, a mixture of confusion and urgency on her face.

He nodded. "Go. Now."

She paused, and for a moment he thought her body had simply shut down. Then she turned, grabbed one of the rungs with two hands, and hoisted herself off the ground. Above, Deveneau had slid the grate aside and climbed out onto the street. The silhouette of his head briefly blotted out the sodium lights from the street.

John began to climb as soon as Tressa was out of his way. Behind him, he could clearly hear feet crashing through puddles.

Tressa reached the opening, and Deveneau hoisted her out onto the street. John hit the opening a second later, scrambling for a handhold. Deveneau grabbed his wrist, jerked him upward, then grabbed his other wrist. He scrambled out of the ground and was struck by the cold night air and the overwhelming stink of the East River. They were in an alley between the club and a decrepit tenement, countless reams of trash bags and discarded cardboard boxes positioned in a metropolis of swill all around them.

His head was spinning as he uttered, "They're still coming."

"Christ." Deveneau bent and slid the grate back into place. His hands were shaking badly now.

John spotted a large dumpster on wheels against the side of the tenement. He rushed to it, calling for Deveneau to help him without looking back. They grabbed either end of the dumpster, shook it. It was full and heavy, and the sound of rats buried deep inside caused Deveneau to jump back and utter a pathetic laugh. With his foot, John popped the wheel locks and they began rolling it with surprisingly little effort. John heard police sirens wailing up the street.

Deveneau uttered another choked laugh. "Goddamn unbelievable." The man's face was torn between a half-grin and the subtle look of fear.

They positioned the dumpster above the grate, and John locked the wheels.

Deveneau finally exploded with laughter. "Son of a bitch!" He punched at the air. "Son of a *bitch!*"

"Come on!" Tressa shouted. The sirens were louder.

Deveneau pushed Tressa and urged her to start running down the alleyway. He paused before following her, acknowledging John with lunatic, enthusiastic eyes. "See you around." Then he took off after his girl, legs pumping through trash bags, his feet crashing through puddles.

John remained standing in the alley, catching his breath, allowing his mind to wind down. *Eleven,* he thought then. *I counted eleven cops when that mirror spun around. How could this have happened here tonight?*

He closed his eyes, shuddered. In his head, all he could hear were the phantom cries from one of the policemen down beneath the club. Looking down, he noticed he was still holding his gun. Absently, he wondered how he'd managed to climb out of the ground and roll the dumpster over the grate with only one free hand.

He heard sirens farther up the street. He could now hear sounds directly below him, too, just beneath the grate. Footsteps in water. People talking. He turned and walked slowly down the alley in the opposite direction of Francis Deveneau and Tressa Walker. He slipped his gun into his jacket, ran his fingers through his wet hair, and stepped out onto the street.

CHAPTER TWO

IT WAS THE SMELL OF FRYING BACON that roused him from sleep.

John rolled over. He could hear grease spitting in a frying pan. Katie was up early as usual, and he rolled casually onto her side of the bed and pressed his face into her pillow. She left behind her the ghost traces of lavender and ginger and the stale-sweet odor of sleep. He inhaled vigorously, then rolled back. There was a tiny, single-paned window across the room, veiled from the outside by a length of fire escape. A glint of sun managed to wink into the room. John winced.

He sat up, abruptly aware of his body. His head was particularly angry. The room appeared to tilt the slightest bit. He paused, hunched over in his underwear, folding his limp hands between his knees and breathing deep breaths. Even his throat hurt. Closing his eyes, rubbing his fingers over the lids, he was aware that he'd dreamt last night . . . though he could only recall flashes of images and feelings—nonsense that may only mean something during the hours of sleep.

A stack of college textbooks sat on the nightstand beside the bed. He thought of his wife at the university. Seated behind one of those uncomfortable wooden desks, the erasable end of her pencil pressed softly to the corner of her mouth . . . maybe her hair pulled back and out of her face. She certainly looked young enough to pass for a regular student—perhaps even a sophomore—and she was also intelligent enough to get by without a struggle. In fact, perhaps the only thing that might possibly set her apart from the other students was her belly—her pregnancy. And in this day and age, he quietly wondered if that would even matter.

Beside the books, slung over the desk chair, was his leather jacket. From where he sat, he could clearly make out what had been the tears caused by the two bullet holes in the right side pocket. While he slept, they had been stitched.

He stood from the bed, and a zigzag bolt of pain shot up from his ankle and coursed through his leg. His right knee looked red and swollen.

With a noticeable limp he crept into the hallway, the sizzle of bacon riding just above the soft lilt of Katie's humming. The hallway was narrow, dark, and cluttered with unopened boxes from the recent move. Peering out from the top of some of the boxes was an assortment of wooden picture frames and ancient photographs—of karate and baseball trophies, of a worn pair of leather ice skates tied together at the laces, of an old sombrero with a green plastic parrot on the brim.

The kitchen at the end of the hall was cramped and ill-lit, with only a single window above the double-basin sink. Katie was examining the uncooperative coffee machine, her body wrapped in a pink cloth robe, the gentle S-curve of her back to him. Coming up behind her, he wrapped his arms around her pregnant belly, buried his face in her hair. He could tell she was smiling.

"Your arms don't make it all the way around anymore."

"I like it," he confessed, rubbing the gentle swell of her belly.

"You like big fat girls?"

"Just you."

"Watch it, buster. You gonna eat anything?"

He shook his head. He was already thinking about last night, and about the confusion that followed his escape through the underground tunnels.

"You should eat," Katie said. She fixed him a plate of bacon, eggs, and toast, and insisted he sit at the table. "You have to go in today?"

He nodded and sat with some difficulty. His knee felt as if it'd been filled with crushed stones. "Yes."

"It's Saturday," she said.

"Hmmm."

Katie had noticed his limp: their eyes had met just at the exact moment he sat down at the table, and John knew his affliction had registered with her. But she didn't say anything. She rarely said anything, rarely asked him about what happened during his long nights working in the dark and the cold. It was a silent pact they'd made once he joined the Secret Service. And in many ways, Katie's sudden interest in earning a college degree, their moving into the new apartment, and even the baby were all just little, menial things—just wallpaper to cover a poorly painted room—in order to keep their marriage and his job separate.

He ate. Through the walls, he could hear the faint drone of someone's stereo. "You got a busy day planned?" he asked Katie.

"Not so much." She ran water from the sink over the frying pan. Steam billowed and hissed. "I'll try and empty the rest of the boxes from the hallway."

"How did we get so much crap?"

"Don't ask me. Most of it's yours. I should really just set it on fire."

"I'll go through it all."

"When?"

"When I have time."

He watched her shuffle from the sink to the refrigerator to the sink again. She was beautiful. Even in the final trimester of her pregnancy she looked almost childishly innocent, naïve even. The sideways glances she would throw him from time to time suggested a certain playfulness only to be admired in a grown woman. She'd somehow grown into absolute purity, with all her half-smiles and casual grazes along parts of his body as they passed each other in a room or the hallway. There was mystique in the way she pulled a curl of hair back behind her ear.

She paused for a moment before the window above the sink, the sunlight striking her in just the right way, and he felt a twang of nostalgia rush through him.

John put his fork down. "What is it?"

"Nausea." She shook her head. "It'll pass."

"You gonna be sick?"

"No, I'm all right."

"Sit down, and stop worrying about dishes and boxes."

"I'm okay." She moved behind him, ran her fingers through his hair while he continued to eat. He could feel her eyes on him, as if she were attempting to wrestle some truth from his skin without his knowledge or assistance. He did not look up at her. With every pause of her fingers in his hair, he felt her concentration grow.

After a while, she said, "Will you see your father today?"

"If I have time."

"You should find the time."

"I want to. We'll see."

"Are you okay?" she said, still running fingers through his hair, her voice a near-whisper now.

"Just tired," he said.

She bent, kissed his cheek. "See your dad," she said.

In the bathroom, he stood for some time before the mirror in his underwear. Twenty-six, with a youthful smile and dark eyes, he possessed the body of a runner, augmented by the well-defined pectoral muscles and biceps of someone passionate about exercise and personal upkeep. He was not a fanatic, though he worked out with some dedication when he found the time. Not very tall, his physique suggested a certain compactness that, in turn, implied a degree of discriminating strength. In his youth he'd been thin and small and, on occasion, he thought he almost caught a glimpse of that child still inside him somewhere, perhaps lingering just beneath the surface of his body.

A faint, puckered scar was visible on his forehead just above his right eye, trickling down from his hairline and quite visible beneath the harsh bathroom lighting.

He showered and dressed quickly. At one point he found himself thinking about his father, and trying to recall the dream from last night, but quickly chased the old man from his mind when he realized what he was doing.

Instead, he focused on the events of last night and, more importantly, on the events to come. He wanted everything as straight as possible in his head before he sat down and said one word to anybody. Thinking of his father only muddled things.

Before leaving, he kissed Katie on the mouth, bent and kissed her belly, and slipped out of the apartment. His wife knew better than to ask what time he'd be home.

Bill Kersh sat on a bench beneath a giant oil painting of two hunting dogs outside the office of Assistant U.S. Attorney Roger Biddleman. Kersh was forty, looked sixty, and smoked like he need not fear death. He sat with his eyes closed, his head back against the alabaster wall, and a pair of headphones over his ears. His shirt was white and wrinkled with one of the buttons undone; his necktie was crooked and spotted with conspicuous burn rings from careless cigarette ash. A heavy, broad-chested Protestant, he was the type of man to ruminate, when left alone, on the intricacies of life and death and all the miserable groaning in between. He found simple pleasure in familiarity and had managed to fashion his personal life in such a way that catered to the predictable. A creature of habit was Bill Kersh.

John approached and sat beside him on the bench. Looking at Kersh's face, the older agent appeared to be in a trance. Eyes still closed, Kersh tapped one of his fingers lightly on the portable tape player that sat in his lap. He smelled faintly of aged tobacco and cheap aftershave lotion.

Without opening his eyes, Kersh said, "Your heartbeat is vibrating through the bench."

"I took the stairs."

Kersh didn't answer, didn't open his eyes. Across from them was the wooden door with the pebbled glass—Biddleman's office. A number of distorted shapes shifted behind the glass.

"Who's in there now?" John asked. He looked at Kersh. "Can you hear me with those things on?"

Kersh sighed and clicked off the tape player. He slid the earphones down around his neck while humming the last few bars of a tune beneath his breath. There was nothing musical about Bill Kersh's humming. He looked John up and down, examining him the way a psychiatrist might take visual inventory of a patient at the first meeting. Bill Kersh was a good man and a talented agent. Though he was older than most of the agents in John's squad, Kersh was seen not as a father figure but, rather, as a jaded recluse with a predilection for the eclectic. His disheveled and awkward presence would have elicited snickers behind his back in a less conscious environment. "You doing all right?"

"I'm fine," John said, looking up at the pebbled glass on the door, "but I think things are gonna change."

"Don't worry about it. How's your dad?"

"Stable."

"All right." Kersh glanced casually down at his fingernails.

He'd chewed them down to the quick. "Katie?"

"She's a trooper."

"Hmmmm." Kersh pushed his head back against the wall. There was a small red nick on his chin where he had cut himself shaving. "These people don't understand what we do. And they don't care to. Don't forget that."

The office door opened, and a pair of suits filed out. They talked in murmurs and acknowledged both John and Bill Kersh through glances from the corners of their eyes. Together, they receded down the hallway, their shoes clacking loudly on the marble floor while their shadows stretched along the wall.

A young woman stepped out of Biddleman's office. "Mr. Biddleman will see you now."

Roger Biddleman's office was spacious and well-furnished, with a wall of windows that overlooked the trinity of One Police Plaza, the Metropolitan Correctional Center, and the gothic steeples of St. Andrews. A number of framed photographs ran along the wood-paneled walls, their glass panes shimmering with the reflection of Manhattan. The carpet was green plush, and the chairs facing Biddleman's desk were upholstered in cordovan leather piped with brass tacks. The entire room smelled of cedar and, faintly, of cigar smoke.

Biddleman stood from behind his desk, nodding at the chairs. He was a tall, narrow-shouldered man with silver-gray eyes and indented temples. He smiled, exposing a perfect row of white, even teeth. "Have a seat."

They sat.

"Roger," Kersh said, folding his hands in his lap.

"Bill." Biddleman eased back in his own chair and massaged his temples. There were dark grooves under his eyes, and a spray of blood vessels was apparent along the extremity of his nose. "I'm not going to stroke you, gentlemen. Last night was a goddamn mess." There were a few papers scattered around Biddleman's desk.

Biddleman shuffled through them now, absently and with one hand, until he selected the one he wanted. "Officer . . . Leland Mackowsky," he read, sounding the name out. He paused and peered at them from above the top of the paper. "Twenty-seven-year-old kid, been with the force three years. He's over at NYU Downtown right now with a shattered collarbone and some massive internal bleeding as a result of last night's shootout. Took a goddamn bullet in the upper chest area, just below his neck. Lucky he didn't lose his face. It's very serious."

"We know," Kersh said. "We spoke with the detectives and the assistant D.A. last night."

"Not to mention the two guys shot and killed behind the bar, John." The attorney's eyes shifted to him. "One of whom you killed." There was disdain in his voice, which John sensed was deliberately obvious. Biddleman's eyes were small and rodent-like, his complexion waxy and pitted. He reminded John of an aged and peeling mannequin. "What the hell happened last night?"

"The cops had been watching Deveneau and his place for a couple of months for narcotics," John said. "They got word the joint was hot, so they hit it. They didn't know we were there, and we didn't know they were coming."

Biddleman drummed his fingers on his desktop. "I think things should have been a little more controlled."

"We're only responsible for ourselves—"

"There should have been better communication, more professionalism displayed. . ."

"Professionalism?" John uttered a laugh. "Come on. You have FBI, DEA, Secret Service, ATF, local cops, transit cops—a million guys with guns and badges trying to lock up the shit. You think we have tea before every operation and discuss it with the world? Shit happens, and last night was just one of those nights."

"I'm not interested in excuses," Biddleman said, "and don't be cavalier with me. We've had this sort of discussion before. You shot and killed someone, then ran away like the criminal you were pretending to be. This isn't a movie set. This is real life, where all your actions have consequences."

John pushed himself back in his chair. He could sense Kersh beside him—an unmoving presence. "I don't need a lecture."

Biddleman sat forward in his chair, his pasty face reflecting in the polished mahogany desktop. "John, you fired the first shot that killed?"

"Yes. He was going to kill the informant. I shot him to save her life."

"Was he going to kill *you?*"

"I don't know what would have happened after he shot her."

"Were you in immediate danger, or were you just pushing your undercover role?"

John felt a burning at the pit of his stomach. For some reason, he thought of his father at that moment: prostrate and unmoving beneath a wall of beeping machinery. "You're out of line," he told Biddleman. "What the hell do you think I am?"

Kersh put up a hand. His voice was steady. "Roger," he said. "Listen, the shooting was justified, you know that. Where are we going with this?"

"We are going nowhere. You agents gave Francis Deveneau a pass. This case is done. No one in my office will touch this thing. John, I personally think you acted out of control, used poor judgment. But that's the Secret Service's problem."

"Jesus . . ."

"Roger," Kersh said, "let's reevaluate this. John's case is still good with Deveneau. We need to flush out his stash of counterfeit, then roll into his supplier. The locals don't have a problem with any of this. The cops and the D.A.'s office said they won't do anything to jeopardize our operation. We're still in."

"I spoke with the D.A.," Biddleman said, his eyes volleying

between them, narrowed and agitated. "Their office is a lot more tolerant than I'm prepared to be."

John locked eyes with the attorney. "Why are you pulling this case?"

"Because you take off through these tunnels while a dozen cops are left to shoot up the place. People are dead, people are injured. Who shot Jeffrey Clay?"

"Clay? He went nuts, started shooting at the cops."

"And now he's dead, too."

"I'm not responsible for the New York Police Department. They can shoot whoever they goddamn want."

"Very intelligent." Biddleman shifted in his chair. "Did it ever occur to you to make your identity clear to the officers, to identify yourself as a Secret Service agent?"

"What?" He sat forward, put a hand on Biddleman's desk. "What the hell was I supposed to do? Stand up, wave my hands, flash my goddamn badge? I'm sitting in the middle of this shit, and you want me to make some damn law enforcement speech?"

"You put other officers at risk by withholding that information. You killed a guy and then ran away. And that's exactly what Deveneau's attorney will say at trial, and the jury will convict us. So it's over. Don't go near Deveneau again, and fuck his counterfeit money. That's all, gentlemen. And I hope I'm very goddamn clear on this."

"You're wrong on this," John said.

"That's all." Both his manicured hands splayed out before him on the desk, Roger Biddleman watched them from beneath his brow and did not move until John and Kersh were up and out of his office.

Outside in the hallway, John kicked the bench. The sound echoed down the hall. "What garbage. Can you believe this?"

"Believe it," Kersh said. He was patting himself down, searching for a cigarette.

"Little worm prick. What about me? So concerned with how things look, the perception, didn't even ask if I'm all right, if I nearly got my head blown off, was I upset, did I shit my pants."

"You're a non-entity. He's an artist—you're a paintbrush. Lose enough hairs or he don't like the feel anymore—he'll toss you and get himself a new one. And remember," Kersh continued, a half-smile tugging at his livery lips, "they went to Harvard, not some state school on an athletic scholarship."

There were high-heeled footsteps moving down the hallway. The attractive young receptionist poked her head around the corner, most likely startled by the sound of the bench being kicked. After a moment, she disappeared again.

"You're full of wisdom this morning," John said after she disappeared. "You must have taken a good dump."

Bill Kersh located his last cigarette and pushed it between his lips. "John," he said, "it was *magnificent.*"

CHAPTER THREE

TWENTY-SIX-YEAR-OLD MICKEY O'SHAY, FIRED up on Thorazine tablets and cocaine, grinned at his reflection in the mirror. For the moment, he was conscious of everything—the ammoniac foulness of the bar's restroom; the cold porcelain sink basin beneath his hands; the spastic pulse in his left eyelid; the vomit at the back of his throat. There was a steady drumming at the base of his skull. He sucked air in between his clenched teeth, grinned wider, spat into the sink.

Winner, he thought, and pushed out the restroom door.

Jimmy Kahn was curled over the gloomiest corner of the bar, a metropolis of empty and half-empty Guinness bottles in ruin before him. Mickey clapped him on the back, straddled a stool while shaking his head.

"I been thinking of this fuckin' song all night," he said, drumming his fingers against the bar. "I know you know it—dum da dum da da dum . . . some shit."

"Have a look," Jimmy said, jerking his head toward the back of the bar.

Mickey turned, saw a spattering of degenerates and hookers, of drunks and underage hoods, and snickered. A young brunette in a flimsy polka-dot dress was laughing with a group of gray-haired men at a table, nodding as if in agreement with the man closest to her. The man lit her cigarette, and Mickey watched her inhale vehemently.

"Fine," Mickey muttered.

"Table by the jukebox," Jimmy said.

"Jukebox," Mickey parroted, turning to look . . . and paused. Still, that drumming slammed at the back of his head, sending bright flashes of color up through his brain. His eyes stung. "Son of a bitch." He pushed the stool out from under him, stood crookedly against the bar. "Son of . . ."

Now Jimmy turned around as well. Slipping a cigarette into his mouth, Jimmy brought one hand up—*slowly*—his forefinger pointing straight into the musty air. "Raymond," he called. "Ray-Ray."

Raymond Selano looked up and froze. The color seemed to drain immediately from his face. For one brief moment, it appeared as though he were about to bolt for the door, then changed his mind at the last second. His eyes, large and brown and wide in disbelief, volleyed between the two men at the bar. Raymond Selano was a scrawny neighborhood punk with an insatiable appetite for petty bullshit—robbery, gambling, assault, anything at all. Like an infectious disease, the kid ran the length of the city, inhabiting dingy bars and clubs from the Upper West Side all the way down to Battery Park.

"Son of a bitch!" Mickey called out again. He rolled his shoulders and sauntered over to Raymond's table. "Where you been, Ray-Ray? You drinkin' alone?" He slapped the palms of his hands down on the tabletop.

"Fellas," Raymond said. He forced a half-smile that came across as a smirk, and dragged his fingers through his greasy hair. "What the hell?"

Jimmy approached, pulled out an empty chair beside Raymond, and dropped himself in it. Compared to Raymond Selano, Mickey thought Jimmy Kahn looked like a prizefighter in a checkered blazer. He chuckled, causing Raymond to shoot an uneasy glance in his direction.

"Ease up, Ray-Ray," Jimmy said. "You got a light?"

Like someone who'd just been struck in the gut by a two-by-four, Raymond took a moment to clear his head before he could react. Absently, he patted down his coat with quaking hands and produced a silver Zippo from a hidden pocket. He flicked it, held it up to Jimmy's smoke, his hands trembling.

Jimmy took a long drag, exhaled a blue cloud to the ceiling. "I said ease up, fella. Don't worry—that twelve hundred's yesterday's news."

"Haven't seen you guys around," Raymond said. There were dark patches beneath his eyes. His chin and the sides of his face were peppered with spider-hair beard stubble. He continuously picked at a red sore at his collarbone below the neckline of his shirt. If he shook any harder, Mickey thought the damn kid's head might roll right off his neck.

"Same goes here," Jimmy said. "You been all right?"

"You look like shit, Ray," Mickey said.

"I been okay."

Jimmy grinned, squeezed Raymond's shoulder. Raymond's eyes twitched, and his head went reflexively back and to one side. "You got something against us, Ray-Ray? You're all tense. See this guy, Mickey?"

"You tense, Ray?"

Compulsively, Raymond began cracking his knuckles. "I want you guys to know," he said, voice cracking, "that I got your money coming. I don't dupe nobody. I just been backed up with some bullshit. Crazy stuff. You know what I'm sayin'? It's just one damn thing after another and before you know it, shit's up to your shoulder blades, you know? You're swimmin' in the stuff."

"Crazy goddamn world," Mickey said.

"It's just, I need to get in touch with a few people, make some calls. It's good, everything's real in-line. Just, you know, wanted you to know that."

"We trust you, kid," Jimmy said. "Forget it. In fact, you can make it up to us tonight. Help out a couple of street thugs like Mickey and me?"

Raymond grinned, now somewhat at ease. His teeth were like busted fence pickets. "Shit," he said, "what you got?"

Jimmy said, "Let's take a ride."

Raymond watched Jimmy rise, watched him crush his cigarette out on the floor, watched him half-walk, half-trot to the bar and knock down the last of his Guinness.

"Got this song in my head," Mickey told Raymond. "Damnedest thing. You know what that's like? You hear it, but you can't think of what it is? Right there. Son of a bitch."

The room seemed to tilt, to spin, to try and shake him off the floor. With one hand, Mickey grabbed the back of a chair, drummed his fingers along it. Looking over his shoulder, he searched for the young girl in the tight polka-dot dress, but she had disappeared. So had the old guy who'd lit her cigarette.

They made it to the Cadillac, although Mickey couldn't recall leaving the bar, and from the back seat he watched the red sodium glare of Manhattan flit past the window, as if in a dream.

Fifteen minutes later and Jimmy was maneuvering the Caddy through a confusion of rundown apartments on Tenth Avenue. It had rained earlier that evening, and now the car crashed through puddles and splashed through ragged dips along the alley. Few lights were on in the windows of these apartments. Time was suddenly an absurdity. Mickey wondered if the eleven o'clock deli was still open.

Brakes squealed. Jimmy pulled the Caddy against one of the tenements, slammed it into park, and hit Raymond with the punchline of some joke he'd been telling. Mickey saw that the clock on the Cadillac's dash read 10:47.

Outside, the air was bitterly cold. Mickey blew plumes of vapor into the air. As if in a parade, the three men pulled their coats closed as they mounted the steps to the rear stoop of one of the apartments. An invisible cat hissed and scurried away through a curtain of metal trash cans. Raymond jumped at the noise, and Jimmy found this hysterical.

"This your place?" Raymond asked no one in particular.

Jimmy rapped both his fists along the door in a circular motion. "Yoo-hoo," he muttered.

After a few seconds, a light came on at the back of the house. Mickey could hear footsteps coming to the door, could see Irish's grizzled form shuffling toward the door through the wire-mesh glass that looked into the kitchen. Bolts snapped and the door creaked open, spilling a soft yellow glow along the wet patio.

"Bastards," Irish muttered, grinning wide enough to split his face in half. Irish was old—late fifties, if Mickey had to guess—and looked like a cement truck fitted with a sleeveless undershirt and tobacco-stained khakis. He had thick, meaty jowls and what looked like a million teeth stuffed into his mouth. His gut was large enough to be obscene.

"What's up, Irish?"

"Jimmy," he said. "Come inside. Cold out there."

They moved into the cramped kitchen and stood around like mopes, their hands stuffed into their coat pockets, until Irish told them to sit inside, relax.

The parlor was dimly lit and cluttered with mismatched junk, presumably accumulated throughout a number of decades. The carpet was thick and kicked up sparks of electricity when Mickey dragged his feet. The entire apartment reeked of spoiled eggs.

"The place isn't too warm," Irish apologized, hitting the refrigerator for some beers. "Old burner. Swear to Christ, nothing works right in this lousy city. If it's not the heater in the winter, it's the goddamn window unit in the middle of summer. Busts my ass."

He distributed the beers around the room. Raymond claimed a chair beside a flickering black-and-white television set. Once seated, he seemed preoccupied with examining the filth on the bottom of his sneaker.

Irish sighed and assaulted his own beer, finishing half the bottle in one tremendous swallow. "And don't get me started on that bitch upstairs and her friggin' cats. I'm tellin' you, boys, you ain't never *seen* so many damn cats. All kinds. Them big fluffy ones and the hairless ones—look like sewer rats. Some of the damn things don't have tails, if you can imagine that."

Jimmy leaned back against the wall, popped the tendons in his back. "You got any food around here?"

"You find it, it's yours," Irish said, finishing his beer.

Jimmy looked at Raymond and held up his own bottle. "You good?"

"I'll do another."

Jimmy flipped his bottle in the air. It spun twice, and he caught it—barely—by the neck as he disappeared into the kitchen.

Irish slipped around a small end table and opened a tarnished pewter box that rested on top of it. "You wanna hit a few lines?"

On Mickey's left, Raymond laughed at something on the television set while wiping saliva from his chapped lips with the sleeve of his coat. "I'm up," Raymond said, sounding a bit more relaxed.

Jimmy returned, his fists loaded with frozen burritos. "Chow's on," he said. Like a knife-thrower in the circus, he began firing the burritos into the air, laughing when Raymond attempted to grab one and nearly fell out of his chair.

"Good stuff here," Irish said, sifting through the little pewter box. He brought what looked like a ring-wrapper from a cigar up to his nose, sniffed it, replaced it inside the box.

Raymond gathered two of the burritos from the floor and examined the packaging. "Damn things are still cold, Jimmy. You ain't heatin' them up?"

"I look like your mommy?" Jimmy said, and produced a .38 from inside his coat. In one fluid motion, he cocked back the hammer, his fingers somehow seemingly unrelated to the expression on his face. He aimed the gun at Raymond.

Raymond uttered a weak laugh, the burritos dropping from his hands and sliding down his jacket into his lap. "Jimmy, what the hell—"

Jimmy Kahn fired two shots in immediate succession. The first one caught Raymond in the chest, jerking the boy back against the chair, his left arm shooting up to his face, his fingers bent into a crooked talon. The second shot caught him in the side of the face, expelling a black gout of blood that splashed against the back of the chair and the alabaster wall beside Raymond's head. A deluge of blood poured from his mouth as he convulsed against the chair, his eyes peeled back into his head, his blood-speckled lip working soundlessly.

"Jesus *Christ!*" Irish shouted, his big hands pressed to either side of his face. "Jesus Christ—in my goddamn *house,* Jimmy?"

One of Raymond's feet snapped out and struck the leg of the small end table, splintering it down the middle and causing the table to topple over. Irish made a noble attempt at rescuing his pewter box, but he was too slow: the box hit the carpet, its lid ricocheting off toward one corner of the room, spilling its contents in a fan of fine powder across the floor.

Raymond's body flailed. Like a sack of wet grain, the kid slid off the front of the chair and hit the floor. A vertical crimson stripe divided the back of the chair into two sections.

Jimmy reloaded the two spent rounds, his teeth chewing at the inside of his right cheek. Mickey watched Jimmy's hands move, watched Irish back up against the side of the wall with a look of absolute disgust on his face. The old man couldn't stop watching as Raymond's spastic leg continued to grind his snort into the carpet.

Jimmy took a step closer to Raymond. He held the gun out at arm's length, slowly rotating his wrist, as if he were having a difficult time deciding which way he liked holding the weapon. He thumbed back the hammer.

"Have some more," he said, and fired three more rounds into Raymond Selano.

Mickey finished his beer and stuffed the empty bottle into the pocket of his peacoat. Like back at the bar, the room began to waver and shift, to expand and deflate . . . as if he were watching it breathe.

"Goddamn," Irish muttered. "Look at this mess."

Jimmy tucked the .38 into the waistband of his pants. He called to Irish without taking his eyes from Raymond's body. "Get some knives and a few plastic bags."

"Goddamn," Irish muttered again. "You bring this shit to my house without tellin' me? You gonna do somethin' like this in my goddamn place, Jimmy, you say somethin'. You don't just do it."

"Plastic trash bags," Jimmy reiterated, "big ones. And a couple of those small sandwich baggie things. I want the hands."

Irritated, Irish shuffled into the kitchen and returned with a cluster of butcher knives and a cylindrical roll of plastic trash bags. He handed the items over to Jimmy, who took them and quickly bent to one knee, grabbed the end of one of the trash bags, and fanned the roll like a magician yanking a tablecloth out from underneath a china dinner setting. A carpet of plastic unraveled the length of the sitting room.

Mickey dropped beside Jimmy, absently scratching at the back of his shaggy head. With little enthusiasm, Mickey removed a slender knife from his coat and jammed it into Raymond's chest.

He winked at Jimmy. "Just makin' sure."

Grinning, Jimmy flicked Mickey's ear and stood. "Help me drag him to the bathroom," he said. "We'll put him in the tub."

Jimmy removed his coat like a surgeon preparing for an operation. Mickey stuffed the collection of butcher knives into his own coat pocket, bent, and grabbed Raymond Selano's hands. With Irish standing in the doorway between the kitchen and the sitting room, the two men carried the kid's body into the bathroom with little difficulty. While he carried the body, his hands slick with Ray-Ray Selano's blood, Mickey finally remembered the song that had been eluding him all evening.

He began to hum.

CHAPTER FOUR

IN THE SOFT RAIN OF MIDDAY, JOHN stood across the street from a group of run-down West Side tenements. The rain helped to calm him. Each time he closed his eyes, he could see the waxy, emotionless face of Roger Biddleman. Even in reflection, Biddleman's forced composure and proctor-like countenance, enshrined in the sanctity of his lacquered office, irritated John to no end. People like Biddleman were an open book, their intentions and motivations so clearly defined that they clouded the air about them like the contrail of a jet plane. And more often than not, their intentions and motivations, John knew, were invariably self-serving.

A taxicab crashed through a puddle beside the curb, and John caught his tired reflection in its passing windows.

Finishing a Styrofoam cup of coffee and shivering against the cold, he crossed Tenth Avenue and passed through a rusted cyclone fence that enclosed, among other things, Tressa Walker's West Side apartment building.

The Secret Service had picked Tressa Walker up roughly two months ago after she'd passed a few phony hundreds at a string of convenience stores around the city. The bills were excellent fakes, and Kersh quickly recognized them from a previous bust, explaining that the printer—some Jew from Queens named Lowenstein—was currently incarcerated. With Tressa's prints on the money, the Service located and detained her for questioning. A search of her vehicle uncovered numerous boxes of Pampers and aspirin, each purchased from a different location with a phony hundred. In her purse, they discovered two more hundreds. A young, frightened junkie with a baby at home, Tressa Walker was quick to give up information. Her boyfriend, Franics Deveneau, had access to the money and had given her a few bills to attract potential customers. The capitalist that she was, Tressa had decided to simply pass the bills herself, pocketing the change from her small purchases. Fearful of what awaited her if she refused to cooperate, she readily agreed to take John into Deveneau's circle.

Tressa's apartment complex was run-down, the brick façade as black as a bruise from numerous fires. He had been here only once before but noticed very little had changed. From behind a chain-link fence, a grouchy Airedale barked at him as he walked by. The noise attracted several pairs of eyes, all of which peered out at him from darkened first-floor windows like the beady eyes of bats from a cave. Above him, a group of messy-looking children sat on a fire escape and watched him the way peasants might watch someone from a faraway land entering their village.

An emergency exit door at the rear of Tressa's building was propped open with a plastic trash receptacle. John stepped over the receptacle and passed into a dark, mildew-rich hallway. The bite of fresh urine struck him. Somewhere far off he could hear a small child crying, some television game show turned up too loud. Tressa Walker lived on the second floor. Though John had been to the building once before, he'd never entered her apartment.

He turned up the stairwell and walked lightly. Graffiti along the stone walls offered advice, such as *phuck off* and *smoke it.* The top of the stairwell faced the door to Tressa's apartment. John knocked once and heard some commotion from inside, but no one came to the door. Casually, he glanced around. The hallway was empty, with the exception of a hungry-looking cat staring at him from its perch on a windowsill.

He knocked again. "Tressa?"

He heard footsteps approach the door, heard a series of bolts turn, and the door cracked open. Wide-eyed Tressa Walker stared at him from the other side of a security chain. She looked distrustful. A single whip of hair curled down over her face, obscuring her left eye. As she began to recognize him, her brow creased and she looked like someone forced to concentrate on too many things at once.

"Uh . . ."

"You alone?" he asked.

Chewing at her lower lip, she nodded, seemed to consider the situation, then undid the chain and let him inside.

"Place is a mess," she said.

The apartment was small and drafty, with only one main living area and a kitchen vestibule as well as a brief corridor that communicated with what was probably a bathroom and bedroom. For the most part, there was no decor—only a conglomeration of junked and salvaged *things:* of splintered furniture and wounded armchairs with springs coiling out like snakes from a den; of crepe garden lanterns, strung together and draped from the ceiling; of mismatched ceramic vases; of dusty record albums fanned out across the carpet; of tiny pictures in wooden frames hanging from the walls, the photographs themselves so small it was impossible to make out any of the faces. Despite the more bizarre artifacts lying around the room—most noticeably, a taxidermic iguana atop an old Zenith—it was these framed pictures that commanded the most attention. It took John a moment to realize why that was: in her own way, those pictures were Tressa Walker's attempt at humanity, at civility. Unlike the ceramic ashtrays and the crepe garden lanterns and the stuffed lizard, those framed pictures were *planned* and were *human.* He, too, had pictures on his walls at home.

"You expecting company?" he asked.

She shook her head and rubbed her left arm slightly before slipping into the kitchen nook, pretending to look busy. Through the single window over the sink, gray daylight cast a dull gloom across a filthy Formica countertop. A light drizzle pattered against the pane. "No."

"Deveneau not around?" He glanced down the hallway, tried to see into the bedroom. The door was closed.

"He's out. Why'd you come here?"

There was a baby's crib in the center of the room, half hidden beneath a swell of unwashed laundry. Like the pictures, this too provided a strangely human touch, though more out of necessity than of want.

"Baby around?"

"Asleep in the other room. So we should be quiet." She crossed the room and gathered some laundry in her arms, clearing a section of sofa. "You can sit."

"I'm okay."

"What is it? Why'd you come here?"

"What's the matter with your arm?"

She looked down at her arm, as if the prominent purple-brown bruise had just now been brought to her attention. It wasn't a drug addict's bruise—she had plenty of those to compare this one to—but rather the sort of bruise inflicted by the wrap of strong fingers around her arm. Someone else's fingers.

"It's nothing," she said. Then to change the subject: "I should thank you for last night. That guy was gonna kill me. I thought I was—" She rolled her shoulders, the events of last night suddenly no big deal. "And then Deveneau—he went ravin' about you after what happened, you know? About how you shot that guy to save my life, then helped us escape."

"I didn't help anybody escape," he said. "I just followed the two of you. I'm not a big fan of getting my head blown off."

"Well, you still killed that guy. I owe you that. So thanks."

He shifted uncomfortably. "I came by to let you know we're dropping the case." There was no need to explain the situation to her, no need to go into detail. Anyway, she wouldn't be interested in such things. They didn't touch her, didn't matter to her, and had nothing to do with her right here, right now.

"What about me?"

"I'm letting you walk," he said. "You and Deveneau."

It took her several beats to find the words, any words. "That's it?" She seemed both relieved and disappointed at the same time, uncertain as to what this truly meant. Absently, she fingered the bruise on her arm; it was the color of an early sunset. "You're just letting me walk?"

"You can tell Deveneau I got hinky after what happened at the club and that I ain't interested in doing business no more."

"Just like that?" Before agreeing to cooperate with the Secret Service, Tressa Walker had been facing what she feared to be some serious jail time. And on top of that, it was also made clear that Child Welfare would be called in to come and take away her baby if she didn't cooperate. Agreeing to take John into Deveneau's circle had afforded her the opportunity to sidestep prison and keep her baby. Now it was evident in her eyes that she did not know what to make of this new information. She blinked twice, quite noticeably, and brushed the comma of hair out of her eyes. "You let me off just like that?"

"Just like that."

"What about our deal?"

"I said I'm letting you slide on this. The whole thing. It's over."

"Then thank you. Again." She moved her pile of laundry to

a different part of the room, desperate to convey a sense of occupation. Her lower lip was being chewed noiselessly—a sign that her mind was reeling.

"Just use your head and clean yourself up. You got a clean slate as of right now, but that don't mean it can't get dirty again real easy."

"Oh, I'm through with it," she said. "I said I was, didn't I? I got a baby to worry about." Her back to him, she fumbled with some plastic baby bottles and carried them to the sink. Lost in concentration, she turned the water on but did not move. "Really, though. Thanks."

"Don't make it be for nothing."

"Right." She turned and dried her hands on a dish towel. "Baby's crying."

"Oh . . ." He stepped toward the door. "I'll go."

Again, she struck him as impossibly young, impossibly naïve. Nothing more than a child.

"Well . . . thank you."

He nodded and slipped out into the hallway.

Manhattan has a way of leading its occupants to certain destinations without said occupants necessarily realizing he or she has been led. This was how John felt when he found himself standing outside NYU Downtown, his father's hospital, later that afternoon.

Inside, nurses filtered in and out of the ICU like women to a confessional—somber and desolate, incapable of or unwilling to meet a stranger's eye. Occasionally, a patient wearing a white paper gown and a lost expression would shuffle down the corridor like someone uncertain of their own destination. Mostly, it was silent.

His father's room was at the end of the hallway, the door closed.

There was a single window beside the door, its blinds drawn. A steel water fountain hung from the wall. He went to it, stared at it for a long time, then bent and drank.

His father. A host of images rushed him—of thoughts and memories, of notions and ideas and complications. For an instant, John almost recalled last night's dream, but it vanished too quickly. His father. Life had thrown the old man a curve and, in doing so, had caused the old man's only child to stumble as well. Standing outside his father's hospital room door now, the hallway so bland and so dry, the sunny slats in the blinds nearly taunting in their proximity, John folded his hands about his chest and leaned against the wall. Stared at the scuffs in the floor tiles. Stared at the wood pattern of the doors along the hallway. Looked up at the light fixtures in the ceiling.

In his mind, he saw the old man as he'd once been—virile and resplendent with strength, alive with a youthfulness that challenged both nature and God. And he had been all of those things not very long ago, which was the most frightening part. In a way, it was not the man's inevitable death that troubled John most; rather, it was the unexpected rapidity with which it was conquering him.

There'd been an old photograph his father had kept on a shelf in the garage when they still lived together in the tiny house in Brooklyn—a photograph of his father in his shiny overalls and fireman helmet, FDNY etched in bold white letters across his broad chest. It was the man in that picture that John always remembered when he thought of his father—a man who never asked for favors, never required the approval of anyone other than himself, whose every move was pre-planned, calculated, and executed to perfection.

A family of two, they shared a home absent of a mother's warmth. Their relationship had been close yet strained, his father inexorably strict. When John had become an agent, his father had showed little enthusiasm. He'd hoped John would have been a lawyer, a doctor—anything better. Not some glorified policeman with a college education.

"Why risk your life when you could have the world?" his father had asked him one evening.

"It's a good job," he'd explained. "This is what I want."

"You have a degree, a college education—"

"Which you need," he'd responded, "to get on the Service."

Unimpressed, his father had waved a hand at him and turned away, mumbling, "You need a college education to take a bullet for the president?"

Now, with one hand, John pushed against his father's hospital door and crept inside the room.

Recumbent and defenseless, almost indistinguishable from the plaster walls and the disposable bedclothes that encased him, the old man slept. His hands lay twisted and gnarled above the white sheet, his knuckles like the turns in a hangman's noose. The skin around his eyes had soured to a dark purple, the eyes themselves sunken into the deep ocular pockets of his skull. He was a child's crude rendition, this old man—his arms riddled with thick blue veins; the honeycombed bulb of his nose slowly receding into his face; the cobweb wisps of angel hair thinned to nonexistence atop his head. A network of broken blood vessels stretched like the roots of an ancient tree across the upper part of his chest. His cheeks had developed a white spray of beard, fine and powder-like. He smelled of medicines and ointments and glucose and, faintly, of urine. Yet, upon closer review, there lingered the underlying presence of Old Spice and Listerine.

Beside his bed on a small fold-out night table were his reading glasses, a few paperback westerns in an oversized font, an iron crucifix, and a gold pocket watch. The watch hadn't been wound in days and had ceased working. Beside the table loomed large, intricate machines and IV drips on steel poles; the catheter tube and bag; a tangle of colored wires leading to a mysterious nowhere; a plastic cylinder that breathed. These things were not silent—they hummed and beeped and buzzed and hissed and rattled. They were, in truth, more alive than the man they supported.

For a long time, John stood by the doorway, taking in the room and its sole occupant with passive detachment. At one point, he considered winding the old man's watch—something about its dormancy irritated him—but found he could not move, could not force his eyes away from the starched topography of his father's bed sheets. That this old man—that his *father*—was here in such a way begged for mourning.

He summoned the visage of his father in a time before the trick of cancer or the magic of death had ever corrupted their lives. He saw him as almost all young boys see their fathers—great and brooding and darkly enigmatic, the possessor of all things strong and powerful, all things superhuman. A small house in a squalid Brooklyn neighborhood with worn carpets and rusted hammers and screwdrivers in every kitchen drawer. A baseball bat and muddy sneakers on the back patio. A motherless home, where the absence of that essential female entity clung like a physical thing to every wall, every bed, every washed and unwashed piece of laundry; where the only evidence of such a woman's existence was a black-and-white photograph at the top of the stairwell, just a few short feet from his own bedroom door. In it, a pale-skinned woman reclined on a hillock of grass in Central Park, a coquettish smile tugging at the corners of her lips. He saw his father coming through the back door and into the kitchen, his face and shirt covered with grime, his boots caked with soot and mud, and as he made himself a fresh pot of coffee, he'd say, "Some fire tonight, Johnny. Flames licked the sky." And John would imagine the flames as tall as skyscrapers bursting through the night in a dazzling display.

The old man stirred.

"Pop," John said.

It took a few moments for the old man's consciousness to take over.

Once his eyes opened, there was a split second of confusion in his stare that was nearly childlike. His rough hands ran along the fabric of the sheet. He looked like someone just brought back to life.

"Pop," he repeated.

"Johnny." The word came out abrasive and uncomfortable, stretched to near incomprehension. The old man ran his tongue out over his cracked lips, priming himself for better articulation. "You're here."

"You feeling all right?" He remained just inside the doorway. With a clammy hand, he pushed his hair from his face.

"Is it late?"

"Late? No, Pop. Do you want something? I can get a nurse."

"No nurse."

"Water?"

"Nothing." His eyes could hardly stay open, an effect of the morphine. "Katie, she's been—"

"She's been here," John said quickly.

"She's been . . . *okay?*" the old man finished.

"Oh, yeah. Yeah, Pop, she's been real good. She's feeling fine."

"That baby's gonna be a boxer."

"That so?"

"Dreamt it two nights in a row. Means *something,* don't it? Big, strong heavyweight. You just wait and see. Come in the goddamn room, John."

He did, moving quickly to the table beside his father's bed. For want of something to occupy himself, John picked up his father's pocket watch and began winding it. This close, he could hear the rasp of the old man's breathing. It was a doomed sound, redolent with the stink of death.

"You're taking care of yourself?"

"Yeah, Pop."

"On the job . . ."

"Yes."

"Ahhh. You don't look so well. You look too tired. I can tell you're not sleeping. Sleep's important. You work crazy hours. It's not healthy. You should sleep more."

"I've been busy at work," John told him. Then regretted it.

"But you should spend time at home. *That's* important."

John set the watch back on the night table. "Katie's been complaining to you about me now?" he half joked.

"She sneaks me in your dinners when you don't come home to eat them. So keep it up then. She's a good cook." The old man smiled, the thin skin at the corners of his eyes split and fissured.

Staring at the crucifix on the night table, John could feel his father's eyes on him. The morphine hadn't numbed all the old man's senses. Again, he felt like a child beneath the storm-cloud parasol that was his father's shadow.

"The baby will be here soon," said his father. There was a certain gravity to his tone now. "You need to think about what you're going to do." After a hesitation, he added, "With your job."

"Pop," he said, rubbing the back of his neck while he craned his head back. "We've been through this . . ."

"What you do . . . it's no way to raise a kid."

"You did it."

"You can do better than me."

"My job's got nothing to do with who I am at home," he said.

Silence fell on the room. John stood there seemingly forever, not saying a word, feeling like the incapable little boy he'd always felt before his father.

"You don't have to come here," his father said after a while, and with so much of his old self that his voice chilled John, "if you're too busy. I understand. These doctors and nurses, they're good here. They keep an eye on me. You don't have to come when you're too busy."

"Don't be ridiculous."

"You know what I mean. You've got things you need to worry about instead of worrying about some old fool in this damn place."

"Stop it."

"I just want you to know I understand."

"Don't be that way. There's nothing to understand," he said. "I wanted to see how you were feeling."

"How I'm feeling . . ." The old man chuckled and wheezed while fanning one skeletal hand above his head, as if to say, *You see these wires, these machines? That, my only son, is how I'm feeling.*

John sighed and slipped his hands into his pockets, took a step away from the bed. "Is there anything I can get you before I go?"

His father watched him with sober eyes. Once, those eyes had been dark brown, almost black. Now they were dull gray, like ash, and seemingly too close together on his face.

"You wound the watch?" the old man asked.

"It's wound."

"Then no," he said, "there's nothing I need."

Later, out in the hallway, John found himself staring out the window through the slits in the blinds. The day had cooled, and the sun had settled behind a stand of buildings off to the west.

He stood, unmoving, for a long time.

CHAPTER FIVE

DETECTIVE SERGEANT DENNIS GLUMLY OF THE NEW York Police Department was nearly killed twice on his way to Pier 76. First, his sedan blew a flat on West 34th Street and as he stepped out of the vehicle to inspect the damage, a taxicab nearly split him in two, swerving at the last possible moment and sparing his life. The wind from the speeding cab caused his jacket to billow and his equilibrium to fail him, sending him reeling back against the hood of his sedan. Taking slow, labored breaths, the detective sergeant righted himself and, knowing very well there was no spare in the sedan's trunk, cursed once under his breath before hailing a cab.

A few minutes later, as the cabdriver was preparing to park off Twelfth Avenue, a rust-colored van slammed into the back of the taxicab, sending Glumly's teeth rattling in his head and causing him to bang his knee smartly against the plastic knob of the manual window roller. The sudden reek of burnt rubber and oil penetrated the cab. Glumly heard the hiss of radiator steam.

"Jesus *Christ,*" he breathed, startled, his mind unable to come up with anything else.

The driver was less confounded. "Sons of bitch!" he shouted out his window.

Dennis Glumly was fifty-one and in good shape. He exercised regularly, ate properly, and took a dump twice a day with the devotion and punctuality of a devout religious fanatic attending Sunday mass. From the cab, he sprinted across the street and headed in the direction of the Hudson River. A native of the city, he barely registered the amphibious, musty stink of the river, and he hurried up to the inland walkway leading toward the piers at a constant runner's pace, his breathing unaffected.

Pier 76 functioned primarily as the city's car tow-away pound. Recently, the city had been discussing the relocation of the pound to a more accessible midtown location to make room for the growing string of high-profile condominiums that had begun creeping up the coast several years ago. As a child, Glumly had exhibited a proclivity for all things large and mechanical, and would spend hours at the piers watching the great ships maneuver in and out of the ports, their hulls dull and iron pitted with protruding bolts as big as a grown man's fist, their wakes white and crisp and frothy. He would try and creep as close as possible to the piers, the pungent stink of fish tremendous in the air, before someone saw him and shouted at him to leave before he got hurt or killed. In all this time, the piers had changed, as had the entire West Side Highway, though there remained an air of nostalgia for him. He was aware of the feeling even now, as an adult and as a cop, searching no longer for great ships and seagoing vessels but for a severed human head.

Brice was the name of the fellow working at the pound who'd discovered the head, roughly thirty minutes ago. A uniformed officer was with him now, as well as a collection of motley roustabouts in soiled overalls and scarves tucked into the collars of their flannel work shirts. A pound attendant in his mid-thirties, James Brice was clear-eyed and lucid, with a rugged complexion, surprisingly nice teeth, and sideburns that dipped down like twin hockey sticks at the lines of his jaw. In another life, Glumly supposed Brice could have been considered movie-star handsome, though after he'd worked so long on the river, the bitter sea air had managed to harden and manipulate his features.

To his cohorts, James Brice spoke of the severed head with great fanfare. "I seen a man dead once, but heads that's on a body don't look the same as heads that's off a body. This one just had some *look*, my God, and I tell you what—whatever the hell's in that river took with it whatever it wanted. Eyes, lips, nose. Gone. Almost didn't look like no head at all, not until I hoisted it up onto the docks to see what the hell it was. But, man, you can't mistake no goddamn head."

"You think the body's down there, too, Brice?" one of the workers asked him.

"Hell," said Brice, "could be *anything* down there—you know what I'm saying? I mean, who even says this is the last head I'll pull outta there? Couple fishin' lines, we maybe pull a whole buncha heads out."

Some men laughed.

The head in question was wrapped in a section of tarpaulin on the floor of the pound's main office. A sallow-looking man named Kroger, introduced to Glumly as the fellow in charge of the pound, stood toward the back of the office, as far away from the misshapen lump on the floor as he could get. Unlike the enthusiasts who had migrated toward James Brice—and Brice himself, for that matter—Kroger looked on the verge of collapse. With his right hand, he supported himself against the office wall, while his left hand fidgeted jerkily with a leather strap that hung from his belt loop. His skin was the color of uncooked fish, and his small, rat-like eyes had to them the irritated squint of a newborn.

"This ain't good," Kroger said upon meeting Dennis Glumly, as if such a declaration warranted reevaluating the entire situation.

A second uniformed officer unwrapped the head for Glumly. Glumly crouched, examined it with a hand to his chin, and, after a moment, whistled.

"Christ in a fedora," he said.

"Somethin', ain't it?" the officer asked for the sake of asking. "The hell you make of this?"

"Well, it's in pretty bad shape. Could have been down there a while."

"Fish got to it."

"Looks like it's male—fella in his forties, maybe. What's this here?" Glumly pointed to a section just above the left temple where the skull had been broken, leaving behind a silver dollar-sized hole in the surface. Behind him, he was aware of Kroger starting to grumble to himself.

"Shit," said the officer. "The fella who dragged the thing out of the river did that . . ."

"Jimmy Brice," volunteered Kroger in a dull voice.

"Said he wasn't sure exactly what it was when he first saw it," the officer continued, "so he used some sort of metal hook on a pole to scoop the head out of the river."

"Oh, for Christ's sake . . ."

"Yeah." The officer almost chuckled.

"You call for divers?"

"No."

"Call for divers."

"You think the body's down there, too?"

Glumly stood, popped his back, and peered out at the river through the grime-smeared windows of the pound office. "Who the hell knows what else is down there," he said.

The officer tossed a corner flap of tarp back over the head and stood. Scratching his brow, he looked in Glumly's direction. "What you got on your mind?" the officer said matter-of-factly.

Glumly just rolled his shoulders.

He didn't tell the officer he was thinking about the severed foot uncovered in a dump last month.

CHAPTER SIX

IN MANY WAYS, COUNTERFEIT MONEY IS LIKE a disease. The bills appear first in an isolated incident, much as a small child in a classroom of perhaps thirty children will all at once come down with the flu. These bills appear throughout the bustle of an enormous city, such as Manhattan, and perhaps fester for some time before they are brought to anyone's attention. Perhaps at a local dive, a cathouse, an expensive Park Avenue boutique. The bills surface like a sneeze and, sometimes, seemingly evaporate into the air before anyone becomes the wiser. Other times, however, the bills—much like a flu bug—become airborne and spread. Soon, that same viral strain crops up in the immune system of every third or fourth child in the classroom—at every third or fourth city block in some major city. A savings and loan bank on West 86th Street becomes wet with fever, and the federal physicians make a house call. And if the strain is particularly virulent, the physicians—the feds—begin keeping an eye out for it. And they see the disease along Lexington Avenue; they study the malignancy beneath the bleeding sodium lights of Wall Street; they follow it through the neon jungle of Times Square; they are aware of cupped hands and coughing fits throughout the seedy alleyways and busted down tenements along Tenth Avenue; prostitutes, all nylon-legged and leopard prints, find themselves infected with it; a shop clerk finds himself feeling and re-feeling the consistency of the disease, holding it up to the light, scrutinizing it, suddenly knowing he is in the presence of some crooked man-made plague. And as with any illness, if left unattended, it is only a matter of time until the entire classroom of children is infected—until the entire city is host to the festering sickness.

And, as is sometimes the case with illnesses, people die.

Within the filth-infested alleyways and poorly lit, subterranean corridors along Manhattan's West Side Highway, one man uttered some nonsensical excuse in a shaking voice and was stabbed in the throat. A second man, a bit quicker than his companion, began to run.

His breath burned his throat. He ran, pushing himself as fast as he could, to beat both God and the devil. At one point he nearly choked on his own laughter, quite certain of his escape. Then he felt something in his right knee snap. With a cry of agony, he collapsed to the trash-littered alleyway, grasping his knee and moaning softly. Hot fluid spread through his leg. Behind him—no, all around him—shadows materialized and solidified, the hint of bodies became actual ones, and footsteps crunched through broken glass along the street.

"You make us run like that, you shit?"

Squirming on the ground, the man closed his eyes, did not open them. He could smell the sewage-stink of the street, could smell the alcohol-rich reek of his pursuers. From behind his eyelids, he watched his friend collapse again, dead in the alley, this time in sickeningly slow motion. The memory less than a minute old, he watched again as the knife blade shot straight out and caught his friend in the throat. There was a dull *plink!* as the tip of the blade pierced through the flesh at the back of his friend's neck and made contact with the concrete wall of the alley behind him . . .

Someone's booted foot stepped on the ground two inches from

his face. He gasped for air, eyes still shut tight.

"You see this? Now I'm outta goddamn breath."

Someone laughed. Nonsensical voices . . .

"What—hey, you got—"

"That's mine—"

"Come the fuck on—"

"Hey, use this, Mickey—"

"I got a hammer—"

"Open your eyes." Someone was very close to his face now. The man could smell his pursuer's breath, could feel its heat pushing against his cheek. "Open your fucking eyes, Harold."

Slowly, Harold did . . . and couldn't make out any details, because his eyes were wet and blurry. There were a few orange streetlights across the street—close, yet at the same time seemingly in another part of the world. These lights smeared across his field of vision like the work of some abstract painter, and were occasionally blotted out as someone stepped in front of them.

"His eyes open?" someone else asked.

"Yeah," muttered the man very close to his face, "they're open. You see me good, Harold? How you doin', my man? You doin' all right? Doin' A-fucking-okay, Harold? Make me goddamn run like that . . ."

Something metal and solid scraped along the ground in front of Harold's face. His vision faded in and out, in sync with the throbbing pain in his right knee. For an instant, his vision cleared up, and he was able to make out what the object was: a serrated knife.

"Mick—" His throat closed up, and he couldn't finish the name.

"I just wanted you to get a good look at what I'm about to use on you, Harold," said the voice just in front of his face—Mickey O'Shay's. "You see what kinda guy I am—lettin' you see it? Big fuckin' knife, Harold, you lousy piece of shit. Heavy one, too. For guys who don't know how to do their fucking jobs."

Then the knife was gone, lifted back off the ground.

There was a moment of absolute, blessed silence. Harold could hear only the rustle of discarded newspapers tumbling down the alley in the wind. In that moment, nothing else existed on the face of the Earth except for him and those tumbling newspapers. Then the hurried movements of feet all around him, and someone grabbed his lower jaw and forced his mouth open. He tried to scream, but no sound came. Fingers pressed painfully into the sides of his face.

"Hold him!" someone shouted. "Get his mouth open!"

He tried moving his head, tried escaping the hand's clasp, but could not. The hand held him down against the pavement. Bright whorls of color exploded beneath his eyelids. Something snaked into his mouth: someone's *fingers.* He gagged, was slapped, and felt the fingers dig down into the soft flesh of his lower jaw. Frantically, he tried to work them out of his mouth with his tongue.

"I want his tongue!"

A sharp, sudden, stinging pain infiltrated his mouth. Liquid flowed freely down his throat, nearly choking him. He felt pain and pressure and the abrupt *chunk!* as the serrated blade of the knife pierced through his tongue and clanged against his teeth. In his agony, he worked his tongue around his mouth to assess the damage . . . only to find that his tongue was no longer there.

"Teach you," said a voice. "School's open."

Then the hammer came down on his injured knee, and an electric charge of pain exploded in his leg. He screamed into the night, his throat full of blood, and the sound of his own agony was suddenly all he could hear, all that existed. Again, behind his clenched eyelids, an image was summoned. Only this was not the image of his friend's death in the alley just moments ago. This image was of a place upstate where his family used to vacation during his childhood, where he and his father would pull large perch from a lake hidden behind a stand of giant firs, and where his mother would sing to them all at night before—

The hammer came down on Harold Corcoran forty-three times that evening.

Yet Harold only lived to feel the eleventh blow.

Special Agent Bill Kersh, who had never married and who had never desired the companionship of a roommate, wholly appreciated the silence of an empty room. When working late, he sooner preferred the company of Charlie Byrd, Benny Goodman, Dave Brubeck, and Billie Holiday to the raucous cacophony of the younger agents. On stormy autumn nights, the soft patter of rain against the office windows soothed him. The look of the darkened cubicles after hours was welcomed, and he would sometimes pause and look up from his work to simply study the emptiness of the office, the way a priest may search for peace in an empty cathedral. On occasion, when he found time to entertain such thoughts, he absently wondered how some of the younger agents viewed him. Not that it really mattered. It was a different generation, after all.

The office was never really asleep. Aside from Kersh, there were always others working the late shift, typing reports, slipping in and out of the office like phantoms through walls. Though he preferred to work alone, their presence did not disturb him; rather, their approaching footfalls in the hallway and their under-the-breath muttering as they stepped from the restroom provided him with some semblance of time and place. There had been times when he'd worked in absolute silence only to find himself staring—quite perplexedly—through the bank of office windows at a rising sun. Watches and clocks served no purpose: easily forgotten, they only ticked away in silence. A living, moving presence, on the other hand, kept him grounded.

He eased back in his desk chair and rubbed his eyes. Before him, the city was black and dotted with colored lights. Glancing at his watch, he saw he only had about ten more minutes before he'd have to head back into the city to meet with Sloopy Black, one of his regular informants, at the Paradise Lounge. Since Biddleman's insistence that Kersh and John sever ties with Deveneau's coterie, Kersh had again immersed himself in his informants and his contacts. Yet despite this revival, Kersh couldn't help but feel that he was looking in the wrong direction. That tonight's meeting with the reptilian-like Sloopy Black would yield no fresh avenues, Kersh had no doubt. He would go merely to get out of the office for a while, to actually walk the streets again like a human being, to smell the air.

Three days since the fiasco at the club, and Francis Deveneau's phony bills were still popping up throughout the city. In the past week alone, the Secret Service had received roughly $100,000 worth of phony notes that were passed in New York, and just about the same amount cropped up in Jersey, Boston, and even Miami. Kersh had a number of the bills laid out across his desk now, most of them individually sealed in plastic bags. The most recent ones were still attached to the description sheets sent over from the various banks that had acquired them throughout the city.

With a sigh, Kersh leaned back in his chair.

Genuine U.S. bills are printed by the Bureau of Printing and Engraving in Washington, D.C. The paper is comprised of 75 percent cotton, 25 percent linen, and contains tiny red and blue fibers throughout. The front of the bill is printed intaglio-style in black ink with green ink used typographically to imprint the note's specific serial numbers and Treasury seal. The back of the bill is printed in green intaglio. Generally, counterfeiters produce their ware by taking photographs of authentic bills, touching up the negatives, and burning the negatives onto plates. Two plates are used for the front—one plate for black ink, one plate for green—and a third is used for the back of the bill. A meticulous counterfeiter may even create two more plates to mimic the strands of blue and red fibers that are embedded in the paper of genuine bills. Due to most counterfeiters' inability to duplicate very minuscule details, quite often the sawtooth points of the Federal Reserve and Treasury seals are slightly uneven and uncharacteristically blunt. However, Deveneau's bills were nearly perfect. The safety features included in the "new money," the redesigned notes, are nearly impossible to duplicate even with the assistance of a competent computer. Yet Deveneau's notes were forgeries of the *old* bills, which made detection that much more difficult. The printer had even used special acid-etched plates to imitate the intaglio printing.

The printer . . .

Charlie Lowenstein.

It was no secret Charlie Lowenstein printed Francis Deveneau's counterfeit money. The Secret Service maintained an extensive catalogue of every phony bill ever to be scrutinized by federal eyes, and when Deveneau's bills had begun popping up like ruptured sores throughout the city several months back, Kersh had recognized them immediately. Lowenstein had been arrested two years earlier during a dispute with a couple of street thugs in Harlem. In Lowenstein's car, the police uncovered roughly $150,000 in counterfeit hundreds. The bills were excellent reproductions, yet they enjoyed no circulation due to Lowenstein's total lack of distribution. A thin, spindly man with ink-blotch eyes, a beaky nose, and a nearly lipless mouth, Charlie Lowenstein was the proprietor of a small printing press in Queens. His talents unbound, he soon found easy money in the printing of counterfeit football and baseball tickets for neighborhood wiseguys. Soon after, he began exercising his talents with the reproduction of U.S. currency. Upon Lowenstein's arrest, the Secret Service assaulted his printing establishment, only to find no trace of evidence whatsoever—much to the Service's indignation. Yet despite the lack of evidence, the Service knew Lowenstein had printed the money, and they had many questions: *Was there any more? Where were the plates? Did he have any partners, any regular customers? How much had he sold?* But just as his stodgy and unaccommodating demeanor dictated, Charlie Lowenstein refused to cooperate with the Secret Service and was subsequently sentenced to five years in prison.

Now, two years later and with Charlie Lowenstein still behind bars, Lowenstein's money had resurfaced. There was no mistake about it—all the incoming bills possessed one of the ten alternate serial numbers found on the counterfeit money taken from Lowenstein's vehicle.

Once the bills began resurfacing, the first thing Kersh did was pay Charlie Lowenstein a visit in his cell up in Connecticut. And just as he'd surmised, Lowenstein refused to cooperate—he merely watched Kersh from across the interview room with dead eyes. Before leaving, Kersh checked the prison's guest log to see who might have been interested in visiting Charlie Lowenstein. Aside from his wife, Ruby, no one had. In a last-ditch effort to catch a break, Kersh had pulled the telephone logs from the Lowenstein residence, on the off chance Ruby Lowenstein had been passing information between her husband and any known criminals. Yet none of the names on the toll reports matched any known street guys. Lowenstein was a dead end.

Kersh stood and popped the tendons in his back. He thought of sleep—thought of his single bed in the remoteness of his apartment, cloaked in darkness, the shade of the tiny window across from his bed drawn against the harsh glare of too many streetlights. Moving across the floor, the carpet crackling with static, he could hear someone running a vacuum down the hallway.

Earlier in the day, a C-note came in with some handwriting scrawled along one side, too small and cramped to read. It was a long shot—what passer would be so careless?—but Kersh brought the note down to the Forensic Services Division nonetheless. The FSD examiners ran the handwriting sample through FISH, the Forensic Information System for Handwriting, to see if they could come up with a match, but it was a futile attempt.

"Just some arbitrary scribble. You were expecting to hit the jackpot?" one of the technicians had asked Kersh nonchalantly.

Kersh only shook his head and scratched at his unshaven throat. He was grasping at straws and suddenly felt very aloof, like a small child abandoned in the middle of a desert wasteland. "You guys have any fresh coffee down here?" was his response.

Now, looking at the money spread out across his desk, he continued to wonder how Francis Deveneau managed to stumble across it. His mind ran over scenarios, too esoteric and bumbling to be spoken aloud.

He shuffled through the description sheets sent in along with the counterfeit money from various banks in the past week: a fake hundred from some expensive downtown boutique; two more from a department store; another hundred from an upscale restaurant. Green and black ink printed on crinkled paper—some folded lengthwise, some dog-eared and damaged, some smeared with grease or frayed at the corners. So many bills . . . so many people to handle it all. There could be hundreds of fingerprints. Pieces of paper. That was all—just *paper.* Paper that ran the world.

What was the solution to the equation? He couldn't see it.

As if startled by some unseen force, Bill Kersh suddenly looked at his watch, grabbed his coat, and shuffled out of the office.

Sloopy Black was the living embodiment of the Paradise Lounge. Like the club, Sloopy was a narrow structure with nondescript features, and his skin was the color of smoke-stained cinderblocks. His eyes were so close together they nearly shared an eye socket, and his teeth—or what remained of them—were encased in so much gold that if a smile was executed, neon lights from the Paradise Lounge flecked off them like stars in some distant galaxy. Around him, like a mist of invisible insects, hung an odor three parts alcohol, one part something frighteningly similar to putrefaction. When he talked, Sloopy was inclined to run his tongue between his thick, livery lips with such feverish rapidity that it wouldn't have surprised Kersh if, on any particular occasion, the man's tongue simply fell out of his face.

Kersh was late meeting Sloopy, and when he first stepped into the Paradise Lounge, he thought perhaps the sleazy creature either had already split or hadn't shown up at all. Then he caught Sloopy's fervent wave from across the club and headed in the man's direction. Of course Sloopy wouldn't skip the meeting; none of Bill Kersh's informants ever skipped their meetings. Meetings made them feel important. Besides, Kersh bought them drinks.

"Hello, Sloopy. Sorry I'm late."

"Awright, Mr. Bill. It's mighty cold outside tonight anyhow." Wasting no time, the incredible flitting tongue made its first appearance of the evening.

"You want a drink?"

"Beer'd be nice." Sloopy was looking over Kersh's shoulder at the Lounge's main stage. A half-nude girl twisted herself between two brass poles. The club was small and oppressively hot, and beads of sweat dotted her body, reflecting the stage lights.

Kersh ordered two beers and did not say anything until they arrived and Sloopy started to drink.

"You remember those counterfeit bills I mentioned to you last week?"

"Oh, sure."

"You heard anything, seen anything since then?"

Sloopy feigned contemplation, contorting the contours of his face until he resembled the twisted crown of a tied garbage bag. "No, no, no cunnerfut."

"Those guys you run with, Sloopy—you think they'd know anything?"

"No, sir. I ast around about it for you. Ain't none of 'em deal in cunnerfut. We all gettin' ourselves cleaned up, don't you know?"

"How's your beer?"

"A little warm. It's good, though. I'll drink it, sure."

Sloopy Black usually slithered around the city with a horde of similar degenerates, eating where he found food, stealing what he could use to get by. The most harmful crimes committed by Sloopy Black and those like him were the crimes they committed against themselves. The morning after a good night, the gray skin of Sloopy's forearms was bruised to a brilliant purple and dotted with needle pricks. On the same mornings, Kersh also noticed a fading resonance in Sloopy's eyes . . . like a roaring fire slowly being starved of oxygen. Yet Sloopy and his ilk were the truest eyes and ears of the city. They crept along the sewer-laden streets on their bellies, sniffing the ground, the air, the people. They knew of murders before bodies were ever discovered; they lived among the refuse of mankind only to become quite adept in recognizing their kin, and found great satisfaction relating such information to anyone who bothered to spare the time and the dollar. Sloopy was no different than any other informant—it was important to listen to what he had to say, lies and all. It was Kersh's job to sift through the muck and compile the salvageable bits of information, no matter how diluted in bullshit they may be.

Kersh tapped a finger on the tabletop to gather Sloopy's attention. "You still got that card with the phone number I gave to you?"

"Sure." Sloopy's eyes lingered on Kersh. "Mr. Bill? You okay?"

From across the room, Kersh watched as the young stripper

swayed over to the edge of the stage, squatted down on her haunches while flipping back her mane of hair, and extended a libidinous smile to the middle-aged gentleman seated at the foot of the stage. She seemed to rise in slow motion, and just as the horizon of her g-string crested the brass railing, the middle-aged man reached out to her, a slender dollar bill folded lengthwise between his fingers, and slipped his stubby fingers beneath the elastic lip of her underwear.

"Mr. Bill—"

Kersh stood up sharply. Without glancing down at Sloopy, he tossed some money on the table and waved his hand at the informant.

"Mr. Bill . . ."

"I'll talk to you later," Kersh said. "I have to go."

He was already moving toward the door.

CHAPTER SEVEN

"What are you doing?" Katie came up behind him and began rubbing his shoulders. The ceiling light threw her shadow across the kitchen table.

"Going over some paperwork," he said. "Is it late?" He was bent over the kitchen table like a monk in prayer. An hour ago, his back had started hurting; now, the pain had grown so dull—or he'd become so accustomed to it—that he hardly felt anything at all.

"Sort of. Do you know what I think?"

"Hmmm?" he responded noncommittally.

"I think we should get some of those fancy Italian fixtures for the bathroom. The real shiny ones."

"What are you talking about?"

"I forget the brand name I'm thinking of . . ."

"I like what's in there already."

"You do not," she said, pushing her mouth against his ear. "You don't even know what's in there. What's in there?"

He shrugged, smiled. Spread out on the table before him were the telephone records for Francis Deveneau's cell phone, going back the past three months. He'd gone over the numbers countless times before, circling and re-circling specific numbers, but he'd been unable to finger another thread, unable to find any other lead.

"They're ugly and pitted," Katie said.

"What are?" He'd hardly heard her.

"The fixtures."

"They're not pitted." Were they? He didn't know.

"And a skylight," Katie continued, whispering in his ear. "A big one, right over the toilet."

"We're on the second floor. You'd be looking at the bathroom in the apartment upstairs."

"I know. Wouldn't that be fun?" She kissed his cheek and examined his face. He felt her eyes on him for what seemed like an eternity, as if she were trying to learn something new about him just by forcing her eyes into his skin. Visual osmosis. He thought of her as the Country Girl just then, as she had been once before, now seemingly so long ago: she the Country Girl from a farm upstate, and he the City Boy who fell hopelessly in love with her. He recalled the first time he'd kissed her and could remember wondering what she thought of him even as their lips were pressed together. Did she like him? Did she *love* him? So long ago, it seemed like someone else's life.

Finally, dejectedly, she stood, the swell of her belly nearly at his eye level. "I'm going to bed," she said, examining her fingernails. "I've got class tomorrow."

"I'll be in soon."

She whispered something in return, but he couldn't make out what it was.

After some time, he pushed himself away from the kitchen table and stared at the walls around him. The place was slowly becoming home. It was rare he found the time to consider things besides his job, but when he did—like now—all the thoughts seemed to rush at him at once, bombarding him until his mind was exhausted by the sheer savagery of the onslaught. He thought of his wife and what it would be like to be a father. Then he thought of his *own* father, and of the cancer that was slowly eating him alive.

There was a small room with an ugly shag carpet at the other end of the hall, mostly crammed with boxes and other displaced items from the move. A sofa was propped up against one wall. An old television set sat on the floor, its screen dusty, with a VCR—a gift from Katie's parents—on the floor next to it. He moved around some the boxes, considering how comfortable it felt to be out of their old apartment.

He examined most of the boxes without opening them, tipping them over to see what was written on their sides. Most of them were filled with Katie's stuff—junk she'd accumulated over time, and more junk accumulated by her parents and passed on to her as if in tradition.

In the bedroom, Katie's breathing was soft and on the surface. He peeled off his clothes and slipped into bed beside her. She muttered something beneath her breath, rolled over, her breathing suddenly deeper.

"You asleep?" he whispered. She was.

When he finally fell asleep, his dreams were a patchwork of irrational sounds and images: off-key overtures and badly performed one-act plays comprised of unskilled actors and illogical symbolism. Somewhere in all the confusion, he dreamt of his father.

When the phone rang later that evening, he awoke slick with sweat, his heart trip-hammering in his chest. Sitting up in the darkness, eyes unfocused, he grabbed his cell phone off the nightstand. Beside him, Katie stirred but did not awake.

"Yeah, hello?"

"Is this John?" A woman's voice.

"Who is this?"

"It's Tressa Walker. John?"

"It's me." It took a moment for the sleep to disperse and for reality to take over. "Tressa, what is it? Is something wrong?"

"I . . ." She was breathing heavy. "John, could you . . . meet me?"

Squinting, he made out the glowing emerald numbers of his alarm clock: 1:15. "Yeah, okay. I'll be at your apartment in—"

"No." Her voice sounded awkward and far away. "Not here. I think . . . I can . . ." She paused, caught her breath. "I know a place. McGinty's, over on Ninth Avenue. It's a small place, stays open real late. I'll go there now. Will you come?"

"McGinty's," he mused. "Yeah, I'll be there."

After he hung up, he found himself crouched over the edge of the bed, his eyes staring off into the darkness of the bedroom while the fingers of his right hand traced the faint scar along his forehead.

McGinty's of Ninth Avenue was dark and bleak and mildly populated. It possessed a dungeon-like quality, with its smoked brick walls and narrow, barred windows. A mahogany bar stood against the wall to the immediate right of the entranceway, behind which a severe-looking, mustachioed bartender cleaned glasses with a towel. To the right of the entranceway, a Naugahyde armchair and a few wooden folding chairs stood beneath framed prints by local painters. The tavern itself was small and boasted only a handful of round, wooden tables. Tonight, only two of these tables were occupied. Two bronze-skinned men in work clothes sat at one, quietly conversing in Spanish over dark beers with thick, foamy heads. They did not look up as John entered the tavern, and they hardly acknowledged the proximity with which John walked around them.

At the second table sat a thin, pale-faced man in a dark overcoat and rimless glasses. He sat *sans* beverage, scribbling something in a spiral-bound notebook with great intensity, his pointed nose only an inch and a half from the page. A constellation of angry scabs dotted the knuckles of his furious writing hand.

Taking such detailed inventory was not a habit he'd acquired from his time on the job. In fact, the tabulation of things—people, places, and all matters of circumstance alike—was a skill he'd honed during his adolescence. The Brooklyn neighborhood where he'd grown up had been no different than an unsupervised home for wayward boys. The gang in which he ran catered to neighborhood troublemakers, abused and neglected street thugs who carried Lucky Strikes in abundance and drank whenever they were able to swipe anything in a bottle. His father's overbearingness had caused him to seek out solace from such gangs and enjoyment from guys who would all later grow up to become gas station attendants, wind up in various prisons, or die young.

Someone shifted in a corner booth toward the rear of the tavern, hidden in shadows. He caught a glimpse of nervous eyes and recognized Tressa Walker. She offered him a wan smile as he approached the booth and sat down.

"Thought you'd changed your mind."

"Traffic on the bridge." He pointed at the collection of empty Guinness bottles that were established in a half-circle in front of the girl. "You looking for a hangover or what?"

She smiled nervously, her eyes dead. From within her coat pocket, she produced a pack of Camels, shook one out, and stuffed the remaining cigarettes back into her coat. She put the smoke between her lips and lit it with the coconut-scented candle from the table. Her first inhalation was exaggerated, and she exhaled with her head nearly all the way back, pale throat exposed. A great plume of blue smoke filtered about her head. The following two inhalations were just the opposite—quick and insincere, as if she were afraid of getting caught doing something wrong and wanted to be done with it.

"What's going on here, Tressa? You look terrible. Something's wrong."

"No, no." She shook her head and actually managed to utter a convincing laugh. "No, it's good. I'm good. I just . . ." Her eyes had yet to meet his. She looked strung-out, wired. John recalled the bruise on her arm from the other day and wondered if Deveneau or one of Deveneau's thug friends had been at her again.

"Just chill out," he soothed, turning and peering about the tavern. The bartender had disappeared, but the other patrons hadn't moved. The scribbler's nose was now just centimeters from his notebook. "Take some deep breaths."

"No, I'm okay. I'm sorry," she said.

"It's all right. Just relax." He was trying to see where the bartender had drifted off to. After a few moments, the bartender returned, his dish towel slung casually over one broad shoulder.

"Yeah." She puffed her smoke, her face cadaverous in the candlelight. "I been thinking about a few things past couple days, you know? Just . . . I don't know . . . going over shit in my head. You don't know, but my life ain't been easy. I mean, I guess you know some of it." She offered a nervous laugh. "I done a lot of things, got involved with a lot of bad guys. I been so fucked up on drugs before and . . . Christ, goddamn it . . ." Her hands trembled, the bones of her knuckles wanting to pushed up through the flesh of her hands. "My father used to kick the shit out of me when I was a kid. He was worthless, a piece of trash. My mother was always drunk, and didn't even know what went on half the time. When I split from there, I just kept doing the same damn things . . . kept getting myself involved with these same damn people . . ." She suddenly looked as though she'd aged twenty years. "Christ, I'm rambling. I'm sorry—I don't know why I started this way."

He just sat in silence, watching her.

"I been arrested a couple of times, been in some pretty bad shape for a while. But now I got that apartment, and it ain't much, but it's mine, and I got it, and I'm payin' rent best I can, and I got my daughter—"

"Don't get upset—"

"Look . . ." And she began rummaging like a madwoman through her purse. "I guess what I'm trying to say is . . . I just . . ." Her chest hitched, and her voice caught in her throat. "Meghan—that's my daughter, Meghan. I have a picture of her here somewhere. You should see her, John—she's the one good thing I got. I ain't all bad, John . . ."

He leaned over the table and pushed his hands down atop her purse, atop her own hands. She froze, looking straight down at the table.

"Take it easy, kid . . ."

Finally, smiling weakly, she just shook her head. "I don't even know why I'm saying all this."

"You in some kind of trouble here, Tressa? Francis been asking questions, giving you a hard time?"

She looked at him then. The faint odor of unwashed hair mingled with cigarette smoke struck him. At that moment, she looked like a portrait of herself painted by an angry and unskilled artist. "I want to help you," she said flatly.

"Me? With what?"

"I know Frankie's source. I know where he gets his money, who gives it to him."

Cigarette smoke, blue and thick, hung in the air between their faces like gauze. There was a wall clock directly above Tressa's head, green shamrocks in place of numbers, its second hand ticking like a pulse.

Tressa leaned across the table, her eyes collective and solemn, her skin gray through the smoke. When she spoke, she did so in a near whisper. "You ever heard of two guys named Mickey O'Shay and Jimmy Kahn?"

"No."

"They're a couple Irish guys from the West Side, run some underground gang. They got their hands in a little bit of everything that goes on around Hell's Kitchen. Frankie got into 'em from a friend of a friend, that sorta thing, and they been feedin' him that fake money for months."

"You said you didn't know his source . . ."

"I lied."

"These guys O'Shay and Kahn—they're printing the stuff?"

"I don't have the dirt on them—only met O'Shay a couple times. Mostly, I'm sayin' this from what I heard from Frankie, and what I heard on the streets. You hang in the right places, and pretty soon you hear somebody whispering their names. They got Hell's Kitchen petrified."

"Over some counterfeit money?"

"You don't know," she insisted. "These guys are like no one you've ever seen."

She paused, perhaps reconsidering her options. It suddenly occurred to John that Deveneau's sources—O'Shay and Kahn—were the reason Tressa's hands were quaking and her knees knocking together beneath the table. He realized something else at that moment as well: that Tressa, too, had taken inventory of the tavern's occupants and had been keeping an eye on them for some time now.

"You want these animals," she continued, "I can get you in. I'll go over Frankie's head, talk directly with Mickey O'Shay. He knows about what happened at the club the other night. I'll tell him you're the guy that was supposed to pick up the dough when everything went to shit and that you ain't interested in dealing with Frankie no more, but still want the bills. But listen—these guys are real sharp. They don't fuck around, in plain English. If they smell something rotten, they'll kill you and me without question."

He shifted in his seat, his eyes watching her eyes watching the tavern. "Why you doing this?"

"I'm still alive because of you," she said. "Plus, you're letting me walk. You're letting me walk and now I still got that apartment, like I said. I still got my daughter. You know what I mean?" She seemed to reflect on something. "I ain't all bad, like I said."

"And you think you can get me into these guys, get me to meet with this guy O'Shay?"

"I'll meet with him, see what he has to say. If he thinks you're a mover and an earner, he'll be interested."

"And this Jimmy Kahn?"

"Never met him. Just know about him from what I heard, from what Frankie says and what I hear around the streets. He and Mickey, they run the show together. They're a death wish. I heard stories about 'em I wouldn't believe about nobody. They're insane. And as far as I know, Kahn tries to keep out of the picture." She produced a second cigarette from her coat and lit it, sucked on it. "There's one thing, though . . ."

"Yeah?"

"I want that witness relocation after this thing's done. Me and my kid—we want outta here. I could never live here again."

"We can get you a change of address . . ."

"Fuck that—you don't know these animals." Her voice rose slightly and cracked. She was conscious of this and quickly brought her voice back down to a whisper. "Change of address won't do no good. I want out of this city altogether. I can put you right in the middle of this insanity, throw you right in with the sharks, but I want to know that you're gonna do right by me and my kid, that you're gonna be able to get us both out."

"Okay, sure. We can work something out."

"Once you meet these guys, you'll understand."

Some realization occurred to her then, and she turned and dug her wallet from her purse. She pulled open the snap that held it closed, shuffled through a wad of receipts, and produced a plastic accordion of small photographs. Tressa delicately laid the accordion out along the table and slid it over in front of John so he could see the photographs.

"There," she said, "that's Meghan."

"She's very cute."

"She was born not breathing and too small. Doctors had to revive her. I thought she was going to die." Tressa Walker smiled to herself. She ran a finger across one of the pictures. "I ain't all bad," she said.

CHAPTER EIGHT

THE NEXT MORNING, JOHN FOUND BILL KERSH tucked away in a dark corner of the Secret Service's library, two levels below ground. It was a small, square, catacomb-like room with poor lighting and no windows. The walls groaned with the weight of numerous leather-bound textbooks and boxes of forgotten files, their musty, ancient smells infused throughout the air. And another smell, this one more foreign and somehow more profound: the sour-sweet stench of age-old sweat, dried and clinging to the air like flapping underwear dangling from a clothesline. Water pipes ran too shallow here, forced up against the walls by incompetent design, interrupting the silence periodically with sounds of running water or toilets flushing upstairs. In the past several years, with the modernization of the government's technology, the Secret Service's underground library had become obsolete. Several times someone had suggested the library—dubbed "the pit" by the new wave of greenhorns—be revamped, that they should tear down the bookshelves to make room for a bank of new computer terminals, though nothing ever came from such suggestions. And although no one could ever say for certain why the library had never been done away with, most would assume it had something to do with man's veneration of all things old and unserviceable—and, fittingly, its only occupants from time to time were those agents themselves who, on occasion, felt a certain kinship with such antiquation.

This morning, Kersh was the pit's only patron. He sat awkwardly in his chair with his back toward the door, curled over a table with his arms folded at his chest. His head was down, his eyes shut, a book opened in front of him. To anyone who happened to glimpse him seated there, Kersh would have appeared deep in concentration. However, in truth, Kersh had been sleeping for several hours, his mind and body detached from time.

"Bill." John came up behind him, pulled out a chair, but did not sit down. Kersh stirred but did not open his eyes. Grinning, John drummed his fists along the tabletop. Kersh jerked, blinked his eyes, and stared confusedly at both John and his surroundings until his senses returned. "You been down here all morning?"

Kersh rubbed his eyes. "Just going over some things."

"Don't you ever go home? It smells like a urinal down here."

"You should smell my apartment."

"Listen," John said, sitting down, "I got a call from Tressa Walker last night, met her down at some bar on the West Side. I don't know what got into her, but she said she wants to help us. She said she's got an in with Deveneau's suppliers, two Irish guys from Hell's Kitchen."

Kersh looked up. He looked very old and pale in the basement lighting. "She told us she didn't know where Deveneau got his money . . ."

"She lied," John said.

"Why the change of heart?" Kersh asked.

"Who knows? Maybe she likes my aftershave."

"Who're the two guys?" Kersh asked.

"Two young guys—Mickey O'Shay and Jimmy Kahn."

"They don't sound familiar. These guys are Deveneau's source?"

"According to Tressa. I ran their names through our files, found nothing on them."

"I'll run the names with NYPD. If they're hanging with Deveneau, they'll have a record. What's the situation?"

"The whole thing seems easy. She said she'd take me in, have me meet with this O'Shay guy."

"Biddleman will be a problem," Kersh said without expression.

"Screw Biddleman."

"John . . ."

"Biddleman said stay away from Deveneau, right? We're not going to Deveneau. We were looking for a break, and we got it. I'm not gonna flush this case twice."

"Biddleman meant Tressa, too."

"Well, he didn't say that to me. Not specifically."

"Just the same, let's keep this quiet until we feel it out. Has the meeting been set yet?"

"Tressa's gotta talk with O'Shay first, see if he'll meet me." He ran his eyes across Kersh's book. "What are you doing?"

For what seemed like a long while, Kersh did not answer. Both his hands were pressed against the wooden tabletop, palms flat. His fingernails were thick and stained a red-yellow from tobacco. Deep bruise-colored grooves under his eyes professed the man's lack of sleep.

He's been up all night, John thought. *Hell, I think he's still wearing the same clothes from yesterday.*

"Come with me," Kersh said finally, his voice dry. "I want to show you something."

Kersh's desk looked like a snow globe someone had turned upside down and shaken. Arbitrary papers littered the surface while a mob of empty and half-empty Styrofoam coffee cups had congregated at one corner of the desk like street hustlers in a bad mood. Flecks of tobacco leaves looked frozen in mid-scatter, like bugs. Numerous cards and plastic bags containing seized counterfeit bills served as the icing on this cake, and as Kersh led John to the desk, Kersh lined up these bills for John to see. John watched his hands work and thought that Bill Kersh's hands actually looked *tired,* if such a thing were possible.

"Sometimes cases are made at the desk and not on the streets, John. Here—this is what came in all last week," Kersh said, still busy organizing the counterfeit money. "You see anything here? Any common denominator?"

"What do you mean?"

"Look at them."

John did. He had seen the counterfeit bills plenty of times before, had gone over and over them just as Kersh had, just as the rest of the squad had. Looking at them again, he could see nothing new.

"I don't get it," he said. "What is it?"

Kersh grabbed one of the bills. Carefully, he refolded it along the lines just as it had been folded in the past. He folded it lengthwise—horizontally—in an accordion-style fold: once in half, then in half again . . .

"What's this look like?" Kersh asked once he'd finished folding the note.

"Huh?"

"Look at it! What's it look like to you?"

"I don't know. It looks like a flattened straw . . ."

"No, no." To John's surprise, Kersh chuckled under his breath and blinked his eyes twice in rapid succession. A fine dark stubble had begun to creep up his jawline. *"Look."* He fluttered the bill in front of John's face. "Who folds bills like this?"

"I don't—" But then it hit him. "Wait . . ."

"Yes." Kersh was smiling, nodding. "Strippers." His smile

grew wider, yet his eyes still looked dead. "This is how a guy folds his money before slipping it into a stripper's g-string."

John plucked the folded bill from Kersh's hands. As if to verify what he already understood, he unfolded the bill, examined the creases, then folded it again.

"See that?" Kersh continued. "It even folds once down the middle, too. Right in half. See?"

"Yeah . . ."

"Smell it."

John brought it up to his nose, inhaled. "Perfume," he said.

"There're five bills that came in last week, all with those same folds. See them? Here—" He pointed to another bill. "Here—" And another. "And here—here. All folded the same way, all smelling like a stripper."

John leaned over the desk, looking more closely at the bills. "Where'd they come from?"

"Just where you'd think a stripper with a lot of money would shop—expensive boutiques, lingerie shops, a fancy restaurant or two. She passed a fake hundred in each place." Kersh shifted through a mess of other papers, produced a folder, opened it. He fished out an index card with another phony hundred stapled to it and handed it to John. "I did some backtracking last night. This one came in this week from First National Bank."

"It's folded the same way."

"Clerk at the bank said a customer named Heidi Carlson deposited it, along with other cash, into her account."

"Let me guess . . ."

"Carlson works weekdays at someplace called the Black Box, near Times Square. Two of our guys rolled into the club after we got the note, asked her about the money—where she got it, could she remember, the whole nine yards. She said she gets paid in cash and assumed that's where it came from. Her boss verified that's how he pays the girls, said he takes in a lot of hundreds every night. Being it was one note and she was depositing it into her own account, our boys figured she got stuck."

"Well unless her boss is slipping her pay into her pants, she's full of shit." He tossed the hundred onto Kersh's desk. "Very good, Billy-boy. I'm impressed. Who were the two guys who went out on this?"

"Steve and Charlie."

"They missed it," John said.

"It's all in the training," Kersh said. His right eyelid twitched, as if wanting to wink. "After work, they hit the gym. Me? I hit the bars."

CHAPTER NINE

THE CLOVERLEAF WAS A SMALL BAR ON the corner of Tenth Avenue and West 57th Street, just a few blocks south of Fordham University. It was a dark, crumbling establishment run by two middle-aged Irish brothers named McKean—one more twisted, hunched, and grotesque than the other. There was a small passageway behind the bar, just before the hallway leading to the storage room that communicated with an underground gambling facility very few people knew existed. Despite its proximity to the university, the Cloverleaf did not cater to students, and on the rare occasion some unwitting underage pupil wandered into the place to see if he could coax a bottle of bourbon from the bartender, one look at the Cloverleaf's clientele turned him quickly around and back out into the street.

There was no sign outside the bar, but Tressa Walker knew the place. She pushed open the front door and slipped inside, thankful to be out of the cold and off the street.

A blast of warm air struck her. Without looking around, she crossed over to the bar and sat on the stool closest to the front door. She kept her eyes trained on the bar, her hands—palms down—directly in front of her. Though she hadn't taken a good look around the place yet, she had seen a number of people stuffed in the dark crevices of the room and was confident of Mickey O'Shay's presence.

As if I could almost smell him. To her astonishment, the thought caused her to break a smile.

The bartender slid in front of her. He was big and muscular with a faint pink scar twisting down the left side of his face. "You need a drink?"

"Guinness."

The bartender filled a glass halfway, waited a full minute as the foam settled, then filled the glass the rest of the way. "Anything else?" he said, resting the glass in front of her.

She touched it with two fingers. It felt warm. "No."

"Kitchen's closed."

"All right."

There was a mirror behind the bar, but it was too cluttered with stickers and decals to give good reflection. Tressa sipped her beer, swallowed mostly foam, and turned her head slightly to glimpse the other occupants scattered about the bar. Trying to seem casual, she scanned faces and finally recognized Mickey O'Shay seated with two other men at a table toward the back. They were in mid-joke, with Mickey setting up the punch line, his hands motioning in front of his face, his eyes animated. She watched the table just long enough to be certain it was him, then turned back to her beer. She was good at reading people, good at comprehending a situation. Though she didn't know Mickey too well, she knew him well enough to know the best way to play him.

Mickey's companions remained at the table for another twenty minutes, laughing at dirty jokes and turning their beer glasses upside down with mechanical exactitude before struggling to their feet and lurching toward the front door. They were older than Mickey and dressed in nondescript brown suits. One of the men leered at her before stumbling out into the street.

Again she turned her head back to the table. Mickey was finishing off his own beer while turning the empty glasses on their sides with his free hand. She watched as he rolled one of the empty glasses back and forth beneath his palm across the top of the table.

Look up, she willed him. *Look at me.*

Mickey emptied his last glass, set it down, and tossed his head back against the wall. He pressed his eyes shut, sucked air through his teeth, and when he opened his eyes again his gaze was leveled on her. She nodded and turned back to her beer with a look of unmistakable disinterest.

"Frankie Deveneau's girl." He was directly behind her a moment later, so close she could feel the warmth of his breath on her neck.

She turned, half-smiled. "I thought that was you, Mickey. Take a seat."

Mickey climbed onto the stool next to her, ordered himself another beer. "The hell you doin' here by yourself?"

"Nothing. Getting some fresh air."

"Oh, yeah?"

"Baby's sick, been keepin' me up. Drivin' me crazy." She watched him rub the sides of his face with filthy hands. His skin looked pale, and his chin was unshaven. With long, flaxen hair and startling blue eyes, Mickey O'Shay was handsome in a universal sense; his features were perfectly symmetrical, his body not muscular but lean, like the body of a long-distance runner. His teeth were small, white, even, and there was something prepubescent about him as well—something Tressa had always noticed but couldn't quite understand. It wasn't any specific thing but, rather, the culmination of his features and mannerisms, she supposed.

"Frank still pissin' his pants over what happened at the club?" Mickey asked, not looking at her.

"I ain't seen him around much," she lied, forcing herself to relax while sipping her beer. It suddenly tasted very bitter.

Mickey chuckled and ran a finger along the rim of his glass.

"Frankie, Frankie, Frankie," he mused.

"We're just lucky the three of us got out without getting jammed up," she added, baiting him with caution.

"That cop die?"

"Huh?"

"That cop that was shot. You heard if he died?"

"No . . . I don't know. I didn't realize it . . ."

"Goddamn it." He laughed again, but there was no emotion in the sound.

If I'm going to do this, she thought, *I'm doing it now.*

"You still looking to move that money?"

Mickey looked at her from the corner of one eye. He was so close she could almost make out her reflection in his pupil. "What?" He said this slowly and under his breath, the way a sinner might begin a confession. "What are you talkin' about?"

"I'm the one who brought that guy to Frankie to buy the stuff."

"So what's that got to do with me?"

"Mickey, Frankie told me who he's getting the money from. I'm his girl."

Mickey looked down at the bar. "Frankie said this guy spooked, took off, that he ain't interested in dealing with him no more . . ."

"He ain't," she said, "so that's why I came here to meet you. After that shit at the club, he don't wanna touch Frank, thinks he's bad luck. Whatever. He ain't scared, but he ain't stupid, either. Come on—Frank's been dealing all kinds of shit outta that club since day one. It was only a matter of time before the place got hit."

"So what about this guy?"

"He still wants to buy."

"How much?"

"Same deal. Hundred grand, same as with Frank. He's anxious. He's got a buyer for it."

"You know him?"

"I brought him to my boyfriend."

Mickey's lips tightened, and a look of distrust flickered behind his blue eyes. A long strand of hair had fallen across his face, dividing his expression. All at once, there appeared to be hundreds of tiny creases beneath Mickey's eyes.

"This guy knows me?" he nearly whispered.

"I didn't drop your name," she said. "He just said he don't want nothing to do with Frank, that he wanted to go directly to Frank's supplier for this thing to happen." She forced a convincing smile that did nothing to soften Mickey's expression. "So here you are—now I'm telling you what he said. Okay?" She winced inwardly—the "okay" made her sound too unsure of herself, too apologetic.

"I don't meet with nobody," Mickey said, turning away from her and swallowing his beer. His boyish profile reminded Tressa of pictures of angels she'd seen in books as a child.

"Suit yourself." For what seemed like an eternity, she watched the bartender change a keg of beer under the bar.

"What's his name?"

"John."

Mickey O'Shay chuckled. "Johnny-John-John." He spoke it like a new word game. "Where's this guy come from?"

"I went to high school with him."

"He Irish?"

"Italian. Don't hold it against him."

"He just pop up outta nowhere like this?"

"Not really. I see him around from time to time."

"Did he shoot that cop?"

"I don't know," she said truthfully. "There was a lot of shooting going on."

"I'm sure it wasn't Frankie-balls," Mickey said offhandedly. "He got away with you guys?"

"Away?"

"Through the tunnels."

"Oh, yeah. Kept his head. I got his number, said I'd call him if I talked to you. So now I talked to you. What you want me to tell him?"

"I don't like making deals with people, new people."

"That's up to you."

"Son of a bitch," Mickey said and finished his beer. He held the empty glass up to his face and examined the bottom. His lips were moist and reflected the neon lights over the bar. After some deliberation, he turned to face Tressa again. "Okay," he said, "I'll meet him. We'll set it up." She watched as he ran a hand along the top of the bar and pushed his finger down in the center of a pile of cocktail napkins. He did this absently and seemingly without notice, as if his hand—his entire arm—were in control of itself.

"Okay," she said.

"What are you lookin' for on this?"

"I guess the same as you'd give Frankie."

"Five percent. And don't worry—I won't tell your old man."

Mickey stood up, stretched, and pulled some wadded tens from his khakis. He tossed two tens on the bar.

"When?" she said.

"When," he repeated, his eyes seemingly lost in a haze of alcohol and complex thought. For a second, Tressa thought he might just fall forward and put his face through the bar. But then something registered inside him and he suddenly looked very sober, very together and alert. "You just better hope this guy don't bring us no problems," he said.

Yeah, she thought, *I hope.*

CHAPTER TEN

THE BLACK BOX WAS JUST THAT—DARK, square, and confined. It was certainly not a tourist stop, not one of the city's hidden dens of fornication now several blocks removed from Times Square; rather, this place was crude and unfriendly, like an injured animal curled up inside a hole in the ground, its silver eyes shining through the darkness. The surrounding streets were dark and narrow, burdened with rats. A single streetlight stood outside the club, a fine mist of water and dust swirling in its dull light. Outside stood an enormous bouncer, and when John and Kersh approached, the bouncer had some frightened street thug by the scruff of his neck.

"You feel like gettin' handy, pal? You wanna fuckin' dance with me? Piece of shit," the bouncer growled. His face looked like the grille of a Mack truck. "Hit the bricks, fool!" And the bouncer delivered a swift kick to the thug's rear, sending the smaller man staggering down the street, dazed and inebriated.

The bouncer turned his attention to John and Kersh. "Fifteen apiece."

John was about to produce his badge, when Kersh nudged him with his elbow and shot him a wink. "It's all right," Kersh said, "I got it." He pulled out two twenties and handed them to the bouncer, who made change and let them inside.

Like most strip clubs, the Black Box was dark and noisy and dense with smoke. Long runway stages stood along three of its four walls. Closest to the front doors was a narrow bar behind which a number of young women in flimsy tops served drinks. The top of the bar was all wood and brass, freshly polished with crocus and marred by countless fingerprints. Opposite the bar stood a bank of pay phones and an ATM.

"Busy night," John mumbled, shoving past two large men in ties. Most of the people were just shapes, just caricatures floating in darkness.

John and Kersh squeezed their way around the bar, pausing before one of the runways. A young Asian girl, desperately struggling to look eighteen, gyrated her buttocks while gripping a brass pole that rose from the stage and disappeared into the rafters. The only things she wore were a pair of tall, white go-go boots and an ear-to-ear smile.

"Lord," Kersh said, rubbing his eyes and tweaking his large nose, "the incense in this place wreaks havoc on my sinuses."

"You mean you're not a regular here?"

"Ha."

"You know what this Carlson girl looks like?"

Kersh rubbed his eyes with the heel of his hand. "No."

John scanned the crowd. The clientele was comprised mostly of middle-aged men in cheap suits showing more scalp than hair. A few younger men had gathered at the foot of one stage, hollering at one of the dancers and waving fistfuls of greasy singles. Beyond them, women in nylons and nothing else filed in and out of bathroom and dressing room doors.

Kersh leaned over and whispered something to a passing dancer who whispered something back and pointed across the room with her chin. Kersh chuckled—he sounded so out of place doing that—and then the girl laughed once, sharply, with her head craned back. Before she disappeared into the crowd, Kersh tipped the girl a dollar.

"Follow me," he told John, and they began snaking their way toward the rear of the club. Smells intensified: lilac and bourbon and sweat—lots and lots of sweat—and something very close to rotting fruit. A few couples were tangled together within the cover of shadow, their bodies propped on tattered couches or smashed against wood-paneled walls. They were oblivious to passersby.

John and Kersh stopped before a small table occupied by a number of young men wearing ski coats and knitted caps and smoking cigarettes. Two men had girls perched in their laps while their friends cheered them on with drunken catcalls and the pounding of beer bottles against their thighs. One of the women, a young black girl, was nibbling on one man's ear.

"Heidi Carlson?" Kersh said.

A few of the men looked up, as did the half-naked nibbler. She was young and attractive, her skin the color of motor oil beneath the neon lights. She wore a sheer bra and a multicolored sarong around her waist, her black hair in loose coils around her face. In the dark, she was mostly eyes.

"Miss Carlson?" Kersh repeated.

"Yes?" The woman pulled herself from the man's lap, straightened her sarong. "Oh—you're the—with—"

"Sorry to interrupt," Kersh went on, "but we'd like to speak with you. Could you give us a few minutes, please?"

"Right now?"

"Right now."

Her eyes darted between John and Kersh. After a moment's hesitation, she nodded. "All right."

The young guy whose lap Heidi had been previously occupying reached out and grabbed Heidi by the wrist, startling her. "Hey!" he shouted. He stood from the chair and glowered at Kersh. He was an ugly bastard, with eyes set too closely together and a row of upper teeth that resembled fence pickets the day after a tornado. "Wait your goddamn turn, buddy."

"Sit down, son," Kersh said, unaffected.

"You think you're my father now?"

John took a step toward the table.

"Let go," Heidi Carlson said, trying to shake her wrist free. "You're hurting me . . ."

"Sit the hell back down," the man told her, his eyes never leaving Kersh's face.

She continued to struggle. "Stop—"

"Listen, Snaggletooth," Kersh said, and casually reached into his jacket pocket to produce his badge. At the sight of Kersh's gold shield, the man frowned and dropped his grip on Heidi Carlson's wrist. Free, the stripper brought her hand up quickly between her breasts. "I can postpone your fun for a few minutes or ruin your next few days. How do you want it?"

The man did not move for perhaps a full ten seconds—he just stood there, his eyes pinned to Kersh, his pockmarked cheeks quivering like thinly sliced slabs of mozzarella cheese, the fingers of his right hand slowly working themselves open and closed.

The waitress Kersh had tipped only moments ago appeared beside the table. Kersh caught her eye and smiled, moving his head slightly to turn his smile on the men as well. He looked like a mechanical clown on rotation outside a candy store. "Sorry about this, fellas," he said. "How 'bout a round of drinks?" Turning back to the waitress, he said, "You wanna load this table up, give 'em whatever they want?"

Some of the guys at the table applauded. Even the frown on Snaggletooth faltered.

The waitress smiled and winked at Kersh. "You got it," she said, and moved around the table to bump Kersh playfully with her hip.

She even managed to snake an arm around his stubby neck. Some of the guys at the table started cheering and laughing.

Kersh smiled wider and leaned over as if to peck the waitress on the cheek. "Put it on their bill," he told her under his breath before turning away.

His hand on Heidi's back, Kersh led the stripper away from the table. "Come on. Is there a place we can talk?"

"In the back," Heidi said, and they followed her to a small door in the wall beside the center stage. She knocked on it once, twice—waited. "Okay," she said, and pushed it open.

It was a dressing room with a wall-length mirror papered with Polaroid pictures on one side opposite a row of lockers and stools. The countertop beneath the mirror was littered with undergarments and makeup cases and countless pairs of high-heeled shoes, all laid out like fresh kills. A twisted nylon stocking sat beside a toothbrush, rolled into a ball. On a rack beside the door hung a number of colorful feathered boas. John saw Kersh eye them ruefully and poke one with his finger. The whole place was thick with the smell of baby powder and cinnamon and more sweat.

"Okay, okay . . ." Heidi said to no one in particular. She crept over to a stool and sat on it, pulling her legs up to her chest like someone suddenly afraid to touch the floor. In this light, she looked much older. Her skin was now the color of ash, but moist with sweat and lanolin, and her body—as tight and well-kept as it had initially appeared—now looked tired and worn from years of misuse. The skin just beneath her chin was black and puckered into scar tissue—something noticeable only in unflattering light.

"You're the police," she said. Her tone suggested she needed to say the words aloud to actually believe them.

"Secret Service," Kersh corrected.

"Again?" She looked disinterested in the whole conversation and only glanced at the agents. "I thought you guys just hung around the president."

"Hmmm," Kersh said, humoring John with a glance. He fished out a plastic bag containing a counterfeit note. "You recognize this?"

"Christ," she muttered. "I already talked to some guys about that."

"Well, now you're talking to us. Where'd you get it?"

"Like I told the other two, probably with my pay."

"Or maybe an admirer handed it to you?" John said.

"Are you serious? You think one of these losers would pop a hundred in my panties? I get tips . . . but not like *that.* I'd remember."

Kersh placed the counterfeit bill on a stool next to her. "I believe you. I believe you would definitely remember a customer who'd give you a hundred dollar bill. And what else you did besides dance for that hundred, I don't care about."

She rolled her bony shoulders, her eyes on the plastic bag and the fake hundred. "Don't know," she said.

Kersh shook his head. "Wrong answer. Get up. Let's go."

Heidi's cavalier attitude quickly fell away. "Shit, you're bustin' me?"

"That's gonna be up to you," John added, "but we're definitely leaving this place now. With you."

"This is bullshit!" She was beginning to get either nervous or annoyed, her eyes again bouncing between John and Kersh. In her agitation, she began picking at the stuffing in the stool cushion beneath her with long, manicured fingernails. "You know that? This is bullshit!"

"Let's go," Kersh repeated, stuffing the counterfeit hundred back into his jacket.

Frustrated, her lower lip working, she stood and grabbed a gaudy red purse from the counter. Reaching out, John intercepted the bag, pulled it open, searched it for weapons.

"Come on," she practically whined.

"Get a coat," John told her without looking up.

She moved to an open locker and pulled out a short leather coat, cut off at the midriff. She proceeded to put it on, but Kersh held up one finger and took the coat from her, searched the pockets.

"Christ," she moaned.

Satisfied, they returned her belongings, and she stood there holding her coat and purse like someone waiting for a bus. Kersh took her by the forearm and led her back out into the club and across the floor to the front doors. John followed close behind, his hands stuffed in his pockets, his eyes darting around the dark room. Outside, the bouncer gave them a questioning look but did not say anything. Apparently, it wasn't unusual for girls to follow men out to their cars.

They moved across the street to Kersh's sedan. His fingers still around Heidi's arm, Kersh tossed John the keys. John stepped around to the driver's side and hopped in behind the wheel while Kersh opened the rear door and ushered Heidi inside. He slid in beside her, slamming the door.

"You don't have to do this," Heidi started in. Her voice was strained, like a violin string about to break. "I was cooperating. Can't help it if I know nothing."

Kersh looked out his window and not at the girl's face. John watched them in the rearview mirror. He had seen Kersh interrogate people many times before but did not understand the reasoning behind such an evasion.

"Sweetheart," Kersh said, "you're bullshitting us. I have five other bills in my office right now that were passed at a few fancy boutiques, a restaurant, a shoe store. You passed them all." It was not a question. And although his tone was deliberate, it was not quite forceful. He could have been reading from the wine list in an expensive restaurant. "Your fingerprints are all over them." This was a lie—the fingerprints had not yet come back from the lab on the newer bills—but the confidence in Kersh's voice could not be contested. "I know you didn't get these bills from your boss at the end of the night. These were given directly to you."

She pushed out her jaw, her eyes narrowing, and noticed John staring at her in the rearview. "Now who's shitting who?" she said.

"All right." Kersh reached back into his jacket pocket and again brought forward the counterfeit hundred. This time, he carefully removed it from the plastic bag and folded it along its creases. He was like an aging magician performing a trick. "All your bills—they all fold like this," he said. "They all have your prints on them, and they all fold like this." He tapped the bill with an extended finger. "Who's been putting them in your pants, Heidi?"

"No." To John's amusement, the girl actually *chuckled.* Shaking her head, black coils of hair bouncing, she rearranged her purse on her lap as if she were angry with it. "No," she said again. "You ain't puttin' all this shit on me. I ain't the only dancer in this club or in this goddamn city. Folded? Goddamn! A lot of people fold money for all kinds of reasons—don't mean nothing. A lot of fucking people—"

"And your prints," Kersh reminded her. His voice remained smooth and serene, the feathered back of a great bird.

She didn't answer. Her head tilted slightly toward the floor, and she stared at Kersh from beneath her brow. At this moment, she wouldn't have surprised John if she either tried to attack Kersh or simply broke down sobbing.

"I touch money all the time," she said finally. "Everybody does. You just tryin' to jack somebody for this, and I'm easy. Shit, if I knew it was fake, you think I'd put it in my bank? Bullshit!"

John watched her from behind the wheel, his eyes never leaving the rearview mirror. He respected Kersh and had no doubts about the man's approach, but he could not sit here like this any longer. For one abrupt and tormenting moment, the image of Katie sitting alone at home surfaced in his head. His hands ached to touch the swell of her belly, to cup a breast, to nestle his face in the soft gossamer of her hair.

The car was suddenly too hot. He slipped the key into the ignition, cranked the engine over, and leaned around the seat to face the back. He must have looked the part, for Heidi Carlson's expression became an out-of-control elevator crashing to the ground, floor after floor. "Listen, you stupid bitch, we got you. Five minutes ago you were shakin' your ass on stage; twenty minutes from now you'll be dancing in the can. They don't tip very fucking good in prison."

She could invoke no response, nor did he expect her to. He was done listening to her warble and whine in the back seat of Kersh's car. Downtown, she'd be a lot more willing to cooperate.

He punched the car into drive and pulled out into the narrow street. He caught Kersh's look in the rearview. Looking away quickly, he said, "Bill, I'm bookin' her. She's done. I'm not playing these silly goddamn games . . ."

"John . . ." Kersh started, and John couldn't help but glance again at Kersh's face in the rearview. Surprisingly, Kersh did not look annoyed or even slightly ruffled. In fact, there was an almost comforting look of satisfaction on the man's face.

"Wait!" Heidi shouted. She pushed herself to the edge of the seat. "Stop! Wait a minute! Wait! Wait! Okay, I'll tell you. I don't want no problems." The stripper reached out and tugged at John's arm. In silence, he turned the wheel and pulled the car to a stop in the middle of the empty street.

"All right, all right," she conceded. "I got the bills. But I swear I didn't know they were fake. Even when I passed them. Not until the bank thing. And I passed no more after that."

John shut the car off.

"Who's the guy, Heidi?" Kersh said. There was something oddly tender in his voice, almost soothing. To John, he suddenly sounded more like a therapist than an agent.

"Who's the guy," she parroted under her breath. Her large eyes were scaling the sedan's windows, the upholstery. She blinked several times; large clumps of mascara were caught in her lashes, visible even in the darkness. "I can't . . . I don't know his name. Saw him a few times before the . . . the night he . . . he hit on me." She was careful with her words. "I'm dancin' and he's watchin', slips a bill in my string. When I'm done, I start takin' out the money and that's when I, you know, realize he gave me a hundred. I was, like, really shocked, you know?" She was talking fast now, not from fear but from anger, and anger made Heidi Carlson unattractive. "I looked around for him after," she continued, "and he was still there, but not by the stage anymore. By himself, sitting at the bar. He was watchin' me from across the room, watchin' me even before I saw him there, and so I went over to him. Bought me a few drinks. We talked for a while. Then we went to his car."

"And no name?" Kersh asked.

Heidi shook her head. "Nothing."

"What type of car?"

"Shit, I don't know. I'm not a car person. Some big, older car, like a dark red color. Like blood. The inside was white and real dirty, cigarette burns all over the seats . . ."

"You ain't saying too much here," John said, "which makes me think you're still playing with us."

"Hey, sugar, I can only tell you what I know." There was a spark of resilience in her voice. "I seen him a few more times—each time the same gig. I dance, he pops me a hundred, a few drinks, and we're horizontal in his car."

"If no name," Kersh said, "what did you call him?"

She laughed at this, and it was a bittersweet sound. She patted the side of her face with one hand, her enormous nails painted red. "Call him? Shit—'Honey,' 'Baby,' 'Sugar,' whatever. The usual crap."

John frowned at Kersh. "She's full of shit. I say we book her ass and try this again tomorrow."

Frantic, Heidi pushed herself in front of Kersh and against the back of John's seat. "Look, that's it, man! I didn't know those bills were fake. I didn't spend time humping that fool for toilet paper. I said—I *said*—" She took a much needed breath. "Listen—I *said* I realized it when I got stopped at the bank. Okay? Goddamn it! That's when I knew he beat me, I swear. I had no fucking *idea,* no fucking *clue,* all right? When your guys came, I panicked. I knew I passed around a few of the bills, but I wasn't gonna take a bust on something I wasn't even in on. I was set up . . . So maybe I wasn't truthful. But, shit, I really wasn't involved—*and I don't know this guy.*"

Still able to maintain a tone of compassion, Kersh asked when she had seen him last.

Catching her breath, her chest hitching, she said, "Three nights ago." She ran those curled, red fingernails across the exposed flesh of her chest, leaving behind white streaks on her tanned skin.

"Did you hit him up about the bills?"

"No." Then, almost as an afterthought, she said, "I mean, I was gonna. He gave me one in the club. I took it but figured I'd hit him up when we went outside. I'll be straight—I was gonna shake him down. Real money for putting me on Front Street. But when we got outside, his car was towed."

The words struck both John and Kersh like a whipcrack across the calves. John looked from Heidi to Kersh and back to Heidi again. *"What?"*

"Yeah. Why?" She had no idea. "First he thought it was clipped, then the fool realized he parked in one of the taxi zones outside the club. The cops hooked it."

Kersh looked beside himself. He was a man unaccustomed to emotions of extravagance, but in the dim light of the car, his face had immediately *changed,* had brightened somehow.

She doesn't even realize what she just said, John thought.

"Where, exactly?" John asked. "The car?"

"Uh . . ." She turned and peered through the sedan's rear

window and back toward the club. The window was fogged and she jogged her head side to side, as if such movement would clear the view. She looked momentarily lost, out of place. *"Somewhere,"* she said. "On the corner by the front of the club, across the street on the other side."

"You're sure it was towed?" Kersh asked. He was still looking at John.

Heidi faced her lap, adjusted her bag. "Positive. He called the precinct, then the pound. He was madder than all hell. Told me it was towed, cursin' his head off, and grabbed a cab and took off. And that was it—that was the last time I saw him. Three days ago." Looking at her captors' faces, the stripper was able to realize she was no longer important. A look of relief overtook her, and she began lightly dragging her exaggerated fingernails across the bronze terrain of her chest again. "Three days ago," she repeated.

"Okay, okay," Kersh said finally, pulling his eyes from John and digging into his jacket. "You see this guy again, call us and stall him. Keep him here in the club. You don't see him in a week, we come back and take you. You got that?" But there was no threat in his voice, and Heidi was no longer buying it.

Just the same, she nodded and accepted the business card Kersh extended to her. "I'll call. I swear I'll call. I'll have one of the boys hold 'em down if I have to. You'll see."

"All right," Kersh said. He leaned across Heidi's lap and popped the door open for her. "Go on."

"I'll call," she reiterated, and pulled herself from the car. She stumbled once by the curb, righted herself, and headed back toward the club down the middle of the empty street.

"You believe this shit?" Kersh whispered from the back seat.

"Yeah, I . . ." John paused, turned, opened the driver's door.

"What?" Kersh called, also stepping from the car. Like Heidi, he staggered a moment as he got out of the car, the crumbling pavement uneven beneath his feet. "John?"

John caught up to Heidi just before she reached the front doors of the club. "Hold on." She turned, still wary. Her purse was covering her chest like a shield. Behind her, the large bouncer peered at them above folded arms. "What'd you do with the bill?"

"Which one?"

"The last one—the one he gave you three days ago."

Her eyes narrowed, and she offered him something very close to a congenial smile. It did nothing to brighten up her features. From nowhere, John wondered why a place like the Black Box had so many mirrors.

Heidi reached into her purse, shuffled around. Moving closer to the club, she used the lights over the door to peer inside the bag. She produced a wad of bills and peeled a hundred from it, held it out. "Here," she said.

He took it by one corner, pinched between two fingers. He'd studied the bills enough to recognize it on the spot.

"Christ." She uttered a laugh, but her eyes were dead. "Such a rip." And she turned and sauntered back into the club.

The bouncer nodded in John's direction. "Knew you two were cops," he said offhandedly.

"Yeah? So how 'bout givin' us our thirty bucks back? Seeing how we're working and all . . ."

The bouncer only stared down at him, his branded arms motionless across his broad chest. Then, surprisingly, he smiled. There was a huge gap between his two front teeth. Then, even more surprising, the bouncer hooked a thick wad of bills from his back pocket, counted off thirty bucks, and held it out to John.

"Come back some night you're not working," the bouncer said, "you and your partner. On me."

Back at the car, Kersh was now behind the wheel. He had the engine running and his head bent forward and very close to the steering wheel. John climbed in the passenger seat, slammed the door, and tossed the thirty dollars into Kersh's lap. The older agent cocked an eyebrow as he scooped up the cash.

"You believe that?" John said, grinning. "Shit!" He slammed a hand against the dash. "Some break, huh? You want me to drive?"

"You wanna do this now? Tonight?" Kersh said.

"What, are you kidding? Let's roll."

Kersh slipped the car into drive and gunned it down the alley. There were streetlights here, and bars of horizontal lights rolled over the car's hood, over the windshield, over the roof.

"Rolling," Kersh said.

CHAPTER ELEVEN

MOST OF THE MEN WHO WORK THE pound at Pier 76 are near-retired NYPD. They wear standard police uniforms, carry handguns, and usually betray an unpalatable disposition toward anyone not associated with law enforcement.

The night was growing late as Kersh wound his sedan along the causeway and onto Pier 76. As they drove, John watched the lights of Weehawken glitter across the Hudson River. He could make out the red and green lights of the tollbooths for the Lincoln Tunnel from this distance as well. So many people living their own lives, oblivious to the things that crept along the world beneath them. He watched the tollbooth lights for some time. The night was windy and clear. With the passenger window cracked slightly, the smells of the river penetrated the car—grim, salty smells. And beneath those smells, somehow hidden and less obtrusive, was the diesel-and-oil reek of the cruise ships that docked several piers to the north.

Cops maintain a different view of the docks along Manhattan's West Side than most ordinary people do. For cops, it is not so much about boats and fisheries and cruise ships weaving in and out of ports, the burning stink of fuel perpetually infused in the air. For them, it is a depot of clues for cases that just moments earlier seemed hopeless. The number of criminal investigations solved, thanks to automobiles seized and searched within the city limits, is staggering. Yet just as often as cases are solved along the docks, they *begin* there as well. The number of bodies pulled from the Hudson River in a year is tantamount to the number of home runs hit by the Yankees in a single season.

Kersh pulled in along a chain-link fence tipped with barbed wire, and double-flashed his high beams at an attendant who was standing by the pound's entrance gate. The attendant swaggered over to the car, crouched down, peered inside. Kersh flipped his badge, and the attendant nodded and waved them through the gate. On the other side of the gate, two gray-haired attendants stood watching the car roll by, one with his arms folded across his chest and the other with hands on hips.

This is where cops go when they get old, John thought, watching the men through his window. *Towed away from the reality of the city streets to this impound lot for cops.*

And for one insane moment, he thought of his father.

The lot was engorged with automobiles of all sizes, shapes, makes, models, colors. Some looked new and shiny in the moonlight; others appeared as brittle as bone and just as lackluster, coated in filth and grime and sea salt. Up ahead and to their right, the pound office stood against the backdrop of night, the lights warm and yellow in the main lobby. Kersh shut down the car, and they both stepped out.

It was cold on the water. Toward the west, John could hear the soothing lap of the river against the dock pilings; to the east, the muffled din of the city was still audible. He zippered up his leather jacket and followed Kersh to the pound office, the older agent humming Beethoven's "Ode to Joy" in an easy contralto.

In contrast to the night air, the inside of the office was stiflingly warm. A tall, gaunt gentleman in a chambray shirt stood behind a large desk. The nameplate atop the desk read *Kroger.* Kroger—if this, in fact, *was* Kroger—glanced up as they entered the office, his face expressionless and his eyes haunted. He had one hand digging around inside an open can of black olives on his desk.

"Help you?"

Again, Kersh produced his badge. "Special Agent Kersh, Secret Service. This is Agent Mavio. We need some information on a car that was towed on 41st Street near Times Square three days ago. Outside a club called the Black Box."

"Three days?" Kroger said, turning to a computer terminal on his desk. His fingers dripped olive juice on the keypad.

"That's right."

"Any other information?" Kroger asked. "Make, model? VIN numbers? License plate, maybe?"

"No numbers. An older, big car," John said. He unzipped his coat, the office uncomfortably warm. "Dark red exterior."

"Yeah, yeah, here it is," Kroger said. "Here's the car." He licked his lips with a small, pink tongue. "Yeah—three days ago. Sure." He tapped faster on the keyboard. "A 1979 Lincoln Towncar, metallic carmine, alabaster interior, plate numbers EGA-419, New York plates. Registered to a—a—to Evelyn Gethers." Kroger whistled. "Lives on the Upper East Side. I'll print the address."

"Evelyn Gethers," Kersh said under his breath. John looked at him, curious to read the older agent's expression. But Kersh had none.

"Name sound familiar?" John asked him.

Kersh frowned, cocked a pair of bushy eyebrows, shrugged his bulky shoulders. His white dress shirt plumed from his pants. Just above his belt and through the fabric of his shirt, John could make out the ribbed band of Kersh's boxer shorts. That sight, coupled with the contemplative countenance on Kersh's face, made John grin to himself.

"Here we go," Kroger said. A printer on the counter behind his desk began spitting out paper. Kroger examined the information, then tore the paper from the printer and handed it over to Kersh. Kroger, leaning halfway across his desk, watched Kersh's face with interest.

Kersh stared at the printout, chewing at his lower lip. "Well," he said, more to himself than anyone else. "Loft on the two hundredth block of East Seventy-second Street."

John frowned. "East Seventy-second? Wow. Nice crib."

"According to her date of birth, she's sixty-four." Kersh looked at Kroger. "You sure this is the right car?"

"Oh, sure," Kroger said emphatically.

"Bizarre," John marveled.

"Hey, uh . . ." Kroger was clearing his throat, looking at them both now from beneath wiry, pepper-colored eyebrows. "This have anything to do with that head?"

"Head?" John said. Kersh did not even look up at Kroger; he was still occupied with the printout.

"That head they pulled from the river a couple days ago. Right here off the dock."

John blinked. "That's a good question," he said, humoring the man. "We'll run some tests back at the office. Thanks."

Kroger interpreted John's sarcasm as genuine appreciation. "Yeah, good thing. Find a head in the river, work slows down like you wouldn't b'lieve. It's one thing they wanna talk about it on their lunch breaks, but we got some work to do here—you know what I mean? Lunch breaks is one thing. Some stories. I mean, it's just a *head.*"

Kersh looked up, folded the printout, and stuffed it into the rear pocket of his slacks. A film of perspiration had materialized on his upper lip. "Were you here when it was picked up?"

"Picked up? The head?"

"The car," Kersh said.

"No."

"Who was?"

"No," said Kroger, shaking his head, "car's still here. Out in the lot. You wanna go see it?"

Kersh just stared. "Yeah," he said.

John said, "We're gonna need a slim jim and a punch."

"I'll get some tools," Kroger said, feeling like a conspirator, "and show her to you m'self."

Evelyn Gethers's Lincoln Towncar was a flashy piece of work, now nestled snugly between a banged-up Volkswagen and a Mercedes with flattened tires. The Lincoln's front end was partially dented, and the windshield boasted a number of conchoidal fractures in the glass. The car's paint job was indeed the color of blood, as Heidi Carlson had suggested. The windows were grimy and covered in filth, decorated with star-shaped splotches of bird crap. Peering through the windows, John could make out the whitish interior—cracked and worn leather. A plastic shamrock with a pair of googly eyes hung from the rearview mirror.

John noticed the lock was open on the driver's side door. Behind him, Kersh and Kroger were busy searching through Kroger's tools for a punch to open the trunk. John grabbed the door handle, popped open the door. He saw Kersh look up in the reflection of the dirty glass of the driver's side window.

"Unlocked," John said, sticking his head inside the car. The dome light in the ceiling was broken and did not come on. "Jesus, smells like a sewer in here." He tried to imagine how anyone could be coerced into copulating in a car that smelled as bad as this one did.

"Anything?" Kersh called to him.

"Empty pack of Marlboros, some loose change in the ashtray

. . . something that looks like a turd stuck to the passenger seat. A Tootsie Roll, I think it is." He leaned farther into the vehicle, holding his breath, and pushed the passenger seat forward. The back seat, too, was virtually empty. "Nothing," he said. "Just a balled up sock and a wet box of tissues."

"Come on—we'll check the trunk," Kersh said, unearthing the lock punch from Kroger's collection, and walking around to the back of the vehicle. He inserted the punch into the keyhole of the Lincoln's trunk, pushed down on it, and popped out the lock. "Love that sound." Stepping back, Kersh dropped the punch on the ground.

John and Kroger gathered around either side of Kersh—three psychics desperate to see the future in the same crystal ball. Kroger was shaking, the cold getting to him. Kersh reached out two fingers and slipped them beneath the hood of the trunk. He hoisted it, springs creaking, till it opened with a bang, and the three men stared inside.

The first one to speak was Kroger. "Son of a bitch," he said, "ain't *that* a sight?"

The trunk's inventory: a ski mask, a bullet-proof Kevlar vest, and a small handgun with a screw-on silencer. The gun was a .22-caliber semiautomatic, often referred to as a "hit" gun. Discreet, compact, and lacking a larger weapon's knockdown power, the .22's smaller caliber bullets are designed strictly to kill, capable of ricocheting off bone to achieve maximum damage.

After a few moments, John and Kersh turned to look at each other in partial disbelief.

"Looks like we're going to need some evidence bags," Kersh said eventually.

CHAPTER TWELVE

A MOLTEN SUN BURNING DOWN ON THE acropolis that is Manhattan's Upper East Side, and a slew of automobiles caught in the upheaval of rush-hour traffic, John steered his Camaro through traffic. His window down, he moved his eyes repeatedly toward the fantastic display of buildings to his left. The radio was tuned to a modern rock station. Beside him, Kersh sat seemingly refreshed despite his lack of sleep. Not for the first time, John wondered what Kersh thought of him. Normally an excellent judge of character, John found Bill Kersh too difficult to crack—a fascinating new species of man. He knew Kersh tolerated most people, and there were a select few he truly detested, but he really could not think of anyone Bill Kersh genuinely *liked.* Which made him all the more interesting to John.

"You get much sleep last night?" Kersh asked.

"Some." He couldn't help but think Kersh was feeling him out. "We could've hit this place last night. Didn't have to wait."

"Doesn't matter. This is going to lead us in some wild circles," Kersh said, almost to himself. "This Evelyn Gethers business. You just wait. I have a feeling." Kersh pushed himself back against his headrest. "Tell me something?"

"Shoot."

"You really listen to this garbage?"

John laughed and turned the radio up louder. "You're pretty damn close-minded for a guy supposed to be so smart."

Kersh drummed his fingers on the dashboard. "Smart? Me? To whom have you been speaking, mah deah boy?"

Turning down 72nd Street, John kept his eyes peeled for Evelyn Gethers's building. The polar opposite of the cramped, filthy network of streets surrounding the Black Box, this section of the city was resplendent and quite visibly teeming with wealth. The buildings were solid and magnificent, boastful in the way some buildings can be. It occurred to John that this must be the only city in the world where the excruciatingly wealthy lived with their asses pressed against the faces of the agonizingly destitute.

"There," Kersh said, pointing to a gold and white awning. "Find a spot down the street."

"Some neighborhood." He could see chrome finish around the ground-level windows and a monkey-suited doorman beneath the awning. "How the hell you think our guy's mixed up with some old woman here? Think maybe it's her son, grandson, or something?"

Kersh bit at his lower lip. He wasn't looking at John, wasn't looking at Evelyn Gethers's building anymore, either. His eyes were set straight ahead, as if some answer lay unfurled in the street before him. He said nothing.

Five minutes later, after a slow elevator ride to the top floor, John was knocking at Evelyn Gethers's door. The hallway—white, meticulously clean, minimally yet sophisticatedly furnished—was a museum.

The door opened and an urgent, severe-looking man in shirtsleeves and a bow tie stood opposite them. His face was ruddy, his nose large and blunt, like the stop on a roller skate. The dome of his head was enormous and absent of even a single hair, his scalp reflecting both John and Kersh. When he spoke, his tone suggested mild irritation and a disinterest in all things living and breathing.

"The police," he said, seemingly addressing himself over anyone else. "The doorman phoned just a minute ago."

John and Kersh introduced themselves and held up their badges.

"Come in," said the butler. He opened the door and stood beside it, emotionless, as John and Kersh entered the apartment.

The place was like something out of a Fitzgerald novel. The main foyer was a massive expanse of herringbone parquet floors and lofty, high-beamed ceilings with crown molding. To the west, a bank of lancet windows looked out upon similar buildings and, beyond those, the colorful, burgeoning ribbon of Central Park. The decor suggested a certain sentimentality toward the forgotten Golden Age, and the walls bled with the colors of exquisite paintings framed in heavy bronze or lacquered mahogany.

"Mrs. Gethers will be down shortly," the butler said. He was standing beside a marble statue of some Greek warrior, the butler's stoic, unenthusiastic posture almost mimicking it. "Is there anything I can get for you two gentlemen in the meantime?"

"We're fine," Kersh said. He was moving slowly around the room, admiring the paintings. "These are—"

"Impressionists," said the butler. "Cézanne, Manet, Monet . . ."

"Are they *real?*"

The butler did not humor Kersh with an answer.

"Mrs. Gethers lives alone?" John asked, watching the butler work. "I mean, aside from you. She have a husband? Any kids?"

"Her husband was C. Charles Gethers, and he is dead. Mrs. Gethers never—" There was a slight hiccup in the butler's speech here as he searched his vocabulary for the most insipid response. He decided on: "Mrs. Gethers never *had* any children."

Who the hell is C. Charles Gethers? John thought but did not ask.

Kersh approached a wall of books and slid one from the shelf. He cracked open the cover and glanced at one of the pages. When

Evelyn Gethers spoke from the top of the winding staircase, Kersh jumped and nearly dropped the book to the floor.

"Company!" she crooned. "This is such a treat!"

John looked up, also startled, and saw the woman standing on the landing directly above a white Steinway piano. She was a slender old thing wrapped loosely in a silk, mint-green gown and matching feather boa. Her hair was perfectly white and glistened with the soft lights of the tremendous crystal chandelier that hung just above her head. Her face heavily made up, her thin arms poking from the fabric of her costume, she stood beaming at them from the landing. Then, slowly and deliberately, she began descending the stairs like an actress making her grand entrance.

Jesus Christ, it's Katherine Hepburn, John thought.

Kersh, too, watched the woman descend the stairwell. He smiled unevenly and presented her with a half-nod as she reached the floor.

"Morris," Evelyn Gethers said, "please see to some coffee. The Caribbean beans, not that imported Mexican garbage."

"Ma'am," Morris the butler said, nodded once, then vanished into another section of the apartment.

"Well," the woman said, moving herself to the center of the room where she could get a better view of her guests. "Isn't this nice?" At this distance she looked her age, and the lights from the crystal chandelier were rather unflattering. Her face was caked with makeup and her eyes were large and colorless, piercing out from behind lashes thick with black clumps of mascara. She'd apparently applied fresh red lipstick, and it was a job poorly done. When she smiled, she exposed a row of teeth that jutted from the gums like villagers fleeing from a plague.

Kersh introduced himself and then John, who nodded without sound. The old woman nodded twice in response to each introduction, the smile never leaving her face. "This is an amazing place,"

Kersh said, genuinely appreciative.

"This room," began Evelyn Gethers, "is a *duplicato* of our room at the Hotel Lungarno in Florence, where we used to vacation quite often in the winter months. Splendid. Really splendid. Florence. You've been, Inspector Kersh?"

"To Italy? Sadly, no."

"Tristemente, it is no longer as it was. No place is. We spent months in Paris as well, stamping down the stones of the Rue Mouffetard, and that, too, has changed. Even the artwork. You've seen my artwork?"

"Very impressive, yes."

She sighed and closed her large eyes, the lids of which were painted an electric blue. "Some things better left to the imagination, but they are not the same. Not for us, anyway."

"Us? You're speaking of your husband?" Kersh said.

"You mean Charles?" She laughed, her throat constricting under the force like a deflating hose. *"Charles* loved the artwork, loved the cities. But Charles was arrogant, even on his deathbed, and cursed like a sailor drunk on rum. But he fit in and loved Paris." She shook her head, her smile faltering, and suddenly looked quite lost. "You'll have to forgive me," she apologized. "My memory isn't what it used to be. It's been a long, long time."

"It's all right," Kersh said.

"Mrs. Gethers," John began, "you're the owner of a red 1979 Lincoln Towncar?"

She blinked once, twice. "The Lincoln," she muttered. Then: "Yes, yes. I own a red Lincoln. It was Charles's car. Temperamental as he was. Won't you both sit down?"

"I'm all right," John began.

"Come," Evelyn Gethers insisted, moving to her sofa. She made room for Kersh, who sat beside her awkwardly, still holding the book from the woman's bookshelf. John remained standing across from her.

"Your car was impounded several days ago, Mrs. Gethers," he said. "What exactly happened?"

"Impounded?" She folded her bony hands into her lap. Her wrists glittered with an impressive selection of diamond bracelets. "You mean, by the police?"

"Does anyone else use that car besides you?" Kersh asked.

"The Lincoln? I don't use the Lincoln." A small, pink tongue darted from her mouth and worked at her lipstick-encrusted lower lip. "I haven't driven in many years. My eyes have gone bad, I'm afraid."

Kersh rephrased the question: "Who usually drives the Lincoln?"

"Oh, that's Douglas," she said matter-of-factly.

"Douglas?" John said. "Who's he?"

"He drives the Lincoln," the woman said.

"What's his last name?"

"He . . ." The woman paused, seemingly lost on the surface of thought. She smiled almost apologetically at John, then turned to show Kersh her smile as not to leave him out.

Morris entered the room carrying a tray of coffee. He stopped just before the granite table and, still holding the tray, cleared his throat several times. John felt like knocking the butler square in the nose, but settled for shooting him a sideways glance. Kersh, on the other hand, thanked him for the coffee.

"Drink, drink," Evelyn Gethers said, reaching for her own cup. Her hand shook, and John was amazed that she managed to bring the cup to her lips without spilling any on herself. "Thank you, Morris."

Morris turned and stalked out of the room like someone suddenly accosted by a great idea.

"Clifton," she said. "His last name's Clifton. We're going to be married."

John shot Kersh a glance, which Kersh returned from over the rim of his coffee cup. "He lives here?" John asked.

"Yes," the woman said. "Well, no. Not all the time, not really.

He has a room upstairs, but he rarely stays. He keeps very busy."

"How old is he?"

"Oh, twenties, thirties . . . fifties. I'm not quite sure." She rubbed the corner of her mouth with a crooked yellow thumb, smearing lipstick. "I don't believe I've ever asked him."

"Where is he now?"

"Now? Well, I believe he's ill. He's sick. This is good coffee."

"He's not here now?" John asked.

"Not now. He's sick. He's in the hospital." The woman nodded toward the coffee tray. "There's another cup, Mister—Inspector?—Mavio. Won't you have some?"

"He told you he was in the hospital?" Kersh asked from beside her.

She turned a smile on him—all teeth and gums and lipstick—and nodded once, blinked her massive eyes. "He called me yesterday," she said. "From the hospital."

John asked her which hospital.

Lips together, she looked up at him as if he'd just asked her what color underwear she was wearing. All of a sudden she looked very hurt.

"There's something you need to know," she almost whispered. "I don't like people passing judgment, so I'd rather just come out and say these things, have the words come from my own mouth to their ears so there's no miscommunication. Do you understand?"

John nodded.

She spoke her words slowly, trying more to convince herself than anyone else in the room: "I loved my husband. I was a good wife. I never complained. Never. Do you understand me? It's important that you understand me, that you understand that. Do you?" But no one answered, and after several moments of silence she straightened her back and sipped some more coffee. "Ah, I remember the place now," she said, suddenly just as cheerful as she'd been when she first greeted them at the foot of the stairs. "The Palazzo. Grand-grand-

grand Palazzo. *Spettacoloso.*"

There was a creaking of floorboards just down the hall, and John turned his head in time to see a shadow drift slowly across the wall of an adjoining room. Morris, he assumed, listening in.

"Would you like to see his room?" the woman said suddenly. "Douglas's room?"

"That would be wonderful," Kersh said, and stood.

They followed the woman up the winding staircase, John lagging behind and peering into every partially opened door. He was already starting to form an impression of the situation in his head. The woman was old, delusional, eccentric, and most likely not without a touch of Alzheimer's. He had little hope that the name she gave them was even real.

She led them into a small, empty room with blue walls and a single window overlooking 72nd Street. In the room was a single bed, made and probably not slept in for some time, a cardboard box beside the bed, and a hand-carved dresser with brass handles and gold-plated molding against one wall. That was it.

"When was the last time he was here?" John asked, bending over and peering into the cardboard box. It was empty. With his foot, he lifted the corner of the bedspread and crouched to peer beneath the bed: nothing.

"Oh, my. Not for some time. I can't remember."

Kersh asked the woman if she could recall what hospital Clifton had called from, if he had said why he was there and what had happened to him. Kersh's lilting voice must have resonated better in Evelyn Gethers's head, for she did not sink back into herself as she'd done when John had asked the question downstairs.

However, Kersh produced no results. Perhaps, the woman suggested, he never even mentioned it to her. "I'm pretty certain I would have remembered, had he told me," she said.

John opened the drawers of the dresser. Empty. Empty. Empty.

In one, a half-empty pack of Marlboros.

"His cigarettes are here," he told Kersh. "Same brand."

There was a closet beside the bedroom door. Kersh slid it open and peered inside. Aside from two very expensive suits and a collection of mismatched hangers, the closet was empty. Kersh wasted no time searching the pockets of the suits, plucking them one at a time from the closet and holding them at arm's length to get an idea of Douglas Clifton's build.

"I bought those for him," the woman said with some despondency. "Smell them. Don't you just love the way a new suit smells?"

"We'd like to leave a phone number with your butler," John told the woman. "In case you happen to see or hear from Douglas again, he could call us, let us know."

"Oh." She was watching Kersh hang one of the suits back up in the closet. "Is he in some kind of trouble?" It was a little late in the game for that question to make its first appearance, John noted, but then again, Evelyn Gethers wasn't shuffling a full deck.

"We just need to ask him a few questions," Kersh said, knowing he needn't go into anymore detail than that.

Evelyn Gethers led them back downstairs where Morris was busy collecting the half-empty cups of coffee off the table. He looked at them through narrow, distrustful eyes, careful to keep his presence at a minimum.

Evelyn Gethers led John and Kersh across the room toward the front door. Kersh, who had also noticed the butler's subtle interest in their activities, presented himself to the man in an amiable enough fashion and produced a business card. Morris stared at it for a second before pinching it between his pincer-like fingers, like someone suddenly unaccustomed to the conventions of the Western world. Kersh made brief mention to the butler about the situation, remaining as vague as they'd been with the old woman.

Morris's eyes shifted toward Mrs. Gethers, then returned to

Kersh. "I don't really know him. He just comes around the house sometimes. Not in a while, though."

Kersh nodded and requested that Morris phone them without haste if Clifton happened to show up again.

The butler continued to look at the business card, aware of the Secret Service emblem emblazoned above Kersh's name, obviously chewing something over in his mind. Then he turned back to clearing off the coffee table.

Kersh leaned over the sofa, grabbed the book he'd taken from the shelf, and proceeded to slide it back into place.

"No, no, no," the woman said, causing Morris the butler to glance over in their direction again. Mrs. Gethers plucked the book from Kersh's hands, held it up to her face as if preparing to read the small print on the leather cover . . . then inhaled deeply, breathing in the musty scent of the book. Eyes partially closed, a soft smile swimming on her face, she gently handed the book back to Kersh. "Keep it," she said. "It's yours."

"Oh, I can't." The older agent uttered an embarrassed laugh. "It's very old. Must be worth—"

Evelyn Gethers merely waved her hand. "Nonsense," she said. "How much crap can an old woman inherit? It's just one other item for Morris to dust."

To this, John expected the butler to grunt and shuffle quickly out of the room. But Morris remained, silent and watchful as ever.

"Really—" Kersh insisted.

"No," she said, adamant, "I won't hear of it. It's yours now. Keep it. And good reading to you, Inspector Kersh." She turned to her butler, her bony hands suddenly hugging her pointy hips. "See them out, Morris. I'm going to the windows for air."

"Ma'am," he said, and straightened up quickly, suddenly disinterested in the coffee cups.

She turned toward the agents, pirouetted with surprising agility, and bade them farewell.

"Gentlemen," Morris said, opening the front door. There was something in his voice, in his demeanor, that caused John to look in the butler's direction and study his face. If Kersh had heard it too, he showed no sign.

He wasn't surprised when Morris followed them out into the hall.

"What'd he do?" were the first words out of Morris's mouth. His breath was stale and awful-smelling. "That son of a bitch."

Stunned, Kersh turned around. "I'm sorry?"

"Clifton," Morris said. "Can you tell me what he did, why you're looking for him?"

"Sir, we—" Kersh began, but John cut him off.

"You know him? What do you know?" he asked the butler. He could almost read the man's thoughts straight from his head, could see them glowing like neon across his bald pate. "Tell us."

"Clifton's no good and not deserving of anything Mrs. Gethers gives him. I see what goes on here, see what he does. He's a hooligan, and I'm not surprised he's in trouble with the authorities."

"How'd this guy get mixed up with her?"

"How does *anything* happen?" Morris spoke in a near-whisper now, his face very close to John's, his breath oppressive. "He used to deliver groceries up to the loft. Mrs. Gethers is elderly, lonely, a little out of it—and she's got a lot of money. This Clifton fellow took advantage of that. He sometimes comes and goes and she gives him money, pays for company, that sort of thing."

"How old is he?" John asked.

"About your age. He's at Bellevue," Morris spat, quick enough to trip over his words. "Bellevue Hospital. I sometimes . . ." Then he caught himself, considered changing his mind, then must have figured *what the hell.* "I sometimes listen in on her calls." He looked embarrassed and a bit peeved at the whole situation. "Her husband was a good man—a good employer and a good friend. I worry about her. This Clifton fellow—he's no good. I knew that from the beginning, but what can I do? She doesn't listen to reason. Plus, he made her happy. I guess it's not terribly bad if she's happy. I don't know. Is he going to jail?" There was some hope in his voice. And although John was positive Morris had some designs of his own, he knew the man *did* care about Evelyn Gethers and *did* want to see Douglas Clifton behind bars. Probably more the latter than the former.

"We just need to speak with him," John told the butler. "I appreciate this."

"I don't know what to do if—"

"Just give us a call if you see or hear from him, all right?"

"Yes," Morris said, glancing down at Kersh's business card. After a moment, he tucked the card into the breast pocket of his shirt, nodded once in a perfunctory manner, then slipped back inside the apartment. John heard him bolt the door on the other side.

"Looks like we're going to Bellevue Hospital," John said once they were riding the elevator to the lobby. "That was some goddamn place, huh? Imagine living like that."

"Amazing," Kersh said. He was flipping through the old book Evelyn Gethers had given him, examining pages the way an archeologist might examine prehistoric tools unearthed from a desert landscape. He paused, his finger on the title page of the book. A small, ironic chuckle lurched from his throat, and John turned in his direction.

"What?"

"Check it out."

Kersh extended the book, his finger pointing to a line of text on the bottom of the title page. The book itself was called *Riders of the Black Storm,* probably an old western. John glanced down at the line of text Kersh had his finger pressed to. It read, *Printed by C.C. Gethers Publishing, Inc.*

"Son of a bitch," John mused.

Kersh smiled and looked up. He watched the numbers on the elevator's panel tick down until they reached the lobby.

Thirty minutes later and they were clopping down a tangle of corridors at Bellevue Hospital Center, searching for Douglas Clifton's room. John's head hurt, and his joints felt tired. And he would have been surprised and a bit ashamed that Bill Kersh had him so easily figured out—that the steely glances Kersh had given him in the car on the way to Evelyn Gethers's were all the older agent needed to confirm his concern about young and abrupt John Mavio. On occasion, he'd caught himself absently trying to imagine Bill Kersh as a child. But that was an impossibility. People like Bill Kersh had never *been* children; somehow, they simply *appeared* one day, dressed slovenly in a wrinkled, cigarette-burned shirt, a stained and crooked tie, and slacks with worn knees. People like Bill Kersh had nothing in common with most ordinary people of the world.

After some confusion and misdirection, John and Kersh found Douglas Clifton's room. Kersh knocked twice lightly, not sure what to expect. The scene at Evelyn Gethers's apartment had left them in a state of suspended amusement, and now they were prepared for anything.

The door quickly opened, startling both men, and a tall, dark-skinned doctor in a white coat stepped out into the hallway. His features were sharp and birdlike, and a dark crop of stiff, curly hair sprouted from his head.

"Can I do something for you gentlemen?"

"Is this Douglas Clifton's room?" John asked.

"Are you relatives of Mr. Clifton?"

John flashed his badge. "We're Secret Service. We want to have a few words with Clifton—"

"Mr. Clifton's in no condition to talk with anyone."

John sized the doctor up, looked for a name plate on his coat. There was none. "Who are you?"

"Dr. Kuhmari, Mr. Clifton's doctor. I'm going to have to insist Mr. Clifton remain undisturbed—"

"Look, I respect what you do. Now respect what I do." There was a small window beside the door—thin and narrow, like windows in a castle tower—but the blinds were drawn and John couldn't see inside. "What's wrong with him? When'd he come in?"

Intimidated by John's forwardness and inability to be swayed by doctoral politics, Dr. Kuhmari delivered a resigned sigh and began massaging his forehead with his brown fingers. "Came in yesterday," the doctor said. "Stumbled into the ER bleeding profusely, hardly even conscious when—"

"Bleeding?" Kersh said. He'd loosened his tie on the drive over, and now a red, raw-looking patch of neck peeked out over his shirt collar. "What the hell happened?"

"Mr. Clifton's right hand had been severed completely. It was bad, and he'd lost a lot of blood."

"Did he say what happened?" Kersh pressed.

"He just said it was an accident, didn't go into detail, but it was severed pretty roughly. Not a clean cut. We had to amputate some more just to clean the area, make it workable. It's not our business to investigate the cause of a patient's accident. I'm a doctor; I just fix the problem."

John resisted the urge to slug the prick. "You gonna be around for a while, if we have questions to ask you?"

Kuhmari glanced at his clipboard, at his beeper. "I'm pretty busy today. You can have me paged."

Kersh thanked him, and the doctor nodded and hurried away.

"Prick," John mumbled under his breath.

"*Doctor* Prick," Kersh corrected, reaching out and pushing open the hospital room door.

The first thing that struck them was the smell—of clotting blood and ammonia and large doses of human sweat. The smell went straight for the stomach.

It was an unusually large hospital room with a single occupied bed alongside an enormous bank of windows. The windowpanes themselves were tinted, making it appear gloomier outside than it really was. It took a moment for their eyes to adjust to the lack of light in the room. Meanwhile, the shape in the bed shifted almost in agitation. John let the door swing closed, blackening the room even more. Across the room, the figure beneath the bed sheets continued to shift restlessly. A soft, pathetic moan escaped the patient's mouth as both he and Kersh stepped farther into the room.

Indeed, the man in the bed was missing his right hand. The arm itself tapered off into a bandaged stump and was propped up in a mechanical sling bolted to a rack above the bed. A network of tubes ran from the wound and were collected in a confusing machine beside the man's bed. The section of gauze bandage at the wrist—the section covering the stump, the actual wound—was blotted with drying blood, so dark it looked nearly black in the poor lighting. The stink of blood in the air was impossibly thick, like the reek of a brutal crime scene.

The man himself looked close to eighty years old, though John knew he was perhaps a little older than himself. Morphine had played a cruel trick on his youth. He was bearded, though not heavily, and he watched both agents approach with muddy, drooping eyes. A crest of dark hair was cropped close to his scalp. Beneath the starched white bedsheets, the man's legs kicked with little strength.

"Douglas Clifton?" Kersh said, his voice low as he moved around the side of the man's bed. "Hello-hello-hello." Clifton's expression suggested his mental status was currently that of a fevered child, and Kersh was quick to catch on.

"He even conscious?" John practically whispered.

"Uh . . ." The figure in the bed began turning at the shoulders, his head turning impatiently from side to side. From the foot of the bed, John examined the man's abbreviated right arm. He could see the muscles and tendons working up the terrain of Clifton's arm where the bandage concluded and skin began. *Phantom fingers,* he thought, wondering if Clifton could still feel his absent right hand.

"Mr. Clifton," Kersh said again, moving a foot closer to the bed. "William Kersh, Secret Service." Kersh paused beside the bed, seeming to consider, then moved in front of the tinted windows and placed his hands on his ample hips. His shadow fell across Clifton's face. Yet Clifton would confess no emotion; his medication had rendered him incapable.

"Do you . . . hear somethin' ringing?" Clifton managed, his voice groggy and inept. The man shifted his gaze from John to Kersh, John to Kersh, his eyes void of cognizance and dulled like that of someone just recently dead. "You hear it?" Those sloppy eyes continued to move wetly in their sockets. Finally, just when it seemed Douglas Clifton was powerless to stimulate that portion of his brain that worked with reality as a medium, Clifton managed a languid, "Who're you?"

John and Kersh shared another glance. Casually, John moved around the other side of Clifton's bed, opposite Kersh. Their dual presence above him and on either side might have intimidated a person not hopped up on meds, but it did nothing to Douglas Clifton.

"What happened to you, Doug?" Kersh said in a serene voice.

Clifton just stared at Kersh. John moved a step closer, but the man did not alter the position of his head on the pillow. This close, John could make out indents in the shape of teeth along Clifton's lower lip, flecked with dried blood.

"Doug?" Kersh held up two fingers, waved them in front of Clifton's face. "What happened to your hand?"

"An accident," Clifton intoned.

"What happened?" Kersh continued, wanting the man to elaborate. He was like a deep sea fisherman, slowly reeling in his catch. "Tell me about the accident."

"I . . ." The man's eyes folded up into his head, as if searching for the information in the deepest recesses of his mind. Then he blinked, turned, and looked John up and down, his eyes cut to slits and eerily sober. "Who sent you here?" he demanded.

"Douglas," John began, "what—"

"Who *sent* you?"

"Nobody sent us. We're cops."

Eyes boring through John, lower lip quivering, Clifton said, "You ain't no cop." Clifton now turned to look at Kersh. "This guy here a cop? He with you? You both . . . the both of you's cops?"

"Both of us," Kersh said. "Do you want to tell us about your hand, Doug?"

"My *hand?*" Clifton's bleary eyes widened. There was an exhale so powerful John was nearly knocked unconscious by the stench. "What about my hand?" His voice was suddenly pleading: a trembling bridge on the verge of collapse. "You have my hand?"

"This is useless," John muttered, disappointed. "This guy's out of it. He couldn't tell us his birthday."

"My hand," Clifton continued. And laughed. He suddenly looked insane. John watched the man's Adam's apple vibrate. "Don't know what you're *talkin'* about. Goddamn." A second burst of laughter. *"Goddamn!"*

A minute later and they were both back out in the hallway. John stood against the wall staring at Clifton's hospital room door while Kersh paced like a caged animal, furiously rubbing his temples. Kuhmari was paged and took a long time coming.

"When's this guy get out of here?" Kersh asked the doctor, one hand still working at the side of his head. He'd bore a hole through his skull before long, John thought as he watched him from against the wall.

"Maybe three, four days," the doctor said, "depending on how well he responds to the surgery."

"Well, this guy's going to be placed under arrest the second he's out of here," Kersh told the doctor, "so I want you to call me before releasing him. Also, you been giving him something for the pain?"

Kuhmari uttered a contemptuous laugh. "Are you serious? Of course. Do you have any idea what kind of pain he'd be in—"

"No," Kersh said, shaking his head, "I don't care. Cut out the meds. We're going to be back tomorrow to talk with this guy. I want his head clear and his eyes on me. Besides, a little pain never hurt anyone."

Kuhmari, not impressed by Kersh's humor, shuffled his feet and glared at Kersh from atop his glasses. When Kersh handed him his business card, the doctor took it without so much as a glance and moved quickly along down the corridor. His shadow had a difficult time keeping up.

John pushed himself off the wall and saddled up beside his partner. "I'm glad you talked with him. I would've knocked him out."

"Might've done him some good—get those neurons firing properly." Kersh winked at him and it made John suddenly feel very tired. The gloom of corridor shadows and the sodium ceiling lights were getting to him, wearing him down. And making him feel somewhat guilty, too. Once again, his mind was with his father, and he was thankful when Kersh spoke, thankful for having something else to think about. "I'm gonna run this guy through NCIC, CCH," Kersh said. "This fool has got to have a record. Meanwhile, I'm gonna rush the prints on those folded hundreds, see if any of this guy's prints are actually on them. Same for the gun and silencer we took out of the trunk. I got a guy who'll dust it for us quick. I want to have as much ammo as possible for when this skel gets out of the hospital. No chances on this one. You wanna grab some lunch?"

John shook his head. It was useless: the hospital's sounds and smells had appealed to a different part of him, a part that wasn't completely cop. "Skipping lunch today," he said. "Think I'm gonna go see me dad."

Kersh smiled, squeezed John's shoulder. "Life's one big hospital visit after another, huh?" Looking in Kersh's eyes, John could tell the man wanted to say more. But he was too slow finding the words.

CHAPTER THIRTEEN

KATIE WAS THERE WHEN HE ARRIVED. AN undetected ghost, he stood just outside the doorway of his father's hospital room and listened while they talked.

"It's this strange, strange thing," he could hear his father saying, "you women have, like some witch's power. Who can understand it? I don't even think *women* understand it half the time."

Katie laughed. He felt a pang of sadness and envy at hearing their candid conversation, at the sound of his wife's laughter. Leaning further into the room, he could see her seated in a small folding chair at his father's bedside, her hand gently on one of his. She looked so young sitting there that her innocence startled him, almost embarrassed him, as if he were the perpetrator of some great crime against her. The tender swell of her belly rested in her lap, hidden beneath an oversized knitted sweater.

"*I* certainly don't understand it," Katie said.

"Well, you're not supposed to. I don't *think,* anyway. That's God's job; leave it to Him, let Him sort things, explain things. But you know, Rachel was the same way, felt the same things."

"John's mother," Katie said. And although it wasn't phrased as a question, the tone of her voice betrayed her unfamiliarity with the name.

"She knew from the first month we were gonna have a boy. She didn't bother considering girl names, and she wasted no time running out every chance she got to buy clothing—little blue pajamas with baseballs on them, anything you'd want. I kept telling her not to get her hopes up, that the baby could just as well be a girl, but she'd say no, no, no, that she knew it was a boy and that was final and I would just have to wait and see. And she was right."

"That's amazing," Katie said. "I wish I'd known her."

"She was beautiful," his father said. "Kind . . . and generous . . . and . . ." He smiled. "All the stuff husbands say, right?"

"It's still nice to hear."

"Well . . ." He pushed back against his pillow, patted her hand. "We were young and carefree and what-have-you. She was a good wife. She . . . she was good . . ."

"Special lady," Katie said. The tone of her voice suggested she craved more information, but dared not ask. Looking up, she noticed her husband standing in the doorway. "Hey, you. Eavesdropping?"

"What are you doing here?"

His father frowned. "That any way to talk to your beautiful wife?"

Katie stood with some difficulty and gave John a one-armed hug. "Had some time before class, figured I'd say hello to Dad."

"She's a good kid, this one," his father said. "Puts up with a crotchety old bastard like me."

"And a crotchety young one at home," she added, grinning.

"How you feeling, Pop?"

"All right." The old man turned to a wall-mounted television set, flipped through the channels with a remote.

Standing between them, Katie looked as though she could feel their discomfort like a solid thing. She crept to the side of the old man's bed, bent and kissed him on his forehead. "Bye," she told him.

"Wait!" His father patted one hand against her arm. "You owe me one name before you leave."

Laughing, Katie picked up her books from the night table beside the bed. "Oh, I was afraid you wouldn't let me get away with it . . ."

"Come on," his father scorned playfully, "you know the deal. One name per visit."

"It's just that I don't think you'll like this one . . ."

"Why not? If it's a good, wholesome name, I'll like it."

Katie frowned, pouted, put a fist on her hip. Her eyes narrowed, and a meager smile crept along her thin lips. "Fielding," she said finally.

"Fielding?" his father said. "This is one of the names you're considering for my grandson? *Fielding?* Sounds like an old Jewish guy. You can't do that to the poor kid."

"I said you wouldn't like it."

"You can do better," he said. "Next time."

She bent and kissed his head again. "Next time," she said. "Always next time. Get some rest and quit watching those trashy talk shows, all right?"

"You're leaving?" John nearly whispered, putting his hand against the small of her back as she brushed past. He followed her halfway out into the hall. "Stay."

"I have class."

"Let me drive you."

"I'll get a cab. I'm a big girl." She rubbed her swollen abdomen. "See?" She caressed his cheek, pinched his chin. Yet she looked upset about something.

"What?" he said. "What is it?"

"The hospital. They're going to discharge him, send him home."

"Jesus. When? Who told you?"

"The doctor. Sometime after Thanksgiving."

"Does Dad know?"

"Not yet. I didn't say anything. The doctor just told me right before you got here. John, this was going to happen sooner or later."

"He'll be all alone in that house. He can be taken care of here. He should stay right here."

"You don't have to convince *me.* But that's not how things work."

"Damn it." He pressed two fingers to his forehead, squeezed skin between them. Turning, he looked at the blinds on the window, at the water fountain against the wall. Things always had a way of falling apart. "Just gonna send him home to die then, right? *Damn* it."

"It'll be all right," she promised. "Now go in there."

"Christ, Katie . . ."

"Quit grumbling."

"I'm not."

"You are. Smile." She hugged him, her belly awkward but beautiful between them. There were no other feelings like it in the world. "Will you be home for dinner tonight, or am I eating alone again?" she asked.

"I'll try to be home."

"I'm making a London broil with scalloped potatoes, seasoned asparagus, apple pie for dessert, all washed down with a nice, smooth bottle of Dom Pérignon."

"Sounds delicious."

"I'd hate to have to eat it all myself." She winked, and turned down the hallway. "I'll save you a couple of hot dogs. Talk to your dad."

Back in the room, the old man continued to flip soundlessly through television channels. When he spoke, he did not look in John's direction; like a greenhorn reporter swiping cues from a teleprompter, he kept his eyes focused on the television,. "She's something, that wife of yours."

"Yes, she is."

"She misses you at home. All your late hours. You should spend more time at the house."

"Pop, please. I'm not a kid."

"Knows for damn certain that baby's gonna be a boy. I had some feeling, too—did I tell you? I guess sometimes people just know."

John's eyes scanned the room—the walls, the bedspread, the tile floor, the machinery beside the bed. He sat in the chair next to the bed, watched the slow rise and fall of his father's small chest from beneath the sheets. He was thankful for the television, thankful that he needn't meet his father's eyes. The disease—even the dying—itself wasn't the worst part; rather, it was the weakness that went along with it. Fathers were not made to be weak, and he was angered by the old man's inability to hold true to that principle. Like a resurrection, the words of Bill Kersh surfaced briefly in his head: *Life's one big hospital visit after another, huh?*

"Heard you talking about Mom," he said.

His father's hand slowed on the television remote. Perhaps he was lost in reverie of his own. "Your mother," he said, his words dry and brittle like ancient cloth. There was no sentiment in his voice. "Katie was talking about the baby, about how she knew it was a boy. I told her your mother felt the same way."

"I didn't know that. You never told me."

"She came up with the name John, too. From the Bible. Said it was bad luck for Catholics to name their first child anything but a biblical name. You got lucky. My choice was Deuteronomy."

"Do you miss her?" The words were out of his mouth before he had time to think about them.

"Every day," his father said, not taking his eyes from the television. For lack of something better to do with his hands, he began flipping through channels again. Faster than before. "She was a good woman."

"I wish I could've known her."

His father began coughing. His frail legs shifted beneath the sheets with the simplicity and helplessness of a small child's, and the television remote clacked against the floor.

"Should I get someone?"

The old man shook his head adamantly, holding one bony hand up to assure John he was going to be all right. When the fit finally subsided, he eased himself back against his pillow, his face flush with color. The linings of his eyelids were rimmed with pink, the sclera tinged a milky yellow. He gasped once, twice for breath before regaining composure.

"You want me to get you some water?"

"No."

"We're going to Katie's parents' house for Thanksgiving," he said from nowhere and thought he felt a small shift in the room's pressure as his father exhaled.

"Oh?"

"She didn't tell you?"

"No."

"We'll just be gone for the day. I'm going to leave the number with one of the nurses in case they need to reach me."

"You should leave early," his father said. "That's the worst day of the year to travel."

"I know, Pop. Will you be all right?"

"I'm not goin' anywhere," the old man muttered, and coughed twice more. They were like small bursts of gunfire. "Just do me one favor tonight, will you?"

"What?"

"At home, on the post by the front door is my black wool coat. Bring it to me."

"You need a coat? Is it too cold in here? I can have them turn up the heat if you're cold, Pop."

"I just want the coat."

"The coat . . ."

"Be careful with it. Don't jostle it around. It's old, and it can tear easy."

John sighed inwardly. Was his father's mind slipping now, too? "Okay," he said after a moment's hesitation.

"Can you do that? If you have time?"

"Sure. Okay."

"Good boy." The television remote was attached to a cable that was connected to the bed frame. His father pulled the cord, retrieved the remote from the floor, and turned the television off. "I'm just a little tired. If I'm asleep when you come back, just put the coat on the chair here."

"Sure."

"I'll see you later, Johnny," the old man said, and turned over on his side.

John stood by the doorway for a long time, watching his father's back. The nape of his neck looked frighteningly tender and unguarded. He remained there for a second longer and continued to watch the old man sleep. He couldn't see his father's eyes and didn't know they were still open.

They had lived in a two-story, semi-detached stucco house on the corner of 62nd Street and Eleventh Avenue in Brooklyn. Summers, the streets would flood with a great storm of children. Cars would crowd as close to the curbs as possible to avoid getting slammed by a rogue baseball. Laughter could be heard well into the night during the summer, permeating the houses along the avenue through screen doors and partially opened windows. Sometimes, if the air thinned enough in the late evening, it was possible to hear the din of a block party halfway across town and, soon, half the neighborhood would begin migrating in that direction: wild animals on the scent of divertissement.

Winters, the moon would rise early from behind the avenue and creep slowly into the sky like a watchful eye, its surface whitish-yellow and swirled with sharp streaks of blue. Winters were usually long and harsh. Neighborhood snowball fights would ensue among the younger children without provocation (to the detriment of working fathers who found it nearly impossible to make it to their cars unscathed by an onslaught of snowballs in the morning). Christmas lights strung from one end of the block to the other, not a single house ostracized from the festivities, all in harmony as things during that time of year should be.

Driving down Eleventh Avenue now, in the cold, gray, snowless afternoon, John found himself subconsciously summoning these memories.

He stopped the car in front of his old home and sat behind the wheel for some time. His father's house sat like a rotting tooth along the avenue. It *had* changed since his childhood, but in the way a young person will eventually change into an old one. The small patch of lawn unkempt, the stone façade nearly pistachio-colored and heavy with mildew. The windows hadn't been scrubbed in some time—since his father had been diagnosed and Katie had gotten pregnant. The driveway pulled up along the left side of the house, comprised of segmented concrete flags. Weeds as thick as forestry sprouted up from cracks in the cement. And beyond the driveway was a small garage, battered and forgotten, ravaged by years of unkind, unyielding weather. Until now he hadn't realized it had gotten so bad, and it bothered him to look at it in such a state.

He got out of the car and crept up the walk, shivering against the cold. Across the street, a group of kids had congregated on the corner, smoking cigarettes behind cupped hands. The lock stuck when he went to turn it, and when he finally managed to push the door open it squealed from age and neglect, piercing the silence of the front hall.

It was dark inside. All the drapes had been pulled closed over the windows. He could just barely make out the semi-familiar shapes of furniture, the stairs at the end of the hallway leading to the second level and, beyond the stairs, the kitchen with its ugly red and gray tile and Formica countertop. Beside the door was his father's black wool coat hanging from the coat rack. On the floor beside the rack were two small suitcases. When his father had found out he'd be spending some time in the hospital for tests, he'd packed his belongings and set them down here by the front door. Then, quite unexpectedly, the old man had suffered a mild stroke and had luckily managed to get to a telephone in time to call the paramedics. The ambulance came and hurried him to the hospital, leaving his bags by the front door like two loyal dogs awaiting the old man's return. Now, looking at the bags, he felt a pang of grief deep inside his chest.

He grabbed the coat from the rack and folded it over his arm.

Before he could realize what he was doing, he had stepped across the foyer and was walking through the condensed living area. He could remember his father's aquarium on the fold-out table beneath the large copper-framed mirror on the wall. He recalled the difficulty with which his father attempted to decorate the house each Christmas, garland and ornaments hanging from every available lip, nail, screw, and doorknob. The year some neighborhood creeps stole Christmas decorations from their front stoop . . .

The kitchen was small and cluttered, and he stood in the doorway while looking the room over. It occurred to him that he hadn't been here since before his father's admittance to the hospital, and it was now like looking at a crime scene: unwashed pots scattered recklessly along the countertop; ground beef, still in the package, rotting in the sink. The coffeepot was still on the stove, cold and defunct.

He was in the middle of making dinner when he collapsed, John realized. Until now, he'd never actually contemplated the details of his father's final moments before the ambulance arrived and whisked him away to the hospital. *He was in the middle of making dinner, and he could have died here—alone—in this house. Maybe a minute or two longer . . .*

Leaving the kitchen, he headed back toward the foyer, but paused as he passed by the stairwell. He turned and looked up. The stairwell itself was dark, but apparently the shades on the upstairs windows had not been drawn, so some daylight managed to seep in and illuminate the hallway. Without thinking, he grabbed the banister and began mounting the stairs one at a time. He stopped at the landing, unmoving. The house smelled stale, empty. Wind blew tree branches against the windows, startling him. He turned and saw his old bedroom door was open a crack. He crossed over to the door, pushed against it gently, though not all the way.

"Christ, Pop," he muttered. For the first time he noticed just how empty the room looked, and a prolonged sadness washed over him. It was as if his father had already passed on and he was here, now, standing in the old man's house like some traitor.

He suddenly realized he was tracing the small scar in his scalp with a pair of fingers.

His cell phone rang.

He slung his father's coat to his left arm, dug his cell phone from his jacket pocket, and quickly pressed it to his face.

"John, it's Tressa. Can you hear me?"

He'd been expecting Kersh to call with information on Douglas Clifton's prints. Hearing Tressa Walker's voice now jarred him, and his mind suddenly slipped back to the night they'd met at McGinty's and how frightened she'd been.

"Yes, yes, go ahead."

"I've only got a minute—"

"I can hear you."

"Mickey's ready to meet you. Outside St. Patrick's Cathedral."

"The cathedral?" He shifted the phone to his other ear. There was an urgency in Tressa's voice, and she was speaking low to try to disguise it. "Sure. When?"

"Thirty minutes," she said, and hung up.

CHAPTER FOURTEEN

STANDING ON FIFTH AVENUE, JOHN LOOKED ACROSS the street at St. Patrick's Cathedral while trying to catch his breath. Before him, the twin spires of the cathedral divided the sky. The building itself loomed there, an ecclesiastic testament to both man and God, surrounded by the abrupt yet suddenly meaningless steel-and-glass rectangles of New York City. A number of people milled around the front steps before the enormous copper doors. He scanned the crowd for Tressa Walker but could not find her. Why would this bum Mickey want to meet here? It was bizarre. Already, he did not like this Mickey O'Shay character.

He mounted the steps of the cathedral two at a time, his hands stuffed into the pockets of his pants, and paused at the crest of stone risers, again dissecting the crowd. Catching his breath after his mad sprint from Rockefeller Center, he feared he was too late. He could find Tressa Walker nowhere. Perhaps O'Shay had changed his mind.

"Damn," John muttered under his breath.

"Here," a woman's voice said from behind him. "John." He turned around and saw Tressa Walker, half-bundled in a thick green coat, standing in the cathedral's entranceway. She looked much smaller than she had the night they met at McGinty's. Her skin looked paler, too—possibly from the cold. She had her coat bundled around something which was pressed to her chest. Not until John made out a distinct little fist jutting from the coat did he realize Tressa had brought along her baby. "John," she said again, a plume of vapor blossoming in the air before her mouth.

"Thought I was late."

"It's cold," she said. "Come on. It's warmer inside."

"Your friend with you?" But, with the exception of her child, John could see Tressa was alone.

"Inside," she repeated, and disappeared behind the large copper doors of the cathedral.

Growing up near the city, John had been inside the cathedral on a number of occasions and, even as a small child, had understood at least some part of the church's power. His father had been a devout Catholic and had taken him to St. Patrick's for Christmas Mass a number of times. He could remember sitting in the pew beside his father and staring at the church in awe.

He realized he was sweating.

There were a number of people slowly working their way around the interior of the church. They were like large fish swimming laps in an aquarium. At his side, Tressa unzipped her coat and shook her hair out from her collar, cradling her child in one arm. Watching her, John was amazed how skewed some people were in this world. He tried to imagine Katie standing here before him, their own child propped against her chest, and the thought made his head spin. He could almost feel the heat from the fiery collapse of morality all around him.

The baby began to fuss, and Tressa quickly popped a pacifier into its mouth to keep the kid quiet.

"Is he here?"

"He's up there in the front," she said, nodding toward the altar.

Two rows of pews stretched out before them like trails of garments. "I'm staying here."

"Are you kidding me? The heck is this?" There were too many people to see Mickey O'Shay clearly. A few people were seated in the pews facing the altar—a collection of necks and heads. "Where?"

"Up front," Tressa repeated, "sitting down."

Slowly, he began walking down the aisle between the pews. He was aware of his footfalls hammering the floor, the heels of his shoes overly loud despite the commotion created by spectators surrounding him. He was always conscious of himself, even under circumstances unrelated to his job: another benefit of having grown up in the streets.

Directly before him, powerful in gold baldachin, humble in alabaster, the grand altar loomed.

There was a man seated in the first row of pews to his left, facing the altar. He could only see the back of the man's head—scraggly, dirty-blond hair—and he could tell he was fairly young just by his posture, but he couldn't make out the man's profile. Not that it mattered; he had no idea what Mickey O'Shay looked like. Before approaching the man, John turned around toward the back of the church, as if seeking Tressa's approval, but the girl was gone.

He stopped at the end of the aisle beside the first row of pews, hands in his pockets, eyes fixed on the magnificent altar. He didn't bother trying to catch a glimpse of the man's face. If the guy was O'Shay, it would play out. "Something, ain't it? Makes you think about some things," he said, shooting for the man's attention.

"You John?"

"Mickey?"

"Sit down."

John sat, his eyes still straight ahead. "This is good . . . that we could meet . . ."

"You still want that hundred grand?" Mickey asked.

"These the same bills I was supposed to get before?"

"The same. How come you don't go back to Deveneau?"

"I don't know any Deveneau."

"Good answer." There was a pause. "We can do the deal right now," Mickey said after a moment.

John turned and faced him. He guessed Mickey to be roughly around his own age, though he appeared much older. His eyes were startlingly blue, his profile—for Mickey O'Shay did not take his eyes from the altar—that of a choirboy. His sandy hair was long and greasy and curled behind his ears. He wore a dull green canvas coat, nondescript slacks, scuffed boots. In all, his appearance was nothing if not disappointing. O'Shay sat there motionless, the collar of his polyester shirt flipped out over the zippered collar of his canvas coat. He looked like some eccentric throwback, a confused and ignorant homage to the Dead End Kids, a street punk who'd somehow struck oil and was now dealing up. There was nothing intimidating about him, nothing in his eyes that professed any semblance of uniformity, of rationalization, of the ability to organize and *be* organized. Less a gangster and more a man who'd just finished scrounging for beer money in his sofa.

"Right now?" John uttered a small laugh. "You wanna do the deal right now? Are you serious?"

"What's the matter?"

"I don't have the money on me. I had to bust my ass to get here in time just to meet with you. I had no notice. Give me a day or two to get my money together and then—"

"You know the price."

He shifted in his seat and turned back toward the altar. "Twenty grand for a hundred thousand."

"You got a pen?"

John blinked, patted the front of his shirt. "I—I don't know . . ."

"Wait." Mickey fished around inside his coat and produced a pencil stub, handed it to John. "Here," he said, then picked up a

Bible from beside him, flipped it open to the middle, and handed it over to John. "And here. Write down your phone number."

He printed his cell phone number on page 887, just above a passage in Jeremiah that said, "The stain of your guilt is still before me." He slid the open Bible across the pew back over to Mickey, who gazed disinterestedly at the main altar. When he *did* glance down, it was only for a second before turning to look at John.

Something flickered behind Mickey's ice-blue eyes—something like a spark in the darkness. But it was there and then gone, too fleeting for John to interpret.

Mickey tore the page from the Bible and stuffed it inside his coat.

"Guess you're not a religious man, huh?" John said.

Mickey stood, his frame unimposing. His eyes remained on the altar. "You know Tressa long?"

"On and off since high school."

"Anything goes wrong with this deal, no one will know her. Or you."

The words were out and John let Mickey say them, though he would have normally slapped the little punk right out of the pew. Instead, he looked forward to slapping the cuffs on O'Shay's wrists. That would be satisfaction enough.

"I'll call ya," O'Shay said.

"When?"

But Mickey O'Shay had nothing more to say: he sidestepped his way out of the pew and mingled among the tourists and spectators until he disappeared in the confusion of St. Patrick's Cathedral.

CHAPTER FIFTEEN

EARLY THE NEXT MORNING, IN A SMALL Midtown diner, John sipped a cup of coffee and watched a roach scuttle across the table. Outside, a light rain fell against the diner's windows, the sound soothing. According to the clock on the wall behind the counter, Kersh was late. And John wanted to get to Douglas Clifton's hospital room within the hour.

After a while, John saw Kersh dart across the street with a newspaper over his head. The man was broad-shouldered and, carrying some extra weight, he ran with the loping, impeded gallop of an injured gazelle. Kersh hit the diner's door like a strong wind, pulled it open, and pushed himself inside while simultaneously exhaling a heavy breath. John raised a hand, and Kersh sauntered over to his table, plodding down in the seat across from him. Catching his breath, Kersh rubbed a hand through his wet hair.

"Weather," Kersh muttered, shaking the drizzle from his newspaper. There was something childish about him—in his face, his mannerisms, his eyes—that caused John to grin.

"You look like shit. Don't you ever shave?"

"You," Kersh said, unfolding his newspaper, "suddenly have more important things to worry about than my personal hygiene."

Buried within the folds of his newspaper was a manila folder. Kersh slid the folder out across the table and opened it, rifled through some computer printouts. "Two bits of information for you," he said, not looking up from his paperwork.

"Oh yeah?"

Kersh slid two of the printouts in front of John: O'Shay's and Kahn's records from NYPD. John's meeting with O'Shay had prompted Kersh to retrieve their information the night before. John scanned the printouts, then muttered, "Son of a *bitch.*"

"Can you believe it? You see those charges? Kidnapping, assault, attempted murder, some robbery sprinkled in there for flavor. All major arrests . . . *but not a single conviction.*" Kersh leaned over the table and drummed a thick finger on one of the rap sheets. "Two murder acquittals on insanity for your churchgoing buddy O'Shay. He's been in and out of institutions half his life."

"I don't believe this. Not from these guys."

"It's there in black and white," Kersh told him, then waved a waitress over and ordered himself a cup of coffee. "This puts a bad taste in my mouth, John. I know you said this guy O'Shay's some dope off the street—"

"He *is*—"

"Nevertheless, you keep this shit in mind every time you meet with this clown—you know what I'm saying? Somebody like this . . . you don't know what to expect."

Something smelled bogus. True, Kersh was right—it was all here in black and white—but he found it impossible to connect that mook O'Shay to the rap sheet in front of him. Bad guys looked a certain way, spoke a certain way, dressed a certain way, operated in a certain way. Often, they were so cliché and so predictable that it was almost ludicrous. Yet here he was, faced with the exception to that rule, and he was surprised and a bit exasperated by his initial miscalculation.

"What else?" he asked Kersh. "You said you had two bits of info for me."

"Clifton's prints on those folded hundreds."

"They came back?" John asked.

"They came back *clean.* His prints aren't on any of the bills."

"Well, that's terrific. Christ."

"Maybe he was careful," Kersh said. "Or just lucky. It happens. Although I thought we'd get at least *one* . . ." Kersh drummed his thick fingers on the table. "Clifton's got a record, anyway. Minor stuff."

"And the gun? The silencer?"

"Hopefully we'll hear on that tonight, tomorrow at the latest. They're checking ballistics."

John looked at the clock again while Kersh sipped his coffee, blew rings across the surface.

"One last thing," Kersh said absently, looking down at his coffee.

"What's that?"

"Don't meet with this O'Shay guy again without telling me first, John."

That same fetid smell still clung to the air inside Douglas Clifton's hospital room. Upon entrance, John and Kersh both expected to find the room's occupant just as delirious as he'd been the day before. However, as they pushed open the door, John was surprised to see that Dr. Kuhmari *had* been intimidated by Kersh and had not administered any pain medication to Clifton, as far as John could tell.

The man writhed in bed, his eyes wide and bloodshot. His breathing was harsh, raspy, filtered through clamped teeth. His dark brush-cut hair had been teased by the mattress in his fitful sleep. He trained his gaze on both John and Kersh the moment they stepped through the door.

Kersh wasted no time. "Douglas Clifton, I'm Special Agent Kersh, Secret Service. This is Agent Mavio. Do you remember us from yesterday?"

Douglas Clifton, who'd probably been told exactly why he hadn't been administered his medication that morning, pushed himself up in his bed, his feet working beneath the sheets. His eyes never left Kersh. Still bandaged and confined to the sling above his bed, Clifton flexed, relaxed, and flexed his injured arm again.

"Don't remember nothin'," Clifton growled. "The hell you guys want?"

Kersh went straight for the obvious. "What happened to your hand, Doug?"

"Why?"

"Curious."

Clifton chewed at the inside of his right cheek. "Get over it," he grumbled.

But Kersh was both calm and relentless. "Really—what happened?"

Clifton's lower lip quivered. The expression on his face was that of a mule repeatedly beaten for its stubbornness. "Get out of here," he practically whispered.

"Don't wanna talk about the accident?" John began, and Clifton's eyes quickly shifted in his direction. "Fine. Let's talk about those counterfeit hundreds you been passing."

Like the shadow of an airplane, a look moved briefly over Douglas Clifton's face. It was that look which immediately gave him away. Yet the man would not comply, and his lower lip began working again. John watched the fingers of Clifton's good hand pick at the frame of the bed. "Don't know what you're talkin' about," he said finally.

"We've got phony hundreds back in our office with your prints all over them," John lied.

Clifton laughed once—sharply—and the corners of his mouth

hooked up into an unsettling grin. "Prints? Fucking *prints?* Yeah? With what *hand?*" He uttered a pained sob and eased his eyes shut. "Don't mean nothing."

John cocked an eyebrow. "It don't? Look at me."

With reluctance, Clifton peeked at John from behind squinted eyes. "Got nothin' to do with me."

"We know you've been slipping phony hundreds to some dancer at the Black Box."

"Bullshit."

"We all know you're full of horse shit here, Doug," Kersh said, the soft tone and abrupt message of his voice contradictory almost to the point of comedy. Yet there was nothing comedic about Kersh's performance. "You have problems, both present"—he nodded toward Clifton's truncated arm—"and future. We grabbed your car from the pound, found some interesting stuff in the trunk. We'll put this whole thing together. Your situation right now is going to seem like a walk in the park. Listen to what I'm saying."

Despite the pain from his wound and the fear that prodded him just below the surface, Clifton's eyes grew calm and lucid, his face growing oddly serene. He pushed his head back against his pillow and tilted his eyes up toward the ceiling. Beside the bed, his heart monitor began picking up tempo.

"Now's your time to talk," John pushed.

"I don't know what you guys are talkin' about," Clifton said. He spoke slow and easy, each word calculated. "Leave me alone. I got no damn hand now. You know what that means? You think I give a shit about what you're saying?"

"You better *start* giving a shit," John said. "You're headed for a room with bars and no Jell-O for dessert. And a guy with one hand, I don't think will do too well in the joint."

"You goddamn guys don't get it," Clifton said, the ghost of that unsettling grin returning to his lips. "I don't give a shit what my prints are on or what you found in my trunk—I ain't tellin' you nothin' and I don't *know* nothin'. I ain't seen that car in days. Any asshole could've stuck somethin' in the trunk. And, shit, I go to clubs all the time, give girls money all the time. I ever slip 'em a hundred-dollar bill? Absolutely not." Shaking his head, that peculiar smile still lingering on his lips, Clifton closed his eyes. Some moisture appeared in the creases. "Ahhhh." A single tear ran down his temple. "I'm tired, and I fucking hurt. Get out."

"This just ain't gonna go away," John promised him.

"You go away," Clifton murmured. "The both of you."

"Where'd you get that money, Doug?" John said, his voice rising. "Who gave you that money?"

"Get out!" Clifton cried, his eyes flipping open, his head coming up off the pillow. His eyes were like two neon bulbs. *"Get out! Get out! Get out! Get out-out-out-out-out!"*

The hospital room door opened, and two young nurses flitted in. One rushed to Clifton's bedside while the other approached John and Kersh, ushering them out of the way. "Gentlemen, please, you shouldn't be—"

John shot a finger out and pointed at Clifton, his eyes just as wild and alert as the man in the bed. *This isn't going away, buddy,* his eyes told Clifton. *I promise you, man. Not by a long shot.*

One of the nurses bent over Clifton, frantic to get the man under control and relaxed. With his good hand, Clifton shoved the young nurse out of the way, his eyes never leaving John's, his abbreviated arm rattling in its mechanical casing. Beside the bed, Clifton's heart monitor began chirping sixteenth notes, the small screen cluttered with flashing numbers and erratic, zigzag lines.

Kersh squeezed John's forearm. "Come on," he said, leading him out into the hallway. "I think we've made an impression."

Later that evening, Kersh arrived alone in the lobby of One Police Plaza and was directed to Detective Peter Brauman of the Intelligence Division. At roughly Kersh's age, weight, and height, Peter Brauman could have worn Kersh's shadow as his own. A dedicated, loyal fellow, John would have been interested to know that Peter Brauman was one of the select few people Bill Kersh honestly *liked.*

Now, surrounded by the soft glow of his desk lamp, Brauman sat reclining in his chair listening to some sporting event on the radio. His back to Kersh, the Secret Service agent watched the man for some time without saying a word, amused by his gestures and scowls at the radio. When Brauman happened to look up in Kersh's direction, he spooked and nearly spilled out of his chair.

"Christ," Brauman said. "Give me a friggin' heart attack."

"Working hard as usual, Peter."

"Smart guy. How you doing? Sit down." Brauman hooked a thumb at a box of pastries that sat on his desk. "Want a cruller?"

"No, I just ate. You got a few minutes?"

"You know it."

Kersh eased himself down in a chair in front of Brauman's desk. Seated, he noticed some tomato sauce on his shirt and scraped at it with his thumbnail. "Last night I pulled up the records on two guys—Mickey O'Shay and Jimmy Kahn. Young Irish guys from the West Side. Got a bunch of arrests but no convictions. Some of the stuff's pretty heavy—homicide, assaults, that sort of thing. You know anything about them?"

Brauman leaned back in his chair and turned the volume down on his radio. "O'Shay and Kahn," Brauman said under his breath. He stood, his chair creaking, and ambled over to a wall of file cabinets. "We got some intelligence files on them going back about two years ago or so. Rumors are they've been involved in some hits, loan sharking, extortion, the usual bag of shit. I just know bits and pieces." He selected two thick folders from the file cabinet and carried them back to his desk. He sat down in a great exhalation. "Supposedly took over Hell's Kitchen. Here." Brauman slid the paperwork around so Kersh could read it. "Pretty vicious guys, as you can see."

Flipping through the files, Kersh whistled.

"Like I said, nothing concrete. Supposedly they've been involved in a lot of shootings, even got their hands in some of the unions."

"You're kidding."

"That's the word."

"What's with the acquittals?" In Kersh's opinion, there were two reasons for the lack of convictions. One: the assaults were against street punks who, in turn, made lousy witnesses. Or two: O'Shay and Kahn had frightened people to the point that they refused to testify against them. Something John had said about Tressa Walker and how frightened she'd been when talking to him about O'Shay and Kahn . . .

Brauman rolled his shoulders and raked his fingers through a graying patch of hair. He looked tired. And it suddenly occurred to Kersh that *all* middle-aged cops looked tired. "Acquittals? If I had to guess, I'd say the prosecution had a difficult time finding anyone to talk against them."

"Why's that?"

Quite matter-of-factly, Brauman said, "Because they're nuts. Real whack-a-doos. They get their way through intimidation. One of 'em—the O'Shay fella, if I'm thinkin' right—he got off a homicide on an insanity plea once or twice, did a few months at some nuthouse upstate. Then he became cured and got out. Some system. I know a detective who's worked some cases, arrested them before." Lacing his hands across his ample stomach, Brauman leaned farther back in his chair; Kersh could hear the rollers creak beneath the man's weight. "What's the deal, anyway? You guys got something on them?"

Kersh, who was instinctually covetous when it came to the divulgence of case information, even with another officer of the law, merely said, "Their names popped up in some counterfeit case we're working. Figured I'd check 'em out, see what came up. Let me ask you—these guys have any connection to a fella named Charles or Charlie Lowenstein that you know of? Guy was a printer."

"Don't ring a bell. I wouldn't know."

"That detective friend of yours?"

"I can give him a call sometime this week, see what he knows."

Kersh frowned, rubbed his chin. "Ahhh—just if you happen to speak with him. Not a big deal."

"Well, if you want to arrest 'em, be my guest. Save us some trouble. Oh," Brauman said, eyebrows raising, "that reminds me. I got your present." He pushed his chair away from his desk and rolled over to a cabinet, opened a drawer, searched. After a moment, Brauman withdrew a plastic evidence bag from the cabinet and rolled back over to his desk, placing the bag on his New York Mets desk calendar. Inside the bag were the gun and silencer recovered from Evelyn Gethers's Lincoln Towncar; stapled to the outside of the bag were the results of the ninhydrin exam. "Lab came back with a hit. Douglas James Clifton is your man. Got some good prints off the twenty-two and a nice fat thumbprint on the silencer."

Kersh leaned forward in his chair and peered at the bag. "Douglas Clifton," Kersh muttered, satisfied. "One-armed bandit."

When Brauman asked what Kersh meant, the Secret Service agent only shook his head and reached for the last cruller.

Time.

It's a volatile thing. Sometimes, it's an abyss. In the swimming moments that occupy the turn around a dark corner in an abandoned neighborhood tenement, time becomes infinite. Gun drawn, heart pounding, sweat prickling and itching the sticky nape of one's neck—time has swallowed that person. He is held captive. Nothing moves, nothing changes. Time has stopped and he is suspended.

Other times, it is like a locomotive barreling through a mountainside tunnel. Yet for an agent, there is no track to guide the way. There is the sensation of losing control. It can be an eternity that lasts for a second, or a second that extends until forever . . .

On the nightstand beside the bed, John's cell phone rang.

"No," Katie muttered, "let it go."

"Can't," John said, completing a line of kisses down his wife's neck before rolling over and fumbling with the cell phone in the dark. "John."

"You sound funny. You're already in bed?" It was Kersh.

"No, no—go ahead. I'm up."

"Just thought you'd want to know—prints came back on the gun and silencer. Douglas Clifton's had his hands all over them."

"Beautiful."

"Well, we'll see how it shakes down," Kersh said. "He isn't the most cooperative soul."

"He'll talk now."

"Let's hope," Kersh said. "You're going to Katie's parents' tomorrow for Thanksgiving?"

"For the day, yeah. You got plans?"

"I help at a church-sponsored soup kitchen every year out in Jersey. Mostly young kids and their mothers, that sort of thing. I'll be there most of the day."

"You gotta be shittin' me . . ." Katie raised her head up off the pillow, but John waved her back down.

Kersh laughed. "Keeps the conscience clean. Better than confession. If there's a God up there, I'm building toward my big retirement."

"You'll get points just for spending the day in Jersey."

Again, Kersh laughed. John pictured him seated in his cramped apartment at a small kitchen table, a can of Spaghetti-O's choked with a spoon laid out before him. Perhaps in the background hums the soft lilt of one of Kersh's beloved jazz records.

"Have a nice holiday," Kersh said. "Send Katie my regards."

"I will. Good night."

He clicked off the phone and rolled back against his wife. Wasting no time, he pressed his lips to her soft neck while she shivered and smiled in his arms. "Bill Kersh sends his regards," he mumbled.

"He's the big, frumpy guy from the office?"

"The very same."

"He reminds me," Katie said, "of a big, messy sofa." She'd only met Kersh once, when they'd bumped into him at a restaurant one afternoon, and she had been impressed with the man's knowledge of artwork, music, theater.

"I'll tell him you said that."

"Don't offend him."

"It won't offend him," he said, continuing to bury his face into the warm, yielding flesh of his wife's neck. "He'd actually like it. Now come here and stop talking . . ."

For an agent on a tedious surveillance, time becomes an opponent. For an agent suddenly plunged into the whizzing heat of an unexpected gunfight, time becomes a threat. For an agent faced with the daunting task of working and reworking undercover scenarios, time becomes a gift.

For John Mavio, time became a decision, and it arrived on Thanksgiving morning.

CHAPTER SIXTEEN

SEVEN-THIRTY THANKSGIVING MORNING, AND THE TEMPERATURE registered at just under forty degrees. The sun was visible only when it passed between the patches of iron-colored clouds that hugged the skyline. Already there was movement in the Mavio home. In the kitchen, Katie hovered around the table like a bee to a flower, filling two large plates with the cookies she'd been baking for the past two days. Humming under her breath, she was a young girl once again, helping her mother prepare food for the holidays. On the counter beside the sink, a small television was turned to NBC, though the Macy's Thanksgiving Day Parade would not begin for another hour and a half.

In the bedroom, John stirred and rolled over, half-awake. He could hear his wife's humming, could hear the sounds of the television set coming down the hall. Outside, he could even make out the early-morning calls of kids out in the street, marching in a parade of their own. Their apartment was situated in a predominantly Italian neighborhood. Italians—particularly *New York* Italians—lived for the holidays. Any annual celebration was an excuse to unload tremendous amounts of food on willing and eager relatives, to clutter kitchens with baked sweets and fresh bread still warm from the bakery. As a child, John had shared a few Thanksgivings with distant relatives, but usually it was just he and his father.

Katie came into the room, yanked open the closet, and stood there with one hand on her hip and her other hand pressed to the swell of her belly. Without looking in her husband's direction, she said, "Wake up, wake up, wake up. Your day off and you're going to spend it in bed?"

"I was dreaming. What time is it?"

"Morning."

"Really? I wouldn't have guessed. Cookies smell good."

"Get up, and get ready," she told him. "We have some driving to do today."

He staggered out of bed at Katie's insistence, was practically shoved into the shower and thrust into a pair of jeans and a sweatshirt. And although some part of his mind was already interrogating Douglas Clifton, he felt mostly at peace with himself and ready to shake his job from him, at least for several hours. It would be nice—pleasant drive to Katie's parents' house, taking in the scenery, spending some time with his wife. To him, it seemed that Katie's pregnancy had progressed in a series of hasty snapshots. Like an absent father sent photographs of his child, surprised at how much the child has grown, he sometimes found himself looking at Katie when she didn't know she was being observed, just capturing her in his mind. There was a rejection he sometimes felt deep within himself when staring at her in this way. As if it was *her* feeling of rejection, radiating so strong that it felt like his own. In a perfect world time would mean nothing, work would be nonessential, and he could spent an eternity staring at his wife.

By eight o'clock there was a strong wind blowing against the side of the building, rattling the windows. The streets filled with shade as the sun was again swallowed up by another blind of clouds. While his wife showered and dressed, he sneaked a couple of oatmeal cookies from the prepared trays and watched the television with little interest. Despite the cold weather, he was in a good mood. It had been a while since he'd felt relaxed.

A chirping sound: his cell phone, still on the nightstand in their bedroom.

Personal calls were always made to the house, so he knew right away the call was work-related. And his first thought was *Kersh.* He hurried down the hall and scooped the phone off the nightstand, pressed the green button.

"Yeah?"

"John." A man's voice—but not Bill Kersh's. He knew the voice, but it took his brain a couple seconds to place a face to it. "John," the man repeated, his voice uninflected.

It was Mickey O'Shay.

"Yeah, this is John."

There was some rustling on the other end of the phone. "Where are you?"

He uttered an apprehensive laugh and glanced back toward the hallway. Quickly, he moved across the bedroom floor and quietly shut the bedroom door. "At home. This—Mickey?"

"I want you to meet me in one hour."

"Somethin' wrong?"

"No," Mickey said. "I got your money with me now."

He thought of the way Mickey O'Shay sat huddled in the front pew of St. Patrick's Cathedral . . .

"Are you kidding me, man?" he said. "I don't have my end. I told you I'd need at least a day." He summoned a forced laugh. "You tryin' to bust my balls here or what?"

"Forget your end," Mickey said. "I'll front it to you."

A rapid sinking sensation overcame him; Mickey had left him no wiggle room.

John breathed heavily into the phone. "The hell you talking about?"

"It's yours," Mickey said. "I'm fronting it. You want it, come get it."

"This better not be bullshit," he told Mickey. "Where you wanna meet?"

A minute later and he was standing in the hallway, watching Katie wrap the trays of cookies in colored Saran Wrap. Her hair was still wet from the shower, strands of it hanging in her face. He watched her work for some time.

She looked up, her hands still holding taut a piece of Saran Wrap. The expression on her face suggested he needn't say anything. "When do you have to leave?" she said.

As he drove, he glanced around the interior of the car to make sure everything looked presentable and in order. The Camaro was not his; likewise, the license plates and registration did not correspond to his home address. It was a seized vehicle, used for undercover work and assigned to him. The registration was made out to a false last name—Esposito: the same last name John used as an alias on his falsified driver's license and American Express card. It would be as John Esposito that Mickey O'Shay would come to know him.

Looking around, he noticed something in the back seat. Hitting a traffic light, he glanced behind him. His father's wool coat lay folded on the seat, forgotten from his mind after he'd taken it from his father's house.

"Goddamn it."

He hit the bridge, and there was already traffic. Why the hell Mickey O'Shay wanted to meet in Manhattan on Thanksgiving Day was beyond him.

He glanced at the clock on the Camaro's console: 8:35. The parade would begin at exactly nine o'clock at 77th Street and Central

Park West, and drip slowly down the park until it turned onto Broadway toward Herald Square. The entire event would last roughly three hours, from nine till noon, and John knew from experience that the city would be a madhouse. Mickey's directions had been to go through the Theater District and wait in his car at the corner of 57th and Ninth. And although the parade would not have trickled down that far by the time he got there, he would essentially be cutting through the parade route, which was cordoned off. Which meant he would have to go down and around Broadway instead of crossing it north of Herald Square.

Son of a bitch, he thought. *There is no way I'm going to make it there in time. No way in the world.*

And Mickey had to know this.

Either he's whacked out of his mind, or he's got something up his sleeve. No one with brains fronts a hundred grand in counterfeit bills to a guy unless he's your brother.

The compact bulge of his gun pressed against the small of his back.

He had been right about the city: straight off the bridge, traffic shuddered to a complete halt. Horns blared, cars edged between other cars and scooted down alleys only to be trapped there moments later. He would have had better luck turning a steamship around in a closet. It occurred to him then that he could probably go up Broadway and flash his badge to gain passage through the parade route, but in the end his instincts warned him away from such an exercise.

Up ahead, traffic broke off into two directions and he got swept up in one lane, unsure what street he was on. Beside him, the driver of a Honda CR-V gunned his engine. In front, some of the cars inched closer toward an intersection and, just as it looked like there was going to be a break in traffic, a mob of people rushed across the intersection, eliciting honks and swears and upraised middle fingers.

According to the console clock, it was already nine o'clock.

Uptown, the Macy's Thanksgiving Day Parade had begun.

He could hear music before he ever saw anything. Marching band music: heavy on the drums, heavy on the horns. And finally, when he *did* see something, it was mostly people and balloons. Handheld balloons, not the massive helium-filled cartoon characters that would soon blot the sky. He moved down an alleyway cluttered with wooden crates and stinking of fish, and popped out onto a crowded section of Eighth Avenue. The sounds of snare drums and brass horns and thousands of feet filled the air. He was aware that he was the only person actually *walking,* actually *moving,* and that everyone else remained stationary along the cusp of the avenue, peering down the block for a glimpse of the parade. Yet all that was visible was the throng of other spectators.

He paused to light a cigarette, smoked it down to the ass, then pitched it in the gutter. He was of medium height and had some difficulty peering over the heads of the crowd that had formed along Eighth Avenue. Two uniformed police officers stood in the street, waving their hands to partition the gathering and create a narrow passageway for people to traverse. One block up, Broadway pulsed as the heart of the parade. A clutch of balloons were let go several yards ahead of him and, briefly, he paused to watch them sail up into the sky.

Scratching at his ears like a flea-bitten dog, he turned and headed east on 57th in the opposite direction of the crowd. Someone slammed into his shoulder but he didn't lift his head, didn't look up. Behind him, a bray of trumpets pierced the air.

Shivering against the cold, vapor billowing from his mouth, Mickey O'Shay moved among the crowd like a ghost unseen.

☘

It was almost ten o'clock when John parked the Camaro at the corner of 57th and Ninth. He was roughly an hour late, and he felt aggravated as he watched the crowd of people mill down 57th Street. Had he missed him already? This was a horrible place to meet, and now John had his doubts whether or not Mickey had ever planned on showing up at all. That notion only angered him more—the thought of the little son of a bitch calling the shots. Was he somewhere right now, laughing to himself? And then it suddenly occurred to John and the revelation was like an electric shock: he had no idea what was going on. Moreover, he had no idea what was going through Mickey O'Shay's mind. For seemingly the first time in the two years since he'd been on the Secret Service, he couldn't think ahead of his target, couldn't outstep him. Peering through the windshield, he watched the bundled onlookers filter down toward Broadway. With the car shut down, it grew cold; he rubbed his hands together to keep warm. How long should he even sit here and wait?

Two short taps against the passenger side window. Jerking his head around, he saw O'Shay's mottled canvas coat and nondescript pants framed within the window. Only the tips of Mickey's fingers could be seen poking out of the cuffs of his coat.

John leaned across the passenger seat and popped open the door. Wasting no time, Mickey climbed in and shut the door, bringing with him the thankless stink of cigarette smoke and the bitter cold. Mickey shook his long hand with his fingers and snorted.

"You're late," he muttered. He looked John up and down, as if deciding whether or not he was worth his time.

"You gotta be kidding me. Maybe you haven't noticed, but there's kind of a big parade goin' on."

Mickey had no interest in small talk. That, or he was still feeling

John out. He craned his head back and peered at the passenger side mirror. "Too many people here," Mickey said. "Turn around and pull into that alley on your right."

John turned the engine over and rolled the Camaro up the street until he spotted the alleyway Mickey had mentioned.

"Right here," Mickey said.

He spun the wheel and eased the car up a slight incline. The alley ran directly behind Roosevelt Hospital. Mickey told him to stop the car before they pulled out onto the hospital's tarmac.

"Yeah, this looks inconspicuous," John mused, peering in the rearview. "But I'm done driving. What's the deal, you givin' me this stuff up front? I'm ready to deal."

"You got a problem with trust?" Mickey said. He shifted in his seat, and John caught another whiff of cigarette smoke.

"Not me," John said. "Not at all."

"I didn't bring the money," Mickey said.

"What are you, yankin' my chain? You don't have the money, the hell did you ask me to come out for?"

"Because," Mickey said, "cops don't work holidays."

"So now I'm a cop?"

"Relax," Mickey said. There was a hint of casualness to his voice—a first for him. "Just wanted to see if you'd show."

The smug look on Mickey's face, coupled with his insouciant tone, made John's blood boil. An image of Katie standing, dejected and heartbroken, over her trays of homemade cookies flashed across his mind. "You little jerk," he said, "I had plans with my family, and you're here wastin' my goddamn time. I should bang you in the teeth."

"So you're a tough guy," Mickey said, still relaxed. He was facing front now, not even looking in John's direction. "I'm shittin' all over myself."

"Get the fuck outta my car."

"Take a couple days to get your money together," Mickey said, "and I'll call you."

"Fuck you and your money."

Mickey popped open the passenger door, stepped out into the alley, and let the door slam shut. For a moment, Mickey O'Shay stood just outside John's car, looking like someone desperately trying to remember something they'd forgotten. Then he dug a pack of cigarettes from his coat, turned, and headed back down the alleyway. John watched him walk away in the rearview mirror, resisting the urge to hop from the car, grab the punk, slam him a few times.

Because cops don't work holidays, John thought. *Also, cops flash a badge and they're able to drive right through a parade route. In other words, cops show up on time.*

"Nice start, pal," he muttered, "but I got your number."

Just then his cell phone rang. Eyes still trained on Mickey in the car's rearview, he answered the phone without looking at it.

"John," he said.

"It's Bill," Kersh said. The connection was poor, and he could hardly make out Kersh's voice. "I hate to spoil your holiday, but I figured you'd want to know . . ."

"What is it?" He watched as Mickey slipped onto 57th Street and disappeared among the mob of people. A second after that, and it was like he never existed. "What?" he repeated. A crash of thunder, and it started to rain.

"It's Douglas Clifton," Kersh said.

"What about him?"

"He's dead."

EARLY DECEMBER

CHAPTER SEVENTEEN

TODAY, IT IS DIFFICULT TO IMAGINE HELL'S Kitchen as having once been a lush, provincial countryside, its landscape defined not by red-brick tenements and fire-scarred shops, but by countless running streams and burgeoning grasslands. Slowly, over time, the region blossomed under the weight of immigrants fleeing their homelands—the Dutch, Italians, Irish, Germans. The land was fertile and strong, and in the mid-1800s, the Hudson River Railroad became the cornerstone on which a changing society was established. The railroad quickly attracted scores of hopeful immigrants, all hungry for work, all anxious to eke out an existence for themselves and their families in this brave new world. Shortly after the addition of the railroad, Manhattan's West Side grew rich with industry, providing the foundation for glue factories and distilleries, slaughterhouses and sweatshops. The air, once pure and untouched, was soon tinged with the metallic reek of the abattoirs along West 39th Street—so overwhelming that, in the summer, everything smelled vaguely of blood. Tenements were constructed close together along what some people called Slaughterhouse Row or Abattoir Place, crammed with families that made their livelihood off the very industry that poisoned their lungs and corrupted their spirits. Runoff from the slaughterhouses pooled along the avenues, causing the gutters to swell with blood. Stray dogs lapped up the gore from the streets. Clothing strung out on clotheslines between tenements reeked permanently of slaughter. The West Side breweries combated the stink of the slaughterhouses with the softer, richer scent of barley and yeast—but mingled, the air simply grew more wet and heavy with stink. In the blink of an eye, the grassy fields and freshwater creeks had disappeared. The fresh air had vanished. And by the late-1800s, Hell's Kitchen had already become what many referred to as the armpit of New York City.

Crime was always an element in Hell's Kitchen, but it wasn't until after the Civil War that the street gangs came to power. As colorful as the smells in the air and the blood in the streets, the gangs of Hell's Kitchen appeared on the scene like schools of hungry piranhas seeking out a meal. There were the Gorillas, the Tenth Avenue Gang (later known as the Hell's Kitchen Gang), the Gophers—each well-versed in the art of strong-armed manipulation and schooled in excessive, merciless violence. Of these gangs, the most notorious were the Gophers. The Gophers were shadows, swirling and shifting like devils beneath the hem of a blue-collar neighborhood. Their presence was known and feared by all. Behind them, a river of blood flowed—somehow much darker and more polluted than the foulness left by the slaughterhouses on West 39th Street. And with the passage of years, their trespasses broadened, enabling them to move beyond petty crime and violent murder and to eventually wrap bloody fingers around the throat of New York City politics.

After World War I, most of Hell's Kitchen's traditional gangs all but fell apart under the weight of a new, more complex society. Other nationalities took up residence in the Kitchen, and the ethnicity grew more and more diverse with the passage of each year. Irish and Italians now had to make room for the inrush of Puerto Ricans, Hispanics, and blacks. There were race riots and bitter crimes committed against specific ethnic groups as the district stretched its arms and began to adjust. And despite the growing difference in culture, the residents of Hell's Kitchen still managed to govern themselves by a strict code of personal ethics. Gangs aside (although sometimes *because* of such gangs), Hell's Kitchen remained a reasonably safe, protected place to live. Criminals and the working class alike prided themselves on their personal beliefs which, among others, included both respect and diligence. An unspoken law dictated the way of the streets, and there would be no mercy for anyone who did not abide by such rules. Illegal drugs were kept under strict control by what street gangs remained, and they hardly ever found their way into the hands of the innocent. The penalties dealt out to anyone who tried to compromise the unspoken drug policy were swift and severe.

In the early '40s, a gang of blacks from Washington Heights began patrolling the streets of Hell's Kitchen looking for trouble. One evening, after drinking too much at a local tavern on 51st Street, the gang jumped and robbed an elderly Italian woman just outside her tenement. After some taunting, they cut the woman's purse with a razor and ripped it from her arms with little struggle. Her face and arms, too, were cut, and she was beaten badly enough to have an eye knocked from her head. Though the woman survived following extensive hospitalization, the members of the Washington Heights gang did not. And in the respected tradition of Hell's Kitchen, no one asked what had happened to them . . . yet everyone took comfort in knowing that the violators had been seen to and appropriately dealt with.

In 1959, roughly forty years before Paul Simon would transform the event into a tasteless and short-lived musical, two boys were brutally stabbed and killed in a gang war on Tenth Avenue. The killings, later called the Capeman Murders, garnered national attention and, for seemingly the first time, opened the country's eyes to the terror of big-city gang violence. Yet this was nothing new to the inhabitants of Hell's Kitchen. For them, it was a way of life.

Young children growing up in the '60s and '70s were well aware of the deep-seated unrest within their own neighborhood, and of the rules of conduct their parents—as well as the streets—were quick to impress upon them. A child of ten was familiar with the names of the neighborhood's infamous members: those jailed or sent to reform schools; those who ran numbers or delivered packages wrapped in butcher's paper; those who had beaten or killed—or beaten *and* killed. And since it sometimes seemed the only lifestyle available to them, many of these children looked up to a slick, neighborhood thug with the same sort of wide-eyed admiration another child might grant a professional athlete. For these children, growing up in the back alleys and corner tenements of New York City's West Side, a future at the hands of the streets was almost inevitable.

Today, senseless brutality runs the streets of Hell's Kitchen. Drugs circulate like secrets whispered behind locked doors. Shops and high-rises all suffer the mark of the graffiti artist: painted neon swirls and loops that serve no purpose other than to desecrate and humiliate. There are broken windows like sightless eyes along the string of Tenth Avenue tenements. Most shop windows have been meshed with wire or simply barred. The once-peaceful Dewitt Clinton Park is now a darkened refuge for the strung-out, the overdosed, the ruined, the hopeless; massive steel barrels blaze with fire, and a dozen dreary shapes crowd around them to keep warm. The stink of the slaughterhouses has dissipated over time, having been overpowered by the caustic reek of the curdling Hudson.

In this concrete valley, there is no law.

Here, violence reigns.

Calliope Candy was a small 1950s-style candy store on the corner of West 53rd Street and Tenth Avenue. Outside, the store's single plate-glass window was shaded by a green-and-white canvas awning. To the right of the window, a flaking wooden door stood ajar, a plastic, water-stained shade half-pulled against the door's wire-meshed, diamond-shaped window. Inside, a small space heater whirred between a stand of gumball machines. A strip of counter ran the length of the rear wall, behind which half-empty wooden shelves displayed rolls of Life Savers, Necco Wafers, bags of M&M's and Skittles, various brands of potato chips and candy bars, and clear plastic packages of strawberry, chocolate, and original-flavored licorice. Resting atop the counter was a large, chrome soda fountain, unpolished and pitted with age. A small, booth-like table stood against one wall beneath a large mirror etched with the logo of the New York Rangers hockey team. Beside the table was a Scooby-Doo pinball machine. With the light of midday falling on him through the plate-glass window, Mickey O'Shay administered a swift kick to one of the legs of the pinball machine. It whirred and beeped.

"The hell'd I say about kickin' that thing?" Irish said from behind the counter, leveling his gaze on Mickey. Unshaven, his hair twisted into spirals, Irish looked about ready to spit nails. "You keep kickin' it, you're gonna bust it. Thing's old."

"You're old," Mickey muttered, eyes on the little silver ball as he worked it through the machine's course. A piece of black licorice protruded from his mouth. "Besides, it bumps up the score."

"Who the hell you cheatin' against?" Irish said. He was trying to piece together a cardboard lollipop display but was having no success.

"Shhh! Don't talk to me. I'm concentrating."

"Well, don't start a fire."

The silver ball rolled down the left side of the machine and was quickly batted by the left flipper before it had time to disappear into the black hole at the bottom of the course. The ball shot up under the force of the hit and ricocheted off a number of circular bumpers. Lights flashed, and buzzers buzzed; orange and yellow lights reflected in Mickey's wide eyes. The score meter on the face of the machine rolled through a series of numbers.

"You gotta be goddamn Albert Einstein to put this thing together," Irish mumbled to himself, giving up on the cardboard display and discarding it beneath the counter. He produced a shot of whiskey and a deck of cards, and began laying out a game of solitaire on the counter. To his right, a distorted rendition of himself began playing the same game in the reflection of the chrome soda fountain.

Five minutes later, Jimmy Kahn double-parked his Cadillac in front of the store, pulled himself from the vehicle, and shuddered at the frigid air. Walking toward Calliope Candy with his mohair sport jacket held together in one fisted hand, he plucked a piece of Juicy Fruit from his mouth and stuck it on the side of the phone booth outside Irish's store.

"Christ," Jimmy said, rubbing his hands together as he entered the store. "Why the hell you keeping the door open, Irish? It's freezing out there." He bent and held his hands above the space heater, kicking the door shut behind him with the toe of his shoe. It creaked, then slammed shut.

"It's refreshing," Irish said from behind the counter.

Jimmy stood, arching his back and staring lazily out the front window. At one time he'd had the natural physique of an athlete, but neglect had eventually allowed it to get away from him. Taking a seat at the table booth, Jimmy pushed his head back and rubbed the sides of his nose between two fingers. Unlike Mickey O'Shay, whose unsupervised upbringing in a fatherless household hadn't prepared him for anything better than the lifestyle he now led, Jimmy Kahn had grown up in a decent middle-class family and had consciously chosen to immerse himself in the practicality of the criminal enterprise.

He had come to this decision at the age of nine, after witnessing a stabbing in the stairwell of his parents' tenement. Two men had approached a young teenager, mouthed some threatening words, and concluded the event by stabbing the teenager in the throat several times with a long, curved knife. Then, after pulling out the teen's pockets and stripping off his shoes, the two men slipped silently out of the stairwell and into the daylight of a summer afternoon. Jimmy, who'd witnessed the ordeal from between the wrought iron bars of the stairwell just outside the apartment where he lived with his parents, sat there for a long time, watching the spreading stain of blood seep out across the yellow tiled floor. He did not view this with the jaded eyes of a youngster, placing the two murderers on some sort of pedestal, reverent and exuding an almost preternatural sense of power. Rather, it simply occurred to him that what he'd witnessed was merely *survival*—that the strong walked away with a handful of pocket change and a new pair of skips, while the weak lay dying in a pool of his own blood. It was a practical concept, one that even he at such a young age was capable of grasping. The weak die, and the strong survive. The doers and the done to's.

Such was the way in Hell's Kitchen.

Empowered by the wisdom attained on that fateful day, Jimmy eventually dropped out of high school to run with the Hell's Kitchen underworld. Fueled less by intelligence and more by an insatiable desire to further himself and his budding career, Jimmy committed himself to a dozen robberies and assaults the way most people commit themselves to academics. Often, the money was pathetic and hardly worth the trouble, but his aggressive nature ignited in him a certain element of intimidation that would prove invaluable in his line of work. The killing of someone who'd tried to rip him off was as commonplace and as necessary to Jimmy Kahn as mandatory layoffs were to big businesses throughout the world.

"Enough already," Irish shouted at Mickey, who was still busy hammering away at the pinball machine. "You're makin' my god-damn head split down the middle!"

Mickey completed his turn, grinning and clapping his hands even when the ball rolled down into the hole and the lights began blinking GAME OVER, GAME OVER.

"New high score," he told no one in particular. His licorice whip was down to a nub, and he sucked it between his pursed lips, still grinning. "I could play that damn thing till it runs outta numbers."

He sat down opposite Jimmy in the booth. He looked wired. Just as Jimmy Kahn was motivated by personal success and used his brutality to attain such power, Mickey O'Shay seemed almost oblivious to his own personal violence. Mentally unstable since childhood and a one-time occupant of several psychiatric institutes throughout his twenty-six years, Mickey O'Shay was like a corked bottle of cheap champagne, ready to explode in a geyser of savagery at the smallest provocation. He ingested a cocktail of Thorazine, marijuana, and cocaine on a regular basis, which dulled to nonexistence any iota of sensitivity that might have been trapped somewhere inside him, and only strengthened his ferocity. Between the two of them and their ragtag assemblage of Irish hoodlums, they had Hell's Kitchen locked down. Fear, force, and intimidation was their calling card. A pack of rabid dogs set loose inside the rabbit hutch that was Manhattan's West Side.

"You bring the book?" Mickey asked Jimmy now, running his hands through the pockets of his coat for a cigarette.

"In the car. You wanna do this now?"

"No, I gotta do dinner at the governor's mansion first."

"Let's go," Jimmy said, and they both stood up and swaggered toward the little shop's front door.

Irish watched them leave. After they piled into Jimmy's Cadillac and pulled onto Tenth Avenue, Irish—whistling to himself and plucking a Sugar Daddy from the wall—ambled over to the front door, pulled it shut tight, and locked it with a series of bolts. Then, turning back around, he passed through a small doorway behind the counter and into the store's back room, which smelled not of peppermint and gumdrops, but of hot grease and metal.

Alphabet City, poisoned by the alkaline stink of the East River, embraced an accumulation of filthy, destitute tenements and squalid, fire-ravaged shops. A few of the buildings had been bought and sold and bought again over the years, traded like cards in a Vegas poker game, casualties of the gradual decline of the East Village. It wasn't uncommon for police to pull a bullet-riddled body from Tompkins Square Park, the victim already gray with rot and age. Likewise, there was always a pusher to be found—whatever you wanted you could have . . . for a price. In certain areas of the city, drugs were controlled by the authorities to the best of their ability. But drugs were still rampant here, as they were in Hell's Kitchen, their distribution fueled by budding entrepreneurs straight from the neighborhood public schools. It was not unusual to find a frozen, malnourished corpse in the lot behind one of the tenements, the corpse's arms black from shooting up, the face frozen in a rigor of perpetual agony.

There was little traffic along the back streets as Jimmy and Mickey drove through the neighborhood. Children of Hell's Kitchen, neither man traveled outside the safety of his neighborhood often, and they could probably count on one hand between them the number of times they'd been to Alphabet City. Hell's Kitchen was a microcosm of the entire city—the entire world, really—and one needn't go beyond that sphere for the length of a lifetime. In fact, if someone left Hell's Kitchen for an extended period, nine times out of ten it was usually to do time upstate.

On the seat between them was a small ledger bound in dark

brown vinyl. The name H. GREEN, embossed in gold letters, was centered on the front cover of the book. It was bound with metal curls of wire.

"How'd the meeting go with that guy John?" Jimmy asked as he drove. Though several days had passed since Mickey and John's meeting Thanksgiving morning, Jimmy was only now bringing it up. That was how he operated: questions were asked when he felt the time was right. Period.

"Pissed him off having to come out for nothing."

"He smell funny to you?"

"No—but it's early."

"Just the same," Jimmy said, "I only want you dealin' with him for now. No sense both of us gettin' fronted. When you meeting again?"

"I said I'd give him a couple days to get his money together," Mickey said. Smoking a cigarette and gazing disinterestedly out the passenger window, he rubbed a hand along the nape of his neck. A group of kids were playing ball in the street up ahead, and Jimmy slowed to a cool fifty-five before barreling through. "So what's this guy's name?"

"Who?"

"The guy." Mickey tapped the ledger with two fingers. *"This* guy."

"Tony Marscolotti," Jimmy said. "We got him for five grand. Let me do the talking. You just keep quiet—and don't say nothin' about the book. Anybody asks about the book, you tell 'em we bought it."

Mickey snorted—a sound which conveyed his mild irritation at Jimmy for even having to bring such a thing up: Mickey O'Shay talked to *nobody* about *nothing.*

They pulled up before a row of small shops—a dry cleaner, a bakery, a barber shop, a camera shop—and stepped out into the cold. Mickey followed Jimmy across the street to a small Italian delicatessen. Two young kids in knitted caps sat on a bench outside the deli, splitting a messy-looking meatball hero. As Jimmy and Mickey entered the shop, both boys glanced up in their direction without moving their heads.

There were a few customers milling about inside, all women. The place smelled strongly of provolone cheese and freshly baked bread. The walls buckled with shelves. Behind the counter slicing ham, a teenage boy in a paper hat watched them swagger around the store but said nothing. Mickey, his hands in his coat pockets, his head down as if to keep an eye on his feet, ambled over to a rack of jarred goods. With little interest, he reached out, unscrewed a jar of green olives, and systematically sucked the pimentos from a handful of them, discarding the little green husks onto the floor.

Jimmy happened to glance up and spot the tortoiseshell bulb of a theft prevention mirror hanging above a restroom door. In it, the entire store was distorted but visible. Directly above him, a lethargic ceiling fan worked in dizzying rotations. A metal chain hung from the center of the fan, remarkably still.

When a thick, ruddy-faced man in his forties shuffled out of the back room, Jimmy moved up against the front counter, his chest nearly leaning on the glass display case. He rolled his eyes down to the assortment of meats and cheeses behind the glass, then brought his eyes back up. Again, he caught the teenager in the paper hat stare in his direction. Then the kid swung his gaze over to Mickey. Mickey had sidled up to the other end of the counter and was standing with one foot over the line that prohibited customers from stepping behind the service counter. He was chewing the inside of his cheek, having finished with the pimentos.

"Tony Marscolotti," Jimmy said as the ruddy-faced man swept by behind the counter. It was not a question—hardly ever did Jimmy Kahn sound like he was unsure about anything, even a person's name. His questions always sounded more like statements, his statements like accusations, and his accusations like death threats.

The ruddy-faced man slowed but did not look up. He was busy carrying a tray of freshly baked rolls. "What can I do for you?" Marscolotti said.

"We're here to collect your vig for Horace Green," Jimmy said.

At the mention of Green's name, Marscolotti paused, setting the tray of rolls on the counter. He brought his round face up and looked at Jimmy Kahn first with an air of anxiety, then derision. "You ain't Green."

"We're collecting for him now."

Marscolotti's tiny black eyes migrated to where Mickey stood at the far end of the counter. Marscolotti didn't stare at him long, however, and was quick to return his gaze to Jimmy Kahn. "I didn't borrow no money from you," Marscolotti said.

"You owe five grand?"

"Green wants his money," Marscolotti said, "tell him to come down and get it himself. Or call me and tell me you're pickin' it up."

Mickey materialized behind Jimmy Kahn, the muscles of his face relaxed, a look of indifference in his eyes. Marscolotti caught that look, and something in its casualness frightened him.

"You want him to call ya?" Jimmy almost laughed. He cocked his head in Mickey's direction and he, too, nearly cracked a smile. "He wants Green to call him so he knows who we are."

"I want you outta my store," Marscolotti said.

"Tell 'im who we are, Jimmy," Mickey said. "Let him know we're okay."

"Couple Irish kids from Hell's Kitchen here to pick up their money," Jimmy said, his eyes on Marscolotti. "Maybe you heard of us—Jimmy Kahn and Mickey O'Shay . . ."

At the mention of their names, Marscolotti's expression fell. His eyes blinked very fast several times in succession, and the muscles in his jaws clenched like machinery. In Tony Marscolotti, the sudden transition from animosity to fear was a rather noticeable one.

Then Jimmy Kahn *did* smile, exposing a row of white, even teeth. "Oh, you heard of us? You think maybe we can move this thing along?"

"Green's got you two collecting for him now?" Marscolotti asked. The tip of a thick, purple tongue poked between his lips, moistened them.

"You don't worry about Green," Jimmy said. "You got that five grand you owe?"

"Five grand." The words came out sickly, devoid of substance. Beside Marscolotti, the teenager in the paper hat set down the sliced ham, moved to a large plastic sink behind the counter, and remained there with his hands on the lip of the basin, his back facing the disturbance.

"Make it six," Jimmy said with little humor. "Consider it a 'transfer fee' for being such a moron."

"You fellas don't . . ." But Marscolotti's words died in the air. The looks on Jimmy's and Mickey's faces, which had at first angered the proprietor, now caused his mouth to dry up and his tongue to feel too big for his mouth.

A woman in a mink coat approached and placed some items on the counter.

"Danny," Marscolotti called from the corner of his mouth. The teenager in the paper hat jerked his shoulders at the mention of his name. "Help this woman down the other end of the counter, will ya?"

Danny turned and moved to the counter without looking at either his boss or his boss's new friends. He reached out and slid the items the woman had placed on the counter down to the register at the opposite end of the shop.

"We don't got all day," Jimmy said.

"I don't have five—*six,*" he corrected himself at the last second, "I been payin' Green a grand a week. One fifty of that is vig."

"Okay," Jimmy said, "we'll keep the same arrangement. Let's have it."

"I don't have it now. He usually comes the end of the week."

"You're wastin' our fuckin' time," Jimmy said. "You ain't paid nothin' in the past few weeks. Green ain't been around. Get the money."

The woman at the cash register cocked her head in their direction, but did not look at them. Danny, as if attempting to rescue the woman from impending disaster, quickly drew her attention to some sale items behind the counter.

Marscolotti shook his head. "I'll see what I got in the back . . ."

"Find it, or I'll take it out of the goddamn register. Mickey'll take a walk with you," Jimmy said, and Mickey was already moving behind the counter, his hands still stuffed into the pockets of his coat. Head down, hair hanging in his face, he looked like a kid about to be reprimanded . . . except for the look in his eyes—those burning embers of detachment, of insanity that loomed just below the surface. Mickey O'Shay had once gotten into an argument with someone at the Cloverleaf. And with Mickey, arguments never *stayed* arguments: he'd beaten the guy pretty badly with a stool—busted the guy's jaw, wrist, ankle, some ribs—and as the guy managed to crawl out of the tavern and over to a police officer who happened to be passing down the street, Mickey stormed from the Cloverleaf and took the top of the guy's head off with his .38. The cop's uniform had been sprayed with blood, the cop's face a startled white.

Marscolotti, with Mickey close on his heels, slipped into the storage room behind the counter. Here, the walls were stocked with shelves of packaged and canned goods still stowed away inside the boxes in which they'd been shipped. Heat from an enormous brick oven blistered the paint from the walls, and the smell of baking bread and seasonings filled the stuffy room. A small wooden desk had been pushed into a niche in the wall at the back of the room, its surface littered with receipts and paperwork. Above it, hanging on the wall by a nail, was a portable radio tuned low and playing Eddie Cochran's "Summertime Blues." And beside the radio hung a framed poster of an Italian countryside.

Marscolotti led Mickey to the desk, pulled out the chair, and bent with some difficulty to the last drawer. Mickey's eyes worked across the paperwork on the man's desk, finding nothing of interest. When the drawer came open, his eyes darted to the man's hands first, then to the interior of the drawer. Inside were a number of rumpled business envelopes and a steel case that resembled a fisherman's tackle box.

"I didn't know you guys were in business with Horace Green." Marscolotti said, pulling the steel box from the drawer and setting it on his lap. He dipped his right hand into the front of the apron he wore and fished out a tangled ball of keys.

"We ain't," Mickey said. "He sold us the book." *After we shot him and chopped him up into little pieces, the lousy Jew bastard,* was what Mickey wanted to say. The memory caused his eyes to gleam.

"Green don't usually come to my place of business . . ."

"We ain't Green," Mickey said.

"It's bad for business, coming around—"

"Shut the fuck up and open the box."

Hands visibly shaking, Marscolotti hurried through his collection of keys until he selected the appropriate one, slipped it into the lock on the box, and popped the lip. Inside, assorted stacks of bills had been stuffed into a slide-away compartment. Before Marscolotti could take the bills out, Mickey's hand was already in there, yanking out the cash like someone tugging at a zipper on a stubborn pair of pants.

"This is? This all you got?"

Marscolotti looked shaken. "Come on . . ."

Mickey reached down and grabbed the box from Marscolotti's

lap, tore the compartments out, shook it, then tossed it on top of the man's desk. It slammed hard against the wood, the sound echoing off the walls.

"Don't look like no grand to me," Mickey said, flipping through the thin stacks of bills. "You're gonna be a pain in the ass. I can tell. You're gonna get me fuckin' started."

"Relax," Marscolotti pleaded. "I'll get it out of the register."

"Move," Mickey said, grabbing Marscolotti by the scruff of his neck and yanking him up out of his chair. He pushed the smaller man back toward the store and out of the storage room. Out here, the customers had left and now Jimmy stood against the cash register, one finger gently massaging the faint scar at his chin. At that moment, if Jimmy's mother were able to see him, she would have sworn her son looked identical to his father, who'd been a respectable accountant and good husband.

"How much?" Jimmy called.

Mickey stepped around the counter and sauntered over to his partner. In his right hand he waved the few stacks of bills. "Looks like seven hundred," he said.

"Enough with the bullshit," Jimmy said, turning to face Marscolotti who, by now, had secreted himself in the space in the wall between two shelves. Yet he was a heavyset man and the majority of his bulk did not fit in the space.

"Let me check the register," Marscolotti said, "I'll give you as much as I can."

But Jimmy Kahn did not even let Marscolotti finish before he was moving across the floor and to the front door. There was a wedge of wood propped beneath the door, and Jimmy kicked this out with two swift knocks of his foot. He slammed the door shut and yanked down the plastic shade, covering the door's window. Outside, the two young boys just finishing up their meatball hero looked up, startled, and took to their heels without further provocation.

"Christ," Marscolotti uttered beneath his breath. His breathing was loud enough to fill the room.

"Mickey," Jimmy said, turning his back to the door. "Hit the fuckin' register."

Mickey hopped back around behind the counter and shoved past Marscolotti on his way to the cash register. Danny, the paper hat-wearing teen, stood a foot from the register, his hands straight down at his sides. The teenager watched Mickey, undaunted by his approach, with the eyes of a stone relic.

"Move," Mickey barked, shoving the teenager out of his way. The kid stumbled a couple of feet, nearly tripping backward over a crate of goods, before righting himself against the back wall. His eyes never left the man who'd shoved him.

Mickey stood with his hands hovering above the keys of the register for perhaps two seconds before he lost all patience and began slamming his index fingers against the keypad. The register drawer did not open, which only frustrated Mickey further, and he began slamming his fists down on the keys, his long hair flailing wildly around his face, his teeth clenched in fury.

"Fuck-fuck-fuck!" Spittle flew from his mouth and a line of it clung to his chin.

"Don't!" Marscolotti pleaded, taking a step closer to Mickey O'Shay.

Mickey slammed another fist against the keys, his left hand up and caught in the tangle of his hair. Shaking his head rapidly from side to side in little spastic jerks, he yanked his left hand out of his hair and slapped the top of the register as if to draw blood. Behind him, Danny's eyes burned into his back. Briefly, partially grinning, Jimmy happened to look in Danny's direction. He recognized the gleam in the boy's eyes as hate, as mounting rage. It was a hard, angry look, too complex and passionate to be frightened. Jimmy could tell the teenager was a stronger person than his boss. He had a hustler's glint behind the burning fury in his eyes, and the obvious familiarity of someone who'd been continuously wronged and abused by someone his entire life. If Jimmy Kahn had been a different person, he might have almost admired the kid.

"Shit!" Breathing heavily, Mickey backed away from the register. He stared at it like someone measuring up an opponent. Not one to be bested, he quickly reached out and grabbed the corners of the machine, preparing to push it over the side of the counter and send it crashing to the floor.

"No!" Marscolotti yelled. His face was red and blotchy, his grubby fingers working over one another. "Let me!"

"Do it," Jimmy called to the proprietor. "Fast."

Somewhat hesitant about breaching the gap between him and Mickey O'Shay, Marscolotti took two ambiguous steps in Mickey's direction. Another bark from Jimmy sent him moving, and he reached over Mickey's shoulders to open the register. He hit two keys and the door sprung open, nearly slamming Mickey in the head.

With one splayed hand against Marscolotti's chest, Mickey sent the smaller man stumbling backward. Not as agile as his employee, Marscolotti managed to catch one foot in a plastic bucket filled with soapy water. His other foot lifted off the ground and, with a groan, the man flipped backward and slammed against the tile floor. One hand shot up to brace himself, or perhaps grasp onto the counter, yet he only managed to bring down a wooden cutting board and tomato slices onto his chest.

Still boiling, Mickey slammed his hands into the register drawer and began pulling out wads of bills. He stuffed some of the money into his coat, tossed some more onto the countertop. Cheeks quivering, he grabbed a handful of change and flung it across the store. A second handful of change was propelled at the tortoiseshell mirror above the restroom door. The coins *chinked!* off the mirror like pellets to a bull's-eye.

Laughing, Jimmy collected the remaining bills from the countertop. From the corner of his eye he could see Tony Marscolotti struggling to get to his feet.

Mickey ruptured. Too riled to even finish emptying the drawer, he planted the sole of his right shoe against the wall behind him, placed both hands once again on either side of the register, and with a great intake of breath—

"No!" Marscolotti cried.

—he shoved the register over the side of the counter. It slammed against the tile floor just inches from Jimmy's feet, plastic bits and pieces flying in every possible direction. And in a whirlwind of hair and flapping coat, Mickey spun on Danny, who'd been staring at Mickey's back throughout the entire fiasco. Mickey's right hand yanked a small handgun from the waistband of his pants. Eyes wide and bloodshot, pale lips quivering and speckled with spit, Mickey brought the gun up to the kid's head and slammed the muzzle against his temple. The kid shuddered, stumbled to one knee, wincing at the sudden pain that blossomed through his skull.

Mickey did not pull the trigger, though Jimmy could tell he wanted to.

"Look at me hard?" Mickey shouted. A dark vein pulsed at his temple. *"You wanna fuckin' look at me hard?"*

Arm stuttering, Mickey jerked the gun away from the kid's head, shook his wild hair into his eyes—then slammed the gun back into the kid's face, striking high on Danny's left cheekbone. Unbelievably, the kid actually managed to pull himself up on both feet again, which only fueled Mickey's rage. His eyes growing wider and wider until they looked about ready to burst, Mickey repeatedly shoved the barrel of the gun into the kid's face.

"You a tough guy?" he shouted, a wad of phlegm getting caught in his throat. "Huh? Huh, tough guy?"

The kid did not say a word. Unmoving and silent, he merely watched Mickey with his right eye (the barrel of Mickey's gun was pressed against his left).

"You *son* of a *bitch!*" Mickey cried, shoving the gun hard enough into the kid's face to finally send him reeling. Danny's legs folded up underneath him, and the kid's body slammed hard against the floor, his head rebounding against the large, wooden crate.

The sight of his adversary bested, Mickey stood above the teenager, catching his breath, suddenly relaxed. The insane flash of light that had been behind his eyes just moments ago was no completely gone. Hair matted with sweat and hanging in his face, Mickey O'Shay adjusted his rumpled coat and slid the handgun into one of the coat's many pockets. Breathing heavily, eyes still on the kid—he was smart enough to know he should remain on the floor, and did—Mickey ran shaky fingers through his hair and uttered a pathetic laugh.

"Come on," Jimmy said casually from the other side of the counter. Mickey's actions had not fazed him. He'd seen Mickey O'Shay at his worst. This wasn't it. "Let's roll."

Mickey turned and hooked a finger at Marscolotti who, by now, had managed to prop himself up on his knees. His pants were soaked from the spilled soapy water.

"You pissed . . . me off," Mickey said between breaths. "We'll . . . be back tomorrow. Have all your fuckin' money . . . ready for us . . ."

Too frightened to even speak, to even acknowledge that he'd heard and understood, Marscolotti just stared at the looming figure that was Mickey O'Shay.

"Hey," Jimmy said, drumming a fist on the countertop. "Let's *go.*"

A grin broke across Mickey's face. He shrugged his shoulders and hopped over the counter, his feet coming down beside the ruined remains of Marscolotti's cash register.

Before they left, Jimmy Kahn shot a glance at Marscolotti from over his shoulder. Then he turned and thumped Mickey on the back, setting him in motion toward the front door. As they left, their long shadows fell across the countertop and the shattered cash register like some impending doom.

CHAPTER EIGHTEEN

"I'VE GOT AN IDEA," JOHN SAID. THE office was busy and Kersh, who disliked the commotion, had transferred some of his reports to the pit. They were both there now, the older agent propped up in a chair at his little wooden table, a scattered assortment of paperwork spread out before him. John, who'd just come in from a street assignment, stood with his arms folded against the wall.

"Your ideas trouble me," Kersh intoned, not looking up from his paperwork.

"I just got off the phone with Tressa," John said. "I told her I wanted to reach out for Mickey. She gave me the name of some candy store in Hell's Kitchen where he supposedly hangs out."

Now Kersh *did* look up. His expression was that of a crotchety old schoolteacher shooting a glance at a rowdy student. "You think this is a good idea?"

"Yeah, I do," John said. "He might need a little push." He offered Kersh a crooked grin. "Coulda lost my number."

He'd decided against telling Kersh about the meeting with Mickey on Thanksgiving Day. Since nothing had been accomplished, telling Kersh would only elicit his disapproval, as the meeting at St. Patrick's Cathedral had done.

Kersh twisted his lips and considered. After a moment, he said, "A *candy* store?"

"That's what she told me."

"Where?" Kersh asked.

"Fifty-third and Tenth." Then, in an attempt to convince Kersh, he said, "Mickey knows I got a buyer, and a buyer don't hang around forever. It's the right move. I should be up his ass about the money."

"So what's the plan?" Kersh said.

"Push the deal. If he's got the money with him—we know he's got a stash—I'll set up the buy for later tonight." John could tell Kersh, too, appreciated the street logic. "Let's do this before it gets too late."

Kersh sighed and shuffled through his paperwork. "My headache's working its way to my knees," Kersh muttered. "Okay, you wanna do this? Let's do it. We drive separately, and I'll hang back a block or two. You really think this guy's gonna be hanging around some candy store?"

John winked at him. "If not, I'll treat you to an egg cream."

It was well into the afternoon by the time they headed out for Hell's Kitchen. John drove a bit fast, his mind two steps ahead of his actions.

The sun was directly overhead when he pulled onto Tenth Avenue. Around him, the sidewalks were alive with people, even in the cold. Just above the tops of the high-rises, interrupted by the skeletal extensions of television antennas, the sky was the color of cold steel, thick with clouds.

The intersection of Tenth and West 53rd was mildly populated, mostly by commuters and taxicabs heading north toward Amsterdam Avenue. Some Christmas decorations had been hung here, in the windows of neighborhood shops and apartments: cheap plastic

Santas, loops of dusty garland, lackluster Christmas balls hanging from pieces of twine.

There were no decorations in the window of Calliope Candy.

John circled the block twice before finding a parking space one block over, and hoofed it back toward the candy store. Kersh, he knew, would remain within eyeshot of the candy store, whether he was illegally parked or not.

There were no customers inside the candy store, even with the *Open* sign still in the window. The place was small and cramped, the levels of shelves along the walls half-empty. A noisy space-heater sat by the door. Behind the counter, a middle-aged man with a sanguine complexion and a faded chambray shirt changed a roll of receipt tape in the cash register. He nodded at John as he approached, his eyes small and rodent-like. There was a large sore at the left corner of his mouth, which he continuously tongued, seemingly without notice.

"Help you with somethin'?" the proprietor said, not pausing in his work.

"I'm looking for Mickey."

The man behind the counter rolled his bulky shoulders. "Nobody by that name works here," he said.

"I know that," John said. "I was told he hangs here."

"Who the hell are you?"

"A business acquaintance," John said. "I think he'll want to talk to me."

The man leveled his eyes on John, sizing him up, trying to convince himself he would have no trouble if things came to blows. He wasn't in good shape, but he was well over six feet and an easy two hundred fifty pounds. Still, something must have dissuaded him from a physical altercation, because he sighed with great exasperation and moved to a telephone that hung on the wall behind the counter. He punched in a phone number, mumbling something under his breath, and waited while it rang.

"Yeah, it's me," the man said, much too familiar. "Got a guy down here, says he's lookin' for you."

"Tell him it's John."

"Says his name's John." Brief pause. "Yeah," he said. "I don't know." Another pause. "All right." With little fanfare, he hung up and turned back to his receipt tape. "He'll be over in five. You want somethin' in the meantime?"

"Sure. Gimme an egg cream."

The man smirked. He turned and grabbed a Coca-Cola glass from the shelf behind him, held it under the soda fountain, pulled the lever. A loop of chocolate syrup drained into the glass. He added milk and seltzer water to the mix, stirred it.

"Not too busy," John marveled, folding his arms and leaning against the counter. He glanced back over his shoulder. Through the window, he watched the traffic motor slowly up Tenth Avenue. Two young boys bouncing a handball passed by the store's window without stopping, their shadows long across the glass. "You scare all the kids away?"

The man chuckled once—a rumbling, truck-like sound—and slid the egg cream over to John. He tossed a plastic spoon wrapped in cellophane next to it while licking the syrup from one finger. "Want a little shot of pepper in it?"

"What?"

A bottle of Irish whiskey materialized from behind the counter. The proprietor uncapped it, tipped it, and shook a tablespoon's worth into the egg cream.

"Wakes up your guts," the man said. "Stir it with the spoon."

John stirred it, took a sip. Winced. "Son of a bitch. It's good."

The man smiled, exposing a row of tar-stained teeth, then nodded toward the front of the store. "Here's your boy."

Mickey entered, wearing a nylon winter coat and a pair of wool gloves with the fingers cut off. His bleary eyes and disheveled appearance communicated to John that Mickey O'Shay had probably just woken up, most likely from the phone call just moments before. He didn't look irritated or cautious—not even concerned—as John had expected he might. He staggered into the store and paused briefly in front of the space heater. Then he turned and, rubbing his unshaven chin, crossed over to the small booth that stood beside a pinball machine. He emptied his weight onto one of the seats.

"Sit down," Mickey told him.

John pulled himself off the counter and sat across from Mickey in the booth. He placed his egg cream on the table between them and Mickey's eyes floated to it, seemed to soften, then turned back to John. When he opened his mouth, his breath struck John like a slap from across the table.

"How'd you know to come here?"

"Tressa told me."

"I figured," Mickey said.

"Listen," he said, "I'm gonna let you know where I stand on this. Last month, I make a deal with somebody. The night I meet with him, the whole thing goes to shit. I nearly wind up shot and almost arrested, and I got nothing to show for it. I meet with you and you sound on the level—then last week you pull this shit on me. I got a buyer for this stuff and probably a couple more, so I don't have the time or the patience to fuck around. If I didn't think I could make a score off this stuff, I wouldn't be here now. So this is kinda like make it or break it."

Mickey cracked his knuckles. "You don't like the way we do business, you—"

"We ain't *doin'* business. Yet. And that's the problem. I want to make sure this is for real, not just somethin' you *hope* you can do."

Mickey snorted and fluttered his eyelids. At that moment he seemed content to sit in this booth, half awake and cracking his knuckles, until the day he died. Again, his casual demeanor provoked John, irritated him. Mickey wasn't just doing John a favor; he stood to make a hefty score himself on the deal. Yet his conduct continually suggested an indifference toward the prospect of moneymaking, which was an attitude very much unlike anyone else's John had ever dealt with.

"You like to talk, don't you?" Mickey said.

"I'm in it strictly for the money," he returned.

"You got your car outside?"

"Next block over."

"Pull it out front," Mickey said, pulling himself out of the booth and heading toward the door. From where he sat, John watched him hustle across the street and disappear into the blackened doorway of a twelve-story high-rise.

"Take it easy," he said to the large man behind the counter, sliding out of the booth.

"You gonna pay for that?" the proprietor answered, pointing a knobby finger at John's egg cream.

Moments later, he was sitting behind the wheel of his car, the engine running to work the heater. His eyes scanned the streets but did not see Kersh's sedan anywhere. A few cars were parked across the street, the unmistakable shapes of heads behind the windshields. Most of the other cars along the street were vacant, packed like crowded teeth along the curb. Hubcaps missing, fenders dented, the sight reminded him of Evelyn Gethers's Lincoln Towncar and Pier 76.

Up ahead, he could see the sun dipping down behind the skyline of high-rises.

Mickey appeared in the doorway of his tenement and started

across the street toward John's car. John noticed he never looked up when he walked, was never curious about or tempted by the world around him. It suddenly occurred to him how dissimilar Mickey O'Shay was from Francis Deveneau and Jeffrey Clay. Both Deveneau and Clay had been your run-of-the-mill thugs, struggling to make some dough and a name for themselves. They happened on an opportunity to pass some funny money and did it with gusto. Tressa had introduced him to Jeffrey Clay, and it had been Clay's greed that eventually led him to Francis Deveneau. And, in turn, it had been Deveneau's greed that initiated their meeting at the nightclub, the boastful Frenchman ready to make a deal. Yet now here was Mickey O'Shay, an arrogant Irish punk who'd undoubtedly spent his entire life traversing the bowels of Hell's Kitchen, committing one fashion of deviant act after another.

Mickey stepped around to the Camaro's passenger side, popped open the door, and slid into the bucket. He slammed the door hard enough to make the window rattle.

"Here," Mickey said, producing a business-sized envelope from within his coat pocket and tossing it onto John's lap. "Put your mind at ease."

John picked up the envelope, pulled back the lip, peered inside. He shook the stack of counterfeit hundreds into his hand. To his surprise, the bills were fresh—crisp and uncirculated, still banded by printer's tape. This suggested Mickey O'Shay was much closer to the printer—the source—than he'd originally thought. Jeffrey Clay's money had been wrinkled and held together by rubber bands, most likely counted by Deveneau, then counted *again* by Clay himself. Either Mickey trusted the printer enough not to count the bills, or he worked in collaboration with him. Whatever the reason, John almost felt the world lurch forward beneath him at the sight of the freshly printed hundreds.

"Looks good," he said, fingering the paper, rubbing a thumb

across the ink. He slipped the money back into the envelope.

"So now, Johnny-No-Bullshit," Mickey said, "it's up to you."

"How much is here?"

"Ten grand."

"How soon can you get the other ninety?"

"A wink," Mickey said. "Now how about you?"

"Tonight," he told Mickey. "Give me three hours, and I'll be back here tonight."

Again, that same look of disinterest passed over Mickey's face. Despite his street-hardened features and coke-reddened eyes, he once again looked like the young choirboy he'd appeared to be on the day of their first meeting as they sat before the altar at St. Patrick's Cathedral.

Mickey glanced at the car's clock. "Make it four hours," Mickey said. "Pull up along Tenth, in front of the store. You wait for me in the car, and I'll come out. You stay in the car."

"Let me keep this ten," John said. "It'll help loosen up my money on the other end."

Mickey plucked the envelope from John's hand.

"I don't think so." Mickey climbed back out into the street. He paused before shutting the car door, his body bent over, his head peeking beneath the roof. "And tell that bitch to quit flappin' her gums about me. She opens her mouth and says my name one more time, they'll be the last words she ever speaks."

"The bills are fresh," he told Kersh back at the office. "He walked right into his apartment and came out with them, untouched, still banded."

"Fresh?" Kersh said. He raised his eyebrows. No doubt the same thoughts were crossing Kersh's mind now that had crossed

John's when he'd first shaken the stack of hundreds into his hand. Kersh set his phone down on the cradle. He'd just gotten off the phone with Tommy Veccio, the agent assigned to keep an eye on Mickey O'Shay and tail him when he left Calliope Candy to pick up the counterfeit.

"Who're we bringing in on this?" John asked.

"We'll have Veccio and Conners on surveillance tonight, couple blocks from the store," Kersh said, unfolding a map on his desk of the West Side District. Early evening, and the number of agents milling about the office had dwindled to a select few finishing reports or going over case files. Kersh's voice seemed to resonate off the walls. "I'll be somewhere along Tenth Avenue, between West Fifty-third and Fifty-fourth, facing the store."

"I don't want an eyeball on this," John said quickly, referring to the agent on surveillance who acted as the stationary hub and lookout who maintained contact with all other units on watch. "You get too close to this guy, and he'll know something's up. He'll spook."

"I think we should play this thing right, maybe get a wire on you . . ."

"Absolutely not! If this guy decides to pat me down, I'm screwed."

"John . . ."

"Trust me, Bill," he insisted. "We get too close to the surface, and this guy Mickey'll sniff us out like a dog. I got this guy, okay? I do. I really do. It'll play out fine."

"You think you can handle too much," Kersh said quietly. "That's not good. You're too anxious."

"I know what I'm doing."

Resigned, Kersh leaned back in his chair. His eyes trailed away from John and focused on the bank of windows that looked out over the city and the setting sun. He looked very old in the light of sunset, John thought, and for the first time since he'd known Bill Kersh he wondered why the man had never married.

"I just don't want you getting too cocky, too pushy on this," Kersh said after a moment.

"Like a kid in a candy store," John said.

Bill Kersh did not laugh.

Following a brief twenty-minute meeting with Kersh and Agent Conners, John drove out to his father's house in Brooklyn. The sky was already ripe with evening by the time he pulled up in front of the house, and he'd spent the entire drive over forcing himself to switch gears and leave tonight's impending meeting with Mickey O'Shay back at the office. Yet even as he parked the car in front of the house, he couldn't shake Mickey's face from his mind.

He leaned over and grabbed his father's coat from the back seat. The feel of the fabric sent a wave of shame through his body, and again he scolded himself for forgetting to bring his father the coat.

His father had been released from the hospital the day after Thanksgiving. Weakened by extensive bed rest and the chemotherapy, the old man had been barely strong enough to lift himself out of his hospital bed. Watching his father move with such difficulty had bothered him. His father had stood, momentarily in pain, at the foot of his bed while he searched the room for his belongings. John and Katie had remained by the hospital room door. When a male nurse arrived with a wheelchair, John's father only shook his head.

"I walked in—" the old man said, "I can walk out."

"Sir," the male nurse assured him, "all patients are released in a wheelchair. Just to get you downstairs and outside. It's nothing personal."

"Dad," Katie said, moving toward the man. She placed one hand around his frail wrist and led him to the chair, assisting him in sitting down.

Outside the room, a young doctor had given John the rundown on his father's medication—what needed to be administered for pain, for sleepless nights, for nausea, for whatever else ailed the man. Yet with half his mind on Mickey O'Shay even then, and the other half stuck on the image of his father slowly wasting away in the small stucco house on Eleventh Avenue, he had to ask the doctor to repeat the information, maybe even write it down for him, so that he could get it straight in his head.

There were lights on in the house now. He entered the foyer and heard movement in the kitchen.

"Pop," he called.

Katie appeared in the kitchen doorway, the bulge beneath her shirt wet with dish water. "Quiet," she said. "He's asleep."

"You're here," he said.

"Made dinner. We talked for a while. It was nice."

He went to her, hugged her.

"What are you doing here so early?" she said, pulling away from him and going back to the sink.

"Had some time to kill, wanted to drop off his coat."

"So you're going back out again?"

"For a little while. How's he feeling?"

Putting dishes into the dishwasher, Katie looked at him, pressed her lips together. She looked tired, worn out. Had it been only recently he had pictured her so young and full of life? And now here she was, looking perhaps ten years older than her actual age, with deep purple grooves under her eyes and the lines around her mouth overemphasized.

"He's in some pain. I know he's getting up too much during the day, but what are you supposed to tell the man? 'Stay in bed and never get out'? He wants to get up, move around the house. What can you say?"

He sighed and glanced down the dark hallway that led back to the stairs. "I'm gonna check in on him," he said.

"You want me to fix you something to eat before you leave?"

"I'm okay."

Upstairs, evening gloom filtered in through the windows. He moved quietly past his old bedroom until he was able to glance in and see his father's withered shape in his own childhood bed. He turned into the room, floorboards creaking, and peered over at his father's shape beneath the sheets. He could hear his father's shallow breathing.

"John?" his father grumbled, clearing his throat.

"You're awake?"

"It's okay. Come in."

He slipped further into the room and set the coat down across the back of a chair. "Your coat," he said. "Sorry. Got caught up in things, had it in my car."

His father waved a thin hand. A pale blue panel of light came in through the bedroom window and fell across the bed, casting pools of shadow in the sunken hollows of his father's face. John turned the desk chair around and sat in it at the foot of the bed.

"You switched rooms," he said.

"This one's closer to the bathroom. Your head bothering you?"

It wasn't until his father spoke that John realized he'd been unconsciously running his fingers along the faint scar creeping down from his hairline. He'd only been thirteen and already in with the wrong crowd—older kids who, in the years after high school, had seemed to vanish like ghosts. His father had forbidden him from hanging out with those kids, particularly in the schoolyard of P.S. 201 at night, when the daytime clamor of neighborhood children gave way to street gangs, cokeheads, and dangerous women, but John hadn't listened. On one particular night, a few words were exchanged between some neighborhood thugs and, soon, fists were thrown. John had been caught in the middle of it. He remembered a broken beer bottle swiping toward his face, the way the blood ran into his eyes and soaked his shirt. His so-called friends had scattered like roaches, thinking he'd been killed . . .

He automatically dropped his hand. "I'm fine."

"I remember that day like it was yesterday," said his father. "Twelve stitches. That bottle opened you up pretty good."

"I should have listened and stayed out of that schoolyard. And away from those jerks."

"You were a hardheaded kid."

"I should have listened to you."

"You want a good laugh?" his father muttered from the bed, his voice barely audible.

"I could use a good laugh," John said.

"I thought I saw Judy Dunbar today when I passed by the bedroom window." Judy Dunbar was the mean-spirited woman who had lived next door to them throughout John's childhood. A nasty, stick-thin creature with pointed features, she'd always professed a strong distrust in doctors and dentists alike and, subsequently, died roughly ten years ago from cancer of the eustachian tube. "I'd just gotten out of bed to use the bathroom," his father continued, "and I thought I saw old Judy Dunbar standing on her back porch, just leaning with her arms folded on the railing and staring out over her yard. Caught her out of the corner of my eye. Course, when I turned back to look there was no one there. But in that split second when I passed by, I was certain it was her, that I saw her. Old Judy Dunbar. You remember her?"

"I do," John said.

"What a cantankerous, bitter woman she was," his father snarled, and coughed up a phlegm-filled chortle.

"She stole my baseball bat off our stoop one year," John said. "Do you remember?"

"You'd hit her car with a baseball while playing with your friends in the street," his father said.

"It didn't do any damage. Just bounced off a tire. But she came out screaming just the same—"

"Wearing that ugly bright green housedress with those big red flowers on it," his father added.

"I remember the housedress. She looked like a Christmas tree."

"And she fired curses at you kids like arrows. You kids laughed at her."

"Just crept up that night while we were asleep," John said, "and snatched my baseball bat from the back porch. She never said anything about it but always kept the bat leaning against her screen door, just where I could see it. I always thought she was tempting me to break in and steal it back. She would have had a field day if I had."

His father sighed and adjusted the blankets about his body. In the brief time he'd been sitting here, the room had gotten much darker.

"It's good we talk like this," John said, knowing before he spoke that the words would come out awkward and stupid.

His father shifted in bed.

John stood, straightened his pants. "I have to get going now. Is there anything I can get you?"

"My coat," his father said, his voice suddenly absent of the strength used to tell the story of old Judy Dunbar.

"Now?"

"Just lay it on the bed."

"All right." He picked up the coat and folded it along the foot of the bed. "Anything else?"

"You're going to work?"

"I have to."

"Then be careful," his father said.

Downstairs, Katie was adjusting the picture on the old Zenith in the living room.

"I'm heading out," he told her. "You're staying?"

"For a while longer," she said, "in case he needs anything. Besides, the apartment gets lonely."

"Stay here, I'll pick you up when I'm done. We'll go home together."

"That's too big a gamble," she said. "You never get home on time."

CHAPTER NINETEEN

THE NIGHT TREMBLED WITH SLEET.

A dull white string of lampposts dotted the intersection of West 53rd Street and Tenth Avenue. The roadway was reasonably crowded. A wet slurry twirled beneath the street lamps' winter glow, sluicing against the posts and puddling on the ice-slicked sidewalks. Yet despite the uncooperative weather, street corners still catered to a certain arrangement of people. A few of the apartment buildings along Tenth Avenue seemed to shudder against the sky, the dark maw of their doorways framing a peeking head or two. Here, the buildings were strung together like pearls along a length of string, each pressed up against the next . . . yet unlike pearls, there was nothing attractive or even adequate about them. Crumbling, twelve-story structures housing squalid little flats, they were more like blackened, rotting teeth crowded into an unaccommodating mouth.

There were lights on inside the Calliope Candy shop, though the store had long since closed for the evening. A few dark shapes shifted in the light, silhouetted like cardboard puppets behind a cloth screen. Above the candy shop's bank of windows, a dull green cloth awning sustained a tough pelting from the weather. The words *Calliope Candy* stitched across the awning in white lettering, seemed to glimmer in the light of the lampposts along the street.

Several blocks away, John Mavio's rust-colored Camaro sat like a predator in waiting, its headlamps and engine off. Enveloped in darkness, the car was hardly visible. There were a number of other parked cars along the street and the Camaro did not look suspicious, out of the ordinary, or unusual in any way—except for one minor detail: the Camaro's windows, shut tight against the storm, were fogged.

Inside, John sat in the driver's seat, his fingers massaging the steering wheel's rubber grip. He was dressed casually but consciously, as if he might be waiting to pick up a young woman for the evening: loose-collared shirt, jeans, Nikes, leather jacket. His hair, jet-black in the murk of the car's interior, was wet and hung in his eyes. With the fingers of his left hand, he raked the hair back from his face. His teeth worked noiselessly on a piece of Wrigley's.

Shifting in his seat, John adjusted his jacket and took a deep breath. He suddenly felt warm. In the inside breast pocket of his leather jacket was a bulky yellow envelope. Inside the envelope was $20,000 in hundred-dollar bills. The bills were divided into two approximately equal stacks, each fastened with greasy rubber bands. The money itself looked worn and tattered but otherwise indistinguishable, and volunteered the faint aroma of turpentine. In the right side outer pocket of his jacket was his gun—a semiautomatic .22-caliber Walther TPH seven-shot (six in the clip, one in the chamber). Specially used by the CIA as a "hit" gun (and rather similar in design to the gun extracted from Evelyn Gethers's Lincoln Towncar), it fired hollow-point, long rifle bullets that expanded when shot. In short, it was a kill-gun for close quarters.

On the dashboard sat what could have been a cigarette lighter, but wasn't.

From the glove compartment, his cell phone tweeted. Keeping an eye on the console's clock, John reached over and yanked the glove compartment hatch down, grappling with the cell phone. It rang a second time before he got it to his ear.

"Yeah," he said.

It was Kersh. "We're hitting the intersection now. It's mildly crowded, but we're gonna hang back just the same. There's some movement in the candy store, too."

"Remember, Bill, I don't want anybody up on this guy. You'll make him hinky."

"Don't worry about us. He won't see a thing."

Still looking at the Camaro's clock, he turned the cell phone's power off and replaced it in the glove compartment. His mind slipped back to only a few days ago—Thanksgiving Day—and to the cold, smoky smell of Mickey O'Shay as he sat in the passenger seat of his car. Now John was suddenly anxious to inhale that smell again. He was an olfactory person by nature, as some people are, and the scent of the city and its occupants aroused not only the agent in him, but also the adolescent he'd once been. It was a rush, the closest thing to ambrosia he would ever encounter. Early on in the first few months of undercover work with the Secret Service, he had established a subconscious correlation between the Service—more specifically, *his job*—and the impoverished streets he'd spent so many dark, lonely hours working. Just as some bankers may have a Pavlovian reaction to the smell of crisp dollar bills, and just as some accountants may associate their office with the smell of wooden pencils and carbon paper and graphite, John remembered the Secret Service when he smelled the salty reek of Manhattan and its ambling destituteness. And now, sitting in wait while watching the car's clock tick slowly through glowing green numbers, he was itchy to get things rolling.

To pass the time, he thought of Douglas Clifton—*dead* Douglas Clifton—who'd been generous and careless enough to leave behind a cache of fingerprints on the .22 and the accompanying silencer. Not that such leverage would prove beneficial in interrogating the dead.

And that was it, wasn't it? All dead ends? All doors flung open only to slam shut again before he was able to pass through? While John had been fighting through Thanksgiving Day traffic to meet Mickey on time and as Bill Kersh served hot plates of goulash to impoverished New Jersey families, Douglas Clifton had decided to take a flying leap out his hospital room window. The last person to see Clifton alive had been Dr. Kuhmari himself. According to the doctor, he'd gone in to check Clifton's vitals fairly early in the morning. Everything in order, the doctor departed the room, intent on heading home to a late Thanksgiving Day breakfast with his family. He made it to the nurses' station, where he administered a number of orders to his staff, handed in his clipboards—and that's when one of the nurses noticed Clifton's monitors had gone dead. Assuming Clifton had knocked the wires loose or even yanked them out in haste, as some patients will do, the nurse hurried into the room. A few seconds later she was screaming and hollering for the doctor, peering out the open window and unable to look at the messy heap that lay broken along the sidewalk several stories below. Kersh had gone to the hospital later that evening to speak with Kuhmari and the screaming nurse. From there, he'd called John and laid out the details.

"Homicide's checking into it, although it sounds like a pretty clear case of suicide," Kersh had said, and John agreed. With Clifton dead, it didn't matter how many goddamn fingerprints they were able to pull from the stuff in the Lincoln's trunk; Clifton couldn't talk if he was dead.

The numbers on the dashboard clock changed and John cranked the key in the ignition, turned the Camaro's engine over, flipped on the headlights, and slowly rolled down the street. He headed east toward Eighth Avenue, having decided to swing down and around to arrive at Tenth. This would suggest the appearance of an approach from the opposite direction. Not that Mickey O'Shay would be conscious of such things, he surmised. It was just how John Mavio operated.

After several minutes, the Camaro turned right onto 51th Street and cruised in third gear past St. Clair Hospital. He made another right onto Tenth Avenue and headed toward the intersection of Tenth and West 53rd Street. A soft drizzle heckled the windshield. Outside, the streets were pitch black and soulless, the darkness disturbed only by the constant stream of swerving headlights. More headlights appeared directly behind him as he approached the intersection, too closely, and he watched their reflection with some intensity in the Camaro's rearview mirror. At the intersection, a horn was blasted and a black Volkswagen Jetta swooped around him and disappeared into the darkness ahead.

Surrounding him stood a number of small, two-story shops behind which larger tenements loomed. Canvas awnings shook in the wind. A sushi restaurant's neon lights attracted his attention, and he worked his eyes over the store's front—the shaded plate of window in the door, the arabesque design etched onto the glass. Sodden balls of discarded newspaper were swept up in the wind and carried away like tumbleweeds along the sidewalk.

His eyes peeled, he inched the car up to the intersection and parked across the street from Calliope Candy. Lights were on in the store, but the shades were pulled. A number of cars were parked here, leaving spaces along the curb like gaps in a smile. If he squinted and caught the cars in front of him at the right angle, John could see that no one was seated in any of them. Relaxing in his seat, he cracked the window two inches, coaxed a cigarette from his jacket. The frigid air wasted no time in violating the car's interior. He spat his gum out the window, silently cursing the cold, and lit the cigarette with a book of matches he kept in the car's ashtray. Took two long drags. The car filled with blue smoke. Casually, his eyes drifted again to the row of shops. Specifically the candy store.

A block or two behind him, Kersh sat in his sedan, his eyes undoubtedly trained on John's taillights. And somewhere up ahead,

Tommy Veccio and Dick Conners sat together in another car, listening to Kersh's occasional radio broadcasts.

Abruptly, like a phantom passing through a wall, a figure emerged from the darkness and began shuffling across the street in John's direction. Silhouetted against the dull lights of the candy store behind him, the figure walked with its head down, shoulders hunched, straggly hair fanned out by the wind.

Mickey O'Shay.

"There he is," John intoned, directing his voice toward the dashboard and the cigarette lighter that was not a cigarette lighter. "Looks like he came out of the candy store."

As Mickey came within five feet of the Camaro, his stride stuttered and he appeared temporarily indecisive as to whether he should gain access to the passenger seat by going around the *front* of the car or the *rear.*

"Fucking dope," John muttered. In his head, he could almost hear Bill Kersh laughing.

Finally, quick as a whip, Mickey swaggered around the front of the car and yanked the passenger side door handle so hard John though it might just break off. Mickey wasted no time occupying the passenger seat, and slammed the door like someone impressed by sharp, insolent noises.

"You got a thing with slamming doors?" John commented.

Mickey just grunted and adjusted himself in his seat. He looked as though he were having some difficulty getting comfortable.

"Cigarette?" John offered.

"No."

He caught a glimpse of Mickey's face in the glow of streetlights and, through the strands of wet hair, he could see Mickey's eyes were bloodshot and muddy, that his lips were dry and peeling. *Probably just finished stuffing shit up his nose,* John thought, then turned away before his lingering gaze made Mickey uncomfortable.

"Shitty weather," John said, trying to engage him. Yet Mickey O'Shay did not feel like being engaged.

"You got your end?" Mickey said. "Let's see it."

"Mickey, you got the shit or what?" He was through playing games and never showed his end first.

Working his peeling lips together, Mickey stuffed a hand into his coat. He extracted a brown paper lunch bag, its lip folded repeatedly. Mickey unfolded it and pulled out a brick-sized package dressed in mint-colored tissue paper. He handed the package to John, who set it in his lap, unwrapped it. Inside were the counterfeit hundreds, fresh and banded just as the others had been. John plucked one of the stacks from the pile, felt it, examined it with one hand. He tossed his cigarette out the crack in the window and flexed the stack with both hands.

"This the same stuff as before?" he asked.

"Exact same."

"It's good quality. All your shit this good?"

"All of it. Now let's finish the deal."

He reached into his jacket and pulled out the envelope containing his money. He held it out, and Mickey's fingers were quick to snatch it, pry it open.

"Count it if you want," he said, "but it's all there."

"I ain't worried about it." There was a serenity to his voice which, to John, said: *It'll be counted eventually. And if you're short a single bill, I'll come gunning for you personally.*

Slapping a stack of the counterfeit money against his thigh, John said, "How much of this can you get?"

The right corner of Mickey's mouth pulled up in a smirk. His eyes looked distant, far away. He flossed the base of his nose with one finger. "As much as you want," he said. "You want more, bring your money. But I don't meet nobody else. Neither do you."

"Fair enough."

"You think about rippin' me off—"

"I got no interest rippin' anybody off. I'm a street guy, not a jerk." He folded the tissue paper back over the counterfeit bills. The traffic lights at the intersection changed, and a steady stream of headlights washed past the car, distorted by the rain and sleet. "Long as there's no bullshit."

"You still bitchin' about what happened on Thanksgiving?" Mickey said suddenly, his voice raised up a notch. "Get over it."

John inwardly shuddered, suddenly too aware of the transmitter designed to look like a cigarette lighter sitting on the dashboard two feet away from Mickey O'Shay's face.

Christ, he thought, picturing Kersh leaning forward in his sedan, making sure he'd heard Mickey's words correctly. *I'm gonna hear it from him now.*

He was careful not to let the curve throw him. In his seat, Mickey sat like someone awaiting bad news from a doctor. His face was slack, sullen, and almost too dark.

John quickly moved forward. "You think you could put together a smaller package for me by tomorrow night?" he said. "I got another buyer interested."

"How much?" Mickey turned to watch the traffic through his window.

"Not sure yet. Maybe ten grand." He was hoping to flush out some information on Jimmy Kahn with a second buy-through, although given Mickey's distaste for small talk he didn't think it would be easy. At the very least, he wanted someone eyeballing Mickey, tailing him if he left the area to pick up the counterfeit.

"That it?" Mickey said.

"For now," he said. "I gotta make some calls first. Gimme a number where I can reach you. I'll call sometime in the afternoon and let you know the deal, give you a couple hours to pick up your end. Things work good, we'll make money together."

"We'll see," Mickey mumbled, now looking straight out the windshield. His left hand dipped into his coat, scrounged around, came out with a pencil. He tore off a section of the brown paper bag and jotted down a phone number. "Here," he said, passing John the number. "It's the number to the candy store. For when you need to reach me."

"What, you *live* there?" John chuckled, looking over the phone number then stuffing it into his jacket.

"Best place to reach me," Mickey said. "I ain't around, you leave your name."

"That guy your personal answering service?" he said, jerking his head toward the candy store.

Mickey just nodded at the slip of paper with the store's phone number on it now in John's pocket. "Somethin' comes up," he said, "call that number, let me know."

"What about knockin' the price down?"

Mickey bit the inside of his cheek, stifling a laugh. "Yeah, sure. Because I like you so much."

John flexed his hands on the steering wheel and shrugged one shoulder. "You're a little high," he said, pressing Mickey, curious to see if Mickey had the authority to drop the price if he wanted. He watched his eyes, tried to read them, studied the ticks at each corner of his mouth.

"You don't like it, hit the bricks."

"Think about it."

"Tomorrow night pans out," Mickey said, "you're lookin' at the same deal. Twenty percent. Bottom line."

John slipped the counterfeit bills back into the paper bag and tossed it behind him on the back seat. "Good doin' business with ya," he told Mickey.

"We'll see," was all Mickey said. And a moment later, he was dodging traffic along Tenth Avenue and heading back toward the candy store.

☘

Back at the office, Kersh was upset. A man of lesser integrity would have been irate, his voice raised, his hands no doubt balled into bloodless white fists. But Bill Kersh was not that man. He sat on the corner of his desk, the hem of his rumpled slacks hitched too high above his socks, one foot—the one off the ground—twitching uneasily. The knot of his necktie was pulled away from his collar, the tie itself twisted like a contortionist. The look on his face was that of a disappointed parent.

"What the hell were you thinking?" Kersh said.

John sat in Kersh's desk chair, labeling evidence bags. On the desk, still wrapped in the mint-green tissue paper and stuffed inside a brown paper bag, was $100,000 in counterfeit hundreds.

"I knew you'd get bent out of shape," he said. "That's why I didn't say anything."

"So tell me," Kersh said. "This guy rings you Thanksgiving morning and you meet him without calling me? Without calling the *office?*"

"It was Thanksgiving. Most of the guys weren't even in. Besides, there was no time. I was late getting there as it was. What the hell would calling the office have done?"

"At least someone would have known where you were," Kersh said. "It was careless. It was *stupid.*"

John slapped the evidence bag down on the desk and looked up at Kersh. "He was fronting me the money. What the hell was I supposed to do? Turn him down? 'No thanks, Mickey, I don't feel like pickin' up free money today'? Come on, Bill, you're talking nonsense."

Kersh slid off his desk. He lingered for a moment with his head facing the darkened bank of office windows, his meaty hands stuffed into the pockets of his slacks. "What about your report? What are you going to say about this in your undercover report?"

John frowned, shrugged. "I was planning to leave it out."

"Oh," Kersh said. "Oh. Okay." He pulled his hands from his pockets and pressed them on top of his desk. Bending down, he cut the distance between their faces in half. "Let me explain something," he said. His voice was not harsh, not preachy. It was Bill Kersh's normal cadence—half simplicity, half heart. *"This is not how we do things.* There are rules we follow and reasons we follow them. This is not a game. I don't need you running around the streets playing Batman. *You* don't need that."

"I think you're getting a little carried away. Relax. It worked out, didn't it?" He offered Kersh a crooked grin—what Katie called his "kiss-my-ass-grin."

Kersh straightened his back, sighed, and folded his arms. The button on his left wrist cuff had fallen off, allowing the cuff to hang open. Tonight, he was bothered by more than just the fact John had left out the details of the Thanksgiving Day meeting. Tommy Veccio had reported in, explaining that he'd kept an eye on Mickey O'Shay all evening, but O'Shay had gone nowhere—just between his apartment and the candy store, and that was it. Which meant the money had to have been in either O'Shay's apartment or Calliope Candy.

"John," Kersh began, "this is a job. A little different than most, maybe, but it's still a job. Doctors operate with the proper equipment—they don't waltz into the O.R. clutching a handful of knives and forks, ready to go to work. That's just not the right way. I'm telling you from experience. You think something's worth it, but it's really not." He rubbed the side of his face. "I just want you to do this like the professional you're supposed to be," he said, then added, "like the professional I know you *are.*"

John pushed back in his chair and didn't say a word.

"Rules," Kersh said. Unfolding his arms, he turned and headed toward the office door. "I'm getting some coffee," he said. "You want?"

"I know what I'm doing," John said, and watched Kersh walk out of the office.

CHAPTER TWENTY

THE PURPOSE OF THE SECOND BUY-THROUGH with Mickey O'Shay was primarily to allow Bill Kersh to sit on him and watch where he went to pick up the money. The problem was Mickey O'Shay went *nowhere.* It was just as Tommy Veccio had informed Kersh prior to the first buy-through: "This guy goes nowhere, Bill. He hangs around the street corner, the candy store. That's it. And another thing," Veccio added, a tinge of humor in his voice. "This guy looks like an extra from an old Jimmy Cagney flick. I'd be surprised if he's got two brain cells to rub together and make a spark. He supposed to be some sort of big deal or what?"

It went down the same this time, too. Mickey O'Shay slipped from his apartment in the early part of the evening, crossed the street to Calliope Candy, and remained inside until John showed up for the buy. Kersh, his sedan parked further west along 53rd Street, sat with his back facing the candy store. Over the years, he'd developed a rather inconspicuous and effective method of backward surveillance: by utilizing the sedan's rearview and sideview mirrors, he was able sit casually behind the wheel and see all the action without ever having to face the suspect. From the sedan, he watched Mickey and could not believe the hood did not have to go to pick up the money.

Surely any second he expected him to pop out of the candy store and start heading down the street on foot. Or maybe grab a cab and head toward Times Square or the Theater District. Yet Mickey O'Shay never left the candy store. Moreover, no one else *entered*—just a smattering of neighborhood kids. Was it possible that the kids were carrying money, that they were used as runners? It was possible, but Kersh thought they looked too young for Mickey to trust them with such valuable merchandise. Then was the money squirreled away in the candy store somewhere? In O'Shay's apartment?

Just as night began to claim the city, John's Camaro pulled up across the street from the candy store, his headlights on. After several minutes, Mickey stuck his head out of the candy store, coughed once into a balled fist, then began crossing the street. He moved with his usual swagger—one that suggested he watched too many movies where the bad guys were heroes and all the cops were dirty.

Mickey entered John's car without saying a word. Around them, the sky was turning a bruised, deep purple. A few pedestrians were hustling home along Tenth Avenue, not a single one interested in the Camaro parked across the street from Calliope Candy.

John nodded toward the candy store.

"You should buy that joint, much time as you spend there," he said. Mickey didn't say a word.

"You got it?" John said.

Mickey produced another package wrapped in mint-green tissue paper, this one much smaller than the first. Mickey did not immediately hand it over to him. Instead, he kept it on his lap and pulled over one flap of the tissue paper, exposing the bills. There was a single banded stack inside—ten thousand in counterfeit hundreds. With one hand, Mickey dumped the package into John's lap.

"Good," John said, examining the bills. "Your guy does good work."

"Where's mine?"

John folded the tissue paper back over the notes and stuffed them into his jacket. He pointed to a crowbar on the floor by Mickey's feet. "Gimme that," he said.

Mickey shot a glance at the crowbar, then looked up at John. "The hell you talkin' about?"

"The crowbar." John opened his door, swung one leg out. He was struck by a blast of cold air. "Give it to me."

Mickey just stared at him.

"You want your money or not?"

Mickey's eyes lingered on John for a moment longer—then he leaned forward, grabbed the crowbar by its hooked end, and handed it over to John without saying a word. If Mickey had any reservations about handing him the crowbar—if for even a split second he thought John might use the tool to bang him over the head and drag him out into the street—his eyes did not show it.

He took the crowbar and stepped out into the street.

"Where you goin'?" Mickey called, not even the slightest tremor in his voice. As if he were speaking the words to convince John of trepidation he did not feel. He remained in the passenger bucket, his eyes focused on the parked car in front of him.

"Gettin' your money," John said, and walked over to the Camaro's rear driver's side tire. Kneeling in the street, he popped the hubcap off the wheel and peeled a small, plastic bag away from where it was taped inside of the hubcap. Leaning over the driver's seat, Mickey watched him in the driver's sideview mirror. John hammered the hubcap back into place and slipped back inside the car, slamming the door and tossing the crowbar on the back seat.

"Had to meet some people before I came here—didn't want the coins on me. You see this car parked somewhere else next week, let me save you the trouble," he said, flipping Mickey the plastic bag.

"Don't bother checking the wheels."

Mickey rolled the plastic bag over in his hands. He took out the money, flipped through it with seemingly little interest, though he did not count it.

"Let's talk about cutting down the price," John said.

"I told you the deal."

"I need a *new* deal." He tapped the pocket of his jacket where he'd stashed the counterfeit. "This is good shit. I wanna keep buyin' from you, Mickey, but you gotta get the numbers down. I'm payin' you twenty points, I gotta make at least another five to make it worth my while. I can get a lot of action on this money, but not at twenty-five percent."

"That ain't my problem."

"I'm just asking you to think about it, talk to whoever you need to . . . maybe we both talk to 'em. I wanna keep doin' business with you, Mickey."

"Who are you?" Mickey said then. His tone wasn't accusatory, wasn't sardonic or laced with any trace of sly humor. It was a straight question. Mickey's eyes lingered on him, awaiting an answer.

"What?"

"Who *are* you?" That same straightforward tone.

"I'm a guy lookin' to make some money," he said, switching to offense. "You ain't interested in making money, in making deals, then tell me who *you* are."

Chewing on the inside of his cheek, Mickey nodded his head and said, "How many buyers you got lined up?"

"What do you care?" It was the appropriate response, yet he wanted to encourage Mickey to keep talking all the same, keep him asking questions. "I move around, make connections, meet people. Like I said—I can move whatever you got. And not just this shit. *Anything.* But the price's gotta be right." He sighed, put his hands on the steering wheel and faced front. A dark blue Pontiac eased past them along Tenth Avenue and turned left on West 53rd Street.

Wheels were turning in Mickey's head; John could see a flicker of thought working behind Mickey's cold, shallow eyes. It was like a suddenly brilliant flame, long since starved of oxygen.

Yet Mickey was through chatting. "You need some more," he said, opening the passenger door, "call me. We'll talk about price then."

"Let me ask you something," he said, peering at Mickey through the door. "You always this friendly?"

Not even grinning, Mickey O'Shay shut the passenger door.

"He's heading back to the store," he said into the transmitter on the dashboard. "Must have one hell of a sweet tooth."

He started up the Camaro's engine but did not pull out right away. He remained, watching Mickey from the corner of his eye.

Kersh, roughly one block away, was also watching Mickey O'Shay. He watched Mickey shuffle onto the curb outside Calliope Candy, his hands stuffed into his pockets, his eyes on the traffic along the street. He looked like someone waiting for a bus. Then one of Mickey's hands appeared from his coat. Kersh watched as he went to the pay phone outside the store, picked up the receiver. After sliding in some change, Mickey dialed a number and remained on the street corner with the receiver up to one ear. With the thumb of his free hand, Mickey scraped at his front teeth, his eyes still on the slow-moving traffic along Tenth Avenue.

"Who're you calling now, buddy?" Kersh muttered to himself, adjusting the sedan's rearview.

Mickey's phone call was brief. After he hung up, he turned and sauntered back inside Calliope Candy. Kersh eased his head against the headrest, his mind lingering on Mickey O'Shay and the candy store. He might just drop in there tomorrow, say he's grabbing some peppermints for his nephew or something. Just to scope out the place, see who was behind the counter. Ideas came quickly to him when he was able to envision his surroundings, when he knew the field on which his opponents practiced.

Kersh's sedan remained parked along West 53rd Street for some time afterward, the car's driver curious to see if Mickey happened to split and head off somewhere. But Mickey O'Shay never came out of the candy store, and the night was quickly upon him.

Starting his car, he backed out of his parking space and onto West 53rd Street, heading toward the Hudson. While readjusting his rearview mirror, he saw John's Camaro drift across the intersection of Tenth Avenue and West 53rd Street. A few cars followed close behind him. Three cars away, Kersh spotted a blue Pontiac Sunbird and felt a sudden needling in the pit of his stomach.

John was being followed.

The blue Pontiac Sunbird had completed two revolutions around the corner of Tenth Avenue and West 53rd Street while Kersh had been on surveillance—probably more, but he hadn't noticed. And now the car was following John down Tenth Avenue.

Headlights behind him caused him to readjust his rearview mirror again. He made a quick right onto Eleventh Avenue, the sedan's engine roaring, and grappled with his cell phone. When he depressed the power button, the screen only glowed a dim green. *LOW BAT* blinked across the screen.

"Shit!"

He tried dialing John's cell phone, nonetheless, but the call would not go through. *Goddamn cell phone,* he thought. *It's got enough power to tell me the battery's low, but not enough to make one stinking phone call.* He tried his radio to reach John, but John had turned his off. He could use his walkie-talkie and get in touch with Veccio and Conners, who'd also been on the surveillance . . . but then decided against it at the last minute. The best way to handle the situation was as indiscriminately as possible.

He spun down West 57th Street toward Tenth Avenue, knowing full well the routes John would take to get back to the office. There was a jam at the intersection up ahead. Some ConEd guys in orange vests and blue helmets had busted half the street open here, and traffic had stalled to a standstill. Horns blared as discourteous drivers spun out into the open side of the street, cutting off less aggressive drivers. The traffic lights were not in Kersh's favor. Slowly, he eased up a few feet behind a white van, his eyes scanning the intersection. He spotted John's car in the confusion of traffic, trying to turn off 57th Street. And a few cars behind him, Kersh could make out the blue Pontiac Sunbird.

Son of a bitch . . .

Squinting, he tried to make out the plates but couldn't read the numbers. A young-looking white guy was behind the wheel, the car's only occupant . . .

Damn . . .

It was probably nothing—perhaps just someone who had been looking for a parking space all day—and from what John had said, Mickey O'Shay did not seem like the sort of guy capable of orchestrating a tail. Still, it did not sit well with him. Bill Kersh would not take that chance.

Behind him, another bright pair of headlights reflected in the sedan's rearview. Squinting, he pushed the rearview off at an angle, casting the reflection from his eyes, and watched as John's Camaro slowly cut across the intersection and began to turn right. Several cars behind John, Kersh could make out the Pontiac edging toward that same direction.

He didn't like the way the Pontiac was pushing its way toward the intersection, somehow more insistent than the other cars around it. Still, he could not make out the license plate.

Traffic was a large part of the city. Bill Kersh did not customarily dislike the traffic, and did not mind the city. Time spent in a jam was usually time to reflect and be alone. Now, however, he felt driven by a certain urgency, a certain gnawing at his gut. Sure, it was probably nothing—yet undercover agents had been tailed before. Why Mickey O'Shay would want to put a tail on John . . . Kersh understood that very well.

The lights above the intersection still had not changed. Two ConEd guys were trying their best to direct traffic around the source of the problem: a giant crater in the center of the street.

Let's move, a voice boomed in Kersh's head, and he gunned the engine and lurched through the intersection. One of the ConEd guys shouted something, then dodged out of the way. Kersh blared his horn. The stream of cars already at a standstill in the middle of the intersection began to reverse or pull forward, as close to the sanctity of the curb as they could manage. A line of traffic cleared, and Kersh's sedan slid quickly between the gap. Someone else shouted something obscene. Fists pumped the air. The sedan shuddered and lurched forward again, closing the gap of the intersection, the front end of his car desperate to pull through the jam and spill out on the other side of 57th Street.

As he crossed the intersection, he angled his car perpendicular to the mouth of West 57th Street, inhibiting the flow of turning traffic. More horns blared. Up ahead, he could make out the diminishing taillights of John's Camaro speeding off into the darkness. And two cars over from Bill Kersh's right was the Pontiac Sunbird, in as dead of a stop as every other car. The driver appeared calm, his face eclipsed by shadow. The two cars between them made it impossible for him to get the tag number.

"Sorry," Kersh shouted from his open window. And since he'd be here for a while, he turned on his stereo and popped in an Art Blakey tape. A rattle of drums shook his speakers and caused him to breathe a sigh of relief.

CHAPTER TWENTY-ONE

"SORRY," KERSH SAID. "HOPE I'M NOT DISTURBING anything."

Surprised by the unexpected company, John opened wide the apartment door and gestured for the older agent to enter. "No," he said, "not at all. Come in. Is everything all right?"

"Sure, sure. I was just in the neighborhood. That's the saying at least, isn't it?" Kersh shook himself off in the doorway—it had started to rain again this evening—and pushed his way inside. Clasped in his oversized hand was a bottle of Luna di Luna chardonnay; he appeared to be squeezing the life out of it.

They entered the kitchen, Kersh uncharacteristically coy. "Hon, you remember Bill Kersh."

"Katie," Kersh said, and nodded once.

"Of course," Katie said, suddenly beaming. "How are you? I'm sorry the place is such a disaster. Maybe you can convince my husband to get some of his crap put away."

"It's really very beautiful," Kersh said, admiring the craftsmanship of the wood paneling, the decorative tablecloth on the small table, the bric-a-brac Katie collected lined along the countertop and the windowsill above the sink. "Congratulations." Then, as if he'd suddenly remembered, he held out the bottle of chardonnay to her.

"Here. A housewarming gift."

"Wow," she said, taking the bottle and squeezing Kersh's forearm with one hand. "Our first housewarming gift." She set the bottle down on the counter.

"Not true. You're forgetting Phyllis Gamberniece's delicious brownies," John said, "topped with a fine sprinkling of cat hair." He went to the refrigerator and grabbed a couple of beers, set them on the kitchen table. "Sit down, Billy."

"Uh . . . I didn't think," Kersh said to Katie, gesticulating at the bottle and still standing awkwardly in the kitchen doorway. "I mean, you probably won't . . . or can't . . . drink any of . . ." He hiked up his pants nervously. "The baby. John's told me you're due the end of February?"

"That's the plan," Katie said. She walked by her husband on her way to the sink and slapped him once lightly on the waist. Winked playfully. "Nice to know he remembered." She tossed a dishrag into the sink. "Are you hungry, Bill? I've got some spaghetti, still hot."

Kersh seated himself at the table with John, who twisted the cap off the man's beer and slid it over to him.

"I don't want to be any trouble," Kersh said.

"No trouble," Katie assured him. "It's still here on the counter."

Kersh took a small sip of his beer and shrugged. John noticed Kersh did not shrug well—that his shoulders were too large and too close to his head for the action to look natural. "Well," Kersh said, "if it's not any trouble . . ." He offered Katie another awkward smile, and it suddenly occurred to John that Bill Kersh was knowledgeable about a lot of things, but knew very little about women. So little, in fact, they apparently made him uncomfortable.

"One dish," Katie said, "coming right up."

"Look at this guy," John said. "Comes to our house, drinks our beer, and eats our leftovers."

"It's good preparation for when you're parents," Kersh said.

John stood, went to the kitchen counter, and took the plate from his wife's hand. "Go get your bath," he said, "I'll do this."

"I can do it."

"I got it."

Defeated, Katie wiped her hands on a dishtowel. "Sorry to spoil the fun," she told Kersh, "but I'm going to get ready for bed."

Kersh stood and smiled. For one crazy moment, John thought the man was actually going to bow down, or kiss his wife's hand. He had to fight off a chuckle.

In the end, Kersh opted for a simple, "Good night."

Katie disappeared down the hall and into the bathroom. A moment later and the apartment shuddered as the water in the bathroom was turned on.

"Tell me something," Kersh said as John crossed the kitchen and set the plate of spaghetti in front of the man. "How did you talk that girl into marrying an ugly, arrogant son of a bitch like yourself?"

"Easy," he said, sitting across from Kersh. "A girl doesn't say no to a guy with a gun."

Kersh laughed. "I knew it couldn't have been your charm."

"You never came back to the office tonight," John said. "I waited around for you. Something come up?"

"Traffic," Kersh said, shoveling spaghetti into his mouth and raising his eyebrows. "Something *did* happen. I mean, I *think* so. Probably nothing. But you know me—better safe than sorry."

"What's the deal?"

"I think someone in a blue Pontiac followed you from the candy store."

"Shit," John said, "I saw that car pulling up along Tenth Avenue during the deal." He remembered watching as it rolled past the Camaro.

"The car pulled around the block at least twice, from what I saw," Kersh said. "Turned onto Fifty-third Street both times. Then, when you pulled out into the intersection, I noticed the car was following a few cars behind you. I turned up on Eleventh and came down Fifty-seventh Street, cut him off at the intersection where they had all that construction."

"Are you sure he was following me?" The idea of Mickey O'Shay setting up a tail seemed absurd. "Could have been a million reasons the guy was driving around the block."

"True, and I'm sure it was nothing, but I just wanted to play it safe just the same. And to let you know, too."

It just didn't sound right. "I don't think it came from Mickey," he said.

"You're probably right," Kersh agreed again. Yet he didn't sound too convinced. "I just figured you should know. This spaghetti is excellent. I should marry an Italian woman."

Cradling his beer in his lap, John leaned back in his chair. "You couldn't handle an Italian woman," he said, though he was still chewing on Kersh's story, his mind elsewhere. "She'd break you down so fast it'd make your head spin."

"You have such little faith," Kersh said. That was when John noticed something else in the man's eyes—something greater than the story he'd just relayed.

"What else?" John asked. "There's something else . . ."

"There is," Kersh said. "You mind if I pop open this chardonnay?"

Several minutes later, with two full glasses of chardonnay in front of them, Bill Kersh said, "I was on Mickey all night. He never left the store, not until you showed up. Not for a single second. Just like when Tommy was watching."

Slowly, John shook his head. "Anybody else go *in* the store?"

Kersh explained about the children, but both knew it meant nothing.

"So he's either got a stash in his apartment—"

"Or someone else's apartment," Kersh added.

"Or in the candy store," John finished.

"Don't know," Kersh said. "You think they're printing it? Him and Jimmy?"

"No—no way," he said, shaking his head. "These are smash-and-grab guys. They're not sophisticated enough to actually be printing the shit."

"What about the store?"

"Guy working there must know the deal," John said. "That's Mickey's business office."

"You know," Kersh said, "the Service isn't going to let us sink much more money into this thing. We're already down twenty-two thousand bucks and we've got nothing to show for it except this guy O'Shay. Soon, Chominsky's gonna want us to bust him, see if we can roll him . . ."

Chominsky was the Special Agent in Charge of the field office. And John knew Kersh was right about him. Dejected, he said, "This guy'll never roll on Kahn. Not in a million years."

"You don't know—"

"I *do,*" he said, pressing the tips of his fingers against the tabletop with enough force to turn them white. "I can smell it just by sitting next to this guy. He won't say boo. And we need to nail Kahn. If we get them both dirty, then maybe they'll cut a deal together, give up the source. But I'll tell you now—alone, Mickey won't cooperate even if he's faced with a zillion years. The guy's not all there."

"Anyone can be persuaded," Kersh assured him. "Loyalty only goes so far."

"I'm not talking about loyalty," John said. "I just think the guy's mind is fractured. And I'm hoping Kahn is smarter." Frustrated, he poured himself some more chardonnay and picked at the bottle's label with his thumbnail. Damn it—if he could have just gotten Mickey to open up a little more . . . just a *little.* "Christ, I don't know." He looked up at Kersh. "So what do we do?"

"We think," Kersh said. "Me, I'm spending more time in what

you so respectfully refer to as 'the pit.' It's like my own personal War Room."

They drank some more, mostly in silence. It was a good feeling—John had not enjoyed the silence of an older man in a long time. Part of his mind was with his father in the little stucco house. He pictured the interior dark, his father's restless shape beneath the covers of his bed. Another part of him remained right here with Bill Kersh, drinking Luna di Luna and liking it. It seemed that contentment and comfort rarely graced him with their presence—that he was always on edge, always moving from someplace to someplace else—but he felt both right now, and very strongly.

"Aside from your horrendous sense of style, some woman somewhere must have fallen for you. How come you never married?" he asked Kersh after pouring them both another glass.

"Almost did," Kersh said. He was leaning back in his chair, his tie undone, a thick fold of red flesh overhanging his shirt collar. There was tomato sauce drying on one sleeve. His glass of chardonnay was precariously balanced on the edge of the table, one of Bill Kersh's thick fingers pressing down against the glass's base. "It's not a particularly original story. We fell in love, did the moonlit stroll through Central Park thing. We talked about marriage. She wanted children desperately, and I wanted nothing to do with them."

John laughed.

"What?" Kersh said, cracking a smile.

"Nothing. It's just you . . ." He waved his hand at Kersh. "Nothing. What's wrong with kids?"

"Not a thing," Kersh said. "They're terrific. Wonderful. Long as they're not mine."

"You're whacked."

"I don't dislike them; I just don't *understand* them."

Smiling, John ran a hand through his hair. Between him and Kersh, they had almost worked their way through an entire bottle of

Luna di Luna. "Did the job have anything to do with it?"

"With what?" Kersh, too, seemed to be in a good place.

"With why you didn't want to have children?" Yet even after a few drinks, he recognized the intent such a question implied. Suddenly, he wished he hadn't said anything.

"No," Kersh said. "Why? Something on your mind?"

"No. I was just curious."

"Are you sure?" Kersh's tone was relaxing, coaxing. It was the tone he used when interrogating people, John suddenly realized, and only now did he understand the full effect of such an approach. Perhaps it was the alcohol, but John didn't think it was. "Look," Kersh continued, "I've been doing this job for a long time. And in that time, I've come to understand that there's really only one thing I need to keep inside my head every day. Just one thing that makes the job possible."

"Yeah? What's that?"

"That it's only a job." Kersh allowed the words to simmer in the air. "You remember that, keep that in mind, and everything else will take care of itself."

He saw Bill Kersh as a preacher, outfitted in folds of black silk, embroidered gold piping around the sleeves and neck, standing before a throng of worshippers, all seeking answers for unanswerable questions.

"You," John said after some time, "drank all the chardonnay."

"You helped," Kersh informed him.

"I got an idea."

"About what?"

"About what to do with Mickey." Setting his empty glass down on the table, he leaned forward in his chair and propped one elbow on the tabletop. "It's a little unconventional, but we can pull it off."

"All your ideas are unconventional," Kersh said.

"Just do me one favor," he said.

"Shoot."

"Promise me you'll agree to it before I tell you what it is."

Kersh laughed, his head back, his enormous Adam's apple vibrating in his throat. He looked astoundingly like some prehistoric animal. When the laughter finally subsided, he set his own glass back down on the table and looked at John with bleary eyes. "Maybe," he said.

"No backbone," John commented.

Kersh paused, rolled his eyes to the left, examined the molding that ran the length of the kitchen wall. Finally, he said, "All right. But it better be good. Now—what's the deal?"

"This guy Mickey don't trust me," he said. "Don't think he trusts anybody, really. I gotta do something that earns that trust, something that puts me in deeper, right on the line with this guy." He twirled the stem of his wine glass between two fingers. "Something he won't expect."

"So what's this brilliant idea of yours?"

"What do undercover agents always do?" he said, not waiting for Kersh to answer: "They *buy.*"

"So?" Kersh said.

"They *buy,*" John repeated. "They never *sell.*"

Kersh rubbed a rough hand across the lower part of his jaw. "I knew," he said, "I shouldn't have drunk all that wine."

CHAPTER TWENTY-TWO

AFTER KNOCKING OFF THE ENTIRE BOTTLE OF Luna di Luna with Kersh, John made a telephone call to a young customs agent named Robert Silvestri at JFK International Airport. Silvestri had grown up in the same Brooklyn neighborhood as John, had even attended the same college. Like John, he was one of the few guys from the old neighborhood who managed to circumvent a life of street crime and privation. With Kersh watching him from above his empty wine glass, John explained the Mickey O'Shay situation to Silvestri.

"Sounds like a real fun guy," Silvestri responded. "What do you need?"

"I wanna turn the tables on him," he said, "spin his head a little bit. I was wondering what you guys might have down there that I could sell to this guy—seized cigarettes, swag, whatever you got."

Laughing, Silvestri said, "Always doing things your own way, huh?"

"That's the *only* way," he said.

"I think we might have just the thing you're looking for," Silvestri said. "Two days ago we seized thirty cases of Canadian whiskey, real high-quality shit. You wanna sell something to a bunch of street punks, you can't go wrong with quality booze."

Though he hadn't found the idea as charmingly amusing as Robert Silvestri had, Brett Chominsky had agreed to the operation the following day. A deal of this magnitude, John assured Chominsky, was certain to flush out some more of Mickey's guys, and maybe even Jimmy Kahn himself—though John silently doubted Kahn would show. Plus, if Mickey went for it, they would have another three grand to play with.

Chominsky made his own phone call to the airport's customs department, then quickly dispatched two agents to pick up the Ryder truck and stow it in the underground garage beneath the field office.

Now, all that was left to do was meet with Mickey and push the deal. He phoned the candy store, and the man who answered the phone told him Mickey was not around. John left a message and his cell phone number.

Reenergized by the thought of turning the tables on Mickey and keeping him aloof, he hit the office gym and ran two miles on the treadmill.

By 1:30, he was in SoHo meeting Katie for lunch before she went to class.

"I'm so big now," she told him as they munched on sandwiches and drank Cokes, "I feel ridiculous walking across campus."

"Why?"

"Everybody stares. I feel old. I'm an old lady to those kids."

"That's not true."

"It *is*. You should see how young some of them look."

"You look beautiful."

"Hmmmm." She smiled. "You're in a good mood today. What set you off?"

He shrugged. "Nothing," he said.

"Well," she responded, "whatever pills you've been taking, keep it up. You just may be salvageable yet."

"Lucky for me."

By three o'clock, Mickey still hadn't returned his call. John tried the candy store a second time, and the guy who answered once again told him that Mickey was not around.

By four o'clock, he'd run two more miles on the gym's treadmill.

He found himself sitting at his desk, staring at the digital readout of Bill Kersh's clock from across the office. Hands folded in his lap, he sat reclining in his chair, the small radio on the corner of his desk broadcasting the Knicks game. Outside, the sky was once again turning to night, and that slipping feeling of time being pulled away was all around him, like the hum of live circuitry.

Mickey had not returned his calls.

Kersh ambled into the office, tugging his coat on while trying to balance a Starbucks cup with the same hand. "It's late," he said. "I'm calling it a day." He kicked one of the legs of John's chair. "Don't look so bummed. He'll call tomorrow. Rats like Mickey always come scurrying at the smell of cheese."

"I know."

"Then go home," Kersh said.

"I'm waiting for you to leave so I can go through your desk."

"Just don't touch the porn."

"Go home, Bill. I'll see you tomorrow."

"Good night, John," Kersh said, moving slowly out of the office.

John remained at his desk for some time, watching the blaze of city lights through the windows and glancing occasionally down at his cell phone. If he left the office now, he'd make it home in time for a late supper with Katie. And given enough time, he could even swing by his father's place. For some reason, his mind summoned the image of the rotting ground beef in his father's sink that night he'd gone to the house to retrieve his father's coat. The old house on

Eleventh Avenue . . . what would happen to it once his father passed on? Could he just sell it, just like that? Surely he couldn't *live* there.

Mickey . . . where the hell are you?

Two agents wearing pressed suits and carrying shotguns walked past his desk. He watched them with little interest.

Where are you?

He left the office five minutes later, his mind still on his wife and their tiny little apartment in Brooklyn. He did not head home, however. Instead, he took his car through the heart of the city toward the West Side. The traffic was unbearable, all major roads congested, and he abruptly knew right at the beginning of his trek that he would not be having that late dinner with his wife or stopping in to see his father after all. Tonight, like most nights, was going to be long. And while part of him *wanted* to be home, a larger part would not allow it. *Could* not allow it.

It was completely dark when he pulled onto Tenth Avenue and slowly cruised along with the traffic heading through Hell's Kitchen. Just before the 53rd Street intersection, he slowed his car to a near-stop directly in front of Calliope Candy. Inside the shop, lights were on and a few people milled about: a father in a tweed coat was holding two young girls by their hands; a thirteen- or fourteen-year-old boy wearing a backpack and holding a skateboard was fingering the little door on one of the gum ball machines. He could see no one behind the counter.

No Mickey O'Shay.

As he drove north along Tenth Avenue, he watched the looming silhouette of Mickey's high-rise recede in his rearview mirror.

He hit the construction at the 57th Street intersection and another stationary wedge of automobiles. Veering off Tenth Avenue, he turned right onto 57th Street. Though the street was somewhat less congested, there were still enough cars to impede his movement. Up ahead, the traffic lights appeared to be on the bum.

Looking around, he was reminded of his Thanksgiving Day meeting with Mickey. It had happened right here on this street.

An hour late and that bastard was still here, waiting for me to show up, he thought now. *What kind of guy stands around on the street corner for a full hour?*

Looking out his window, he noticed what looked like a small, nameless pub behind him, just beyond the intersection. A Guinness sign hung in the darkened window. Below that glowed a green neon clover.

Because hanging around is easy, he thought, *when you can watch a guy through a bar window.*

Maneuvering the Camaro through the traffic, he managed to make his way to the small alleyway that led to the back of Roosevelt Hospital—where Mickey had told him to drive that day. He turned his lights off and parked midway along the darkened alley. Stepping out of the car, he shivered against the cold and pulled his leather jacket closed. Moving back toward the street, he was conscious of the rustle of city rats beneath discarded newspapers and inside the giant dumpsters that lined the alley.

The pub was warm and small, accommodating only a few tables and booths toward the back, and a selection of mismatched bar stools along the front of the bar. A decorative mirror in the entranceway had the word *Cloverleaf* stenciled on it in calligraphy, which he assumed to be the name of the pub. Across the room, an old-fashioned jukebox was rolling through an old Johnny Cash number.

Tonight, the tables and booths were empty. Only the barstools were occupied, the company diverse. He claimed the closest stool, seating himself next to a meaty woman with red, blotchy forearms and a face that looked like someone had massaged it with the business end of a rake. Beside her, a muscular man in a leather coat and a handlebar mustache puckered his lips around the head of a bottle of Killian's. They were relatively quiet, compared to the stifled laughter and drumming of fists coming from the opposite end of the bar.

The bartender stepped in front of him, placing his hands on the bar, and asked him what he wanted.

"Gimme a Guinness."

"See your ID?"

"Seriously?"

The bartender looked irritated. "Come on, pal."

John removed his undercover wallet from his pants and showed him his forged driver's license. Satisfied, the bartender made his way down to the other end of the bar to pour the drink.

Leaning forward, he peered down toward the opposite end of the bar. Huddled there, standing, were four guys with twice that many glasses of beer in front of them. Out of the four guys, John only recognized one: Mickey O'Shay.

The rest of the guys in Mickey's company looked just as young, just as degenerate. They coalesced in a semicircle around O'Shay, who stood among them not as a peer but as their better; this was obvious in the stately bravado exhibited by him in his mannerisms, his facial expressions, the way he carried his body. Watching Mickey O'Shay at the end of the bar, John was back in college, peeking up during an exam to study the faces of the classroom cheaters. And Mickey, secure in familiar company, was the biggest cheater he'd ever seen.

A thought occurred to him. Could one of the other guys be Jimmy Kahn? He remembered how disappointed he'd been upon meeting Mickey after the way Tressa Walker had talked about him. Couldn't one of these losers be Kahn? They all looked equally unimpressive.

Mickey's eyes shifted in John's direction. A look of distraction swam across his face. It was the look of uncertain recognition, stimulated by a change in surroundings. John returned the look, held it steadier than Mickey seemed capable of, and did not look away until Mickey did. Mickey's companions did not even seem to notice.

"Four fifty," the bartender said, placing the beer in front of John.

He paid the bartender, aware now that Mickey's eyes continued to dart over in his direction. He didn't have to look up, look over at him, to know that. Facing forward, he sat and sipped his beer. It was too thick, mostly head, and tasted like motor oil.

In the mirror behind the bar, John watched Mickey's reflection approach, step around him. A second later and Mickey appeared on his right, leaning against the bar.

"Mickey," he muttered.

"The hell you doin' here?"

"Drinkin'. What's it look like?"

"You come all this way for a beer?"

He took another sip of the beer, set it down on a cocktail napkin. "Actually, no. I came here lookin' for you. You're like the Invisible Man, Mickey. Been tryin' to call you at the store all day."

"Yeah? Well, ya found me."

Mickey O'Shay was drunk. And not only drunk—John could tell he'd recently snorted something up his nose or shot something into his arm. He'd been around enough drug abusers—both during his career and growing up in Brooklyn—to recognize the hollowed eyes and quivering cheeks of the recently blitzed.

"Irish tell you I was here?" Mickey said.

"Who?"

Mickey shook his head, blinked his eyes. "Never mind. What'd you want?"

"You gonna piss off your friends, ignoring them like this?"

"Don't worry about them. What'd you wanna see me about?"

John picked up his beer and lifted himself off his stool. "Come on," he said, moving toward a booth at the back of the tavern.

Mickey pushed himself off the bar and somehow managed to close the distance between the bar and the booth without falling on his face. Back at the bar, Mickey's friends shouted something in unison, downed a shot of whiskey each, then hollered at Mickey for abandoning them. Without the courtesy of vocalization, Mickey shot out a single hand in their direction, palm out, but did not take his eyes off John. The crowd of hoods at the far end of the bar broke out in more laughter and ordered another round of shots.

Mickey climbed into the booth and sat opposite John, who was now lighting a cigarette with a candle from the table. He looked at Mickey from over the top of the candle, raised his eyebrows.

"Want a smoke?" he offered.

Mickey licked his lips. "Gimme one."

No matter how grand or how insignificant, the giving of an object to someone else subconsciously created a hierarchy between the two people. John, being aware of this, readily handed over one of his cigarettes to Mickey. Holding the candle up to Mickey's face while he inhaled, he lit it for him. The flame threw the skel's face in stark relief.

"Uh," Mickey sighed, taking a deep drag. With his fingers, he pulled his hair back out of his face.

"You all right?" John said. "You don't look so hot."

Mickey took another drag. His eyes looked like divots in a skull. "What's goin' on?"

"I'm doin' you a favor," he said. "Opportunity just fell into my lap, and I'm throwing it your way before I go someplace else."

"What is it?"

"I just got my hands on thirty cases of Canadian whiskey. Real good stuff. Thought you and your friends might be interested . . ."

"Where'd you get it?"

"Canada. What the fuck difference does it make?"

"How much?"

John shrugged, pinched another hit from his cigarette. "Hundred bucks a case. Three grand, all in. Whattaya say?"

The pale husk of his cigarette dangling from his mouth, Mickey rubbed his hands together in a parody of slow motion. Behind him back at the bar, his friends cheered and pounded down another shot.

"That good?" Mickey said.

"Less than half price. Ask around."

"Sounds good," Mickey said. His dead eyes clung to John through a thick cloud of cigarette smoke. "That's a good price. You wanna be paid in the gaff?"

John considered, then shook his head. "No," he said. "This deal's for somebody else. I need cash."

"I can let you know tomorrow."

"Don't waste time on this," he said. "It won't be around long."

The gears were turning in Mickey O'Shay's head.

See how far you can push him, a small voice spoke up inside John's head. *He's as burnt as a fuse right now. See what else he'll say . . .*

"Come on, I'll buy you and your friends a drink."

Mickey finished his cigarette and tossed the butt to the floor, crushing it beneath his heel. More casually than John would have expected, Mickey turned to shoot a glance over at the rowdy group of guys at the end of the bar. Sniffling once, he turned back to John and said, "They ain't my friends."

"I'll buy 'em a beer anyway."

Whatever trace of accessibility he'd seen just moments ago in Mickey's dead eyes was now gone. The man who returned his gaze was again the cold, unreceptive delinquent he'd been during all their prior meetings. Whatever door John had thought he'd managed to open had just been slammed shut in his face.

Mickey did not say another word. He simply stood from the booth, his greasy hair falling in front of his face like a veil, and hovered above the table for a disquieting length of time. His eyes were again hard, sober, alert . . . and distrustful. Borrower or lender—all of a sudden, none of that seemed to matter. In all, the look on Mickey's face was one John thought he recognized, if only for a brief moment.

Then Mickey turned away and sauntered back to the bar. As he approached, one of the guys in his group clapped him on the back while a second guy began chanting what sounded like an old Irish drinking song in a whiny soprano.

And it suddenly dawned on him where he'd seen Mickey's expression before . . .

On *himself.*

It was the hardened, suspicious stare of a street kid.

John was nearly home when his cell phone rang. It was Mickey.

"Let's do the deal," Mickey told him. His voice was flat. John could hear wind whipping against the receiver. "Get your shit ready and I'll call you tomorrow, let you know where to bring it."

John glanced at the car's clock. It was pushing eleven o'clock. "That fast, huh?"

"You said you wanted to move on this," Mickey said. "So let's move." A dull *click,* and Mickey hung up the phone.

Somehow I knew this was going to be a long night, he thought, quickly dialing Kersh's cell phone from memory. It rang several times before a groggy voice muttered, "'Lo?"

"Get your shoes on, sweetheart," John said. "You're going back out."

JFK International Airport is consistently hectic. Even in the deepest hours of night, people drift about like patients in a psyche ward, their eyes unfocused from a lack of sleep, their arms and shoulders overburdened with suitcases and duffel bags and brown paper shopping bags. As a child, John had been fascinated by airports, and had found enjoyment in watching the planes take off and land through the great panels of windows that looked out across the runways. Visits to the airport had been infrequent back then, limited to the few times out-of-state relatives would come to visit him and his father. Now, as an adult and an agent, he no longer appreciated airports for their ability to challenge the minds of preadolescent youths; the spell had been broken the first time he'd boarded a plane heading for Glynco, Georgia, to begin his Secret Service training.

It was dark now, the runways indistinguishable from the night except for the tails of guide-lights that ran their lengths. Waiting for Kersh to exit the bathroom, John leaned against a support post and gazed introspectively out the bank of large windows. He could see himself in the window's reflection, his arms folded about his chest, his hair too long, his posture still frighteningly similar to the young boy he'd once been. He was standing too far from his reflection to make out the details of his face, but he was fairly certain he still even *looked* like that little boy. Did he look anything like his father? And would his son—if he *had* a son—someday look like him?

Kersh's reflection appeared beside his. "You okay?" John asked him.

"Uh," Kersh groaned. Wearing a shirt and tie, his slacks hiked too high above the tops of his socks, Kersh pushed one sweaty hand against the support post and took some weight off his feet. "Got the runs."

"Why the hell did you put a shirt and tie on, anyway?"

"I take pride in my appearance," Kersh said, leaning forward against the support post.

"Yeah," John snickered, "right."

"John!" a voice shouted from farther down the corridor.

"Rob," John said, meeting the man halfway and giving him a one-armed hug. "How you been?"

Robert Silvestri, hands on his hips, nodded fervently up and down. "All right, man, all right." He was tall and slender, with a fine crop of curly black hair at the top of his head. His eyes were dark and beseeching, his jaw perfectly squared.

"Rob," John said, "this is my partner, Bill Kersh."

"A pleasure," Kersh said, peeling himself from the support post and shaking Silvestri's hand.

"Rob and I grew up in the same neighborhood," he explained. "This guy hit the longest home run on Shore Road I've ever seen. Swear to God, the thing flew for miles. To this day, I don't think anyone's ever found the ball."

Silvestri laughed. He had a strong, masculine laugh that suited his face and body well. "That's only because you were the lousy son of a bitch pitching that game," Silvestri said.

John shook his head and told Kersh not to pay any attention to the man.

"Come on," Silvestri said, turning back down the corridor. John and Kersh followed—Kersh a little bit slower. "You cook this plan up all on your own, Johnny?"

"It was Kersh's idea," John said.

"Don't pass the buck to me, buddy," Kersh murmured from over John's shoulder.

"Shouldn't be a problem," Silvestri continued. "I have a few papers for you to fill out just to cover all the bases, but that's really about it. I also got a couple guys to give us a hand loading the stuff. They're packed in some heavy crates. At least a two-man job. Did you pull your truck around to the hangar like I said?"

"Right around back."

"The guards give you any trouble?"

"Yeah. Had to shoot and kill 'em."

Silvestri brought them to a set of locked double-doors. He slipped a large key into the lock, twisted it in two complete revolutions, then bumped one of the doors open with his hip. Leaning against the door, he motioned John and Kersh through, his eyes lingering on

Kersh as he passed.

"You okay, pal? You look green."

"I get airsick at airports," Kersh said, stumbling through the doors.

Silvestri closed the door behind them, washing the room in darkness. Then, following a series of loud clicks, giant floodlights installed in the high ceiling came on one by one, filling the room with light. They were standing in a large cargo hangar. A concrete walkway wove through the hangar, bookended on either side by stacks of wooden crates and large boxes wrapped in plastic Bubble Wrap. Some of the stacks nearly scraped the ceiling, towering above them like buildings. A forklift the size of a large truck stood silently in one corner, *The Old Heave Ho* stenciled in black on its side.

"Some sight, huh?" Silvestri said, scratching casually behind one ear. "You wouldn't believe the kind of crap some bastards try bringing into the country. Never in my life did I ever imagine there were so many colorful ways to smuggle drugs into this great nation of ours. I could tell some stories."

Two strong-looking men appeared from behind a column of wooden crates, their brows already beaded with sweat, the armpits of their matching white polo shirts stained yellow. One of them—a dark-skinned guy with bad teeth—carried a number of leather weight belts over one arm.

"Hey, guys," Silvestri said. "Jerry, you wanna get that door up?"

Jerry, the guy not carrying the belts, waved a finger in Silvestri's direction and hustled around toward the back of the front of the hangar.

The dark-skinned guy approached and distributed the weight belts to the three newcomers.

"My buddy's gonna need a larger size," John said, poking a finger at Kersh's gut.

"Now's not the time to be pokin' there, Mavio," Kersh said. "I might blow a hole through these pants."

Toward the front, the hangar door began climbing toward the ceiling, accompanied by the growl of churning gears. Cold night air rushed in.

"I'll show you the stuff," Silvestri said, buckling the weight belt around his waist. He led them toward the front of the hangar, to a pyramid of nondescript wooden crates stacked just higher than their heads.

John whistled. *"Beautiful."*

Arching his back, his weight belt looped over one shoulder, Kersh said, "When I pictured them in my head, I didn't think there'd be so many . . ."

Above them, the giant hangar door shuddered to a standstill.

"Wanna see?" Silvestri said, walking around the pyramid and grabbing an industrial-sized crowbar from a wall of tools. He jabbed the tapered end of the crowbar beneath the lid of one of the crates, pushed down on it like a lever. Teeth clenched, face turning red, he finally managed to pop the top off. Inside, the corks of several tightly packed liters of whiskey stared up at the ceiling.

"That's a lotta booze," John marveled. He moved across the hangar's threshold and unlocked the back of the Ryder truck, slid the door open.

Kersh bent before one of the crates, worked his hands around the edges until he found the best possible handholds. "This a one- or two-man job, don't you think?" he huffed, then stood, trying to hoist the crate himself. It lifted at an angle off the floor, but it was too heavy for Kersh to move it by himself.

John hopped down from the Ryder truck and back into the hangar. With two fingers, he tapped Kersh on the shoulder. "Leave these for the young guys. You'll blow a gasket."

Standing, breathing hard, Kersh scratched his temple. "I should argue with you," he said, "but I'm not." Turning, he made his way to a metal stepladder and eased down on top of it.

"Okay," John said, clapping his hands. "These crates ain't

gonna move on their own."

"Two guys per crate," Silvestri said, his shirt rippled by the wind. "They're heavy."

With Silvestri's assistance, John hoisted the first of the crates onto the back of the Ryder truck. From his perch on the stepladder, Bill Kersh watched.

They worked for roughly forty-five minutes and when they finished, hands blistered, bodies covered with sweat, backs and knees sore from bending and lifting, they staggered out onto the tarmac to breathe in the crisp winter air. John winked at Kersh, sagged his shoulders to feign exhaustion . . . but Kersh could see in the kid's eyes that he was more ready to go than ever.

Patience, kid, Kersh thought, winking back.

Around them, it began to snow.

CHAPTER TWENTY-THREE

THE SMELL OF FORMALDEHYDE AND ANTISEPTIC DETERGENT seeped out into the main office of Morton Cheever, the district's head medical examiner. The hallway was uninspired, its floor comprised of phlegm-colored tiles, and the walls a drab bone-gray. The tube lighting in the ceiling never worked properly, and there was always at least one bulb burnt out along the hallway. Some metal folding chairs lined one wall, directly opposite a cramped, glassed-in booth that now stood vacant. Shafts of daylight filtered in through grimy, cracked windows.

Dennis Glumly stood before a square, wicker table in the center of the room, its top laden with magazines and—of all things—coloring books. Across from him, at eye-level on the wall, hung a calendar with pictures of frisky kittens. It was Morton Cheever's little joke, to make the outer part of the coroner's office look like a regular doctor's waiting room . . . or even a nursery school. Morton Cheever, Glumly knew, was a man of many morbid little jokes.

Cheever greeted him outside the autopsy room, his portly little body cloaked in a white lab coat. A gaudy Christmas tie hung from his neck, the bottom half of the tie speckled in drying fluids Glumly did not wish to consider. Blinking his left eye as quickly as a hummingbird moves its wing, Cheever shot out his right hand and grasped Glumly's own. The M.E. pumped hands twice, firmly, then worked a finger around the perimeter of his eyeball.

"How you been, Dennis?"

"Taking it easy. The hell's wrong with your eye?"

"Spilled some . . . some powder . . . got some in my . . . eye—*damn it!*" He blinked twice, opened both eyes wide, stared directly at Glumly.

"It's red," Glumly said.

"Hurts, too." The eye started to water, and Cheever blinked several more times. "Patricia's well?"

Glumly nodded. "She keeps busy. Started some yoga class or something last week. One of our neighbors talked her into it. Half the time I see her now, she's nothing but Lycra and headbands. I keep telling her she doesn't need to spend money to feel healthy. She could go outside, run around the block. Exercise is free. Thanks for calling me, by the way, Mort."

"Wait a while," Cheever said, turning and leading Glumly down the hall and toward the autopsy room. "You may not thank me once you see the condition this fella's in."

The autopsy room was small and poorly ventilated. The smell struck Glumly like a slap in the face, strong enough to add pause to his gait. Without turning toward him, Cheever grabbed a jar of Vick's and handed it over to Glumly in one pudgy, outstretched hand.

"Thanks," the detective muttered, quickly applying a dab of Vick's beneath each nostril. "How can you stand it?"

"It's probably like working cleanup at the Bronx Zoo," Cheever said. "After a while, you get used to it."

A number of stainless steel tables were erected in the center of the room, mostly unoccupied. The table closest to them, however, boasted a curious hump beneath a stained yellow sheet. A smaller table had been placed beside this one, on which a dizzying array of knives and scalpels and syringes lay.

"I don't know what it is," Cheever was saying as he pulled on a pair of green rubber gloves. "Every time it gets cold, right around lunchtime—right now—I get this tickle in the back of my throat. Like a drip, though, you know? But only when the weather's cold and only around noon."

"You've got too many allergies to be doing this job," Glumly told him, his eyes tracing the shelves of pharmaceuticals and other implements. Cheever's desk was shoved into the farthest corner of the room, littered with paperwork. On the wall behind the desk, a number of framed drawings hung—artwork from Cheever's kids.

"Jillian tried getting me to do that Amish country thing once," Cheever said. He was searching along the counter, peering beneath scattered paperwork and folded aprons for a particular item. "You know, that place up in Pennsylvania? Figured it'd be an experience, you know? See the countryside, what have you. Fifteen minutes into the country, still miles from the Amish, and my face ballooned up like I'd just gone ten rounds with Mike Tyson. I mean *bad.* Kids thought it was hysterical and I could tell Jillian was holding back a smile, too . . . but I swear, it was like my sinuses turned evil. Country life ain't for me. I don't know how the Amish do it. Give me this smoggy, congested, fluorocarbonated air any day. You can keep your countryside. Ahhh . . . there you are, you bastard . . ."

Cheever pulled a small bottle of Visine from beneath a bundle of towels and slipped it into the breast pocket of his lab coat. Pivoting on his heels, he turned to the covered lump on the table and motioned Glumly over with a wave of his hand.

"And here's our man of the hour," Cheever said, peeling back the yellow sheet like a magician at the climax of his greatest trick.

"Oh, goddamn," Glumly muttered.

What sat on the stainless steel table was a partially-rotted, nude male torso. Ravaged by weather and hungry animals, the tissue had turned a sickening blue. It looked spongy, its texture like cheesecloth. Deep slashes emphasized the torso's ribs and ran along the pelvic region. Its genitals were completely gone, leaving behind only a spongy mass of ravaged, blackened tissue. The head and limbs had been removed, the wounds themselves now congealed and black with dried blood. White nubs of bone protruded from these wounds and Glumly was immediately reminded of the time he'd seen a kid fall off the gymnasium bleachers in high school, and how his elbow had torn through the flesh of his arm.

"Nice lookin' fella, huh?" Cheever said. "Decapitation was the cause of death."

Glumly winced inwardly.

"Most of these injuries you see here were sustained postmortem," Cheever continued, "no doubt by rats and dogs and whatever else happened to get at it while it sat in that back lot. Goddamn rats always go for the testicles. Of course, rats didn't slice this guy's head and limbs off." Cheever pointed a gloved finger at the serrated skin just below the right shoulder. "These limbs were cut, were hacked off, most likely with a heavy, blunt object. I'm guessing an ax. Pretty hastily, too. Same with the head." Then, with a slightly crooked smile, Cheever added: "*Your* head."

"It's a match?" Glumly said.

"Oh, yeah. The DNA from the head you found is a perfect fit. Sorry to say it's the *only* fit," he added. Glumly did not have to ask Cheever to elaborate—he knew exactly what the medical examiner meant. He'd been finding body parts all over Manhattan for two years now. Most were still unidentified.

"Any distinguishing marks on the body?" he asked Cheever.

"Some scar tissue. No tattoos or piercings or anything like that, though." Cheever bent over the body, his face astonishingly close to the chest of the victim. With his gloved finger, he prodded at two tiny, circular incisions made in the upper chest cavity. The sound made by yielding flesh was enough to roll Glumly's stomach. "See these?" Cheever said. "Bullet holes. He was shot twice in the chest."

"I thought you said the cause of death was decapitation—"

"Oh, I did," said Cheever. "He was shot, just not *killed* by the shots. One bruised the aortic arch, just millimeters from being fatal. The other collapsed the left lung, zipped around to bust apart a couple of ribs, and wound up lodging itself in the left kidney. Small caliber bullets, but they did a hell of a lot of damage. Zigged around, smashed through a lot of bones. I've opened him up in the back. Wanna see?"

"I'll take your word for it."

"Your loss," Cheever said amiably enough.

"The bullets were still in the body?"

Cheever jerked a thumb back over his shoulder. "Small Tupperware container on my desk. I wrapped them in a plastic bag. Make sure you don't take my lunch by mistake."

Glumly scrounged around the mess on Cheever's desk until he found the clear plastic container. He popped off the lid and pulled out a Glad zipper-lock plastic bag. Inside the bag were the two rounds. The rounds were damaged, bent out of shape from having crashed through bone. Still, looking at them, he could tell they were .22-caliber rounds.

"You'll let me know if you come across anything else?" he said, stuffing the plastic bag into his pants pocket.

"Sure, sure," Cheever said. Finished with the corpse, the little man straightened his back and pulled off each rubber glove with an audible *snap!* "This reminds me," Cheever said then, "of a finger I found when I was just a kid. Was playing in some filthy back lot with some friends, sifting through crap like kids do, and wham—sure enough, I find this finger. Mean, ugly thing—all worm-eaten and stuff. But I was fascinated. I had no idea how it got there and didn't mention it to my folks. I hid it in my room in one of those plastic globes used to display autographed baseballs. I thought it was the most amazing thing I'd ever seen. The nail fell off after about a week, and it just went downhill fast after that." Cheever smiled in reflection, his hands on his portly hips, one cordovan shoe tapping on the tile floor. "I'm only kidding, Dennis. When I was a kid, I collected baseball cards." He tossed his rubber gloves on the counter and sighed. "Everybody thinks you have to be weird to do this job for a living."

"Now why would you say that?" Glumly said.

CHAPTER TWENTY-FOUR

MICKEY DID NOT CALL UNTIL FIVE O'CLOCK the day after the pickup at JFK, leaving John to worry most of the day whether or not he would call at all. He still didn't have a full grasp on Mickey—not just yet—but the meeting with him the other night at the Cloverleaf offered a glimmer of hope. For the first time, he'd glimpsed Mickey O'Shay unguarded and in his own environment. He'd always been confident in his approach as an undercover agent, but sometimes—no matter how well you played the part—some people remained distrustful. It was the nature of the business. Half the time if they didn't figure you were a cop or a snitch, they assumed that you were just as rotten as they were, and that you were only biding the time before you ripped them off. If greed was the motivation, and its result the hidden treasure, then a certain level of mutual contentment made it possible to unlock the dark chest. Cutting the deal to sell Mickey and his gang thirty cases of whiskey had rocketed him up into a whole new stratosphere.

At least, he hoped.

When Mickey finally did call, he refused to give John the details of the meeting over the phone. John immediately agreed to split for Hell's Kitchen without a second thought. Kersh wanted to set up a full surveillance, but somehow John managed to convince him to keep it small scale. Surprisingly, Kersh offered little resistance and agreed to cover John on his own.

Outside the candy store, Mickey was hanging around by the street corner, slumped against a pay telephone, his eyes impassively scrutinizing the passing cars. Traffic already heavy along Tenth Avenue, John could find no place to park. Last night's light snowfall hadn't been enough to hinder the city, but it had been enough to freeze the roads. He pulled the Camaro up in front of the store and nearly hopped the curb. Pumping the brakes, he slowed to a stop and popped open the passenger door for Mickey. Behind him, a woman in a hunter-green Lexus blared her horn at him.

"Hurry up," he told Mickey.

Mickey shuffled into the car and pulled his legs up, slammed the door.

"I can't park here," he said.

Mickey jabbed a finger on the dashboard. "Drive around the block."

With the woman in the Lexus still leaning on her horn, he inched the Camaro back into traffic and hooked his first right onto 54th Street. Here, traffic was just as bad, and he had to slam on the brakes immediately after making the turn to avoid smashing into the back of a city bus.

"Sometimes I hate this goddamn city," he muttered under his breath.

"How well you know the West Side?" was Mickey's first question. Nothing about John surprising him at the Cloverleaf, nothing about how shitfaced he'd been during their conversation. He was like a different person, an alternate Mickey O'Shay, a doppelganger.

"Depends," he said.

"There's a bar called Pickernell's down West Fifty-third Street, halfway between Tenth and Eleventh avenues. You know the park down there? It's right before the park."

"Okay."

"You got a truck, right?"

"A rental," he said.

"Park it outside the bar tonight around two o'clock. I'll be out front waiting for you. Come by yourself. I'll get some guys to help us unload."

"I'm getting paid on delivery," he said. It was not a question.

"You'll get your money," Mickey said. "Stop the car."

"What?"

"Stop."

John pulled over to the curb, just barely avoiding another collision. Mickey jerked open the passenger door and swung one leg out onto the curb. "This traffic," he muttered, and slammed the door behind him. John watched him disappear down the street back toward Tenth Avenue in his rearview mirror.

I really hate this son of a bitch, he thought.

Back at the office, a team of three agents was assembled for the meeting later that night. They targeted the location of Pickernell's on a map of the West Side and considered the strategic placement of their surveillance vehicles. It would be difficult—the positioning of the bar, in tandem with the lack of traffic that far west, would provide little cover for anyone within eyeshot. Finally, Kersh decided the best thing to do was to have one vehicle stowed away in a back alley along West 53rd Street, opposite the bar. A second unit with two more agents could hang down by the park. John sat and listened to the plan, uncomfortable with the proximity of the surveillance vehicles. Yet Kersh was passionate about the vehicles' locations and would not budge.

After the meeting, he noticed Kersh brooding out in the hallway, a lukewarm cup of coffee in one hand.

"What's up?" he said, coming up behind him.

"I think you should wear a wire tonight," Kersh said, staring down at his cup.

"No way."

"Listen to me," Kersh said, looking up. "You're walking into this thing tonight expecting to leave with three thousand dollars of Mickey O'Shay's money. Once you bring the liquor to him and his pals, what's to stop them from keeping the three grand and blowing your head off?"

"For a lousy three grand?"

"John, man, I don't know. I haven't felt right about this since I pulled Mickey and Kahn's records."

"I'm not wearing a wire," he said, adamant. "We got thirty cases to unload, and they sure as shit ain't gonna let me sit there and twiddle my thumbs while they move it. I'm not gonna bounce around wearing a wire, Bill. That's ridiculous. Anyway," he added, "wire or not—they wanna pull their guns, they're gonna do it."

"Then what do *you* do?"

"If I wear a wire, you need to get closer to monitor it. We're not blowing this."

It was not the response Kersh was looking for. Still, it was the truth and they both knew it.

He arrived home around ten o'clock and crawled into bed just as Katie came in from the shower. Wrapped in a towel, her hair up in one hand, she jumped when she saw him sprawled out across the top of the bed.

"What the hell are you doing here?" she nearly gasped. "Jesus Christ, you scared the hell out of me . . ."

"Surprise," he said, grinning. "I only have a few hours."

"You're going back out?"

He nodded.

"I hate that," she said, moving to the closet.

"Don't get dressed," he told her. "Come here."

Smiling, she pulled the towel from her body and hurried quickly to the bed, not quite comfortable with the shape of her new body. He hugged her, kissed her, cradled her head against his chest. Her scent was clean and strong, undeniably female, and it filtered through his nose and coursed through his lungs with ferocious intensity. Still . . . his mind was not totally here with her: it volleyed between her and *out there,* making a drop-off to Mickey O'Shay and the rest of the Dead End Kids.

"I asked Dad if he wanted me to stay at the house with him," she said.

"Yeah?"

"He said no. He said you'd be lonely."

"What'd you tell him?"

"The truth. That you're never home anyway."

"It's just for a little while longer," he promised, kissing the top of her head. "Is he feeling okay?"

"Hmmmm . . ." She was half-asleep.

Again, he kissed the top of her head. Held her against his body, feeling the gentle curve of her belly against his side.

Once he was certain Katie was asleep, he pulled himself out of bed and crept down the hall to wander around in the dark until it was time to go.

CHAPTER TWENTY-FIVE

THE STREETS WERE DARK, QUIET. THE CLOSER he drove toward the piers, the more he was aware of leaving the rest of the living world behind. The Ryder truck's cab smelled ambiguously bad. The vinyl seats were cracked and torn, gaping yellow foam protruding from the fissures like organs from a mutilated body. Someone had glued three pennies to the truck's peeling dashboard, all three Lincolns face-up.

Up ahead, John saw the dotted traffic along Eleventh Avenue. Beyond the street, he could make out the dark ink-spot that was Dewitt Clinton Park. Coasting, he studied the passing brick buildings on either side of the street through the grime-flecked windshield. Outside, the night was cold, black, motionless. Sporadically, a small group of snowflakes would pat against the windshield, immediately melting. He had the truck's heater cranked up and pumping.

Just as Mickey had promised, halfway down the quiet stretch of West 53rd Street, a jutting black awning stretched out over the curb to his left. The narrow window—dark and foreboding—displayed an unlit neon *Open* sign and the word *Pickernell's* printed on the glass in yellow lettering. John eased down on the brake and felt the truck shudder to a halt. He switched it to *park*, shut off the headlights, and sat in the idling truck, his eyes scanning the street. Straight ahead on Eleventh Avenue, the occasional vehicles buzzed past the mouth of the 53rd Street. To his right across from Pickernell's was a trash-littered alleyway and a fenced-in auto parts shop. Kersh was back there somewhere, keeping his eyes on the bar across the street.

The truck's clock read 2:02 A.M. Blowing into his hands to keep them warm, he shifted in his seat and peered at his sideview mirror. Behind him, the street was empty. Even with the windows closed, he could hear the din of traffic along both Eleventh and Tenth Avenues.

Mickey materialized from behind the fence of the auto parts shop. In the moonlight, he looked like an apparition. Unmoving, Mickey stood there behind the fence for a single beat, the fingers of his left hand curled through one of the links in the chain fence. Then he dragged his boots down off the curb and plodded across the street, his head down, the red eye of a cigarette glowing in the darkness.

Mickey cracked opened the truck's passenger door and climbed into the cab. "Let's go," he told John, plucking the cigarette from his mouth between two fingers.

John dropped the truck into drive. "Where?" he asked.

Mickey pointed up ahead, toward Eleventh Avenue. "Go down, take a left."

He let his foot off the brake and rolled down 53rd Street toward Eleventh Avenue. Silently, he hoped Kersh would be discreet if he chose to follow . . . which he would, John assumed.

"Where we going?" he asked, crossing between a gap in the traffic along Eleventh Avenue and hanging a left.

"Just drive," Mickey said, in no mood for conversation. "I'll tell you when to turn."

To their right, the dark spread of Dewitt Clinton Park rifled by.

"Hope you got guys," he said to Mickey. "Stuff's pretty goddamn heavy."

"It's taken care of," Mickey promised, still smoking his cigarette.

He cracked the window an inch, blew the smoke out, then flicked the butt out after it. Then he jerked a thumb to the right, acknowledging one of the side streets leading down to the West Side Highway and the piers. "Turn here."

John spun the wheel, and the tires slid on some ice. He was unfamiliar with this section of the West Side, had missed the street sign, and was unsure exactly what street they were on or where they were. Around them, the night seemed to have suddenly grown darker. The street itself was barely wide enough for the truck to make it down. On either side of the street, two-story brick buildings crowded against one another like vagrants desperate to keep warm. He could see no other cars, though he could hear vehicles droning back and forth along the avenue. They sounded very far away.

"Slow it down," Mickey said. A few yards ahead and to the right, a small, fenced-in parking lot spread out before them, wedged between two ramshackle, vacant buildings. The fence gate was open, and Mickey told him to drive the truck through it. Glancing in his sideview to see if Kersh had followed down the street—he hadn't—John obliged.

The truck hopped a stone curb and trembled, its undercarriage rattling like thunderous applause.

"To the end," Mickey said, jerking his chin toward the rear of the parking lot. The lot ended at a peeling picket fence, overgrown with weeds and vines and wild shrubbery. To the left, a whitewashed brick garage clung to the back of one of the shops, fronted by a graffiti-laden metal door.

Mickey told him to swing the truck around and line the back up with the garage door.

"What happened to Pickernell's?" he asked.

"What?" Mickey countered. "I said I'd meet you there." He opened the passenger door and jumped out. "Let's go."

John shut the truck down and climbed out of the cab, still rubbing his hands together. A single streetlight on the other side of the wooden fence offered minimal light. Mickey was on the other side of the truck; only his shadow, distended and freakish pooling along the pavement, could be seen.

Bill Kersh's warning rose up suddenly in John's mind: *Once you bring the liquor to him and his pals, what's to stop them from keeping the three grand and blowing your head off?* Kersh's ghostly voice surfaced like a white flag on a battlefield. Yet instead of shaking the warning from his head, he used it to prime himself, to siphon power and strength and build his confidence. Build his *will.* He was not thinking about death—was not thinking about his wife and his father and his unborn child. Now, he was only thinking about Mickey O'Shay and himself. And the gun buried inside his jacket. Nothing else mattered, nothing else existed. He understood the volatility of time, had even experienced it during the shoot-out at Deveneau's club, but now was the first time he was fully *aware* of it: that the here-and-now was a fleeting, ridiculous, impossible thing that could either kill you or spare your life. A moment's hesitation could be the difference between soaking in a hot bath or riding in a body bag. In his mind's eye, he watched the replay of the albino going down behind the bar, his eyes suddenly blank and stupid in his head, his grasp on Tressa Walker abruptly disengaged. He'd pacified Kersh—or had at least attempted to—by insisting that Mickey and his gang would not pull a rip and kill him . . . but in reality, he did not exactly believe that. In fact, standing in the parking lot contemplating the ephemeral qualities of relative time, he'd never felt more suspicious and dubious of Mickey O'Shay in all the time he'd known the man.

Mickey appeared around the back of the truck, lighting another cigarette, his teeth rattling in his head. He turned, his profile temporarily illuminated by the single street lamp on the other side of the wooden fence.

John, hands stuffed in his pockets, walked over to him. "I bum one of those off ya?"

Mickey scrounged around in his coat pocket until he found a wrinkled pack of Kools. He shook one out, and John plucked it from the package and popped it into his mouth. Taking Mickey's lighter, he lit the stick and inhaled deeply enough to fill his shoes with smoke.

"Christ," he muttered, exhaling. "At least my lungs will be warm."

A bang echoed through the parking lot, followed by the grind of rusted gears. A sliver of yellow light fell across them as the metal garage door was lifted. In the widening shaft of light, John could make out several pairs of legs moving about inside the garage.

"Your guys know how to make an entrance," he muttered, hooking another drag from the Kool.

Through the open garage door, three guys sauntered out onto the parking lot, their bundled forms silhouetted by the dull yellow backlight of the garage.

He recognized at least one of the guys from the Cloverleaf—a small, wiry guy with nervous eyes. The guy directly to his right was a bit huskier, with a round, doughy face topped in a red knitted cap. The third guy was taller than the other two, his face somehow more well-defined. His eyes were set deep in his head, creating the appearance of a brooding thoughtfulness, and his chest was broad beneath the pullover and checked sports coat he wore. While these other two guys seemed to fit perfectly into Mickey O'Shay's clique, this guy seemed just a little off-center, a little more shrewd, a little less confrontational.

Mickey flicked his cigarette off into the night. "Fellas," he said to the two guys behind the taller one. Then he turned to John. "This is my partner, Jimmy Kahn."

"How's it going?" John said, and pumped Jimmy's hand twice.

Jimmy's eyes fell all over him. "Nice truck."

"You should see what's inside," he said. Emulating Mickey's famous head-nod, he acknowledged the garage. "What is this place?"

"Back of a bar," Jimmy said. "Storage."

"Before this goes down," he said, "I just wanna make sure we're straight on the money."

"Three grand," Jimmy said.

"You got it?" he asked.

Jimmy rubbed a finger beneath his nose. "Help us unload this shit—then you get paid."

Without a word, John turned from them, the truck's keys clanging in his hand, and moved back toward the cab. He felt their eyes on him, had their attention, and even saw Mickey's shadow move when he opened the driver's side door and climbed inside. Without hesitation, he turned the truck's engine over.

Mickey appeared outside the window. "The hell you doin'?"

"You want what's in this truck," he said, "you give me my money."

Laughing, Mickey took two steps away from the truck, his arms out at his sides. He turned to Jimmy Kahn and yelled, "Hey, Jimmy! This guy wants his money! Let's do this, already!" He held his hand up, palm facing John. "Come on."

He shut down the truck and hopped back out onto the parking lot.

"Here," Jimmy said, fishing a wad of bills secured in a plastic bag from his coat pocket. He thrust it toward John, Jimmy's eyes uncomfortably on him.

He took the money, opened the bag. "This all of it?"

"Three grand," Jimmy said.

John smirked. "Would have jacked up the price if I knew it included labor." He tossed the truck's keys over to Jimmy, who caught them with a swipe of his hand.

Jimmy moved to the rear of the truck, unlocked the door. He motioned for one of the other two guys to give him a hand. Together, they managed to push open the door. Jimmy remained standing on the rear bumper, looking into the back of the truck for several seconds, not saying a word.

"Well?" John initiated.

"That's all thirty?" Jimmy said.

"All thirty. Count 'em."

Still standing on the bumper, Jimmy turned to the scrawnier of the two nameless men. "Go get me that hammer and screwdriver from the back," he told the lackey. The kid turned and hurried back into the garage.

How many guys they got working with them? he wondered. It was obvious just by his presence that Jimmy Kahn called the shots—and yet Mickey had introduced them as partners. *Are these two goons running this entire operation?* He thought of the counterfeit money, banded and freshly printed. Were they printing it themselves? *And Irish,* he reminded himself. *Don't forget Mickey said something about a person named Irish the other night.*

The scrawny guy returned with a hammer and a large flathead screwdriver. He handed them over to Jimmy, who positioned the tapered end of the screwdriver in the crack beneath the crate's top. Once he felt it was secured, he slammed the hammer down on the back end of the screwdriver, driving it deeper beneath the lid. The gap widened. Wood creaked and splintered. A moment later and the crate's lid broke upward.

Jimmy tossed the tools onto the pavement and reached his fingers beneath the lid, lifted it. Nails were pulled from the housing. With an upward jerk, he managed to pull the lid completely off. He tossed that, too, to the pavement with little interest.

"One, two, three . . ." He was counting the bottles inside. Leaning over, he selected one of the bottles, slid it from the crate. Holding it by the neck with one hand, he sloshed the amber liquid around while examining the label.

"Looks good," Mickey said beside John.

"Don't give a shit how it *looks,*" Jimmy muttered, and unscrewed the bottle. He took two sizable swigs, winced, bared his teeth. Capping the bottled, he nodded to himself and tossed it over to Mickey.

Mickey took his own swig, then made a face similar to Jimmy's. Wiping his mouth with the sleeve of his coat, he uttered, "Stuff tastes like *piss!*" Then he laughed—sharply—into the night, a billow of vapor trailing off in the wind. "No, no," he said, "it's good."

"It's good," Jimmy repeated, hopping down from the truck. "Canadian whiskey. Good deal. Where'd this stuff come from?"

"Canada," John said.

Jimmy smirked with the right corner of his mouth. "No," he said, "that's not what I mean."

"I know. But what's the difference?"

"This your deal?" Jimmy said.

"Most of it."

Hands on his hips, Jimmy paced backward toward the rear of the truck again, tabulating something in his head. "All right," he said finally, "let's get this shit inside, stack it up by the back."

The two lackeys wasted no time climbing into the Ryder truck and lifting one of the crates.

"They heavy?" Mickey called over to them, already downing his second or third mouthful of whiskey.

"As a bastard," said the burly guy, climbing down from the truck with the crate and nearly missing his footing.

"It's got a ramp," John said. "Unlatch it. It slides out. You guys'll break your necks doing it that way."

"Shit," mumbled the burly guy. "Set it down, Sean."

John turned and watched Jimmy and Mickey head over to a wedge of stone steps beside the garage, passing the bottle of whiskey back and forth between them. Together, they moved like equal pieces of the same machine, and any notion of hierarchy John had originally supposed lay between them was now obliterated. Seeing them now, he could tell they *were* partners, fifty-fifty straight down the middle. He could tell just by the language of their bodies, by the confidence they bounced off each other.

They sat down on the stone steps, the bottle now in Jimmy's hands, and John averted his gaze. Out on the street, a car crept by and he hoped it wasn't Kersh slipping in too close. But the car did not stop—it continued down the street toward the docks.

"Slipping! Slipping!" the scrawny guy—Sean—shouted as his companion struggled to set the crate down on the ground.

"Hold up," he said, helping them slide the crate out of the way. "Here." He undid the latch just above the truck's bumper and pulled out a steel ramp from beneath the truck bed. "Slide 'em down," he told them. "Don't break any."

Sean began dragging the crates to the top of the ramp while John and the burly guy—he introduced himself as Donny—moved them together into the garage. In the garage and out of Mickey and Jimmy's line of sight, he pressed Donny.

"You know these guys long?"

"Who? Mickey and Jimmy? Kinda."

"They good guys or what?"

Donny shrugged. "They're all right." The man seemed unimpressed.

Back at the truck, John was helping take down another crate when Jimmy shouted his name. Looking up, he saw Jimmy waving him over.

"Come 'ere . . ."

He walked over to where Mickey and Jimmy sat. In the bottle, the whiskey was now down to the label.

"Sit down," Jimmy said. "Let those bums do that."

"I'm with you," he said, and eased himself down onto a stack of discarded wooden planks. Letting out a deep breath, he ran his fingers through his hair.

"Here," Jimmy said, tapping him on the arm with the bottle of whiskey. "Warm you up quick."

"Thanks." He took a mouthful, held it a moment, then swallowed. It screamed all the way down his throat. He was suddenly aware of just how cold his hands and feet were. A second swig and he passed the bottle over to Mickey.

"Where you from?" It was Jimmy who asked, though he wasn't facing John; he was busy watching Donny and Sean empty the Ryder truck.

"Brooklyn," he said. "Bath Avenue."

"How you know Tressa Walker?"

"Went to the same high school," he said.

"Which one?"

"Lafayette. You know the area?"

"Bath Avenue," Jimmy mused, taking the bottle from Mickey. "You a hookup guy? In with the guineas?"

"I'm on my own," he told Jimmy. "But everybody's hooked up to somebody. Who you attached to?"

Jimmy executed his half-smirk again and jerked his head in Mickey's direction. "This guy," he said.

The urge to bring up the counterfeit money was great, but if he brought it up now it would be too conspicuous, like dropping a grenade in a foxhole—soldiers are going to scatter. It was possible that he could work around it, maybe head down that path and hope Jimmy Kahn was careless enough to start talking, but he didn't think Jimmy Kahn ever would.

The bottle came around to him again, and he swallowed another mouthful. This one sent the parking lot listing to the left. Beside him, Mickey pointed at the two guys unloading the truck and mumbled something practically inarticulate to Jimmy. Yet Jimmy must have understood, because he started chuckling under his breath and plucked the bottle from John's hands. John didn't know quite what to make of Jimmy—it was still too early—but he'd been around Mickey enough by now to tell Mickey's impenetrable veneer was slowly sloughing off. With each sip from the bottle, he was regressing to the accessible hood he'd been at the Cloverleaf. It was as close to being friendly, he assumed, as Mickey ever came. With any luck, maybe *Mickey* would initiate a conversation about the counterfeit money . . .

When the bottle made it back around to him, he was aware of Mickey watching him from the corner of his eye, a drunken grin threatening his lips. He took two large swallows, his eyes on Mickey.

"Uh . . ." He wanted to hang his head between his legs and moan but wouldn't give in. Handing the bottle to Mickey, he noticed that Mickey's hands looked blurred. And so did his.

Wonderful. Now I'm getting shitfaced.

Mickey drank, passed the bottle to Jimmy. Jimmy knocked back enough to fill a small teacup. They drank like troopers, their postures becoming more and more relaxed, their conversation more and more flowing. They talked for some time about hockey and about their best scores on some pinball machine, Jimmy's eyes never leaving the two guys unloading the truck, while Mickey's eyes remained on the circulating bottle.

The plan had been a success. He'd thrown them a curveball, and they'd swung. Now they knew he was a player, a go-to guy, and that put them at ease just a little. There would be no more surface-level bullshit with Mickey O'Shay. He was now at the next stage of the game.

When the final crate was loaded into the garage, Donny sat his bulk down on the bumper of the Ryder truck (his weight caused the truck to list) and the little guy—Sean—just stood beside him. After he caught his breath, Donny got up and took a few steps in their direction, arms outstretched. Despite the cold, his face was red and blotchy from perspiration, and he was panting like a dog.

"Hope you fuckers didn't wear yourselves out watching us work," Donny said. "That bottle looks heavy."

"Shut the fuck up," Mickey growled, pulling himself to his feet.

Jimmy, too, got up and tossed the now-empty bottle in the grass behind them. Unzipping his fly, he voided a hot ribbon of urine onto the stone steps. Then without saying a word, he walked around the side of the garage, no doubt to inspect his laborers' work.

"Drank it *all?*" Donny was moaning, peering over the side of the stone steps and down at the empty whiskey bottle in the grass. "Goddamn."

Eyes swimming in his head, John caught Mickey staring at him through the wet tangles of his hair.

Don't look at me like that, he thought. *I'll knock you right the hell down, Mickey Mouse.*

"All right," John muttered, and stuck out his hand for Mickey to shake. However, his face remained stoic and unwelcoming. Following a slight hesitation, without even looking at John's hand, Mickey grabbed it and shook it once, firmly. "Where's Jimmy? I wanna say good night."

"Jimmy's gone," Mickey said, turning in a loose half-circle and heading around to the other side of the garage.

"What? Already?"

Mickey didn't answer. His back to John, he walked with his hands stuffed into his pockets, his head cocked toward his feet in his usual manner. Watching him leave, John felt a resurgence of frustration rise up inside him, more potent than any amount of alcohol he could consume. Sitting, shooting the shit, opening conversation . . . and the bastard just *disappears?* As if he'd never been here in the first place. It wasn't just that *street guys* didn't behave that way—it was that *people* didn't behave that way. Damn it, they made him feel too off-guard.

He watched Mickey's shadow disappear around the side of the garage like a ghost. Something Tressa Walker had said to him last month when he'd met with her at McGinty's came back to him now, the context of her words unexpectedly more profound than they'd been that evening: *These guys are like no one you've ever seen.*

Maybe. But that didn't mean he couldn't play them just as hard. Harder, if he had to.

The door to the garage came down in a series of rattles and bangs. It hit the ground hard, the sound like the report of a pistol in John's head, and was locked from the inside. Several moments later, beyond the fence and across the street, he heard car doors slam and the engine of a large car kick over. Not moving, he stood in the parking lot and listened as the car took off down the street, its headlights glimmering through the slats in the wooden fence at the opposite end of the parking lot.

These guys are like no one you've ever seen.

It was the voice of a ghost, a prophet.

CHAPTER TWENTY-SIX

"DON'T GET TOO COMFORTABLE," KERSH SAID JUST as John was about to sink down into his desk chair.

"What's up?"

"Chominsky's waiting on us in his office."

John pulled off his leather jacket and hung it on the back of his chair. "Whatever it is, let's just blame Veccio."

"You feeling all right this morning?"

Rubbing his temples, John said, "Never better."

Kersh picked up a large dictionary from his desk, held it a few feet over the desktop—then dropped it. Some heads in the office turned. The sound slammed into John's head, rocketing through his ears.

"Christ," he muttered.

Grinning, Kersh said, "That's what you get for partying with the Irish." Then he handed him a fresh cup of coffee. "Here," he said. "Just to let you know I've been thinking about you."

"You go on ahead," he said. "I'm gonna hit the bathroom."

"Take some aspirin," Kersh said. "You look like garbage."

❦

Bill Kersh entered Chominsky's office following two quick knocks on the door.

Chominsky was seated behind his desk, a box of doughnuts resting at the corner of his desk, two men in suits seated in chairs before him. Both men shifted their gaze to the office door as both he and Kersh entered. The man closest to the door Kersh immediately recognized—Peter Brauman, in a pressed suit and tie. The other man was rather staunch and at first appeared slightly irritated, one hand pressed neatly in his lap while the other held what appeared to be a fruit shake.

Kersh nodded at Brauman. "Peter."

"How you doing, Bill?"

"Hanging in."

Chominsky pushed forward in his chair. "Where's Mavio?"

"He'll be here in a few minutes," Kersh said, pulling a chair from the wall and dragging beside Peter Brauman. "What's going on?"

"Bill," Chominsky said, "this is Detective Sergeant Dennis Glumly, NYPD."

"Bill," Glumly began, "we've got a unit that's been keeping an eye on Mickey O'Shay and Jimmy Kahn for just about two years now. We've set up surveillance around the candy store on Fifty-third and Tenth, on O'Shay's apartment, all over the neighborhood. We've even got a loft rented down the street and a makeshift HQ at John Jay College."

"Why are you keeping tabs on them?" he asked Glumly.

Glumly blinked. He had long, feminine lashes and steel-colored eyes. "I was going to ask you guys that same question," Glumly said, quite matter-of-factly. "Few weeks ago I saw you parked around the intersection by the candy store. Long story short, I saw you there a few more times and made another car that smelled like feds. Got me curious."

"O'Shay and Kahn are part of a counterfeit investigation," Kersh said.

Glumly nodded. "Doesn't surprise me. Those guys are into everything."

"Bill," Peter Brauman spoke up, "I didn't really emphasize just how bad these guys are when you came to me the other night."

"I saw the reports," Kersh said.

Brauman shook his head. "You don't understand . . ."

A quick knock on the office door and they all looked up. John stepped in, closing the door behind him, and nodded at the men.

Chominsky started to make the introductions. "John, this is—"

Dennis Glumly's fruit shake fell on the floor. "Holy *Christ!*" It looked as though he were about to topple out of the chair, his eyes never leaving John's face. A mottled expression of perplexity and shock blossomed across his face, and he brought his hands up in a parody of surrender. "Holy *Christ!*" He couldn't help but repeat the phrase.

Likewise, Peter Brauman looked as if someone had just dropped a cinder block across his feet and then slapped him in the face. He, too, could not keep his eyes from John; he stared at John as if to confirm his reality.

"Holy *Christ* . . ."

About to pull another chair over to the group, John stood frozen in place. "Did I miss something?"

"I don't . . ." Chominsky attempted.

Kersh looked at Peter Brauman, shook the man's arm. "The hell's going on, Pete?"

Then, quite surprisingly, Peter Brauman snorted an astonished laugh and rubbed the side of his face with his hand.

Looking directly at John, Dennis Glumly said, "Brett . . . you're not going to believe this . . ." The detective shook his head as if to clear blurred vision. To John, he said, "I'm Dennis Glumly, NYPD."

"John Mavio."

"John," Glumly repeated. Then he, too, laughed. "Son of a bitch! John, we've been . . ." He couldn't manage the words. Finally, after pausing a moment to collect his thoughts, Glumly said, "How long have you been undercover?" He seemed amazed by his own words.

John knitted his brow. "What's going on?"

Just as confused, Brett Chominsky turned to Glumly while running a finger along the left side of his face. "Dennis?"

Resignedly, looking at John, Glumly said, "I was just explaining to Agent Kersh that we've had a surveillance set up on Mickey O'Shay and Jimmy Kahn for close to two years. And we've been watching you, too, for the past couple weeks."

"Me?" He sat himself down in a chair beside Kersh. Then it hit him, and he smiled. He just couldn't help it. "You guys thought I was the real deal, huh? Another player on the field . . ." He shot Kersh a wink and said, "There's your blue Pontiac."

"Goddamn," Glumly muttered, matching John's grin. "John, man . . . *how the hell did you get in with these guys?"*

"Hold up," John said. "Why are you guys here?"

Glumly filled John in about spotting the Service's surveillance vehicles around the candy store. "Figured there must be something big going down if you guys were involved."

"Counterfeit case," John said.

Glumly nodded. "So I've learned."

Kersh waved a hand. "Wait, wait—back up." Turning to Brauman, he said, "What's the deal with these guys? You said you didn't give me the whole story that night I came to see you . . ."

"They're animals," Glumly interrupted, without waiting for Brauman to answer, "connected to about fifty unsolved homicides throughout the city. I'm talking brutal shit—shootings, shakedowns, chopping people up into little pieces and scattering the parts like birdseed. Past year I've been picking up limbs all over the West Side. Some are probably contract hits, the rest for intimidation. They've got the entire West Side petrified, and we're getting concerned. Six months ago I arrested O'Shay as the prime suspect in a murder rap—butchered some guy in a bar bathroom. Shot him in the knees, poked out one of his eyes, then blew two holes in his head. Ten, maybe a dozen people were in the bar, but I couldn't get a single witness. I had a snitch put it on Mickey, but he wasn't there and wouldn't testify. Every time we get close, people change their minds or simply vanish into the air." With a straight face, Glumly added, "Or the river."

John watched as Glumly's eyes again came to rest on him. He'd been soaking in all the details of the detective's story up to this point, trying to imagine just how a pair of Hell's Kitchen hoodlums had come so far so fast. If what Glumly said was accurate, he suddenly understood why Tressa Walker had been so frightened of them that night in McGinty's. He also understood what it must have been like for her to come out and confess what she knew to him, and to take him into the center of their world.

Looking at John, Glumly said, "They hang around street corners like teenagers and sit inside that candy store almost all day. Occasionally they'll shoot out to the Garden for a hockey game, but that's it." Glumly jerked his chin at John. "You show up, we thought maybe we'd get somewhere. A new player."

"*We* got somewhere," he told Glumly.

"Yeah," Glumly said, leaning back in his chair, his left leg bouncing. He noticed his spilled shake and leaned over the armrest of his chair to scoop it up and set it in the half-empty box of doughnuts on Chominsky's desk. "Yeah, kid, you're goddamn right you did. I don't know how the hell you pulled it off, but you're like a gift from God. I would never have believed an undercover could get into them. They only trust the shit they grew up with." His features darkened. "But you don't know these guys like I do." There was a respect in Glumly's voice now that John had not expected from the man upon their introduction. It seemed very much out of character. "You deal with them, you think everything's fine, then they turn on you for no reason and you don't see it coming."

"I can handle myself."

Kersh shot John a look, then turned to Glumly. "Who's backing them?"

"The gang is Mickey and Jimmy," Glumly said. "They have a few steadies, but everyone else is just a straphanger, a nickel-and-dimer. They can grab any kid in the neighborhood. These jerks have a hell of a reputation on the streets, and they attract more shit than the can at Port Authority."

"They're a cancer spreading across the West Side," Peter Brauman added.

"Never in a million years did I think anyone could get *inside,*" continued Glumly, this time almost to himself.

"What do you want?" John asked Glumly, feeling both Kersh's and Chominsky's eyes suddenly upon him.

A humorless grin threatened the corners of Dennis Glumly's mouth. He was a man, John realized, who appreciated such directness. "I want you to put them away for us," Glumly said flatly. "For *everyone.*" He raised one hand, as if taking an oath. "I understand you're pushing your counterfeit case," he added, "but you're in there now and you can get a hell of a lot of info, and you're a witness that will testify. We can build some case on them."

"Wait, wait—hold on," Kersh quickly interrupted. "Our concern is bringing these guys in on counterfeit charges, and flushing out their source." Kersh turned, now addressing John more than anyone else. "If they're this nuts, our best bet is to get in and out quickly."

Glumly was adamant. Still looking at John, he said, "You got the keys to the kingdom here, kid. We'll never get another shot at these guys. We'll do whatever you want to help. John, you can make two years of wasted time turn into something."

"That's not the reason John's in there," Kersh insisted.

"Wait," John told Kersh. Already Kersh did not like his tone. "Why not take advantage of this? I'm in there. As long as things are cool—"

"John . . ."

"No." He turned from Kersh and looked directly at Chominsky. "Boss, what do you think?"

The agent in charge sat forward in his chair, elbows on his desk. "Let's think it over," Chominsky said.

Before the end of the day, John was called into Roger Biddleman's office. It was a meeting he'd been expecting, although he would have gone home a happy man had he not heard from the attorney all day. The call from Biddleman came exactly twenty minutes after John and Brett Chominsky decided John would go for it.

As the light of day dimmed over St. Andrews Plaza, Assistant U.S. Attorney Roger Biddleman sat behind his desk in a haughty three-piece suit, reprogramming the speed-dial on his cell phone when John entered his office.

The first thing he noticed was Biddleman's friendly new smile. *"John,"* Biddleman said, stretching out his name until it achieved maximum significance. He quickly stowed his cell phone away in his desk. "Have a seat."

He dropped in a chair that had been deliberately placed less than two feet away from the front of Roger Biddleman's desk.

"How've you been?" Biddleman asked.

"Got a pretty bad hangover, actually."

"Uh . . ." The attorney's left eyebrow cocked. Quickly averting his eyes, he began rifling through a series of computer printouts lifted from his desk. "Brett Chominsky brought me up to speed on your dealings with Mickey O'Shay and Jimmy Kahn. Your stunt with that liquor was a nice touch, by the way."

Stunt? he thought. *Go take a shit.*

Reading from his notes, Biddleman said, "You've got them for selling counterfeit money on . . . two occasions . . ."

"No."

Biddleman looked up. "I'm sorry?"

He said, "Just O'Shay. Kahn's involved, but I haven't hooked him yet."

"Kahn . . ." Biddleman rifled through more of his notes. Finally, he just set the entire stack on his desk and stared over at John with his rodent-like eyes. "This could be big, John. These guys . . ." He tapped the stack of notes. He'd done his homework. "These guys are some pretty bad players. They done half the stuff NYPD thinks they have, they'll both be sent away for a very long time."

John shifted in his seat. No doubt Biddleman was already imagining the headlines. The case was a prosecutor's wet dream.

"I'm going ahead with the wire taps on the candy store's phone. Also, the pay phone on the corner and the one in Mickey's apartment," Biddleman continued. He'd been struggling to represent an accommodating, friendly disposition . . . but he could overlook John's inimical stare no longer. "We've had our disagreements," he said then, a hint of surrender in his voice. "I'll admit I can be—" he paused, "sometimes . . . *inflexible.* But you understand." He laughed, abruptly and cheerlessly. "Anyway, from here on in, I want you to know that you have my complete and devoted support on this case. We're going to crack this thing wide open together, John. You're a good agent; you can make things happen."

"Last time I was here you said I was a pain in the ass, that I should be disciplined. What's with the change of heart?"

Biddleman shifted uncomfortably, unnerved by John's tone. "I was upset. The mix-up with the cops, the shooting and all." He executed a halfhearted shrug, then straightened in his chair. "I can't help but feel that you're still upset with me," Biddleman said, his eyes narrowing, his thin lips pressed tightly together.

"Good," John said, getting up. "For a second there I thought you misunderstood."

In the dark and noiseless apartment, John moved down the hallway with his shoes off. A small light over the kitchen sink cast a somber glow on the countertop. A single plate, a lone cup of half-finished coffee, remained on the kitchen table. Beside it, a napkin was balled as if in anger.

In bare feet, he crept into his bedroom and stood for some time in the doorway, his eyes caressing the gentle curves of his wife from across the room. It occurred to him that the past few months of his domestic life equated to countless moments exactly like this one: standing alone in the dark, watching his life continue on without him. He felt pinned to a sedentary wheel, flattened and incapable of movement.

Time would not stand still for him.

He recalled a summer afternoon during their courtship spent at Coney Island. Katie's laughter blossoming in the humidity, the runnels of diamond-shaped perspiration making slick her neck and dampening her brow. She'd lost a shoe while riding the Tilt-A-Whirl and found an extra ream of tickets in her purse from a previous visit to the park; he'd slammed the hammer down on the strength meter and rung the bell. In a showy display of irony, she'd won him a stuffed panda at the Shoot-For-Loot booth, and it had been an ugly thing with creepy red eyes. They'd laughed about it. She'd called it the Devil Bear. Lost somewhere over time.

Time . . .

Katie's guardian angel, he remained standing in the bedroom doorway, unmoving, for a very, very long time.

LATE DECEMBER

CHAPTER TWENTY-SEVEN

THERE WAS BLOOD ON THE CONCRETE FLOOR.

Dino "Smiles" Moratto lay in stasis, poised like a turtle spun on its back, his eyes betraying the conflagration of fear, anger, and utter humility that had collected inside him. From his left nostril flowed a scarlet ribbon of blood; it traced like a river down the contours of his face, over the hideous scar that hooked the left side of his mouth into a perpetual grin, up and over the rugged swell of one cheek, finally dipping down into the valley of his left ear. Beside his head, Dino's blood pooled as if from a busted pipe. A smaller, somehow darker puddle lay smeared by his left arm in a rainbow arc. He worked his mouth noiselessly, his tongue pushing against bad air, his long hair fanned out like the posterior of a peacock on the floor behind his head.

Mickey O'Shay stood above him, breathing heavily. His hands still balled into fists, blood smeared across the knuckles, they remained at rest in the position that had finally sent Dino "Smiles" Moratto to the floor.

Behind Mickey, a few guys in worsted coats and cargo pants—John Mavio among them—shifted uncomfortably, most of them silently hoping the fight was finally over. Set atop a small table across the room, a Sony radio was tuned to Sly and the Family

Stone's "Higher."

Nobody moved. And for one brief moment, it seemed no one ever would.

Then something clicked behind Dino's eyes—consciousness, perhaps—and he managed to roll over onto his left side, pressing his face into the syrupy pool of his own blood. He brought one hand up and pawed feebly at the air. There was something utterly pathetic about the action. He was like a wounded animal, ignorant of the events which had led him to such a state . . .

The room was dim and spacious with a low ceiling, directly beneath the floor of the Cloverleaf pub. Weekends, the room served as an underground sanctuary for professional gamblers engaging in business—cards, dice, whatever the trend. Sweaty, greasy fives and tens, twenties and fifties covered the stand of card tables on those nights. Fight nights, a small black-and-white television set was pulled from behind the bar and propped in a corner. Cigar smoke and cheap cologne circulated through the musty air, mingled with the voracious cheers of guileful street hustlers and fist-pumpers.

Dino shuffled across the floor, a rattle deep in his throat. His nose was still bleeding like a fountain, leaving behind a constellation of blood on the concrete floor.

"Funny-man," Mickey O'Shay said, finally dropping his arms. Over the passage of several days, he had grown a small thatch of hair at his chin. At the moment, two bright red globules of Dino Moratto's blood were suspended in the wiry hair. "You're a real tough guy, Moratto, fuckin' guinea bastard. You're real tough with your nose busted open."

The night started out like any other night with Mickey O'Shay: suffused in a bleak haze of pot smoke and alcohol. Mickey, John, and some nameless tagalong had dropped into the Cloverleaf well after dark. As usual, Mickey had gone straight for the restroom while John and the tagalong ordered themselves a beer. Mickey's primary infatuation was with booze—lager, whiskey, bourbon, Irish cream, any goddamn thing he could get his mitts on. For the sheer grandiloquence of it, the animal had downed a shot glass full of lighter fluid the night before while John stood and watched. And he'd spent the rest of the evening vomiting on himself, his eyes no more vacant than they'd been at any other point during the day. Frequently, Mickey chose to augment his daily toxin intake by smoking several joints down to the roach. And when he felt like it, he'd snort a line or two of coke into each nostril with such enthusiasm one would assume the act provided for him some sort of sexual gratification.

When Mickey had returned from the restroom, his eyes were blistered and beaten. Though they'd just shared a lengthy conversation about Islanders hockey on the walk down the block to the Cloverleaf, Mickey pulled up a stool beside John and did not say a word to him. He motioned for a beer without speaking a word to the bartender, either. John, a quick study, knew better than to initiate a conversation. Mickey O'Shay was socially inept to the point of near retardation. No social graces whatsoever, he spoke when he felt like it and ignored everyone the rest of the time.

Some guys had been making noise at the other end of the bar, and John could tell they were beginning to irritate Mickey. Some loudmouth with a scar on his face began arm wrestling one of his buddies, and Mickey casually turned to watch the event. Drinking his beer in small sips with one elbow propped up on the bar, he could have been lulling himself to sleep. When the match was over and scar-face was deemed the victor, the crowd turned and marched down the small hallway that communicated with a declivity of cement steps which, in turn, led to the underground storage cellar cum gambling establishment.

Without saying a word, leaving his beer on the bar, Mickey had risen from his stool and affixed himself to the rear of the crowd. John, too, stood and followed Mickey and the rest of the men down the narrow hallway. The mob led them to the end of the hallway and through a small, trapdoor-like passageway cut into the floorboards.

Downstairs, the spacious underground bar stank of urine, alcohol, and stale cigarette smoke. The men milled around, talking in loud, booming voices, oblivious to Mickey, who remained leaning against the frame of the door at the bottom of the stairwell. He was like a ghost on a different plane—invisible almost to the point of nonexistence in this world.

Then, in what John would later recall as a confusing blur, things began to happen.

Dino Moratto, the victor of the arm wrestling match, started to shout something at some of the other men, smiling a disfigured smile. He moved to a small radio that sat on a table, turned it on, rolled through the stations.

For several moments, Mickey had remained brooding in the corner, unnoticed by Dino and his friends. The things that set Mickey off were not intelligent, calculable, *understandable* things: he was a firecracker that exploded at will and without provocation.

In a rush, Mickey had stormed Dino and slammed him in the face. The sudden burst of movement caused John to take a reflexive step backward, as it did most of the other spectators. Blood immediately ruptured from Dino's nose. A second slug from Mickey, and it suddenly looked like a number of Dino Moratto's friends would jump in . . . but then something *happened.* Somehow, by the grace of God, they must have caught the homicidal glint in Mickey O'Shay's eyes, because everyone froze in mid-step. The color abruptly drained from their faces, their lungs at a standstill in their chests. The hammer of heartbeats filled the room.

"What—" Dino had managed, and was slugged again.

There was no real power behind Mickey's punches—just a brutal, senseless ferocity. Most of the punches did not even connect, and he wound up boxing his opponent several times on the ears and cheekbones with the sides of his arms. Dino moaned, shuddered, attempted to defend himself . . . but it was a futile attempt. Mickey had hit him without notice, without warning, and was unrelenting.

Now, with Dino moaning and slobbering at his feet, Mickey ran his bloody fingers through his hair. In two steps, he closed the distance between him and the radio, picked it off the table, and smashed it on the floor.

Let this end here, John thought. Mickey, as unpredictable as he was, might kill the bastard, might follow him and his friends out into the street and shoot them all. He was aware that any confrontation outside the bar or on the street would alert Kersh, who was sitting in his car and parked in an alley. If Kersh came over, things would go to hell. Fast.

End here, John thought again.

Things didn't end.

Mickey stalked over to where Dino Moratto lay. Behind him, Dino's friends were slowly closing in. Despite Mickey's reputation, they were no doubt planning to make a move, though they still hadn't been able to work up the courage. Crouching on his haunches, Mickey reached out and tore the back pocket off Dino's pants. He took Dino's wallet, gutted it like a fish, and stuffed the few bills he found into his coat. Standing up, he dropped the wallet on top of Dino's head. And giggled.

In the two weeks John had immersed himself in the hopeless and violent world of Mickey O'Shay, he had come to understand just what Mickey was: an enigma. *Understanding* Mickey was *not* understanding him. It was knowing that at any moment he might lean over and slap you contentedly on the back . . . or grab you around the neck with hooked fingers. No time spent undercover could have prepared him to deal with such an animal. And slowly, as the days crept by and he spent more and more time consorting with the boys of the West Side, the cloth began slipping from the painting, soon to expose the whole picture for what it was.

For the most part, Jimmy Kahn stayed out of the picture. He lived in a comfortable apartment on the Upper West Side, drove a Cadillac—was, in fact, the only one of the West Side boys who even possessed a driver's license—and seemed to be the only one with any sense of ambition past the bottle. When he wasn't around, which was quite often, his boy Mickey ran the streets in his absence, brutal and intimidating enough to fill in for an entire squad of Jimmy Kahns. And Detective Glumly had been right: everyone else was just a straphanger, a bullshit street punk who made some quick cash selling their muscle to Mickey and Jimmy's endeavors.

And there were *plenty* of endeavors: extortion, robbery . . . they had their claws in a little bit of everything. They were not smart guys. More like rats, like piddling thieves. If they stumbled across a box of rosary beads, they would try to hock them. An abundance of anything, in their eyes, could yield some sort of profit. Yet despite their lack of a traditional business sense, which had propelled the Italian Mafia to the front pages, they were raking in the dough. Eavesdropping on cryptic conversations while hanging around Mickey, coupled with attaining information from the wire taps Roger Biddleman so enthusiastically employed, John found his mental picture of Mickey O'Shay and Jimmy Kahn gradually broadening. And so was the scope of their crimes.

They had a piece of the dock workers' union, the factories, the canneries across the river. They had a piece of the theatrical union and were collecting big money from the Theater District. Even the limousine drivers whose job it was to chauffeur eminent performers, actors, and musicians to their respective engagements paid a kickback to the Irish boys of Hell's Kitchen. Kings of the "no shows," they would approach the foremen of local construction sites and demolition crews and suggest two or three of their boys be added to their payroll, showing up to the site only twice a month to collect their paychecks. Their names and reputations struck unmitigated fear in the hearts of anyone who knew of them. No one would say no to them, would stand in their way, would attempt to jerk them around. Mickey O'Shay and Jimmy Kahn were not window-breakers; you fucked with them, you'd better kill them.

Yet through all the wire taps and conversations overheard by John and the Secret Service, Jimmy Kahn remained elusive. He was always close by, but never actually on the scene. And although the West Side Boys spoke of him frequently—especially Mickey—it wasn't enough for a court of law. By the end of two weeks, the Secret Service had enough burn on Mickey to lock him up for years . . . but not a single conclusive thing on Jimmy Kahn.

Upstairs, Mickey reclaimed his seat at the bar and finished his beer. He did not say a word. Dried blood matted his hair. Then, looking at them, he uttered, "Gotta take a whiz," and stumbled into the bathroom.

Sometime later, Dino Moratto and his boys climbed up out of the basement and collected themselves around the bar. Dino now held a bloodied, wadded piece of newspaper to his nose, his eyes all funny.

When Mickey returned, the Irish lad did not even look in Dino's direction. He simply sat himself back down on his bar stool and ordered another beer and a shot of Wild Turkey. Mickey never ordered for anyone else, no matter who was in his company. When he drank, he was utterly and completely alone, with the rest of the world shut down all around him.

The bartender placed Mickey's drinks in front of him, then swung down to Dino Moratto's end of the bar. Dino and his boys were settling up, half of them already to the door. John tensed, watching the slowness with which they moved. Even the eyes of the little tagalong beside him grew wide, unable to look away from the passing mob. Only Mickey did not budge, seeming not to notice. With one finger, he rubbed the bottom of his empty shot glass, then stuck it in his mouth.

"Jesus. The hell happened to you?" the bartender asked Dino as he moved through the crowd toward the door.

For a brief instant, Mickey *did* look up. His eyes locked with Dino's in the mirror above the bar, the strength and intimidation of their individual glares incomparable: even Dino Moratto's *eyes* were no match for Mickey's.

Dino quickly looked away. "Nothing," was all he said, and he and his crew slipped out into the night.

John knew, after spending roughly two weeks on and off with Mickey, that there was no way he would ever befriend Mickey. In the world of the street criminal, there were no such things as friends. They'd met in cars and in clubs, bars, and pizza joints throughout the West Side. Young Irish hoodlums filtered in and out of the group like flies buzzing a dung heap. He was spending all this time hoping for a morsel, working simply off the feeling that something might happen. In this time, there had been no transactions, no deals, with John's intention being to alleviate some of Mickey's distrust, thus achieving further access into the guy's personal life. And, if possible, to Jimmy Kahn. From the onset, Kersh did not like the idea and did not want him pushing his undercover role any more than necessary. Kersh still thought fishing for information and asking too many questions were bad ideas. The Secret Service made a pact with the NYPD, motioning Roger Biddleman as ringleader, but John was making his own decisions. Similarly, Detective Dennis Glumly and the NYPD left it in John's hands; they wanted guns from the Hell's Kitchen boys to hopefully match ballistics with unsolved homicides, but knew he was at the helm. Moreover, the Secret Service wanted to flush out the counterfeit investigation, but would not push John.

In fact, only two people were impatient about the operation.

One was Roger Biddleman, who had suddenly become John Mavio's new best friend—or so Biddleman thought, anyway. The attorney spent several hours a day researching Mickey O'Shay and Jimmy Kahn, and conferring with the NYPD about all their alleged crimes. To Biddleman, John had become his most important tool: the longest available stick with which he could poke and prod a sleeping cobra.

The other person was John himself.

In short, he wanted Jimmy Kahn.

Mickey left the Cloverleaf about twenty minutes after Dino Moratto and his friends. He left without saying anything to anyone, not leaving a dime on the counter, and slipped out into the night by himself.

Creep, John thought, sipping his beer and watching Mickey's skulking form pass by the bar's only window.

Beside him, the no-name tagalong finished off his own beer and began searching through the pockets of his coat for money to pay his tab. A loose dollar here, a handful of change there—everything he found was plucked from his coat and pushed into a disorganized heap on the bar. John watched him from the corner of his eye. The kid was young, maybe eighteen, and had a purple-brown bruise along one cheek. There was nothing youthful in his demeanor, however; his features were hard, his brow perpetually creased in either thought or confusion. Downstairs, the kid had watched Mickey slam Dino Moratto with a look of subtle veneration on his face. Now, in Mickey's absence, he looked lost and out of sorts.

John pushed his beer glass off to one side. He hooked a cigarette from his shirt pocket, lit it, inhaled. The nameless kid's eyes caught his in the mirror above the bar. "What's your name?"

"Ashleigh."

John nodded toward the front door. "You gonna follow him

around all night?" he said, meaning Mickey.

"No," Ashleigh said after a short pause, which confessed that yes, he had planned on doing that very thing.

"You know him long?"

"Not really," the kid said. He seemed uncomfortable talking about Mickey. "Know him from the neighborhood. What about you?"

The bartender was sweeping a dishrag along the counter at the far end of the bar, his movements deliberately slow.

"No," he said. "Don't really know him."

The kid counted his money and left no tip on the bar. Heading toward the door, he turned and nodded in John's direction. "See you around," Ashleigh said.

CHAPTER TWENTY-EIGHT

SEAN SULLIVAN, THE MEEK-LOOKING KID WHO'D helped unload the whiskey from the Ryder truck, was a cutter. Both his arms, from the wrists and up past the elbows, all the way to the shoulders, were covered in scar tissue. The thin, reddened puckers along his skin were so numerous that it seemed a trick of the eye.

"Did that one with a straight razor when I was fifteen," he said, almost proudly. He and John were seated in a small booth toward the back of the Cloverleaf, a billow of cigarette smoke wafting about their heads. This evening, the bar was fairly populated, some of Mickey and Jimmy's boys crowded around the front of the bar, pounding back shots and growling at each other in intoxicated banter. "Sliced my shit right up."

"What the hell for?" John said.

"For?" As if the question made no sense. "I just fucking *did* it." The kid rolled up his other sleeve. "Look at this one." Another road map of scars was revealed. Sean pointed to a particular scar distinctly shaped like a six-sided star. "Star of fucking David. You know what that is? It's a Jew star. In memory of Jacob Goldman. So I never forget him. You know who Jacob Goldman is?"

He shook his head. "No."

"Course not," Sean said, now more to himself than John. "I'll tell you about him someday." The kid smiled weakly. The way the light struck his face, he almost appeared to have no skin at all—just a skull with eyes. "I'm in a good mood tonight," Sean continued, "and I ain't gonna ruin it talking about that son of a bitch."

A twisted shadow fell across the table. John looked up and saw Mickey O'Shay standing above him, a cigarette poking from between his lips, his eyes hollow and glassy.

Mickey looked at Sean Sullivan. "Hit the bricks."

Sean pulled himself out of the booth and pushed his way through the crowd toward the bar. He walked timidly, like someone ashamed of his own trespass. Wasting no time, Mickey quickly claimed the kid's seat across from John, puffing hard on his cigarette. His fingers were stained brown from the nicotine.

"What's going on?" John said.

"How come you can't move any more money?"

John leaned back in the booth, his eyes scanning the crowd of people around the bar. He felt his bowels tighten and his heart skip as his eyes fell on Bill Kersh, seated at the bar and sipping a gin and tonic. Kersh was facing in his direction, though his eyes were unfocused, one hand busy in a bowl of unsalted pretzels. Then Kersh's eyes *did* focus on him, looked straight at him, and it seemed like their eyes locked for an eternity.

"I told you, Mickey, your price is too goddamn high. I can't move shit when I'm paying twenty points."

"Get better customers," Mickey said.

"You wanna do business, drop your price. Have a sit-down with your guy. Me and you'll go, try and negotiate a better deal."

Mickey's mind was working.

Somewhat impatiently, John said, "Well . . .?"

Mickey's eyes jerked up in his direction, seemed to flutter in their sockets, then held their ground. In a toneless voice, Mickey said, "What about guns? Think you can move some guns?"

CHAPTER TWENTY-NINE

THE CALM RISE AND SWELL OF THE Hudson, mingled with the traffic along the West Side Highway, was an everlasting symphony. The water was cold and muddy, the color of slate, and hugged the iron pilings along the river. Summer months, the piers were always hot and busy. Winters, they were as barren as an arctic landscape. Even the dock workers, packaged in corduroy coats, thick canvas pants, and broadcloth shirts, seemed less formidable this time of year, as if something inside them had slowed and frozen along with nature.

Standing outside his Camaro while smoking a cigarette and sipping coffee, John's eyes trolled the piers. Behind him, the great hulking framework of the *Intrepid* lay enormous against the steel sky, its hull moored to the piers by links of iron chain. Up ahead, a Hindu guy pushed a hot dog cart along the bulwark, his yellow-and-white-striped umbrella pulling slow rotations in the wind. A number of cars were parked along the street and a few people were out along the promenade, though the afternoon was bitterly cold and windy. Of those cars, one of them was Bill Kersh's sedan.

John took a labored sip of coffee. He was coming down with a cold, could feel it slowly working its way through his system, and attributed the onslaught of such an illness to the unconventional hours he'd been keeping with Mickey O'Shay and his crew. Last night, he'd recognized the initial breath of fever down his spine and along his neck. There were also deep brown grooves beneath his eyes, and his skin had taken on a jaundiced hue. From the oncoming illness or a lack of sleep—he did not know which.

He'd spent very few hours at home the past couple of weeks. What little time he had was spent languishing in the dark of the apartment like a thief and a stranger. Either Katie was asleep in bed already, or she had left to spend the night at his father's place. Whatever the case, he was alone. And when sleep finally found him on these nights, it was restless and cruel, like an afternoon half-sleep, his mind filling with loud images and the phantom cracks of gunshots.

Finishing his coffee, he tossed the Styrofoam cup into the nearest receptacle. It did little to warm his insides. Pausing, he looked out over the Hudson and tried to attain from the great river whatever peace he was able. It was very little.

Sucking the last bit of life from his cigarette, he pitched the butt over the bulwark railing and turned his head to one side, his hair whipping against his face in the wind. He could make out the back of Kersh's sedan wedged between two other vehicles along the promenade.

A beat-up Toyota pulled up behind the Camaro and parked. A sputter of exhaust billowed from the tailpipe. The driver kept the engine running. John could make out two people in the car—the driver, and a second person in the back seat.

One of the back doors opened. Mickey O'Shay stepped out.

A small part of his mind had hoped Jimmy Kahn would accompany Mickey on the gun deal, but the driver was not Kahn—just another one of their straphangers.

"You're late," he said, watching Mickey move around to the trunk of the car. This afternoon, Mickey O'Shay's eyes were inanimate and slow. "It's freezing out here, and you're late."

"Come here," Mickey said, motioning for him to approach the Toyota's trunk. Mickey slipped a key into the trunk and popped it open.

Peering into the trunk from the curb, John could make out two wool blankets rolled up into balls, a pair of corduroy pants, an old hockey stick, and other senseless junk. Mickey pushed most of this stuff aside and grabbed the lip of the carpet that lined the interior floor of the Toyota's trunk. Like a doctor undoing a bandage, he peeled back the carpeting with exaggerated care. He was wearing black wool gloves with the fingers cut out.

Revealed within the well of the trunk was a large white canvas bag closed tight with a drawstring. Fisting one gloved hand and breathing warmth into it, Mickey struggled to work the canvas bag open with only his left hand. John took a step down from the curb and moved beside him. The trunk stank of exhaust and gasoline. Standing there, he began shivering beneath his leather jacket and sweater, yet at the same time could feel blisters of sweat dripping down his neck and along his ribcage.

Fever, he thought. *I think my goddamn fever just hit.*

He felt his entire body grow tired in an instantaneous clap. His head suddenly felt too big for his neck. The cup of coffee he'd just downed now seemed like a bad idea. A small moan escaped him, and he slid his hands into the pockets of his leather jacket; his right hand fell upon his gun.

"Okay," Mickey breathed, a plume of vapor wafting from his mouth. He slid a .32-caliber semiautomatic from the bag and rested it on the trunk's carpeting.

"You said this was a new gun. It looks dirty."

Mickey shrugged. "It's been layin' around."

"How many more you got?"

"Maybe a dozen right now," Mickey said. "A hundred or so by next week. Two hundred apiece, no discounts. You interested?"

He nodded, peering over the lip of the trunk at the gun. *A hundred or so by next week?* he thought. *Jesus Christ!*

"What about this one?" Mickey said. "Think you can move it?"

"I can," he said, "but I don't got the cash on me now."

"Take it," Mickey said. "I trust ya. Pay me when you move it."

The driver's side door opened and a severe-looking kid with a pug face and deep-set eyes stepped out. He had the unlit nub of a cigar tucked into the right corner of his mouth and was wearing a knitted Islanders cap. His lips were full and purple in the cold, resembling two cuts of liver.

"All right," John said, and Mickey quickly replaced the .32 in the canvas, pulled tight the drawstring, and sat on the bumper of the Toyota while John took the gun and put it in the trunk of the Camaro. The kid with the cigar was leaning against the open driver's door, trying without much luck to light the end of the stogie with an uncooperative Zippo. The kid eyed John from beneath the ribbed band of his knit cap. As if in approval, the kid nodded once, then looked with some disappointment at his Zippo.

"How's Jimmy?" he said, slamming the Camaro's trunk and moving back around to the rear of the Toyota. His nose was running, his eyes starting to tear from the wind. He could feel his muscles tightening. "Haven't seen him around in a while."

Mickey had shut the Toyota's trunk and was sitting on it now, tugging at his gloves. "You gonna be around tonight?" Mickey said, ignoring his question.

"Depends. What's up?"

"An opportunity," Mickey said. "Because I know how much you like making money."

The .32 was like an early Christmas present for Dennis Glumly. With an expression of excitement on his face—or, rather, the closest thing to excitement the man was able to muster—he admired the weapon on John's desk like a child peering in a shop window at a brand new bicycle. After John detailed his conversation with Mickey for both Glumly and Brett Chominsky, the NYPD detective rushed the gun out of the office to check ballistics and prints. If the gun could be traced to an unsolved homicide, there would be one more thing to stick against Mickey O'Shay. And if *Kahn's* prints happened to be on the gun . . . well, it would be the only real evidence they'd have against the man.

Downstairs, Kersh was in the pit, going over reports and sipping a Diet Coke.

"You hiding out?" John said, coming up behind him.

"As much as ever. What's the deal with this thing tonight?"

He explained to Kersh what Mickey had told him—to meet outside the candy store at eleven o'clock if he wanted to make a couple extra bucks.

"If we're lucky, he's set up a meeting with his source," he said, pulling up a chair across from Kersh at the table. In the warmth of the pit he felt a little bit better, but knew that his fever was gradually climbing. "I've been bugging him like crazy to get those points down."

"Maybe," Kersh said. He didn't sound too convinced.

"I want to set them up for one more big buy," he said, "hopefully flush out Kahn. We get him dirty, we can close this thing."

"And if he doesn't show?" Kersh said. "If he *never* shows? What do we do then? Keep chasing these two bastards for the next twenty years, John?" Perhaps bothered by his own sudden passion, Kersh paused, relaxing. "Look," he continued, "I see you getting wrapped up in this thing, and it bothers me."

"We've already talked about this."

"The past month you've been slinking around in the mud with these assholes, getting half-bombed every night—getting *sick*—and for what? To get inside their *heads?* To see if *maybe* someone tips you off about some bullshit hit they did eight months ago in goddamn

Queens? That's not why we're here, John. And it's not worth it."

"Trust me," he said, "and we'll get the whole ball of wax. I'm okay, I can handle myself. I'm not about to give up on something after all this time just because it's too hard. You know me, Bill."

"I know," said Kersh. "That's what scares me."

CHAPTER THIRTY

BY ELEVEN O'CLOCK, TRAFFIC HAD DWINDLED ALONG Tenth Avenue. Pulling his car up outside Calliope Candy, John had the heater cranked and the defroster running. On his hands he wore leather racing gloves—warm enough to keep the cold air at bay, yet workable enough to permit maximum dexterity. His jacket zippered almost to the neck, he could feel sweat coursing from his armpits and rolling down his sides. But still his face was cold, his lips numb even with the heat pumping, and he was still aware of the faint throbbing at the center of his hands.

Lights were still on in the candy store, but the shade had been pulled, making it impossible to see inside. To his left, cars coasted along the street. A few people hurried across the intersection, the collars of their coats pulled tightly around their necks.

There was a streetlight on the corner of Tenth and 53rd Street, a few feet away from the telephone booth outside Calliope Candy. A figure stood there in the darkness, hunched over in the cold, his face shielded from the streetlight and his back facing John. The figure was definitely male, but too short to be Mickey. There was a restless motion to the man's body as he rocked uneasily on his feet, his eyes out over the intersection.

As if he had read John's mind, the figure noticed the car and moved toward it, hopping down the curb—*Mickey does not hop,* he thought—and approaching the driver's side door. The figure bent down, his face inches from the window, and peered inside.

It was Sean Sullivan.

He rolled down his window.

"Hey, John."

"Sean," he said. "What the hell you doin' out here?"

"Mickey said to meet 'im," Sean said, his teeth chattering in his head. "Said he's taking me someplace."

John's eyes darted to the transmitter stashed inside the casing of the cigarette lighter. It was resting on his dashboard, pointed toward the passenger seat. It was windy outside; there was a good possibility Sean Sullivan's words got lost in the wind. But if not, then there would be no doubt that Bill Kersh, who was parked one block over on the corner of Tenth and 52nd Street, had heard.

"You goin' with us?" he asked Sean.

The kid shrugged his shoulders. "He didn't say nothing 'bout you."

"Where's Mickey now?"

"Inside," Sean said, nodding his head in the direction of the candy store.

"Well, get in the car before your freeze your balls off."

"Shit, thanks."

Sean hurried around the front of the car while John popped the lock on the passenger door. The kid climbed in and plopped down in the seat like someone who'd been on his feet all day. He pulled the door closed—did not slam it like Mickey—and immediately held his hands up to the vents in the dashboard.

"Christ," Sean said, looking him over. "Man, you don't look so good. You sick?"

"A little."

"Flu?"

"Don't know," John said. "Probably."

"I just got over one . . ."

"You know anything about tonight?" John asked.

"Nope," Sean said, rubbing his hands together. "Just said to meet 'im here. Eleven o'clock. That's all."

John could see some of the scars along Sean's hands as he held them up to the vents, a striking pink discoloration against the cold, white flesh of his skin. "How'd you get hooked up with Mickey?" he asked, peering past Sean and at the front of the candy store. Still no movement.

"They know my older brother. Been in Rikers last two years."

"You been runnin' with these guys long?"

"On and off," Sean said. He was young and impressed by the violence Mickey and Jimmy dispensed, and by the power their names held. They were sacred in his eyes—John could tell that just by looking at the kid, and by the way the kid looked at them—probably more inspiring than any adult male figure had ever been to him. For Sean Sullivan, the two Irish hoods from the West Side were heroes, and his association with them was a privilege.

Still, he was just a kid—maybe eighteen or nineteen—and his patriotism to Mickey O'Shay and Jimmy Kahn seemed a grievous, complicated thing.

"Lotta guys up this way make some money workin' for Jimmy and Mickey," Sean said. "Figured I'd get in on it."

"They have you do anything besides moving whiskey off trucks?" He tried to make it sound like a joke.

"Shit, yeah," Sean said. His pitch suggested he thought of John as someone to impress.

"Like what?"

"Stuff," Sean said. "Just stuff."

"Where you from?" John asked.

"Right here."

"You still live here?"

"Of course," Sean said.

Looking at the kid now, John could tell that this was a potentially big night for young Sean Sullivan. The kid had started to sweat.

"Hey," Sean said, opening his door. "Here he is."

Mickey had stepped from the candy store looking as vacant as usual, the stick of a Tootsie Pop jutting from between his lips. He crossed over to the car and jerked a thumb at Sean, motioning for him to get into the Camaro's cramped back seat. Sean managed with some difficulty while Mickey chucked the Tootsie Pop down the street.

Once inside the car, Mickey motioned for him to head down Tenth Avenue.

"What's the deal?" he said before pulling out of the space. "You didn't say nothin' about this kid coming."

"So?"

"So I'm not a goddamn taxi, picking people up and dropping them off."

"There's a place on Eighty-fifth Street," Mickey said. "The Samjetta. You know it?"

"No."

"Bar and grill. We're going across the street from there," Mickey said. Like his phone calls from the pay phone on Tenth Avenue, his apartment phone, and the telephone in the candy store, he spoke cryptically, his intentions demanding interpretation.

Pulling out onto Tenth Avenue, John said, "What's across the street?"

"Liquor store."

They drove mostly in silence, with the majority of the chatter coming from Sean in the back seat. He spoke of nonsense and seemed to choose his words with tedium, eager to impress Mickey, or at least prove to him that he was one of the gang. And Sean

Sullivan was not quite part of Mickey and Jimmy's gang. Thinking of quiet, subdued Ashleigh who'd not spoken at the Cloverleaf the entire night, and of the guy in the knitted Islanders cap who'd driven Mickey to sell John the .32, he knew that Sean Sullivan did not truly fit in. Which bothered John. Was it so obvious he, too, did not fit in? Was this the roundup, the weeding out?

Driving, he glanced in the rearview to see if he could spot Kersh's car following them.

He couldn't.

As Tenth Avenue turned into Amsterdam, the traffic grew more congested. Mickey got lost and had them circle the block a number of times. They eventually continued west until they hit Riverside Drive.

"The hell's going on here, Mickey?" He could see the lights of the Henry Hudson Parkway at the other end of Riverside Park from here.

Mumbling to himself, scratching his head, Mickey told him to turn around and head back toward Amsterdam Avenue.

Traffic grew thicker, and Mickey began to collect his thoughts once they reached Amsterdam.

"Stop-stop-stop," Mickey said, leaning forward in his seat and peering through the windshield. A row of shops and restaurants lined the street, accentuated by the lights of passing vehicles.

"Where?" he said. Across the street, he could see the Samjetta —a family-style steakhouse with a brick front illuminated by red and yellow neon lights. It looked like no place Mickey O'Shay would have anything to do with.

"Slow down." Mickey turned and looked out his window, his nose only two inches from the glass. He was pointing across the street, opposite the Samjetta. "There's a, uh . . . you see that liquor store up ahead? See the alley? Turn in there. Go around back."

The alleyway ran between a liquor store and Pat's Laundromat, dark and narrow. John maneuvered the Camaro through it and stopped alongside a huddle of trash cans. A stand of doors without knobs lined the walls of the brick alley. He caught a glimpse of Sean's white face in the rearview. The kid looked about ready to wet his pants.

He'd made up his mind long ago that he could shoot and kill Mickey without hesitation if he even suspected something off-kilter. Now, wedged between the brick siding of two stores, the thought resurfaced in his head. He knew there would be no use trying to arrest him, trying to subdue him if Mickey decided to break bad. Mickey would not give him the opportunity. He would be like a wild boar ensnared in a trap: there would be no way to cut him loose or even cage him. The only option was to kill.

Mickey got out of the car and headed down the alley to one of the doors embedded in the brick wall. Sean was quick to follow, already pushing against the passenger seat and pulling himself from the car. He nearly stumbled getting out of the car, managing to keep himself from crashing to the ground only by catching the wall with both hands at the last possible second.

"In an alley just before Eighty-fifth Street, off Amsterdam," he said to the transmitter on the dash. "Couple doors back here. Looks like they lead to the back of the shops. We're going inside."

He slipped the cigarette lighter transmitter into his jacket pocket, although he was certain he would be out of Kersh's range once he stepped inside the building. Regardless, he shut the car down and got out. Behind him, he was aware of the traffic droning down the street, and the louder idles of the cars stopping along the rows of shops. Mickey knocked against one of the doors and stood there, digging in one ear with the pinkie of his right hand. Like someone suddenly struck by a momentous thought, he dug a filthy cigarette from the breast pocket of his green coat and stuck it behind his other ear.

As John approached, the alley door creaked open several inches. There was no discernible light inside. Mickey placed a hand on the inside of the door and pushed it open, wasting no time with a leisurely entrance. On his heels, Sean Sullivan, slack-faced and wide-eyed, crept over the threshold while John counted three beats in his head. He didn't know what to expect—a series of gunshots or the shouts of haughty laughter. He heard neither.

Casting one final glance toward the street at the mouth of the alley, he crept inside the building and heard the door slam.

Around him, darkness prevailed.

Parked along Amsterdam Avenue, Bill Kersh chewed disconcertedly on his left thumb.

"Goddamn kid," he muttered. His mind regressed to earlier that day and to their conversation in the pit. It wasn't so much John's words that had bothered him—he was young and anxious and willing to take risks, and a lot of what the kid said made good sense. No, what bothered Kersh was the way the kid had *looked,* like someone just off a caffeine rush. John was wired, too wrapped up in the case. That same machinelike quality that Kersh had noticed in him the night they loaded up the Ryder truck with the Canadian whiskey was still there, yet it had changed in some way. His tenacity had turned into urgency and was slowly driving the kid over the edge. Too much more of this and Kersh feared—

But he didn't want to think about that. Hopefully it would all be over soon. Brett Chominksy was not one to be swayed by the opinions of Roger Biddleman and would pull the plug after too much time, no matter what evidence John happened to bring to the table.

At least, Kersh *hoped.*

Looking at the row of shops across the street, he noticed that Pat's Laundromat and a liquor store stood on either side of the alley's entrance. The lights were on in the liquor store, the neon pink *Open* sign sizzling in the window.

Kersh was torn. His instinct told him to give John a few minutes in the store before strolling inside, posing as a customer, casing the joint. Yet John had gotten his fingers into him as well, and some part of him—however small—told him to bide his time and give the kid a chance, see what happens.

"Where the hell are the lights?" Mickey said somewhere ahead of him in the darkness.

His eyes adjusting, John could see a faint strip of yellow light on the floor across the room. Light from behind a closed door, he imagined. The place smelled strongly of cigar smoke and provolone cheese.

His hand was in his jacket pocket, his fingers around the hilt of his gun, when the lights came on.

They were standing in a storage room with a large fan humming in a caged casing embedded in the far wall. Around them, cases of beer were stacked to shoulder height, some on handcarts and still wrapped in cellophane. *Playboy* centerfolds were taped to the walls, and there was a clipboard hanging from a nail above a case of Amstel Light, a pencil dangling from it by a greasy length of string.

A thick-shouldered man with graying hair stood by a closed door—the door leading out into the store, most likely—with a look of mild amusement on his face. In a T-shirt and checkered flannel pajama pants, he looked as if he'd just been roused from sleep.

"Keep your voice down, Mickey," the man said, scratching between the folds of his unshaven chin. "The hell's the matter with you?"

Uninterested in conversation, Mickey pulled the cellophane from one of the cases of beer and proceeded to bust open the carton. From between two stacks of cased beer, Sean watched Mickey without expression, his fingers working themselves into the fabric of his pants.

Sighing, the man by the door said, "It's warm."

"Don't care," Mickey said, pulling out a bottle and twisting off the cap. He drank half the bottle in two huge gulps, spilling some down the front of his shirt.

"What are we doing here, Mickey?" John said, his eyes shifting from Mickey O'Shay to the guy in the checkered flannel pants.

The guy in flannel looked at him. "Your friends want beer, Mickey, they pay for it. I ain't runnin' a goddamn charity here."

"Take a walk," Mickey said, initiating the man's retreat back to the front of his store.

John turned his gaze on Mickey, who sat passively atop a stack of crates finishing off his beer. "We gonna get to the point now, or what?"

"I know you're a mover, John," Mickey said. "There's a bartender across the street that needs to disappear. Five grand split between the two of you for the hit."

"Are you for real?" he said.

Mickey didn't answer, didn't even bother to meet his eyes.

"Who is this guy?" he asked. "And why me and the kid?"

"Forget it," Mickey said. "That don't matter. What matters is if you two do the job or not. Bartender's name is Ricky Laughlin. I'll give you guys the guns to do the job. You can keep 'em along with the money after you're done."

"How come you don't do it yourself?"

"Guy's *expecting* it to come from me," Mickey answered, almost with a laugh.

That's not it. He wants to test me, to own me.

Mickey pulled himself off the cases of beer and shrugged off his coat. "He's across the street right now," Mickey said. "Go over there, check him out, case the joint. You want the job, give me a call in a couple days."

With nothing more to say, Mickey slipped two more beers from the case and started loading up his coat.

John looked at Sean, saw that the kid had nearly run his fingers down to the bone against the fabric of his pants. Sean looked over at him, too, uncertain if he should speak or not. There was a fire in his eyes—the same look a kid gets when his old man entrusts him for the first time with the keys to the family car.

"Come on," John said, turning and heading for the door.

Outside, he found himself scanning for any signs of Kersh's car at the mouth of the alley. If Kersh had kept on their tail, then he was playing it smart and hanging back a block or two.

"Holy *shit!*" Sean said, walking quickly at John's side toward Amsterdam. "He ever call you for a hit before?"

"Nope."

"Goddamn! I mean, like, this is the real deal."

They paused at the curb to wait for a break in traffic. Across the street, the lights of the Samjetta were reflected in puddles in the street and on the windshields of passing cars. He took two quick glances in both directions and could not see Kersh's sedan, which meant nothing. Bill Kersh had long since mastered the art of camouflage.

"The Samjetta," John said, for the sole benefit of Kersh, who might now be within range of the transmitter in his pocket. "Looks like a steakhouse."

"What do you think this guy Laughlin did?" Sean asked.

"Beats me."

Between a break in traffic, the two of them scurried across the street like rats. Sean slammed through a puddle and unleashed a string of foul language. And despite the large neon letters announcing *The Samjetta* just above their heads, Sean turned and was about to continue down the street.

"Hey," John said to him, opening the front door of the restaurant. "Over here, Sean."

In the moments before they entered the restaurant, their images were reflected in tinted windows along Amsterdam Avenue.

The Samjetta was a cozy restaurant with a smattering of tables and booths to the right of the front doors, and a long mahogany bar to the left. The walls were alternating brick and polished wood, adorned with miscellaneous clothing from different generations. Tonight, there was a fair amount of traffic in the place, though there were still a few tables open. The bar, too, was only mildly crowded—mostly men in business suits sitting in small groups.

Sean headed immediately for the bar, but John grabbed him by the forearm and directed him over to one of the empty tables.

The kid looked annoyed. "What's wrong?"

"We'll sit here."

"That him?" Sean was already straining to stare at the bartender from across the floor.

"I don't know. Could be."

The bartender was tall and slender with a crop of black hair trimmed close to his head. He sported a goatee and a diamond stud in his left ear. From where he sat, John could make out the bluish swirls of a tattoo on the side of the bartender's neck.

"I think that's him," Sean said, unable to peel his eyes from the bartender.

"Hey." John drummed a finger on the table to attract the kid's attention. "You're gonna do this, huh?"

"What? The hit? Shit, yeah. Why?"

"You ever hear of this guy before?"

"Ricky Laughlin?" Sean shook his head. "No way."

"Must've done *something.*" John looked Sean over. "What's the deal with that star you carved on your arm? You said you'd tell me later."

That seemed to collect Sean's attention. Jarred by the question, the kid turned and faced him, the excitement drained from his face.

On the tabletop, his fingers were pushing against the polished surface, as they'd done against the fabric of his pants just a few minutes ago. He looked like someone trying to smooth wrinkles out of the wood.

"Jacob Goldman, you mean," Sean said.

"Yeah, that's the name, I think."

"Just someone I want to remember."

"He's that important you gotta carve a star in your arm?"

Without hesitation, Sean said, "To me he is."

"Come on," John urged. "Tell me."

As if to enhance the story, Sean rolled up his sleeve and exposed his filleted arm. Beneath the harsh lighting above their table, the scars looked almost purple and plumped out to grotesque exaggeration.

"Jacob Goldman was a guy who had a lot of money," Sean said. "He was married four times. His fourth wife was my mother, and she split with him. I don't know where they went or even if they're still married. This," he said, pointing to the star-shaped scar, "reminds me of that bastard. Every day. And I'm gonna find him someday. All the money in the world won't save him then."

"Had to carve it in your arm?"

"I see it every day," Sean Sullivan said.

"That why you follow Mickey O'Shay around?"

Uncomfortable, Sean shrugged. "Where you from?"

"Brooklyn."

"Around here, you're either with Mickey and Jimmy, or you're chased by them. That's fact. These guys don't mess around. You wanna make some money, they're the go-to guys."

"How well you know 'em?"

"We're pretty close," Sean said. John could tell that he was lying, that the kid was no more a part of Mickey and Jimmy's group than John was. "I do some jobs for them, stuff like that. Ain't nobody out here tells them how to do business. Not even the cops. Cops are fucking *scared* of 'em, man." The right side of his mouth hooked up into a partial grin. "All the bars pay 'em kickbacks. Most of the unions down there, too. If there's money bein' made in Hell's Kitchen, Mickey and Jimmy get a piece of it."

"What about people who don't wanna pay? What about bars that don't pay them kickbacks?"

"Show me one," Sean said with little humor. "Everyone's scared to death. Even the guineas want to work with them."

"Get the hell out of here. The *Italians?*"

"It's true," the kid insisted, now beaming with a corrupted pride. "Listen," he continued, "you wanna hear something crazy? I mean, like, absolutely fucking nuts?"

"What's that?"

"Just something I heard, something I—"

"Yeah?" John pressed.

Sean leaned closer to him from across the table, his voice dropping an octave. "There was this bookie, some Jew bastard named Horace Green, collecting loan-sharking debts for a while in Hell's Kitchen. Mickey and Jimmy get wind of this, they pay him a little visit, tell him they want a piece of the action. They tell him they'll keep an eye on him, make sure nobody comes around and rips him off. Protection, right? Well, Green tells 'em to forget it, that he's got the Italians already watching his back and he don't need a couple Irish punks from the West Side buggin' him. Anyway, all's cool for a couple nights. Then Green shows up in the neighborhood again to collect some vigs, probably in a good mood and everything, and at the end of the day he stops off for a few drinks at a neighborhood bar, right? Later, as he's comin' outta the bar in the middle of the night, there's Mickey and Jimmy, leaning against the guy's car. This bastard Green tries worming his way around them, probably startin' to blubber like a goddamn baby, but Jimmy and Mickey, they don't let nothin' go—you know what I mean?"

"What happened?" His forehead was burning up with fever, his hands again throbbing beneath the table.

"They kill him," Sean said flatly. "Jimmy shoots him twice in the chest, they take his keys, dump him in the trunk of his own car. Drive to some warehouse and—get this shit—*the motherfucker is still alive in the trunk when they get there.*"

"You serious?"

"Swear to Christ, John, that's how I heard it."

"So they kill him at the warehouse . . ."

"Chopped him up," Sean said. That vague smile was back on his face, his eyes aglow and teeming with bombast. He was like a parent bragging about his son's home run in Little League. "Cut the bastard into pieces with an axe—his head, his legs, his arms. Diced him like a Chinatown fish. It's how they make people disappear, is what I heard. They call it doin' a Houdini."

"Where'd you hear this?"

Sean waved away the question. It was unimportant. "I heard it. And you ain't even heard the best part yet. They grab this guy Green's loan-sharking book and start going around the city collecting the guy's vigs! I heard that, thought it was the funniest damn thing in the *world.* Can you imagine?"

"I think whoever told you this story's full of shit," he said.

"I don't think so, man. I mean, I know these guys. These ain't just stories. This is the way it is down here."

John turned and glanced over at the bartender, watched him flirt with an attractive Asian woman in tan pants and a red sweater. Without looking at Sean, he asked him how many other people Mickey and Jimmy killed.

Sean Sullivan rolled his shoulders. He suddenly looked very, very young beneath the glow of the restaurant's lights.

"Word on the street," Sean said, "they worked a lot of guys."

CHAPTER THIRTY-ONE

For a moment, the recording of Sean Sullivan's voice rendered the occupants of Brett Chominsky's office speechless. Then, as Chominsky leaned over and turned the tape recorder off, there sounded a tremulous exhale from where Roger Biddleman stood before the large bank of office windows.

Kersh, who had recorded the conversation via John's transmitter last night, sat before Chominsky's desk, his arms folded, his eyes unfocused and distant. He hadn't shaved this morning, and his chin looked like a loaded pin cushion.

John stood by the closed office door, his back against the wall, his hands stuffed into his pants pockets. Throughout the length of the recording, his eyes had volleyed from Kersh to Chominsky to Biddleman like someone watching a three-man handball game. Each had a different expression on his face: Kersh's was one of perdition, Chominsky displayed an uncharacteristic incertitude, and Roger Biddleman looked like someone who'd just been dealt four aces in a poker game and was doing his best to keep a straight face.

"Jesus," Chominksy said, the first person to speak. "Who is this kid again?"

"Sean Sullivan," John said. "Maybe nineteen years old. Said he's been doing jobs for Mickey and Jimmy for about five months now."

"Do you believe him?"

"I believe that someone *told* him that story, yes," he said.

"But do you believe the *story?*" Chominksy elaborated.

"I do, yes."

Chominksy frowned. "Are you sick? You look sick."

"I'm all right."

Chominksy turned to Kersh. "Bill?"

"Green . . . Horace Green . . ." Kersh muttered to himself. He pushed back in his chair, frowning in consideration. "That name sounds so familiar. Horace Green . . ." He paused, then looked up at Chominsky. "I think," Kersh said, "we need to first figure out what to do about this hit on the bartender."

"Ricky Laughlin," John said.

Chominsky asked John why he thought Mickey had offered him the hit.

"To see who I really am," he answered evenly. "And because he thinks he can own me."

Kersh shot him a look.

"When is Mickey expecting an answer?" Chominsky asked.

"Couple days."

"Any suggestions, Bill?"

Sighing, Kersh unfolded his arms and set the palms of his hands flat against his knees. He looked like someone about to commence with prayer. "We have John take the hit," he said. "Meanwhile, we'll have the guys from NYPD approach this guy Laughlin, tell him that they got word someone's looking to bump him. We'll get him and stick him in a safe house in Queens until this thing is over." He looked at John, and his eyes were dead. "Can't do a hit on someone if they disappear."

Biddleman had been listening intently to the conversation. Safe houses, hits, and protective custody were catch phrases that defined a career-making case. Any more discussion and the attorney would no doubt begin salivating all over the rug. Yet he kept his countenance reserved, his hands pressed neatly together at his waist, his predatory eyes shielded behind a veil of modest concern.

"Doing a Houdini," Chominsky muttered to himself, pulling the cassette tape from the recorder. "What a bunch of animals. Here." He handed the cassette over to Kersh. "Make some copies."

Kersh stood, the creases in his pants remaining. He walked out of the office, followed by Roger Biddleman, who took his time crossing the room. The attorney paused to smile at John.

"Good job, John."

John simply nodded and watched the attorney slip out into the hallway.

"What about you?" Chominsky said, reclining in his chair. "How do you feel about all this?"

"What do you mean?"

"I mean you look like you've got malaria. And I'm aware of the hours you've been putting in with these guys. You sure you feel okay?"

"I feel like shit, but I'll be fine. Just a cold. Haven't been sleeping too well."

"When's the baby due?"

"February." Having Brett Chominsky mention his unborn child was tantamount to hearing Muhammad Ali discuss the fundamentals of nuclear physics. As much as he could remember, he hadn't even mentioned his wife's pregnancy to Chominsky.

"You agree with Bill's approach to this hit?"

He nodded. "Sounds good."

"John," Chominsky began, pushing forward in his chair, "if you feel you're in over your head—"

"No." His tone was harsher than he would have liked. "I feel good about this. Some more time, we can bust this thing wide open."

Chominsky continued staring at him for several moments in

silence before sitting up again and turning toward his desk. "Just know," Chominsky said, not looking in his direction, "we can stop this thing whenever you feel it's necessary."

"I know," John said, turning toward the door. "I know."

Out in the hallway, John moved quickly toward the bathroom. There, he ran his hands beneath the faucet, working the feeling back into his fingers. He recalled an evening outside the candy store, standing on the curb in the freezing rain while Mickey and another guy talked in whispers by the pay telephone. In his mind, he could see the red-rimmed lids of Mickey's eyes staring at him from over a table at the Cloverleaf, his face hard and unyielding, saying, *What about guns? You think you can move some guns?* And coupled with that, the ghostly articulation of Sean Sullivan saying, *Diced him like a Chinatown fish. It's how they make people disappear, is what I heard. They call it doin' a Houdini.*

Behind him, the bathroom door swung open and Roger Biddleman entered. The attorney did a double-take in John's direction, then smiled at his reflection in the mirror.

"Come to take a load off my mind," Biddleman said, still grinning.

John shut off the water and grappled with a handful of paper towels.

"Pretty impressive, getting that kid to open up like that," Biddleman said. He saddled up to a urinal and relieved himself with great fervor.

"It's just talk."

"Well, I was impressed." The attorney finished and turned toward the sink, rested his hands on his hips. Instead of washing his hands, he leaned forward over the sink basin to examine his nostrils in the mirror. "You know what would be amazing? If we could get Mickey on tape talking about chopping that bookie up. I mean, can you imagine the impact that would have on a jury, just hearing this guy describe his own brutal crime?" Biddleman turned and faced him, his hands still on his hips. "I like to think we're on the same page here. At least . . . on the same *team* . . ."

"You want me to push Mickey for details on Green's murder? Get him on tape?" Yet even as the words came from his own mouth, he knew Roger Biddleman was right. And it wasn't just the notion of sending Mickey O'Shay away for a very long time that ignited something within him; it was the trepidation involved in pumping Mickey for that information. Another level; another condition to be bested. As he'd told Kersh, he was not doing anything for Roger Biddleman. It was all for himself, to see how far he could go, see how deeply he could submerge himself in Mickey O'Shay and Jimmy Kahn's world.

Suddenly, the prospect of pumping Mickey about Horace Green's death appealed to him.

He turned and looked at Biddleman, standing with his back toward the mirror, his hands still on his hips.

"You want it," he said, "you got it."

Katie was studying at the kitchen table of John's father's house when he arrived. She heard him approach but did not turn and look up from her textbook immediately. Finally, as he lingered in the kitchen doorway, making noise with the zipper on his leather jacket, she spoke.

"There's Tylenol in the upstairs bathroom under the sink," she said. "Take something before you get pneumonia."

He came up behind her and placed one hand on the top of her head. Like a curious bird perched on a branch, he peered over her head and ran his eyes over the spread of textbooks.

"Exams?" he said.

She closed the book. Turned in her seat. Looked at him. "You don't look well."

"I'm just tired."

"Are you going back out tonight?"

"No," he said, pulling off his jacket, "I'm here tonight. Or home. Wherever you want to be."

"Are you hungry? I just made tuna fish sandwiches, but I can make you something hot . . ."

Draping his jacket over the back of one of the chairs, he shook his head. "How's Dad?"

Her eyes held him, unmoving. For a second, she appeared to him like a stranger. She no longer looked young and full of energy. Over the past couple weeks, something had changed inside her—in her face, in her eyes, in the lines around her mouth. Had it really been just recently he'd thought of her as a young schoolgirl? Imagined her at Coney Island, losing a shoe on the Tilt-A-Whirl? What had happened to that red-eyed panda bear she'd won for him, anyway?

"You're mad," he said, smoothing back her hair.

"He's real sick, John," she said. Tears filled her eyes. "I mean . . . you know . . . it's coming down to the end here and . . ." But her voice trailed off.

"And?" he said, but she just shook her head. "What?"

"Nothing."

"I'm gonna check up on him," he said, not knowing what else to tell her. And even as he turned down the hallway and moved toward the stairs, he could feel his wife's eyes on him.

Upstairs, only the dim yellow light from the hallway bathroom was on. The door itself was half-closed, casting a thin sliver of light along the otherwise dark carpet.

His father was in his childhood bed; the old man turned his head in his direction when he entered the room.

"Hey, Pop, how you feeling?"

"John . . ." His father's voice was paper-thin. John felt his own body tremble at the sound. "I need . . . help me . . . up . . ."

"Pop . . . what?"

"Bathroom," his father managed, pulling back the bedsheets from his withered body.

"Wait," he said, "I'll help you."

It was like lifting an empty husk. The old man couldn't have weighed a hundred pounds. He closed one hand around his father's wrist, felt bone, shuddered. A second hand went to the old man's back, and it was like caressing some exotic desert plant. He felt helpless, powerless, impossibly small. He hated himself for his weakness, hated himself for his inability to fix things, mend things.

"You've been taking your medication?"

But his father was too weak to respond.

Though the bathroom was only a few feet away, it seemed an eternity. Together, they walked like children, like two generations of an incapable breed. And halfway to the bathroom he found himself wishing for the journey to be over, for them to reach the light, because his mind was reeling now, speeding like a runaway locomotive . . .

"Help," the old man said, trying to inch open the bathroom door.

"Relax, Pop, I got it . . ."

The bathroom was overly bright. He winced and tightened his grip on his father's wrist, his father's frail back. He could feel the shift of the old man's shoulder blades through his cotton pajamas.

Here, in the light, they were both exposed.

"Do you . . . Pop, do you need . . ."

He was trying to pull the man's drawstring on his pajamas while maintaining balance at the same time. In his arms, his father felt nonexistent, like a prop, like the faint memory of the person he'd once been.

"Shit, *Dad*—"

His father was not cooperating. One of the old man's hands flailed out, knocking his son's hand away. One of his bare feet lifted an inch or two off the tile floor, toes rigid . . . then the heel stamped down.

"Pop—"

A foamy string of vomit dribbled down the front of his father's pajamas. Shocked, frightened, John snapped his head up and saw his father's eyes had rolled back into his head. The flailing hand continued to flail at his side, the fingers working in meaningless semaphore.

"Katie! Katie!" In an instant, his father's body collapsed in his arms. Holding him tight, he could feel the seizures wrack the old man's body. "Katie! Call an ambulance!"

There was pounding on the stairwell—footsteps?—and the lights in the bathroom suddenly seemed too bright, too comic. The lid of the toilet seat cracked down against the porcelain with deafening abruptness.

And standing there in the throes of fever, his father convulsing in his arms, John saw the world sway and bend before his eyes.

The rest of the evening was spent in a blinding delusion of sharp hospital light fixtures and the stink of latex and antiseptic.

John remained staring straight ahead at the blank hospital wall, Katie asleep with her head on his shoulder. His face held no expression; his eyes had softened to a dull gray. The steady course of Katie's breathing beside his ear did little to soothe him.

A young female doctor stepped out into the hallway clicking a pen. "Mr. Mavio?"

Secluded behind a green plastic curtain in the ICU, his father lay unconscious in a bed that looked ridiculously large for him. He had become, in just a couple months, a shadow of the man he'd once been.

"Your father's suffered a severe stroke caused by a buildup of pressure in the location surrounding the tumor. He's currently unconscious, though if he should ever regain consciousness, it will not be without complete dysfunction of all motor skills, including speech and, according to his papillary response, vision loss . . . hearing . . . paralysis . . ."

The words faded around him, broken like clouds of smoke in the air.

"Thank you," he said to the doctor and slipped out into the hallway.

Katie was still asleep in the waiting room, her head against the back of her chair. He paused just outside the ICU and watched her for some time before heading down the hall toward the bathroom.

There, in his own soundless way, he cried.

CHAPTER THIRTY-TWO

Corky McKean, one of the two brothers who owned the Cloverleaf, had a face like a whipped pit bull and a spine as crooked as the contours of a woodpile. His hands were big—lumberjack's hands—with curled, blackened nails at the tips of his fingers. Scarred by adolescent acne, Corky's cheeks resembled two tic-tac-toe boards, separated by a nose as flat as a bottle cap.

As the day manager, Corky rarely remained at the Cloverleaf after dark, but the sudden snowstorm that had accosted the city just prior to his routine departure caused him to loiter behind the bar, smoking a Macanudo while seated on a keg of beer. He was notorious for his hatred of snow—feared it, some said—ever since he spun off an icy road and slammed into a tree somewhere upstate. Now he continued to peek through the Cloverleaf's narrow window while he smoked to watch the storm's progression. He silently hoped it would let up soon: he had a can of baked beans and a couple of skin flicks at home that he was anxious to abuse.

John entered in a gust of wind and snow, and hurried straight for the bathroom. The Cloverleaf had become familiar to him over the passage of weeks. As he walked the length of the room, he offhandedly took notice of the faces at the tables and around the bar. Some he recognized—Boxie, the old boozer, was seated at the end of the bar; likewise, the kid in the knitted Islanders cap hugged a table toward the back of the room—and some he did not.

The bathroom was empty. John pushed open the stall door, slipped inside, and attempted to work the busted lock to no avail. The stall was tiny, hardly large enough for someone to stand upright, let alone sit down on the toilet. The back of the stall door was decorated with crude graffiti and at least twenty different phone numbers. Behind him, the flecked rim of the toilet bowl prodded the backs of his knees.

John unzipped his jacket and lifted his fleece pullover above his waist. There was a pocket sewn to the inside lining of the fleece, in which a reel-to-reel recorder the size of an audiocassette was secured. A wire from the recorder was taped to his chest and ran the length of his upper body, capped by a minuscule microphone just below the neckline of his shirt. He adjusted the reel-to-reel against his stomach and straightened the fleece, then his jacket. He hated to wear the wire, but knew it was better than using a portable transmitter; it was more reliable for recording and, blessedly, did not require the surveillance team to crowd too close around the Cloverleaf.

By the sink, John slipped his gloves off and stuffed them into the back pocket of his jeans. Jiggling the handles on the sink, he waited for the water to turn warm before he slipped his hands beneath the stream and briskly rubbed them together.

Back at the bar, someone had selected a U2 song on the juke. It played softly, the volume low. He pulled himself up onto a stool, rubbing his eyes with the heels of his hands. His illness was in limbo now, debating whether it was leaving him or preparing for one final, devastating assault.

Corky McKean, rising from his keg and snuffing the life from his cigar in a glass ashtray, ambled his way over to him. "What'll it be?"

He shook a finger at a coffee machine that sat on the counter, resting on top of a stack of soggy magazines. "Think I can get a cup?"

Picking at something in his teeth, Corky turned and began rifling through a box of mugs. He found one, poured half a cup of coffee, and set it in front of him. Bringing the mug to his lips, John noticed—quite aware of the irony—the letters NYPD stenciled in white across the side of the mug. The coffee was lukewarm and tasted like baking soda, but he didn't complain.

Since the recording of Sean Sullivan had been presented to the Secret Service, Roger Biddleman, and Detective Glumly of the NYPD, two connections had been made. According to the detective, he'd recently uncovered a decapitated head and the remains of a male torso plugged in the chest by two bullet holes made from a .22-caliber gun. After hearing Sean Sullivan's recording, Glumly backtracked and pulled all known dental records for all the Horace Greens in and around the city. One of the records matched the teeth in the severed head: Horace Green from Queens, New York.

The second connection made was that the .22 retrieved from Evelyn Gethers's Lincoln had been the gun used to shoot Green twice in the chest. A second sweep for fingerprints resulted in the same conclusion the first sweep had yielded—that only the deceased Douglas Clifton's prints were on the gun. Hearing this information, something had rattled and turned over inside John's head, though he couldn't quite put his finger on what it was. There was now another connection between Douglas Clifton and Mickey and Jimmy, other than just the counterfeit money; now they shared a *murder.* But how did it all connect? And each time, just when John thought he was able to make some sense out of the equation, his thoughts dispersed like blown dust.

A cold wind struck his back.

Mickey entered the Cloverleaf alone. John turned when he heard the door open and watched Mickey cross the threshold, his thick-soled boots leaving puddles of slush on the hardwood. Mickey's eyes rose to meet John's, but the creep didn't sit down beside him; instead, Mickey made his way around the other end of the bar and sat by himself. When Corky McKean turned his mongrel face to him, Mickey ordered a shot of Irish cream and a Guinness—what Mickey referred to as a milkshake.

John watched Mickey from over the rim of his coffee. *Already twenty minutes late from the time we're supposed to meet,* he thought, *and now the asshole's drinking beer and pretending he doesn't know me.* Yet he'd come to expect such behavior from him.

When John finished his coffee, he set the mug down and folded his hands on the counter, making no attempt to disguise his aggravation. Mickey continued to look in his direction, and surely he could tell John was growing angry, but he did not say anything and would only turn back to his beer and stare at the glass with the glazed-over look of a young child.

Finally, John got up, paid his tab, and began heading toward the door.

"John." Mickey's voice was not urgent, merely conversational.

He turned, flipping up his jacket collar, and did not say a word. A shaft of moonlight crossed his face from the single window beside the door.

Grinning, shaking his head, Mickey motioned for him to come over and sit beside him. Still annoyed, he crossed the floor and claimed the stool beside Mickey.

"What's with this silent shit?" John said. "Thought you were being watched or something."

"You and that kid Sullivan discuss the job?" Mickey said, turning the bottom of his beer glass toward the ceiling.

"We'll do it."

Still grinning, Mickey faced him and nodded. Their faces were too close; he could smell the alcohol coming off Mickey in waves.

The stink made his stomach angry. The guy's eyes looked like the black, soulless eyes of a catfish.

"Good," Mickey said. "We leave here, I'll get you the guns. You got what you owe me for the other one yet?"

"In my car."

"Good deal."

Outside, they crawled into the Camaro and drove in the direction of the candy store and Mickey O'Shay's apartment.

"Money's under your seat," he told Mickey.

Leaning forward, Mickey reached under his seat and pulled out four fifties bound together by a paper clip. Without saying a word, he folded the money and stuffed it into his coat.

"How come you didn't just come to me about the hit?" he asked after a few moments of silence. "Why bring that kid Sullivan in?"

"What are you talkin' about?" Mickey said. He was bent slightly forward in his seat, his eyes dull, his tongue prodding the inside of one cheek.

"This thing ain't exactly a two-man job," he said. "I could use the whole five grand."

"Just making sure the job gets done," Mickey said. "I'm payin' out five grand. Whatever you work out with the kid is your business."

"Had a couple drinks at that bar the other night with him," he said, forcing a grin. "Actually, he told me the funniest goddamn story about you and Jimmy and some Jewish lone shark . . ."

"What?" Mickey's exasperation was like a strum on an out-of-tune guitar. Immediately, he had become rigid in his seat, the long strands of his hair set in motion by the hot air gusting from the console vents.

"Said you grabbed this guy, this bookie, cut him up and took his book. Said you guys were collecting from the book. I just thought that was the funniest damn—"

"What the hell are you talking about?" Mickey spat, turning

to face him and leaning his right arm along the console. Something inside Mickey O'Shay had snapped. The look in his eyes now was too similar to the look on the night he'd clobbered Dino "Smiles" Moratto. "Why the hell are you bringing that up?"

"Jesus Christ, Mickey, relax! Sit the hell back and relax. All right? The hell's the big deal?"

"Sullivan told you that?"

"Yes—"

"Where'd he hear it? Who told him?"

"I don't know. Didn't ask."

"What else did he say?" Mickey was breathing heavy now, his nostrils flared, his lips pressed tightly together. "That little asshole . . ."

"Nothing, nothing—what? Mickey, man, chill the fuck out."

Mickey remained silent for several seconds, his eyes boring through the side of John's head. John could almost taste the shock and anger coming off Mickey in undulating waves, like burning jet fuel in the air. Then, like an engine ticking down, Mickey slowly adjusted himself in the passenger seat, pushed his head back against the headrest, and placed the palms of his hands flat on his knees. His breathing regained a slow, labored consistency. Staring straight through the windshield, Mickey said, "Why you bringin' that up?" His voice was low and inconspicuous again, though the outer layers of his tone still bristled with tension.

He shrugged, glancing at Mickey from the corner of his eye, then back at the road. "It was just talk. Forget it. But if you don't like what this kid says, why you putting him with me?"

"Quit talkin' about that."

There was suddenly no doubt in his mind that Mickey and Jimmy had committed the very crime Sean Sullivan told him about. And not just that—it was the hidden rage, the quick snaps and breaks in Mickey's character that reinforced the notion, and forced John to wonder just how many other people Mickey O'Shay and Jimmy

Kahn had murdered.

He pulled the car along Tenth Avenue, the tires peeling through slush. The streets had been plowed, but the sidewalks were still blanketed in snow. A few pedestrians trudged through the snow, their heads down, swaddled in thick winter coats and billowing scarves.

He stopped the car in front of Mickey's complex, letting the engine idle. In all the time he'd spent around Mickey O'Shay, he hadn't once been back to the guy's apartment. He pictured a one-room flat with bare walls and peeling plaster; a litter of empty beer bottles strewn about the floor; hardly any change of clothes; an unmade bed with stained, yellowed sheets.

"Wait here," Mickey said, and stepped out into the night. He did not head up to his apartment, however, as John had anticipated; instead, he hustled across the street and dashed into Calliope Candy.

"He's going into the candy store," he said, drumming his gloved fingers on the steering wheel. A line of cars slipped along Tenth Avenue, Kersh's sedan among them. John caught the passing taillights of Kersh's car just as it rolled by, and he watched it continue up Tenth Avenue and turn left onto West 53rd Street at the intersection. Darkness all around him, a light snowfall pattered down on the Camaro's windshield. He watched it with some indifference, recalling his childhood winters in Brooklyn.

Mickey appeared across the street with a brown paper bag under one arm. Even beneath the glow of the street lamp, he looked capable of blending into the brick façade of the candy store and out of sight at will. Yet Mickey was incapable of keeping himself hidden for very long. People like him never stayed hidden, no matter how much heat was on them. There was always something else that eventually coaxed them from their holes and out into the limelight again, always a piece of bait dangling from a hook to whet their appetite. All the circuitry in Mickey's body was wired to a central hub driven by greed and blistering insanity.

Teeth chattering, Mickey hopped back in the car and slammed the door. Opening the bag on his lap, he peered inside, reached in with one hand. He pulled out a .25 Beretta and handed it to John.

"There's another one in here for Sean," Mickey said, "plus ammo. And take a look at this."

Mickey removed a narrow cardboard box from the bag, popped open the lid. The box was stuffed with newspaper. Shifting the paper aside, Mickey produced a short, black, cylindrical metal tube with a dime-sized opening at one end and screw-on threads at the other: a silencer.

"Jesus Christ. Where'd you get that?"

"Got a guy who makes 'em for us. High quality. What do ya think? Think you could move any of these?"

"In a heartbeat. How many you got?"

"A few right now," Mickey said, "but they're sold. I can get you some more in a couple days."

"What's the price?"

Mickey shrugged. "Two hundred."

"That's about the price of the guns," he said.

"I can go one seventy five," Mickey said, "but that's it. Besides," he continued, stuffing the silencer back into the box, "guns you can get anywhere. *These* things though . . ."

"Can I buy that one from you?"

"You got the money now?"

"Not on me, but you know I'm good for it. I can get it to you tomorrow."

"Like I said," Mickey muttered, stuffing the box into his jacket pocket, "these are sold."

John took the bag from Mickey's lap, poked around inside, and examined the second gun. Nodding his head, he replaced both weapons back into the bag, rolled it closed, and stashed it away in the back seat.

"You talk to your guy about dropping the points on the counterfeit?"

"You know," Mickey said, "I been thinking about that. I can drop the points down to fifteen percent."

"No," he said. "Still too high, Mickey. I can't earn off that."

Mickey stuck out his lower lip. "Okay," he said, "ten percent."

John hoped the presumptuous look on his face didn't register with Mickey. Ten percent meant they were most likely getting the money directly from the printer after all. And how suddenly Mickey had dropped the price—

"Ten percent . . . *but here's the deal,*" Mickey added, the timbre of his voice rising. "You buy a million from us."

He uttered a laugh and turned away from Mickey. "A *million?* Shit, man, you growing this stuff in your *house?*" He whistled, pushed his head back against the headrest. "That's a lot of money coming from my end. At ten percent, that's a hundred grand."

"Is that a problem?" Mickey said.

"Yeah," he told him, "but it's worth a try. It's gonna take me some time to line up customers. I wanna get everybody in line before I make that kind of buy."

"How long?"

"At least a couple weeks. But I'm interested. Ten percent gives me a lot of interest."

"I know," said Mickey.

"In the meantime," he said, "see what you can do about those silencers."

"How many you want?"

He considered. "Can you do five?"

"No problem."

"I'll see how quick I move 'em, then maybe we can talk about more."

"Don't—" Mickey's words died in his mouth as his eyes locked onto something just past John's head. And just as he was about to turn to see what was going on behind him, a quick rapping sounded against the driver's side window.

A uniformed police officer stood on the other side of the window, inches from his face.

Without waiting for John to roll down the window, the cop pointed toward the intersection with two fingers. His face a bleached white, his eyebrows knitted together, the cop shouted, "Get this car outta here now! You can't park here, buddy. Move it! Move it!"

He switched the car in gear just as Mickey popped open the passenger door. For one crazy instant, he visualized Mickey pulling a gun from the waistband of his pants and firing round after round into the police officer, sending the officer crashing against the front of the building behind him in a spray of blood. It was frightening just how quickly his mind managed to summon such an image, as if he'd known for some time just how close to the edge Mickey really walked—just how *gone,* how mentally *fragile*—and how quickly things could go bad.

"Move!" the officer shouted again, flecking the window with spit. "Now!"

Mickey slammed the door shut and hurried across the street toward Calliope Candy. The top half of the silencer box, too big for the pocket, jutted like a bone from his coat. The streetlight on the corner painted his shadow in great leaps across the piling snow that covered the sidewalk.

Not once did he turn to look back.

Rolling a handball between his hands, resting one leg up on his desk, John said, "They're looking to unload the last of what they got. That's why they've dropped the points. And that's why they want me to take the whole million."

The glow of his computer screen reflected on his face, Kersh nodded. He was picking apart a Styrofoam cup, with little interest, and rolling the broken pieces into tiny white balls. They'd just finished listening to the reel-to-reel recording made earlier that day. At the part where John had pushed Mickey about Horace Green's murder, Kersh stood, paced around his desk, like a basketball fan whose team is down by five points with seven seconds left on the clock.

"A deal this big," John continued, "will flush out Kahn."

"Jimmy Kahn," Kersh muttered to himself. He'd been listening to the recordings made from the wire taps daily, and had been ultimately disappointed. Mickey had his greasy fingers into everything, but there was still nothing concrete on Jimmy Kahn. Even when the two of them spoke over the phone, their messages were so cryptic or so insipid that they proved nothing but a waste of time.

"Another thing," he said. "I think they're making the silencers in the candy store."

"Glumly picked up that guy Laughlin today," Kersh said. "The bartender."

"And?"

"Big guy collapsed like a little girl," Kersh said. "If he's scared of Mickey O'Shay, he isn't saying. Said he didn't know anyone who'd be after him—but Glumly pulled his record. Guy's been arrested a couple times for moving drugs. Mostly marijuana."

"There could be a million reasons Mickey wants him dead." He shook his head and rubbed his forehead. "Or no reason at all . . ."

"Glumly's moving the bartender to a safe house in Queens for a while. Cable TV, hot meals. Probably the best the punk's ever lived."

"Meanwhile," John said, "let's make sure we can get the flash money for this counterfeit deal and hope Kahn shows, 'cause the boss-man isn't gonna part with a hundred grand."

"Kahn may show for the silencers," Kersh said. "That's fifteen years mandatory right there."

He could tell Kersh was uncomfortable about the million-dollar deal. However, John didn't know if Kahn would show just to sell him silencers; in the past, he'd only showed when John was selling. And even if he did, John had to get him involved with the deal; just being there was not good enough. They could put Mickey away for life, but Kahn would eventually be back on the streets. And in the time he'd spent around them, John was quick to realize that with Jimmy Kahn on the streets, another Mickey O'Shay would always came along. That was the problem. For this thing to be successful, they'd have to nail them both for a long, long time. Maybe Bill Kersh would be satisfied with a cheap bust for Jimmy Kahn, but John wouldn't.

"Anyway," Kersh said with exaggerated zeal, "it's late and I'm tired. I'm going to go home and watch the Discovery Channel until I fall asleep. There's a killer special on prehistoric sharks I've been dying to see." He stood and struggled with his jacket. "You should go home, too. You look about eight months behind on your beauty rest."

Kersh left, and for a while John listened to the larger man's footfalls creak down the office corridor. There was the familiar grind of the elevator being called to their floor, the *ding!* of the bell as it arrived, and the lethargic *swoosh* as the elevator doors opened. After a second or two, the grinding started up again, and he listened to the elevator slowly descend.

Closing his eyes, he reclined in his chair, squeezing the handball in one hand. The events of the past two months whizzed through his brain like a video on fast-forward. It wasn't until the phone at his desk rang, startling him that he realized he'd fallen asleep.

It was one of the agents at the duty desk. "John. Wasn't sure you were still here."

"What's up?"

"There's a woman here to see you. She looks pretty upset."

"Her name?"

"Says her name is Tressa Walker."

The handball rolled to the edge of the desk, paused for a moment . . . then fell off; it bounced a few feet away from the desk, then began rolling across the floor to the wide bank of office windows. Looking up at the windows, John saw his face reflecting back at him.

"I'll be right there," he said, and hung up the phone.

CHAPTER THIRTY-THREE

INSIDE A SMALL, WINDOWLESS INTERVIEW ROOM ON the main floor of the New York field office, Tressa Walker sat at the end of a long rectangular table with her white, fisted hands pushed into her lap. When John opened the door and stepped inside, the young woman looked up nervously. For a split second, she looked as though she wanted to rise and quickly run out of the room. Fear and confusion registered on her face, pulling the lines of her mouth and eyes into sad fishhooks. It had been close to a month since he'd last seen her, and it now looked as though the girl had aged twenty years.

"Tressa," he said, moving into the room and shutting the door behind him, "what are you doing here? You can't come around here like this. You wanted to talk, you should have called me."

He took a seat not across from her but beside her, with one empty chair between them. Her eyes had a difficult time staying on him, or in any one place for any length of time. She looked much more frightened now than on the evening at McGinty's. The worry in her face prompted him to lean forward in his chair, suddenly worried that something had gone wrong, horribly wrong.

"What?" he said. "What is it?"

"They're asking questions about you," she said in an unsteady voice. It was as if she were confessing her sins to a priest, embarrassed by her misdeeds and terrified of the consequences. "Mickey and Jimmy. They're goin' around the neighborhood asking about you. They saw me tonight, cornered me, started pumping me for information. I didn't . . . I mean . . . when I saw them, saw who they were, I knew right away something was wrong. Christ." Her body was trembling. "John, what the hell's going on? What's taking so long?"

"First of all, calm down."

Nodding rapidly, she formed her lips into a wide circle and sucked in a deep breath.

"What did they want to know?" he said. "What did you tell them?"

"I didn't tell them nothing," she insisted. "They cornered me, scared the *shit* outta me. I thought . . ." She fell silent, not needing to continue. Tressa Walker had thought she was going to die.

"What did they ask you?" he pressed her. "What did they say about me?"

"No, nothing," she said, shaking her head. She fumbled a cigarette from her purse and lit it with one shaking hand. "Just . . . they just wanted to know stuff . . . I don't know . . ." She pulled a long, hard drag from the smoke. The insides of her cheeks almost touched. "I can't give 'em answers for all their questions, John. I'm gettin' scared. They start askin' me things I don't got answers to, I screw up and say the wrong thing, they're gonna *know.* These guys don't play around. What the hell is taking you so long to get them?"

"We're working it." He tried to sound confident and convincing. "We're close, but it takes time. You just have to chill out. It's all right."

"It's *not.* They're still trying to move the money through Francis, you know, but he don't have no buyers lined up. And really, he's too goddamn scared to deal with them anymore." Another pull on her cigarette and John thought her eyes would roll back into her head. "This is taking too long, and I don't like it. I wanna get out of the city now, get away from them. I don't like where this is going. That witness protection thing we talked about—you gotta get me out of here *now* . . ."

"Listen to me—Tressa, you have to stay calm. They're just pushing you—that's all. We've been doing some deals, and they're starting to trust me now—"

"They don't trust nobody."

"If we move you out now," he continued, "it'll raise suspicion. It's better for you to hang here until this thing blows over. They're just trying to put a scare on you, see if you tell them anything. As long as you *don't,* there's nothing to worry about."

But he could see from the look on her face and from the nervous shift of her eyes that any further pressuring by the West Side boys would surely result in her collapse, regardless of what the penalty might be. What had seemed like her ticket out of Hell's Kitchen just a short month or so ago now seemed like a death sentence.

"They been trying to find out where you come from, who you've dealt with," Tressa explained. "They been whispering your name all through Hell's Kitchen, see if anybody's ever heard of you. John, they find out you're Secret Service, they'll fucking cut me, fucking *hurt*—"

"Relax."

He realized then just how fragile a foundation the entire case was built on. One word—one false word, false action, false *anything*—put a lot of people in danger.

"This thing's almost over," he told her. It was a promise he made to himself more than to her. "A little while longer and we'll grab them. Just hang in and be smart. Nothing bad is gonna happen."

Looking down at her lap, she said, "I hope so."

Yet she already sounded defeated.

CHAPTER THIRTY-FOUR

On the morning of December 23, roughly fifteen hours before he would have a gun pointed at his head, John Mavio awoke early and in a good mood. Slipping his pants on, he turned to watch Katie sleeping in bed. She stirred and twisted her body around to stretch across the width of the mattress. She'd grown accustomed to sleeping alone; he could tell just by the way her body curled into a comma, taking up both sides of the bed simultaneously even in her sleep. That was the way he'd sometimes find her when he would come home at night.

He walked silently down the hallway and crept into the spare room at the front of the apartment. There were still boxes here from the move—now just mostly his junk—and the television and VCR had been propped on a stained butcher block. Beside the television, Katie had erected and decorated a scrawny-looking fake tree for Christmas.

Silently, in the gloom of morning, he began wrapping his wife's Christmas presents.

In the days since Tressa Walker's surprise visit to the field office, he'd purchased two more guns from Mickey, neither of which had been linked to any unsolved homicides or possessed any of Jimmy

Kahn's fingerprints. And in the passage of those days, he could feel the urgency to move things along like a festering disease at the pit of his stomach. Each subsequent time he met with Mickey, he found it very difficult to put Tressa's face out of his mind. The nervous sound of her voice served as a constant ticking inside his head. He feared it was only a matter of time before the cracks in the structure of his undercover operation started to show.

"You're up early," Katie said from the doorway.

"Did I wake you?"

"Not you," she said. "The phone. Didn't you hear it ringing? Bill Kersh is on the line."

On the phone, Kersh sounded more energetic than usual.

"What's up, Bill?"

"Sorry to ruin your day, but we gotta roll out."

"What's the matter?"

"You'll never guess who just called me."

Morris, Evelyn Gethers's butler, stood outside a strip of storefronts along the Bowery. Dressed in gray Brooks Brothers slacks, a pin-stripe shirt, and a long black coat, he looked out of place among the subverted streets and devastated buildings. More incriminating was Morris's black El Dorado, buffed to a dull shine and idling in a street surrounded by burned-out VW Beetles and an old Comet stripped of its chrome.

Following Kersh's phone call, John had headed into the city and met Kersh at the field office. Now, in Kersh's sedan, they both pulled up together behind Morris's Cadillac. Morris approached John's side of the car and began speaking before he was even out the door.

"I thought I should call you, thought you should know. It's—come with me—it's up here."

The road rose to a slight incline. John and Kersh followed Morris up the sidewalk. To their left, five-story tenements pressed against the colorless sky. To their right, a chain-link fence surrounded a series of dilapidated storefronts, each of their windows soaped, their fronts the bleached color of bone. Metal roll-down doors covered some of the entranceways, most of them locked with industrial-sized padlocks and chains.

"We've had this space for years," Morris continued. "It's all Mr. Gethers's stuff. His wife refused to part with it after his death, so she had it all tucked away here. It's all junk, really, but it has some sentimental value to her, I suppose."

Morris led them through the fence and over to one of the storefronts. They lined the street here, identical brick buildings with spray-painted steel roll-down doors. Some of them had numbers painted above the doors, but time and the elements had caused the numbers to fade. Most were hardly legible.

While Morris dug around for a set of keys in his coat, John rubbed his gloved hands together, exhaled warm breath onto the palms. The day before Christmas Eve, but one would never notice down here: the streets looked vacant, the windows in the buildings like blind, gaping eyes. As far as he could see, the only evidence of red and green were the cheerless bulbs of the traffic lights at each intersection.

"Here we are," Morris muttered, finding the appropriate key. He bent and slipped the key into the zigzag niche at the base of a padlock. The lock was as large as a grown man's fist. It popped open, and Morris slid it from the loop that held the giant roll-down door closed. "I'm going to need some assistance . . ."

Bending down, giving his hands one last rub, John grabbed the lip at the bottom of the roll-down door and helped Morris hoist it off the ground. It opened with surprising effortlessness. Above their heads, the beams that secured the door rattled and clanged like the chains of Marley's ghost. There was a grinding of gears that echoed through the dull afternoon. One final push, and the door locked in place.

Behind the roll-down door was a smaller door, accessible after a simple turn of the knob. Morris reached out and unlocked this door, too, turned the knob, and held the door open.

The inside of the place was dark, and it took their eyes a few moments to adjust as they stepped inside.

"What's that smell?" Kersh said, taking small, shuffling steps and sniffing the air.

John recognized it, too. It smelled like the computer room back at the office, after the ink jet printers became too hot and overworked.

Morris felt along the wall for a light switch. He clicked it on, throwing shadows into corners and crevices.

John whistled.

At first glance, the stuff that filled the room looked like junk jettisoned from the Museum of Natural History's basement. Packaged wooden crates lined most of the walls, unlabeled and in a variety of sizes. The center part of the room served as a collage of ancient, mismatched artifacts: splintered furniture; a number of headless dress-maker's dummies; a large mattresses, sodden with mildew and folded into an upside-down V; a dusty leather trunk with brass buckles; what appeared to be an interior door of a house, the knob and hinges still attached; a bookshelf littered with wires and cables and hoses coiled like snakes. And that was only the beginning. The room went far back, most of it cloaked in shadow. With each step closer to the rear, more and more of Charles Gethers's forgotten relics appeared, like great reaches of stalagmites.

"Come toward the back," Morris said, already on his way past the junk. It was like maneuvering through an obstacle course. "Like I've said," the butler continued, "Mrs. Gethers has kept this place running for some time. She obviously pays the electric bill, but as you can imagine, no one comes here often and the bill is not much. However," he added, swinging one leg around a large ceramic lamp with some difficulty, "I've recently received the electric bill to cover the past several months. It was through the roof. I thought there had to be some mistake, so I called the company—but they insisted it was correct. So I figured I'd come down here and see what the heck was going on. That's when I discovered this."

Morris stopped abruptly toward the back of the room, and John nearly slammed into the man's back. Behind him, Kersh grunted and knocked over the ceramic lamp Morris had been careful to avoid.

The first thing John noticed were the two large machines that rested against the back wall. He immediately recognized them for what they were: dry offset printing presses. That was the smell he and Kersh had noticed upon entering the storage room—the smell of ink. Lots of it. He was aware of Kersh saddling up beside him, then pausing, just as dumbfounded by the presses as John. When they finally averted their eyes, they glanced at each other with a twin look of amazement on their faces.

This was where the money was printed.

Yet the printing presses were not what Morris had taken them here to see. The butler was looking in the direction opposite of the presses, pointing to a jumbled swath of clothing balled against the floor. Behind the clothing was a New York Jets duffel bag, the canvas dotted with specks of spilled ink. More ink had dried like syrup on the cement floor behind the duffel bag.

"These are his. Clifton's," Morris said. "I recognize his clothes." He turned to the agents, scowling. "That bastard's been living here."

It occurred to John that Morris was not aware Douglas Clifton had taken a nosedive out his hospital window last month. And although the butler would have undoubtedly received some great satisfaction from the knowledge, John did not say anything to him about it.

Instead, he walked slowly around the printing presses. "These presses," he said. "Mr. Gethers . . ."

"He was in publishing," Morris said. "It was his career. As you know, it turned him into a very wealthy man. These were his first two printing presses, I believe, when he was developing magazine prototypes, mockups . . . those sort of things." Morris cleared his throat. "Is there something wrong? What about these clothes? What about Mr. Clifton?"

"He had access to this place?" John asked the butler.

"Apparently he does," Morris said, "though neither myself or Mrs. Gethers knew about it until now."

"Anyone else?"

"Anyone else what?"

"Have access to this place?" John said. He bent down and peered around the side of one of the presses, then turned and glanced over at the pile of Clifton's clothes and the Jets duffel bag. The clothes looked hardened, molded to one another. They hadn't been worn in some time.

"Just myself and Mrs. Gethers," Morris said. Then, after a pause, he added rather unwillingly, "And, I suppose, anyone else our friend Clifton passed the key along to. Do you think he'll be back here this evening?"

Considering the mess Clifton must have left on the sidewalk below his hospital window, John said, "Doubt it." He leaned closer, looking at the spilled ink on the floor. "Bill . . . come take a look at this . . ."

"What?" Kersh said, leaning over one of John's shoulders.

"This ain't ink."

"What is it?" But at the last second, something clicked at the back of Kersh's throat, and John realized the older agent suddenly knew *exactly* what it was.

"Blood," John said. "Coagulated. Almost dry."

"I'm sorry?" Morris said, taking a hesitant step closer to the duffel bag. *"Blood?* Whose?"

If I had to guess, John thought, *I'd say this is where Douglas Clifton lost his hand.*

"John." There was an excited tremor in Kersh's voice. He felt the man's fingers close around his shoulder. "John . . . take a look . . ."

Turning his head to follow Kersh's finger, his eyes landed on a Rubbermaid trash receptacle, the triangular ecru corners of paper jutting from above the receptacle's rim. *Printing* paper.

Kersh went over to the receptacle, tipped it at an angle, peered inside. With one hand he fished out crinkled sheaves of paper, held them up, examined them in the light. Many of the discarded sheets of paper had partially printed hundred-dollar bills on them.

Cocking a thin eyebrow, Morris said, "What're those?"

"Waste," Kersh said, tossing the paper back into the receptacle. "Dry runs."

"Excuse me?"

John lifted some articles of clothing. They were damp and stiff, and he moved several articles in a heap at one time. Large, black roaches had taken up residence in the sodden channels and darkened creases of the clothing; they scattered like dust the moment they were struck by light. The powerful, coppery smell of blood mingled with the moist reek of mildew made his stomach caterwaul and roll over.

Reaching over the pile of clothing, John grappled with the zipper of the Jets bag, and with a series of rigid tugs he managed to unzip it.

"Bill." His own voice sounded very far away. "Bill, I got your Christmas present over here."

Inside the duffel bag and wrapped in lengths of cloth were the plates and negatives necessary for printing counterfeit hundred-dollar bills.

And buried beneath the plates and negatives was a million dollars worth of phony notes.

Back at the field office, John and Kersh set to work bagging the counterfeit money. Though John had wanted to leave the storage garage exactly as they'd found it to avoid arousing Mickey and Jimmy's suspicions, he knew the money needed to be confiscated. Now, at his desk, he'd counted it a number of times, examining the quality of the print, the matching serial numbers to the bills purchased during previous buy-throughs. These, like the other stacks he'd gotten from Mickey, were also banded and crisp. They even *smelled* new.

"This was it," he said to Kersh, who sat across from him at his desk. "This was the million they wanted me to move."

"I still can't imagine how they managed to print this much," Kersh said. "Or how they got their greasy hands on Lowenstein's plates and negatives."

"I wanna call Mickey," John said out of the blue, "set up a buy for the silencers tonight."

"Tonight? John, tomorrow's Christmas Eve."

"We don't need a whole team. Just you and me. We'll make it quick."

"You're hoping Kahn shows to sell the silencers?"

He was. He would have much rather nailed Jimmy Kahn for counterfeiting, but they had no direct evidence linking him. And now, with their counterfeit money mysteriously taken from the storage room, the million-dollar deal would be called off . . . unless they had a stash someplace else, which he didn't think they did. They had Mickey O'Shay by the balls, could lock him up for the rest of his life. If selling silencers was the only thing they'd be able to pin on Jimmy Kahn, then that would be better than nothing. Right now, he didn't want to think about Kahn slipping through his fingers.

"I just think we should pick up the pace," he told Kersh.

Kersh sighed. "What's the matter? Doesn't anyone make plans for the holidays anymore?"

CHAPTER THIRTY-FIVE

THERE WAS A STILLNESS TO THE NIGHT that seemed to presage some imminent disaster. Beneath the somber paleness of a midnight moon, the streets were wet and forbidding. Light traffic trickled north in a constant wave. Through the Camaro's windshield, John could see warm, yellow lights on in many of the high-rise windows. Christmas, like most everything else, came to Hell's Kitchen differently than to other parts of the city. Times Square and the Theater District, which flanked the eastern border of the Kitchen, celebrated festively, all shimmering lights, glitter, and glamour. Additionally, the more upscale locales along the Upper West Side, teetering on the cusp of a frozen Central Park, enjoyed a holiday ripe with new promise. But the residents of Hell's Kitchen were different. Their holidays were personal, quiet, and sacred, spent only with the closest of family members and in the solidarity of one's home. For them, there was no glittering lights or street decorations. There were no promises of good things to come.

Earlier on the phone, Mickey had been surprisingly receptive and anxious to meet with him. "Five silencers sittin' here waitin' for ya," he'd said, the hint of joviality in his voice more than just peculiar. Katie, on the other hand, had not been so pleased to hear her husband was putting in late hours around the holidays.

Now, as his eyes bounced between the console clock and the illuminated window of Calliope Candy, John just wished Mickey would hurry the hell up. As usual, the shade on the candy store window was pulled, but he could make out nebulous gray forms moving behind the shade toward the rear of the store. An indeterminate number of people were inside.

A figure appeared on the corner of Tenth and West 53rd Street—slumped, shoulders hunched. He knew immediately it was Mickey O'Shay.

"Mickey's coming down Tenth," he said into the transmitter. "He's alone."

Mickey got into the car, slammed the door, and slid his hands through his hair. He exhaled with great exaggeration, frosting his side of the windshield in a cloud of vapor.

"You're in a good mood," he said, looking at Mickey's profile silhouetted in front of the candy store's window. "Must be getting everything you asked for this year."

"Almost," Mickey said, turning to face him.

"Jesus Christ . . ." He shook a finger at Mickey's face. "You got—"

"What?"

"Your nose is bleeding."

A dark tassel of blood trickled from his left nostril and over his lips. It was a wonder he couldn't taste it.

"Shit," Mickey muttered, flipping down his visor and peering at his reflection in the small, rectangular mirror. He touched the line of blood with one finger, with the delicacy of someone pressing a finger to fine silk. "Look at that . . ." He pulled off one of his fingerless wool gloves and blotted his left nostril with it, keeping his head cocked slightly back. He remained in this position for several minutes—John watched the clock tick by—until the bleeding stopped and Mickey slipped the bloodied glove into the breast pocket of his coat.

"You know," John said, "me and Sean been sitting outside that restaurant for over a week now. That bartender Laughlin ain't showing up, and I'm wasting my time."

"Yeah," Mickey said, "I heard he ain't been around."

"So what's up with that?"

Mickey shrugged and glanced again at his reflection in the visor's mirror. "You see him, take the hit. You don't, then forget about it."

"Just like that? I could use that five grand."

"The hell you want me to do? Guy's a drunk with a big goddamn mouth. Somebody either nailed him first, or he just drank himself to death. Works for me either way." This final notion seemed to strike a chord with Mickey, and the corners of his mouth jerked upward into a bitter grin. Turning away from the mirror, his lips still stained with blood, Mickey said, "You got the money?"

"Yeah," he said. "Where's the silencers?"

Mickey blinked his eyes in what seemed like slow motion. "They're up in my apartment," he said. "Come on—we'll get 'em." One of his hands, the one still wearing the glove, pawed feebly at the door handle.

"Why didn't you just bring 'em down?"

"Five of them," Mickey said, his voice disjointed.

"Go up and get 'em," John said.

That same hungry grin was again threatening Mickey's lips. "Come on," he said. "Come on up."

He didn't like the look on Mickey's face. Again, he recalled Tressa Walker's nervous warning, remembered the way she shook and the way her eyes darted about the interview room.

They're asking questions about you . . .

"It's freezing out there. Why can't you just bring 'em down?" he said, suddenly conscious of his gun stashed away in his jacket pocket.

But Mickey's demeanor was softer than usual, probably from the coke he'd snorted, and he wouldn't let it go. "Come on. I'll show 'em to you. Five of 'em. Let's go." And he was out on the sidewalk before John could utter another word.

The instant John opened his door, a strong wind shook his body. It was damn cold. He could feel the rumblings of his fever boiling inside his stomach, could feel a mechanical throb at the center of his head.

Mickey was already halfway across the street.

He felt vulnerable walking across the street. Traffic along Tenth Avenue had dwindled to only a few passing motorists. Somewhere in the darkness, he knew Bill Kersh was silently cursing his name.

The money for the silencers was stuffed in an envelope in the inside pocket of his jacket. Once in Mickey's apartment—once the silencers made an appearance—he'd tell Mickey the money was back in the car somewhere. As long as Mickey didn't think he had the money on him, he might not try anything stupid in the apartment . . .

Mickey slipped into a tenement doorway and disappeared into the darkness. John hurried across the street, his footfalls echoing dully on the cement, and hopped the curb on the other side. His right hand in his jacket pocket and around the hilt of his gun, he passed through the tenement doorway and followed Mickey down a chilly, green-tiled corridor. A vent in the wall pumped cold air into the hallway. Overhead, fading fluorescent tube-lights hummed in their fixtures. They sounded alive and angry, filled with bees.

At the end of the corridor, Mickey hunched before an elevator, waiting for the doors to open. He did not look in John's direction, did not acknowledge him, and could have faded into the tiled walls with ease if he so desired.

The elevator doors opened, and John expected—*something.* The soft *ding!* and his hand tightened around the gun in his pocket, his finger lightly on the trigger, ready to start shooting at anything that might spring out of the elevator at him. But nothing did.

Mickey entered the elevator in silence and held the doors open for him.

The elevator hummed slowly up the floors, coming to a shaky standstill on the ninth floor. The doors opened and Mickey remained standing with his back against one wall, his eyes more lucid now than John had ever remembered seeing.

"Go on up to the roof," Mickey said. "I'll meet you there with the silencers."

They're asking questions about you.

Mickey stepped out into the hallway, and the elevator doors closed behind him. Running his eyes down the panel of buttons, he selected the top floor.

On the roof, the wind was fierce and unrelenting. The moment he stepped onto the tarred roof, he felt his body surrender to the whim of the wind. Before him, the lights of the city seemed to stretch on for an eternity.

Pulling his jacket tight around his body, he took a number of steps away from the door and out across the roof. Bullied by the wind, he could feel his fever returning with frightening rapidity, could feel his gloved hands trembling while they pulled tight the corners of his jacket. The throbbing in his head was tremendous now.

He stepped closer to the edge of the building. Twelve stories below, vehicles negotiated the one-way streets of Hell's Kitchen like rats in a maze with no reward.

Behind him, the tin door of the roof banged open. John spun around.

Mickey appeared in the doorway, half masked by night, and shuffled over to where John stood at the edge of the roof. In Mickey's hand was what looked like a .25 Beretta, held waist-high and pointing off to one side like an extension of his body.

The wind, coupled with the din of traffic, was all John could hear.

Mickey stepped up to the edge of the building and casually peered over the side. Like a bird, he seemed undaunted by the height. Mickey's eyes shifted from rooftop to rooftop, then settled momentarily on John. His eyes were bloodshot and raw-looking, the pupils dilated to pinpoints.

"You nervous?" Mickey said, facing back out over the city.

"Cold."

From his coat pocket, Mickey produced a silencer. With little emotion, he began screwing the silencer to the muzzle of the gun. His hair, bullied by the wind, covered his face.

"There's been some problems," Mickey said, his eyes still trained on the lights of the city.

"Like what?"

"We ran your plates," Mickey said, now turning to look back at him. He looked drained of life and as hard as granite. "They don't match your car."

"So what?"

Slowly, Mickey continued to screw on the silencer. "You come from nowhere. Nobody knows who the hell you are."

"That's better for you," he said. "I'm not hot."

"What happened to Ricky Laughlin?"

A peal of thunder far off in the distance seemed to underscore the question.

"Mickey," he said, pulling his coat tighter around his chest, "you got somethin' to say, say it."

Mickey O'Shay leveled the gun at John's head.

In an instant, the world seemed to freeze. Everything that had mattered just moments before suddenly ceased to exist. The world, in all its infinite authority, was now nothing larger than the breath of two mammals. Looking at Mickey O'Shay, John felt no fear inside his body at all—just an unrestrained hatred for his opponent, and for the fact that his *own* world could be deleted so completely and indifferently by the actions of a petty *nothing,* a lousy bullshit *noth-*

ing. It had come to this, and he was already imagining their deaths, their bodies spiraling down the side of the building and to the street below. He would die here tonight and resigned himself to that . . . but refused to die alone. One jump, before Mickey could even fire the gun, and a strong tackle would send them both over the edge of the roof . . .

Mickey turned and pointed the gun out over the city, pulled the trigger and fired two quick rounds. The gun bucked in his hand, and the silencer coughed twice and belched out a cloud of smoke.

John started breathing again.

"Hear that?" Mickey said, grinning. "Sounds like a goddamn baby fart." He fired two more rounds out over the street. One struck a tenement window on the other side of Tenth Avenue, shattering it. Mickey did not seem to notice. Still grinning, his eyes glowing, he held the gun out to John. "Wanna try?"

CHAPTER THIRTY-SIX

THE MORNING OF DECEMBER 24, AND IT was just another day in Hell's Kitchen.

Sitting at the bar in the shaft of daylight, Mickey ordered himself a drink and watched the lights of the jukebox across the room. Corky McKean, wearing a mistletoe necktie, placed the drink in front of him without bothering to look in his direction.

"Working the late shift tonight, Mickey. Goddamn holidays."

Mickey hardly heard the man. His brain was pulling slow revolutions in his head, and he could feel a migraine coming on. Once, when he was sixteen, he'd suffered a migraine so bad that he'd collapsed at the top of a tenement staircase and tumbled, unconscious, all the way to the bottom. When he awoke two days later, he was propped up in a bed with a busted nose, three fractures ribs, a broken wrist, a bruised coccyx, and an assortment of lacerations.

Thinking about John Esposito and the counterfeit money only made his headaches worse. Depending on his mood, Jimmy Kahn's opinion of Esposito vacillated, and he constantly unloaded his suspicions on Mickey. Some days, Jimmy was certain Esposito was a snitch. Other days, he didn't know *who* the guy was yet still wanted to do business with him. Jimmy's wavering opinions were starting to push Mickey over the edge. He respected Jimmy's opinions, but by this point, he could give two shits about Esposito and his background. They'd been dealing for over a month. If something was going to come down, he was already in the middle of things. Not that he was afraid. Besides . . . snitch or not, when Esposito's time was up, all bets were off. Good night.

Now it seemed like a million years since they'd gotten involved with the counterfeit money. In reality, it had only been a number of months ago, right after the whack-and-hack job on that Jewish bookie, Green . . .

Horace Green's death was quite fitting for the bastard: slow and painful. The only thing Mickey O'Shay despised more than a loan shark collecting vigs in his neighborhood was a *Jewish* loan shark collecting vigs in his neighborhood. And the night he and Jimmy had surprised him coming out of the Cloverleaf . . . Christ, the look on the bastard's face had been *priceless.*

"I thought we told you not to come around here no more," Jimmy had said. They were leaning against Green's car, refusing to move.

"And now he's drinking at our bars," he added.

Jimmy was relentless. "How much you collect tonight?"

Green said it was none of their business. But he looked frightened.

"Taking money from my neighborhood," Jimmy said, "looks *very much* like my business. What do ya think, Mickey?"

"I think we should check his book, see how much he collected."

There'd been a brief struggle to retrieve Green's book, but the bookie was quickly defeated. Jimmy had flipped through it and then passed it along to Mickey. Smiling to himself, Mickey had said, "Looks like you do pretty good for yourself, Green." Then he'd slipped Green's book into the waistband of his pants.

"Give it to me," Green said, his voice shaking, his body trembling against the trunk of his car.

"You don't need it no more," Jimmy said, pulling a .22 from his jacket and pointing it at Horace Green's chest. They were separated by only a few feet. "We're taking over your business."

Jimmy fired twice, and Green's body collapsed against the trunk of his car, folded at the waist, then toppled to the street. They snatched his car keys, stuffed Green's body in the trunk, and headed out to a warehouse down by the piers. Once there, in the seclusion of the warehouse, they popped the trunk to examine what other goodies Green might have been carrying . . . and noticed Green was still alive.

Mickey immediately burst out laughing. "Jimmy, Jimmy, *Jesus!* This fucker hangs in there!"

Jerking a thumb over one shoulder, Jimmy muttered, "Drag 'im out."

They'd used the warehouse before and had stocked it with implements for just such an occasion. Jimmy went to one corner and pulled back a burlap cloth from a pile of tools. With little emotion, he selected an ax and carried it back over to Green's car. By this time, Mickey had managed to pull the bookie out and drop him to the cement floor. At their feet, Horace Green struggled on his back, blood soaking his shirt and tie and bubbling out of his throat. He looked like a worm that had been stabbed with a sharp stick.

"Good," Jimmy said, kneeling over Green. "Give you one last chance to cut us in for a percentage, Mr. Green. Whattaya say?"

Green coughed up a gout of blood. His face was the color of dead fish, his eyes wide and blind and staring.

Jimmy leaned over Green's face, turned an ear to Green's mouth. In a high-pitched, cartoon voice, Jimmy muttered through the corner of his mouth, *"Just take the book, Jimmy! Just take the book!"*

Mickey started laughing.

"Very nice of you, Mr. Green," Jimmy said, back to his own voice. He stood and raised the ax over one shoulder. "Seein' how you're out of commission and everything . . ."

The ax came down, and Mickey broke out in another gale of laughter. Again, and he began to sober up and watch Jimmy work. Jimmy swung like a madman, his teeth gritted, his pale skin and cropped hair flecked with blood. Once he tired, he handed the blood-slicked ax to Mickey and told him to finish. "Keep going," Jimmy told him, "until nothing's left."

Blood spreads quickly on a concrete floor. Mickey got it under his shoes, in his hair, on his clothes. Yet he worked like a professional, his eyes never off his target, his hands blistering and muscles cramping but never slowing down.

Once Green had been adequately dismembered, Mickey dropped the ax to the floor, walked past Jimmy, who sat smoking on an overturned plastic bucket, and vomited in the corner. Beside him, Jimmy didn't say a word. And when he'd finished emptying his stomach, Mickey wiped his mouth with his sleeve, staggered over to Jimmy Kahn, and bummed a smoke from him.

In the end, the only items they wound up keeping from Green's car were the plates and negatives used to print counterfeit money. At first, they didn't even know what they were exactly—they'd never gotten involved with the counterfeit racket before, and they had no knowledge of printing. But then it quickly dawned on them.

"Keep 'em," Jimmy said.

"For what? To sell?"

"To hold onto," Jimmy said.

"How do these things work, anyway? Like . . . whattaya do?"

Jimmy just shrugged. He was unrolling a length of plastic bags.

"Why you think he had 'em in his trunk?" Mickey asked.

"What am I, his mother? The hell should I know? Here—help me wrap him up."

They didn't find a use for the plates until roughly one month later, when Douglas Clifton, one of their sidekicks, appeared on the scene with some news.

For some time, Clifton had been bleeding the bank account of some ritzy old broad from the Upper East Side. In only a short amount of time, Clifton had managed to work his way behind the wheel of the old woman's car, and was given a key to the house, his own bedroom and closet (complete with wardrobe), and spending money.

"How old is this broad?" Mickey had asked him once.

With little interest, Clifton had said, "I don't know. Maybe like sixty."

"Sixty? Jesus Christ, that's like my grandmother! You gotta *fuck* that?"

After some time, Clifton had gotten wind of an old shop-turned-storage warehouse in the Bowery the old woman owned. Swiping a set of keys, he headed down there one day to check the place out. It was like a museum of crap, but Clifton didn't know shit from sugar cubes and figured Mickey and Jimmy might be interested in cleaning the place out and seeing what they could move. Mickey headed down to the warehouse with him one afternoon to take a look around. Unimpressed, he told Clifton there was nothing worth a dime in the place . . . and then he spotted the two printing presses, and the bent and rusted wheels in his head began turning.

"What're these?"

"Beats me," Clifton said.

"They look like printing tables—presses—like where—you—"

Clifton did not understand the importance of the presses until Jimmy Kahn took a trip to the warehouse with Mickey and, *yes,* they agreed they *were* printing presses. They explained to Clifton about the plates and the negatives, and about killing Horace Green. Clifton seemed both amused and chagrined by the story and, at one point, the gun used to shoot Green twice in the chest was stashed in the trunk of the Lincoln Towncar Clifton drove around in.

Enter Harold Corcoran.

Corcoran was a small-time hustler who, at one time, had been employed as a printer's assistant for a printing press in the Bronx. When he found the time, and if the money was right, he would forge documents for some of the neighborhood crews. Over time, however, his predisposition toward cocaine and marijuana cost him that job and eventually landed him in a rehabilitation facility somewhere upstate. He served three months and was back on the street the same day of his release, getting his feet wet all over again.

Having worked some paltry jobs in Hell's Kitchen in the past, Corcoran had become friends with Jimmy Kahn, and Corcoran's father had even known Jimmy's parents. One October evening, Jimmy, along with a sharp-faced Greek named Moonie Curik and a nineteen-year-old runner named Gavin "Duster" O'Toole, drove out to Long Island to knock over a liquor store. There was a scuffle, and Jimmy shot the guy behind the counter twice in the face, killing him. It had been Harold Corcoran who'd holed Jimmy, Curik, and O'Toole up at his place in Long Island until everything had cooled down.

Corcoran was a difficult guy to get in touch with. It took Jimmy a few days to track him down, but when he finally did, Corcoran nearly began salivating at the prospect of hooking into a counterfeit operation. When he requested to examine the printing presses, Jimmy and Mickey drove him out to the Bowery warehouse that same day. There, Corcoran looked the machines over and nodded once, impressed.

"You can do this?" Jimmy said.

"Sure," Corcoran replied. "I mean, its gonna take some money to get things started—there're supplies and everything—but you got the presses, the plates and negatives, and that's the hardest part."

"How much money we talkin'?" Mickey wanted to know. He didn't approve of laying out cash to guys like Harold Corcoran. He'd even been tempted to suggest he and Jimmy try and work the presses by themselves and screw everybody else. But Jimmy had been negotiating with the Italians for some time, and some of their business savvy had rubbed off on him. Whereas Mickey had always been a believer in the quick buck, Jimmy was actually beginning to *organize* things, set things up. It had been Jimmy's idea to break into the unions, the clubs, the construction outfits as well. Jimmy Kahn had lofty aspirations.

"I'll have to figure it out," Corcoran said. "There's paper, ink . . ."

"Figure it out," Jimmy said, "then let us know."

Meanwhile, Jimmy busied himself with contacting potential buyers. His plans were to run off a couple million dollars and sell the money in lump sums to four or five different customers, who would in turn move it on their own. Both he and Mickey could get more for the counterfeit, Jimmy knew, if the bills had not been previously circulated. By selling to all his customers at the same time, he'd ensure he and Mickey made a healthy profit. Needless to say, his intentions were on the mark but his connections were lacking. Neither Jimmy nor Mickey knew the first thing about moving counterfeit bills and found it difficult to make suitable connections. Francis Deveneau was one connection—he could move the bills through his club via a network of operatives. But it turned out to be more difficult than they'd thought.

Mickey and Jimmy would occasionally drop in at the warehouse and oversee the operation, but they new very little about the printing of counterfeit money. One evening, while creeping around the warehouse after hours, Jimmy discovered a trash can full of wadded sheets of paper, each with hundred-dollar bills printed on them. When he later confronted Corcoran about the trash, Corcoran assured Jimmy that there was a lot of throwaway involved in printing phony bills, and that he'd just have to trust him. Problem was, Jimmy *did* trust him.

It seemed that the production of the phony bills was running smoothly since Jimmy and Mickey had set the project in motion, up until about four months ago. Before they sold a single counterfeit note to anyone, Jimmy was approached one evening in McGinty's tavern by an Irish guy in a suit and tie named Danny Monahan. After a few lines of conversation, Monahan produced a crisp hundred-dollar bill from his shirt pocket and laid it on the bar in front of Jimmy.

"Take a look at that," Monahan said, an impetuous grin breaking across his face. "What do ya think?"

"This?" Jimmy said, picking up the hundred and examining it. "This a fake?"

"Looks good, don't it?"

"Where'd you get it?"

"Some fella. Figured maybe you'd be interested."

"Yeah," Jimmy said, fingering the bill. "Can I take this one?"

"I can sell you a whole stack," Monahan offered. He was older than Jimmy and the rest of the West Side gang, holding down a tolerable job at an accounting firm. Yet Jimmy knew him from his dealings throughout the West Side. Not a permanent fixture in Hell's Kitchen, Monahan was a late bloomer who, in his middle age, was still trying to cut himself a piece of the underground pie. To Jimmy Kahn and Mickey O'Shay, guys like Danny Monahan were a joke—somebody to harry when there was time to kill—but the counterfeit note caught Jimmy's eye. The following evening, he showed it to Mickey.

"I been goin' down to the warehouse, watching what's goin' on," Jimmy told him. "This bill . . . this is one of ours."

"Huh?" Mickey held it up to the light, examined it. It looked real enough to him.

"I been watching everything," Jimmy continued. "At night, after Corcoran leaves, I take some of the papers out of the trash and bring 'em back to my apartment." He plucked the note from Mickey's hand and slammed it on the bar. They were at the Cloverleaf that evening, and patrons of the 'Leaf knew better than to look up at the slamming of fists. "This is one of ours," Jimmy continued. "The serial numbers match."

"What's that mean?"

"It means," Jimmy went on, "that Corcoran ain't happy with five percent and he's selling this shit out from under us."

Jimmy had negotiated a 5 percent cut for both Harold Corcoran and Douglas Clifton on any batch of counterfeit they were able to sell. Now, according to Jimmy, one or both of the bastards was fucking them in the ass and selling the shit throughout the city.

The idea seemed implausible to Mickey. "You sure?" He could not fathom why someone would think they'd be able to rip them off.

"The fucking *numbers* are the same," Jimmy repeated.

"Those shits," Mickey growled. "I told you we gave them too much room, that we shoulda watched them closer. Now what?"

There was a pause as Jimmy considered their options. There was over a million dollars of counterfeit printed already. If they used their heads, they could start moving what they had before the bills sold by Corcoran or Clifton or whoever, made much of a circulation.

Jimmy and Mickey had approached Corcoran one night at the warehouse, playing it cool, and asked him about the money. As expected, Corcoran denied selling the counterfeit under their noses.

"I don't know," Jimmy said. "You're spending a lot of money printing this shit, Harold . . ."

Almost frustrated at their intrusion, Corcoran said, "Jimmy, man, there's a lotta fucking waste that goes into the production. You see the trash? You see what we're throwin' away? It costs money to print this shit, man."

They let it go at that, though neither Mickey nor Jimmy believed Harold Corcoran had told them the truth. And some time later, after spotting Corcoran in a club, Mickey approached the printer and demanded to know just what the hell was going on.

"Hey, hey, hey," Corcoran said, the palm of one hand up in defense. He was sitting at a bar with some friend of his, a black guy named Fee Williams. "What'd I tell you before, Mickey? I don't know nothin' about this. I ain't sellin' your money, man. Think I'm crazy? Now chill out. Let me buy you a drink."

Mickey, who happened to be in the company of some of his own friends, was in no mood for drinking with a traitor and a thief. "Either you come clean with me right now," he told Corcoran, "or you and your nigger friend are gonna see God tonight."

"You know what?" Corcoran said then. His tone was quite unapologetic. "You're one crazy piece of shit, Mickey—you know that? Got some nerve, accusing me of somethin' like that. I wouldn't rip you guys. Jimmy's like family to me. You think you're being ripped, I'd go see your buddy Clifton instead of wasting time poking me . . ."

It is difficult to say what made Mickey murder both Harold Corcoran and Fee Williams that night as they stepped from Toby's Bar on West 41st Street, but it was not solely about the counterfeit money. Some of it was Corcoran's attitude—the way he held his hand up in front of Mickey's face, the way he spoke to him in front of the guys. It could have also been Fee Williams, Corcoran's black friend, who set Mickey over the edge: Mickey was a dedicated racist who thought blacks and Hispanics and Italians and anyone else who was not what he considered "white" deserved to burn in the hottest depths of hell. Or it could have been something as simple as his mood that evening. Regardless, when Corcoran and Williams stepped from Toby's Bar, Mickey O'Shay and his boys were outside waiting for them.

"Mickey—" was all Corcoran managed to say.

The gleam of a knife appeared in Mickey's hands. It shot out in a swift, decisive streak and embedded itself into the soft flesh of Fee Williams's throat, pinning the man against the brick alley wall.

Corcoran began to run, but he would not make it very far: he tripped and spilled to the street like a cripple. Above him, Mickey and his boys walked circles, staring down at his exhausted body. He was held down and, with the same knife, his tongue was cut from his head. Following that, someone produced a hammer and, amidst a storm of insanity, the West Side boys took turns beating Harold Corcoran to a bloody pulp.

Mickey's one hope was that Corcoran would live long enough to feel the worst of the pain.

Later, Jimmy was somewhat incensed by Corcoran's hasty disposal. Killing Harold Corcoran left them without a printer, which meant whatever money they had printed before Corcoran's death was all they were going to get. Taking Corcoran's advice, Mickey suggested they approach Douglas Clifton and see what he had to say. "Maybe," Mickey suggested, "they got a stash of it somewhere."

If Douglas Clifton had any of their counterfeit hidden, they'd get him to give it up. One way or another.

Clifton had been spending a lot of time at the warehouse, confident that there were salvageable, salable antiques among Evelyn Gethers's dead husband's junk. The night Jimmy and Mickey approached him, he was half bombed from smoking too much weed and had several days' beard growth sprouting from his face. As the door was lifted and Mickey and Jimmy entered, Clifton struggled to pull himself to his feet and achieve some semblance of sobriety.

"Hey . . ." Clifton righted himself against a wall, his features seeming to swim across his face. The entire garage was veiled in a thin haze of smoke and reeked of pot. Clifton's words came out slow and stupid. "You guys . . ."

Jimmy was in no mood for games. "What's been going on with our money, Doug?"

Rubbing a hand across the nape of his neck, Clifton managed to turn around and run his eyes over the two printing presses and, beyond the presses, at the duffel bag full of printed counterfeit. "What about it?" he said, his throat scratchy and dry. "It's here . . ."

"You and Harold Corcoran been ripping us off," Mickey added, "been selling the shit from under us. How much you got left? How much you guys print that we don't know about?"

The fear in Clifton's eyes—sober or not—registered immediately. "I wouldn't fuck you guys! Christ, come *on.* What am I, an idiot?" And he tried a frightened laugh. He sounded pathetic. "I don't—I mean, you—the fuck do I know 'bout printing money?"

Jimmy was relentless and unemotional. "How much you got left, Doug?"

"No!" Clifton shouted, his fists balled, his face flushed. He was no stranger to the stories that circulated around about the brutality of the two West Side boys, no stranger to the jobs they'd pulled and the people they'd ripped apart.

Mickey circled around the printing presses, his hands stuffed customarily in his pockets. Before him, his shadow bled across the concrete floor.

Jimmy took a step closer to Clifton. "How 'bout we make a deal, huh?" Jimmy said.

Distrustful, Clifton stammered, "Wuh-what deal?"

From behind, Mickey grabbed Clifton's shoulders and pulled him back with amazing force. Clifton, too stoned and frightened to react, spilled to the floor, cracking his head on the cement, and howled like an injured coyote. He struggled to roll over and away from Mickey, but Mickey held him to the floor with little difficulty, both his hands squeezing the flesh of Clifton's upper arms. A wide grin on his face, Mickey hung his head directly above Clifton's, their noses only inches apart, the curled and wet strands of Mickey's hair tickling the sides of Clifton's face.

Jimmy came forward, pulling a long knife from inside his jacket. Kneeling down, he managed to pin both of Clifton's legs to the floor, Jimmy's knees pressing heavily into the man's thighs.

"The deal," Jimmy said, snatching Clifton's right wrist with the speed and accuracy of a snake's strike, "is that *you* take something of *ours,"* and he pressed the point of the knife slowly into the tender flesh of Clifton's wrist, "and *we* take something of *yours."*

Jimmy slammed the knife all the way through Clifton's wrist; the knife point chinked dully against the cement floor on the other side. Douglas Clifton screamed, and hot, rancid breath rushed up into Mickey's face, the entry wound in Clifton's wrist spilling over with blood. He continued to struggle, but his terror coupled with fresh pain had immediately weakened him.

Jimmy continued to slice through Clifton's wrist, pausing briefly when the knife blade struck bone. Gritting his teeth, Jimmy worked the knife through bone and gristle, streaks of Clifton's blood spraying his face.

The deed was completed in a matter of two minutes. When finished, Jimmy slowly rose to his feet, a bit out of breath from the rush of adrenaline. He held the bloodied knife in one hand and Douglas Clifton's severed right hand in the other.

"Good deal, right?" Jimmy said, taking a few awkward steps backward.

Mickey released Clifton and stood as well. All the fight had drained from Clifton's body. Even now, Clifton was capable only of pulling himself into a fetal position, his abbreviated right arm tucked under the folds of his shirt. His back hitched, though he was still too shocked to emit a single sob.

"You come up with the money you and Corcoran stole," Jimmy told him, his shadow washing over Clifton's tortured body. "We'll see you in a couple days. You don't have the money when we come back, I take off another piece. Got it?"

Clifton could not manage an answer, but it was evident that he got it. In the end, they *always* got it.

Mickey took Clifton's keys to the print shop warehouse, shouted at the cripple to get the hell out of his sight, and locked the warehouse door. And like any street hustler who had grown up within the cold embrace of Hell's Kitchen, Jimmy and Mickey kept good on their word: they visited Clifton some time later at Bellevue Hospital, and it was all they could do to keep from busting out laughing at the sight of the sorry son of a bitch.

"What?" Jimmy said, moving to the side of Clifton's bed. "You ain't gonna shake hands?"

Clifton had the look of someone too doped up to recognize faces, but his eyes quickly widened at the sound of Jimmy Kahn's voice. As he turned to Jimmy, his lips began to tremble.

"You look like shit, Stump," Mickey said, leaning against the wall by the door. With his left hand, he reached over and locked the door. "Smells bad in here, too."

"Uh . . ." Clifton tried to speak.

"We're back, just like we promised," Jimmy told him. "Now—you gonna let us know where you're keeping the money, or do we have to make another withdrawal?"

Clifton's eyes went glassy. His dried, peelings lips were working, but no sound was coming out of his mouth. Jimmy reached out and squeezed Clifton's bandaged stump. Clifton grimaced in pain, his eyes pressed shut and squirting tears, his teeth clenched and bared.

"This is gonna be a slow and painful process, Stump," Jimmy nearly whispered, his lips just a few inches from Clifton's ear. "I can tell. Your buddy Corcoran's already rotting in a dump somewhere. Be smarter than him, and tell us where you're keeping the stash."

"I swear . . ." he managed between breaths, "I don't—*know*—anything about . . . the . . . *money* . . ."

"You're gonna have a hard time lying to us without a tongue, Stump," Mickey said from against the wall.

Clifton started to weep. *"Fuck,"* he groaned. "Oh, God . . ." Teeth chattering in his head, he sobered up as best he could and stared at Jimmy with dead eyes. "Corcoran's been printing . . . extra bills . . . selling them with some guy . . . Patrick Nolan . . ."

"Patty Nolan?" Mickey said. They'd worked some deals together in the past.

"Corcoran's been moving it around the city," Clifton continued, his face still twisted in pain, "and Nolan's been going to . . . Florida . . .Boston . . . fuck, I don't know." He took a deep breath, and his eyelids fluttered. For a moment, Mickey thought Corcoran might pass out.

"Where's Nolan now?" Jimmy asked, and looked over to Mickey. Mickey just shrugged and folded his arms.

"Don't know," Clifton croaked.

"You have any of the money? You know where it is?"

"Nolan has it."

"Son of a bitch," Mickey mumbled from across the room.

"I'm a fair guy," Jimmy said, releasing Clifton's injured wrist. "We'll come back when you're feeling better. Meanwhile, you better get in touch with Nolan, get him to bring you the counterfeit."

But Douglas Clifton would never get in touch with Patrick Nolan.

The next morning, he would throw himself out a window . . .

Now, still nursing the same drink at the Cloverleaf, Mickey felt his migraine intensifying with the memory of those events. What a goddamn mess. And now with both Clifton and Corcoran dead, they had no way of finding Patrick Nolan. They'd checked most of Nolan's haunts, asked a number of his friends about his whereabouts, but no one knew where he was. When John Esposito showed up, they started moving the money again. But Jimmy was becoming aggravated and distrustful by the whole situation—the counterfeit money was now only a reminder of how they'd been screwed by Corcoran, Clifton, and Nolan—and he wanted nothing more than to move beyond the entire ordeal. Screwed or not, they were making money off Esposito and that was all that mattered to Mickey.

Behind him, the Cloverleaf's door opened and a gust of cold air entered. Craning his head around, Mickey saw Jimmy Kahn step into the bar, his nose red and his lips chapped. He was dressed in a button-down shirt and checkered sport jacket, and his hair was greased back into a ducktail.

"You ready to go?" Jimmy said.

"Wait a while. Have a drink."

"No time for drinks. Come on."

Reluctantly, Mickey followed Jimmy to the street and hopped into the passenger seat of Jimmy's Cadillac. They drove most of the way in silence.

"How come we're meeting with these guys so early?" he asked Jimmy after growing bored with flipping the dial on the radio.

"This is when they wanted to meet," Jimmy said. He turned and looked Mickey over. "You could have put on some clean clothes."

"These *are* clean. Besides," he added, "I ain't tryin' to impress nobody. Especially some friggin' wop. I don't see why we're wastin' our time with these grease-balls. I don't trust 'em for shit."

"We wanna spread out of the Kitchen, make some real money, these are the go-to guys."

"Fuck 'em. They're afraid of us. Why the hell should we work with 'em when we can just run 'em off?"

Jimmy frowned. "Don't be an idiot."

"I'm serious."

"Just keep your mouth shut, and let me do the talking."

They pulled up outside a fancy Italian restaurant on Canal Street—all red brick and tinted glass, royal blue awning, candles flickering on the other side of the windows. In the car, Jimmy checked his gun, then slid it back inside his jacket. Mickey did not mind Jimmy's lofty career aspirations—they had helped them get *this* far—but he did not understand why his partner had such an infatuation with the Italians. To Mickey, they were relics, throwbacks to a forgotten time, dinosaurs in an evolutionary pool. Their operations were overburdened and convoluted, their reach wide but unimpressive. In fact, he and Jimmy had done more throughout the West Side in just a few years than the mob had been able to accomplish in roughly a decade. They were an old breed trying to operate in a new society. Why Jimmy Kahn thought they were so important, Mickey did not know.

Inside, the restaurant was quiet, gloomy, and mildly populated. The walls were brick and decorated with wreaths of garlic and shelves of canned goods, the labels striped in red, white, and green. Dean Martin was piped through speakers suspended in the rafters.

"I don't even see a bar," Mickey muttered, following Jimmy through the restaurant. Jimmy paused to talk to a silver-haired man in a dark suit and tie who must have been in his early seventies. The man nodded once, glanced over Jimmy's shoulder at Mickey, then pointed to a set of wooden doors at the back of the restaurant. Jimmy thanked the man and motioned for Mickey to follow him through the doors.

They stepped into a dark, brick-and-mortar room with a low ceiling and an unoccupied stage, complete with stripping poles, at the center of the room. Booths lined the walls in a semicircle around the stage, and an unattended bar stood against the far wall. The lighting was poor—mostly dimmed overheads and candlelight—but Mickey could make out a few people huddled together in one booth, playing cards, smoking, and sipping cocktails.

He and Jimmy approached the booth, Jimmy in the lead. One of the men seated on the outside of the booth glanced up at them. He was overweight and balding, most likely in his mid-fifties, with thick patches of fleshy skin beneath obsidian eyes. His nose was enormous and looked porous, like a sponge. Mickey recognized him from a newspaper photograph Jimmy had showed him some time ago: Angelo Gisondi.

"Jimmy," Gisondi said, breaking into a crooked smile. His teeth were perfectly even and bleached white. "Good to see you. I'm glad you came."

"This is my partner, Mickey O'Shay," Jimmy said, nodding in Mickey's direction.

"Nice to meet you," Gisondi said.

Mickey nodded, disinterestedly.

"Come on," Gisondi said, pulling himself from the booth with some effort. He knocked a large, bejeweled pinkie ring against the tabletop and urged his companions to continue their poker game without him. Leading them to another booth toward the back of the club, Gisondi said, "Can I get you boys anything to drink?"

"No, thanks," Jimmy said, and slipped into the booth opposite Gisondi. Mickey, unimpressed, sat beside his partner, slouching in his seat, the greasy fingers of his right hands drumming the tabletop.

Gisondi set his own drink down in front of him. "Jimmy," he said, "I have to say, I've been impressed with some of the things I've been hearing about you." Smiling, the old man turned his eyes on Mickey. "The *both* of you. You guys are young, getting your hands in a lot of things—and in a lot of people. That's good. Again, I'm impressed. Like anything else, you start out small and gradually . . . you spread your wings. You learn who to trust and who to keep an eye on. You learn a lot of things." Still smiling, Gisondi held up one finger. It was plump as a sausage. "You learn just how important money and friends are. Am I right?"

To Mickey, this sounded like a steaming load—who was this guy, anyway? Did he think he and Jimmy were a couple of street hoods who'd been jacking hubcaps for the past two years?

"Yeah," Jimmy said, nodding.

"Because those are things you cannot afford to take for granted,"

Gisondi continued, "no matter how much money you make or how many friends you *think* you might have."

Across the club, Gisondi's friends broke out in laughter and someone lit a cigar. Mickey could hear poker chips being counted and slid across the tabletop.

"Jimmy," Gisondi went on, "I want to work with you guys. I'm willing to bankroll specific operations, even supply you with some protection, in return for a percentage. I think this could be good for all of us."

"How much percentage?" Mickey asked, looking up sharply from the table.

"Something reasonable," Gisondi provided. "We can work out those details at a later date. Now, there are more pressing issues to discuss. Do you mind if I'm honest with you?"

"Sure," Jimmy said.

A small, lizard-like tongue darted from Gisondi's mouth, moistened his lower lip, then disappeared back into place. "Some of your behavior has raised eyebrows with a few of the men I work with. In truth, not everyone believes we can profit from our union. I think they're wrong, but I *do* think you should take something into consideration for this relationship to prove lucrative."

"What?"

"This isn't the 1920s, Jimmy. Days of shooting up saloons and killing people in the streets are over. Men like us do not operate that way anymore. That's for niggers up in Harlem. You have to be selective. Too much attention from the wrong people is a very bad thing, Jimmy, and it doesn't make the work any easier. Talents like yours deserve to be respected and used properly, not flaunted all over the city for bravado's sake. What I'm telling you is the truth. Sometimes, subtlety is more persuasive."

"Okay," Jimmy said, "you make sense, Mr. Gisondi. I appreciate it. Me and Mickey are gonna discuss your offer. In the meantime, would you mind doin' me a favor?"

"Name it, Jimmy."

"There's this guy we been dealin' with, fella named Johnny Esposito from Brooklyn. You ever heard of him?"

Smacking his lips, his eyes shifting from Jimmy to Mickey, Gisondi slowly shook his head. "Esposito? Not familiar."

"We'd appreciate it if you'd ask around about him, see if any of your guys recognize the name."

"This guy been giving you trouble?"

"No," Jimmy said, "just a new face on the scene. I like to know who he is—that's all."

Gisondi smiled. He looked like a shark. "That's good," he said. "Sure, Jimmy, I'll ask around, see what comes back."

Jimmy shook Gisondi's hand. Turning with his hand still extended, Gisondi looked at Mickey. That shark-like grin was still on his face. Nodding, Mickey shook the old man's hand and slid quietly out of the booth.

"One more thing, Jimmy," Gisondi said, still seated in the booth. "There's a loan shark, Horace Green, who does business up your way. He's been missing for some time now. No one's seen him around, you know? I was wondering, maybe you guys heard something, know something . . ."

"Horace Green?" Jimmy said. Shaking his head, he added, "Nope. Never heard of him."

CHAPTER THIRTY-SEVEN

"ESPOSITO BUY THOSE SILENCERS LAST NIGHT?" JIMMY asked, seating himself beside Mickey in a corner booth at the Cloverleaf. They'd driven back from Gisondi's restaurant mostly in silence, the car radio on and turned low, Mickey sipping from a bottle of bourbon wrapped in a brown paper bag. Like the tide, their relationship hinged on a veritable ebb and flow of conversation. Even between each other, they hoarded words the way misers hoard gold coins, and rarely spoke when there was nothing to say. Tonight, however, it was evident Johnny Esposito was on Jimmy's mind.

"Bought all five," Mickey said, then gave his partner a brief recount of the events on the roof. When he'd finished, he was discomforted by the look on Jimmy's face. "What?" Mickey demanded.

"This guy," Jimmy muttered. Around them, the Cloverleaf was unusually crowded and noisy. On the jukebox, Dean Martin was doing a lilting rendition of "You Belong to Me," and a woman's laughter briefly rose above the din of surrounding conversation. "This goddamn guy," Jimmy went on. "Something about him don't sit good with me, Mickey."

"You worry too much."

But Jimmy did not look worried. Rather, his brows were knitted together in deep thought, his eyes narrowed and focused on the tabletop. Behind him, a group of young guys laughed loudly at some joke, and one of the guys accidentally bumped Jimmy's shoulder, but Jimmy hardly noticed.

No, he was not worried at all.

He was *thinking.*

"We're making money off him," Mickey continued, displeased that his evening of drinking and smoking and zoning out had been interrupted by his partner's paranoid concerns. "What the hell difference does it make now?"

Jimmy did not answer. Lost in concentration, he pulled himself from the booth and meandered over to the bar.

The Cloverleaf's door opened, and Mickey could hear traffic skirting along West 57th Street. Patrick Nolan entered with a good-looking brunette, smiled and held up a hand to the few faces he recognized around the bar, then led his woman over to the only unoccupied table in the joint. Mickey watched as the couple exchanged a few lines of conversation, then Patty Nolan departed for the restroom.

Mickey stood.

In the restroom, Patrick Nolan found himself alone in the cramped little room. Humming a Prince tune under his breath, he relieved himself with gusto, then hopped over to the sink to wash his hands and examine his teeth in the water-stained mirror. His mind was still fully occupied with the brunette sitting at the table outside. The furthest thing from his mind at the moment was his trip to Miami and Harold Corcoran's counterfeit money.

The restroom door eased open. A slice of Mickey's reflection appeared in the mirror above the sink, and Nolan looked up, then turned around and faced him.

Staring at Patrick Nolan made all the events of the past year rush back to him: Horace Green; the counterfeit negatives and plates; the printing presses; Johnny Esposito; Douglas Clifton and Harold Corcoran; the way Corcoran had cried out like a wounded dog while Mickey cut the man's tongue from his mouth. And now . . . Patrick Nolan.

He knew Nolan from the neighborhood, had worked some bullshit deals with him in the past, and had at one time respected the reputation the man was trying to shape for himself. But that was some time ago, and things had changed. Now the bullshit deals Patty Nolan orchestrated were small-time and, in all honesty, rather pathetic. Nolan was in his thirties and looked maybe a decade older than that. With some hard work, the right hookups, and a bit more motivation, Nolan could have grown to become a powerful entity within Hell's Kitchen. He'd done his share of robberies, extortion, even murders—but he was a smalltime street hustler at heart and had never managed to break away from that.

"Patty Nolan," Mickey said from the restroom doorway, grinning. "Ain't seen you around. Been hiding out?"

"Mickey . . ." Nolan spoke the name slowly. He returned Mickey's grin, then turned back to the sink. He glanced up once at Mickey's reflection in the mirror while continuing to wash his hands. A vein throbbed along the left side of his head. "Shit, guy, how you been?"

"Not bad. Where you been, Patty?"

Nolan kept his eyes on the sink. He turned off the water and rubbed his hands together like someone trying to start a fire, shook water into the basin. "Had some business out of town. You know how it is."

"Yeah?"

"You know . . ."

"Some good-lookin' broad you rolled in with. You pick her up out of town?"

Nolan laughed nervously. "Jimmy around?"

"Don't know," Mickey said.

"Well," Nolan said, moving toward the paper towel dispenser, "you tell him I said hey. And Merry Christmas. You too, Mickey." There were no paper towels in the dispenser. Seemingly struck by this—as if he were disappointed in the lack of bathroom supplies—Nolan snorted and forced a second grin while wiping his hands down the length of his pants. Turning toward the door, he nodded once at Mickey, brushed past him, and moved down the narrow hallway.

Mickey watched Patty Nolan leave. Then, before stepping back out into the bar area, he turned and looked at his own reflection in the mirror above the restroom sink. He could feel his migraine coming on again, bubbling up from the base of his neck and up over the top of his skull in an arch. In the mirror, his reflection appeared blurry and unfamiliar. Squinting, he tried to make out his features . . . and found that he couldn't.

He grinned.

Winner, he thought.

Back at the bar, the jukebox was rumbling through some psychedelic 1970s number. The lights had been dimmed and the clamor of numerous conversations mingled with the chime of clinking beer bottles. Corky McKean was behind the bar, smoking a fat Cuban cigar and still wearing his mistletoe necktie. Corky enjoyed working nights during the holidays: the tips were slightly more generous.

Mickey spent the remainder of the evening in a corner booth surrounded by a few guys from the neighborhood. He drank modestly, which was unusual for him, and smoked only one cigarette for the duration of the festivities. One by one, the Cloverleaf's patrons dispersed into the night, stumbling home along the dark, wet streets beneath a winter sky. At one point, Mickey saw Patty Nolan's girl rise from the table, squeeze Nolan's shoulder, and slip out the door. Nolan remained, pulling himself from his table and staggering over to the bar. There, he met with a number of his friends. Drinks were bought and passed around. Someone shouted something about the

Yankees, but Mickey could not make out the words.

A few more people left the bar. Christmas Eve, and the dregs of Hell's Kitchen all had someplace to be. Mickey O'Shay's most vivid memory of Christmas was when he was fifteen and spent the holiday in a juvenile facility upstate. He recalled a snowfall from a window in the cafeteria and how some grotesquely fat kid eating beside him had started throwing a fit, screaming for his mother—his mother—where was his mother? Some of the inmates had snickered at the fat kid, some had cursed at him and thrown things at him, and some had simply stared in mild amusement. Mickey, too, had stared . . . but there had been no amusement on his face, no compassion, and no ridicule. He'd just stared, hypnotized by the way the fat kid's body shook, the way the flesh hung in winged flaps from his arms, the way two guards dragged him out of the cafeteria. That night, as a Christmas present to himself, he replayed the image of the trembling, shrieking fat kid over and over again in his head. And enjoyed it.

At eleven o'clock, Mickey slid from the corner booth and moved down the narrow hallway toward the trapdoor stairwell that led to the underground club. Dragging one hand along the wall, he descended the stairs and remained below ground for some time. When he finally emerged, not too far behind him was Jimmy Kahn, straightening his sport jacket.

"Killian's," Mickey called to Corky McKean, slapping one hand on the bar and sitting in the empty stool beside Patty Nolan.

Nolan turned and eyed Mickey up and down, then focused his eyes further down the bar where Jimmy Kahn stood leaning against the jukebox.

Corky McKean disappeared from behind the bar and returned a moment later with Mickey's beer. Swinging a dishtowel over one hunched shoulder, Corky turned and headed for the Cloverleaf's storage room.

There was a vibe in the air, and Patrick Nolan's few companions were not comfortable with it. Simultaneously, the group of them set their unfinished drinks on the bar, shrugged on their coats, and began moving toward the door. Nolan, too, apparently had designs to leave, for he knocked down the last of his gin and tonic in one gulp and began buttoning his own coat.

"Wait awhile," Mickey said, not looking at Nolan. "Hang around."

"It's late," Nolan said, continuing to button his coat.

Jimmy walked the length of the bar and occupied the bar stool on the other side of Patrick Nolan. Only then did Nolan's hands slow up and finally cease buttoning his coat. Not looking at either Jimmy or Mickey, he placed his palms on the top of the bar, his fingers splayed.

Sipping his Killian's, Mickey did not utter a word. Occasionally, his gaze would shift to Nolan's in the mirror above the bar, but for the most part he was occupied with his beer.

Jimmy smiled and reached into his coat pocket. "You got a nice tan," he told Nolan. "Where you been?"

"Around. What's going on, Jimmy?"

"Mickey and me, we got somethin' for ya." Jimmy produced a small white box tied with a red ribbon. He placed it on the bar, tapped it twice with an index finger, then slid it in front of Nolan. "This is for you."

Mickey got up from his stool and moved to the jukebox. He selected a Sam Cooke number, then turned and made his way to the front door. Nolan jerked his head in Mickey's direction at the sound of the turning dead bolt.

"Go ahead," Jimmy said. "Open it."

"What is it?"

"*Open* it."

Nolan's gaze lingered a moment on Jimmy. Then he turned and looked down at the small white box with the red ribbon. He brought one hand up and pulled the knot out of the ribbon. In the polished mahogany of the bar, he could see Mickey passing behind him. Taking a deep breath, he unwrapped the gift and took off the lid.

Patrick Nolan stared inquisitively at the object in the box. "The hell *is* it?" Then he suddenly knew *exactly* what it was: someone's tongue. "Oh *shit* . . ."

"You don't get it?" Jimmy said, picking up the box and the lid. "Lemme show you." He placed the lid back on the box, brought it to his ear, then worked the lid of the box like the mouth of a puppet. In a high-pitched voice, Jimmy said, "You been rippin' us, Patty! You been rippin' us off!"

Patrick Nolan suddenly looked very angry. "Fuck is this all about, Jimmy?"

Jimmy just smiled and slid the box back over to Nolan.

Behind them, Mickey picked up a chair from one of the tables, lifted it over his head, and slammed it down on the bar beside Nolan. Nolan shrieked and jumped in his seat, holding one arm up over his eyes. The chair splintered into pieces. One of his hands bleeding, Mickey grappled with a busted chair leg, freed it, then wielded it like a baton.

"You been ripping us, Nolan!" Mickey shouted, pointing the chair leg at the man.

With as much placidity as he could muster, Nolan assured Mickey that he had no idea what he was talking about.

Mickey prodded Nolan's shoulder with the chair leg. "The counterfeit money. How much you been moving? How much you got left?"

"There's *nothing* left," Nolan said, "and I wasn't ripping you guys. I worked out a deal with Corcoran. You got a problem with that, you work it out with him."

"You're full of shit," Mickey scowled. Nolan had known he was ripping them off all along—Mickey could tell in Nolan's eyes, in the way he looked when Mickey confronted him in the restroom, and in the way he had avoided Mickey all evening.

"That's not how this works, Patty," Jimmy said. Nolan glanced at him but seemed uncomfortable leaving his eyes off Mickey for too long. "You fucked up our deal. How much money you make moving this stuff?"

"No," Nolan said quickly, "forget it. My deal was with Corcoran. I didn't know he was ripping you."

"You're lying," Jimmy said.

"Don't play bullshit games with me, Jimmy," Nolan said. His face had turned red, and his eyes had narrowed. "I ran these streets longer than you; I know the setup. You think you can shake me down, you're out of your minds. I'm not one of them kids who wants to smell your shit."

Nolan stood and pushed away from the bar. His anger was coming off him in waves, boiling the air. Hands stuffed in his pockets, he moved quickly toward the door, then paused and turned to face them. He jabbed a finger at Mickey. "This little weasel follows me out, I'll rip his fuckin' head off."

Breathing heavily, white-fisting the chair leg, Mickey stood heaving like an ape. He turned and looked at Jimmy.

Jimmy waved one hand. "Let him go," he muttered quietly, getting up to unlock the front door.

Nolan stared Mickey down, his eyes rimmed with hatred, his sallow cheeks quivering. Finally, after a moment, Mickey dropped the chair leg on the floor. But he did not move his eyes from Nolan's.

"You—" Nolan began, but was immediately knocked against the bar following a sound like the crack of a whip. Behind him, Jimmy stood holding the wooden coat rack, its polished wood post marred by a vague circle of hair and blood. Without hesitation, Jimmy brought the clawed feet of the coat rack down on the small of Patrick Nolan's back.

Nolan screamed and crumpled to the floor, one hand clawing for Jimmy.

Mickey grabbed his chair leg from the floor and proceeded to swing at Nolan's head. He managed to hit him only once before Nolan grabbed the chair leg and yanked it clean out of Mickey's hands. Lurching forward, runnels of blood running from his scalp and into his eyes, Nolan rushed Mickey and drove his head into his chest. In an expulsion of breath, Mickey was slammed back against the wall, suddenly victim to Nolan's pummeling fists.

Jimmy swung the coat rack again, breaking it in half across Nolan's back. Again Nolan cried out, but his fury was relentless and he refused to cease beating Mickey.

One of Mickey's hands managed to snake up the wall and close around a clutch of darts stuck into the dart board above his head. Eyes closed, he swung the fistful of darts in a curve toward Nolan's face. There was a wet, crunching sound, and a spray of warm liquid along Mickey's knuckles as he drove the darts into the side of Patrick Nolan's face and neck.

Nolan's fists suddenly stopped coming, and Mickey opened his eyes. Before him, Patrick Nolan's eyes had gone wide, the pupils ridiculously small, the left side of his face decorated with the colorful feathered plumes of the darts and smeared with his own blood. Nolan's jaw worked noiselessly, and blood poured from his mouth. He looked lost, pained, frightened, shocked. But those were just passing emotions, and in an instant, his body seemed to spasm with an electrical jolt, and his eyes refocused on Mickey.

"Uhhh . . ." His hands closed around Mickey's throat and began strangling him. Mickey landed an elbow to Nolan's face, tried shoving the darts further into his face, but there was no stopping the man—

Until Jimmy appeared at his side and drove a ten-inch knife into Patrick Nolan's belly.

Immediately, Nolan's hands dropped away from Mickey's throat.

Gasping, sputtering, Mickey curled against the wall and pushed himself out of Nolan's reach. But Patrick Nolan would be reaching for things no more: with a number of quick, upward jabs, Jimmy continued to bury the large knife-blade into Nolan's gut. Nolan's shoulders hitched with each stab. Jimmy finally pulled away, his arms covered in blood. With the knife still embedded in his abdomen, Nolan staggered comically against the wall, his eyes suddenly distant and blind.

In a rage, Mickey sprang up and rushed Nolan. He grabbed the man by a clutch of hair with one hand, another hand against one shoulder, and drove the man's face straight into the brick wall. Yelling, he spun Nolan around and pushed him across the floor, driving Nolan's face through the glass bubble of the Cloverleaf's jukebox. The shatter of glass was followed by a display of electrical sparks. Sam Cooke's voice slowed in an instant to a dull, impeded baritone, then died completely. Nolan's body twitched a number of times, his face through the juke and impaled on shards of glass. Blood ran down the length of the jukebox and pooled on the floor.

Nearly out of breath, Mickey managed to summon a choked laugh. "Check it out," he muttered. "Patty Nolan just broke into the music biz."

"Come on," Jimmy said, reaching out and grabbing the ruffled collar of Nolan's coat. With a sturdy yank, he managed to pull Nolan from the jukebox. Broken glass clattered to the floor. Like a ventriloquist's dummy, Patrick Nolan was lain out on the floor, his sightless eyes unfocused and facing the ceiling. The force of his face through the jukebox glass had torn most of the darts from the side of his face and neck. A few jagged pieces of glass poked up from ragged wounds at his neck and cheeks.

"Don't look so good no more," Mickey muttered, staggering over to the bar and finishing his Killian's. In the hallway, Corky McKean watched them in silence, his arms folded, one foot tapping on the floor.

Sometime later, just as a light snow began to fall along Manhattan's West Side, Mickey O'Shay and Jimmy Kahn dumped Patty Nolan's body into the Hudson River. They worked mostly in silence and spoke only after the body had been discarded and they were in the Cadillac on their way back home.

"I been thinking about the counterfeit we got left and this guy Esposito," Jimmy said. The glare of streetlights washed over his pale face as he drove.

In the passenger seat, Mickey nodded while looking out the window. "Esposito," he muttered to himself. "Esposito-ito-ito . . ."

"I been thinking," Jimmy repeated. Turning onto Tenth Avenue and pulling up outside Calliope Candy, he said, "Here's what we're gonna do . . ."

Somewhere over the river, winter lightning filled the sky.

CHAPTER THIRTY-EIGHT

THE CLOVERLEAF WAS NOT TOO BUSY.

Standing in the doorway, John pulled off his leather gloves and skirted his eyes around the room. The bartender stared disconcertedly out the window at the freshly fallen snow, lusterless in the tarnished gray of midafternoon. Across the room against one wall stood a table where the jukebox had been previously. Mickey and Jimmy sat there, picking at the labels of their beer bottles and watching a basketball game on the small television set mounted in the rafters above the bar. Mickey noticed John but did not hold his eyes to him; rather, he took a swig of beer and turned back to the television.

It was December 31, the last day of the year. A light snow had fallen intermittently over the past two days, depositing powder and slush on the streets and sidewalks. John and Katie had spent a draining Christmas morning at the hospital, sitting at his father's bedside. Unable to do anything more for the old man, the doctors had transferred his father to a room just down the hall from the ICU. "A nice, quiet room," one of the doctors had told John. "Intensive Care's hectic. You can sit with him and not be disturbed here." Quiet or not, in reality it was the room where people went to die.

"This wouldn't have happened if they'd just kept him here,

looked after him," he'd muttered.

"You don't know that," Katie had said. She was standing behind him, one hand on his shoulder.

"He was alone too much."

"He wasn't," she'd insisted. "We were both there as much as possible."

"I wasn't."

"John, you were there that night when it happened, just the same as me. There was nothing we could have done. We knew it was going to come down to this. We knew . . ." She had more to say, but her voice trailed off nonetheless.

"Do you think he's in pain?" he had asked her.

"I don't know," she'd said truthfully. "How are you?"

"I'm fine. Don't worry about me."

"I *always* worry about you."

They'd eaten Christmas dinner with Katie's family. John had spent half the evening thinking about his father, and the other half thinking about the West Side boys and their counterfeit money. He recalled the evening on the roof, and how Mickey had pointed the gun at him. Five silencers. There had been no prints on the silencers themselves; however, the boxes were covered in not only Mickey's prints but the prints belonging to a man named Glenn Hanratty, known to his friends on the West Side as "Irish." Irish was the proprietor of Calliope Candy. Kersh had matched up the prints on the silencer boxes to a set of prints taken from a box of Junior Mints he'd purchased at the candy store, sold directly to him by "Irish" Hanratty himself. Still . . . they had nothing solid on Kahn, and John couldn't help but feel that time was running short.

John pulled out an empty chair and sat at the table with Mickey and Jimmy. The pain was back in his hands, and he alternated pressing his thumbs into his palms to work out the numbness.

"Haven't heard from you guys in a while," he said. "Thought maybe you changed your minds."

"You want a beer?" Jimmy said, and held up one finger to Corky McKean behind the bar.

John glanced up at the basketball game, then over at Mickey. The skin under his right eye was purple-black and shiny, the lid slightly swollen. Two cuts, now hardened and scabrous, broke open the flesh at the tip of his cheekbone.

"What happened to you?"

Mickey chuckled and drank some beer. "Christmas present," he said.

"Could be a good look for you," John said, and Mickey chuckled again. The bartender came over and set a bottle of Killian's on the table, then sauntered away without a word. John took a swig and winced at the taste. It was too cold and too early to start drinking with the West Side boys. Resting the bottle back on the table, he turned again to Mickey. "So what's up?"

Mickey had called him just an hour before, requesting they meet at the Cloverleaf. The agents monitoring the wire taps had immediately contacted Bill Kersh, who'd met John at the office and wired him up in case Jimmy Kahn started talking about the counterfeit money. Though there had been no mention of them discovering the money or plates, and though negatives had been taken from the Bowery warehouse over the wire taps, there was a good chance Mickey and Jimmy had already found out. It was in the hope that Jimmy might talk after all that John had worn the wire. Now, as he sat at a table beside Jimmy Kahn, such an idea seemed ridiculous. Was this guy playing smart, or had he just been lucky so far?

"Nothing's up," Mickey said, his eyes still on the television. "Haven't seen you in a while. Wanted to make sure you were still around."

"Where would I go?"

Mickey rolled his shoulder and brushed his greasy hair from his eyes. "Don't know," he said. "Sometimes people just disappear."

"Well," he said, "I'm still here. And I'm still interested."

Chewing the inside of his cheek, Mickey only nodded. He seemed terrifically unenthusiastic. If they didn't want to discuss the million-dollar counterfeit deal, then why had they called him here? In all the time he'd known them, and through all the drop-of-a-hat mood swings, one thing had remained constant: they were not sociable. They did not chill out with friends from the neighborhood, did not *do* anything. Even their drinking was less for fun and recreation than for occupying those long hours of daylight prior to an evening of crime and corruption.

When neither Mickey nor Jimmy responded, he said, "Ten percent's good, but I'm having some trouble getting the money fronted—"

Mickey's eyes swung in his direction. "Drink your beer." The words seemed to tumble from Mickey's mouth and lay solid and wet on the table. Mickey's eyes remained on him a moment longer, impressing upon John the extent to which Mickey did not wish to discuss business at the moment. Beside him, Jimmy Kahn kept his eyes trained on the basketball game, uninterested in the wave of unease that had just rushed across their table.

John stared back at Mickey, unflinching, until Mickey finally turned back to the television.

He wanted to talk about the money but didn't want to push it. He ordered another beer for both him and Mickey. John drank his torturously slow. Jimmy and Mickey watched the basketball game and, when he was able, John watched them. There was something so cavalier about them that made him want to crack them both across the teeth. And as the minutes ticked by and the daylight turned to dusk, he grew more and more irritable.

Finally, he pulled some bills from his jacket and threw them on the table. "It's getting late," he said. "Think I'm gonna hit the road."

"Wait," Jimmy said, standing up. "Hang around for one more drink."

Jimmy went to the bar and leaned against one of the stools, waiting for Corky McKean to return from the back room.

There was a moment of awkward, balanced silence between him and Mickey. That disapproving look was back in Mickey's eyes, but a hint of something else seemed to soften his features. What was it?

Then, finally, Mickey said, "You been having any luck gettin' those customers lined up?"

"Some."

"How much longer you think you'll need?"

He was waiting for Jimmy to leave the table, he realized. *This way we could discuss whatever we want without involving his partner.*

Jimmy was playing it smart.

"I'm having some trouble getting some of the money up front," he said. Maybe if he let on that he was having some difficulty lining up the money, Jimmy might be brought in to negotiate another deal.

"Ten percent's a good deal," Mickey said.

"It's not that," he said. "Just . . . some of my guys ain't comfortable fronting that much money. You know what I mean?"

"Eight percent," Mickey said.

John had been rubbing his hands together while they spoke. Now he stopped and just stared at Mickey. "What?"

"Eight percent," Mickey repeated. "But you round up your end and we do the deal in two days."

Apparently they didn't know the money was missing. It was also apparent that, for whatever reason, they wanted desperately to move it. Eight percent was ridiculously low.

"Can you handle that?" Mickey asked him.

"Eighty grand in two days," he muttered, considering. "Yeah,

I can work that."

Mickey appeared to relax. "Good," he said, leaning back in his chair and bringing his beer to his lap. "Good."

"Let me ask you something," John said, nodding toward the bar and Jimmy Kahn. "He don't trust me or what?"

"Jimmy?"

"I didn't need to waste my whole goddamn day here waiting for him to leave the table . . ."

Mickey chugged the rest of his beer and said, "Don't worry about Jimmy."

Sometime after dark, John left the Cloverleaf and crossed West 57th Street to his car. He turned over the engine and radioed Kersh, who was sitting in his own car farther down the street. Kersh was surprised Mickey had dropped the points so much and was not completely comfortable with Mickey's sudden burst of generosity. John, on the other hand, was gratified that the deal had finally been set up. In two days, when Mickey discovered the money was missing, Jimmy Kahn would have to get involved. There would be no way around that. Mickey was crazy, but he wasn't stupid enough to approach John alone. As far as Mickey and Jimmy knew, John had been going around the city collecting money from people expecting to buy counterfeit money. Neither Mickey nor Jimmy would allow that opportunity to pass them by.

Jimmy would get dirty . . .

Pulling out onto West 57th Street, John forced his mind to switch gears. It was like living a double life, and the past two months had been draining. He felt like a man dangling by a wire, spinning in midair, the weight of his own body stressing the wire more and more. The last day of the year, and he could only hope the New Year would bring with it a sense of serenity.

He would take Katie to the hospital, and they would sit with his father for some time. Then they would go home together and wait out the rest of the year by themselves, in each other's arms, in the dark.

He never knew he was being followed.

CHAPTER THIRTY-NINE

A DARKENED TENEMENT HALLWAY. THROUGH THE WALLS, soft cries of a baby could be heard. Then after a few moments, the crying stopped.

Mickey O'Shay crept up a narrow bend of stairs, his shadow like a stretched black cloth on the wall beside him. At the second floor, he paused on the stairwell landing before pushing through a large metal door. The hallway reeked of urine and mildew, sour like rotting citrus fruit. His footfalls were muted on the floor. Someone's television was turned up too loud. At the end of the hall, a cat froze and stared directly at him beneath a darkened window, the feline's eyes reflecting the bulb in the single light fixture in the middle of the hallway ceiling.

Slinking like a thief along the gloomy corridor, Mickey paused outside an apartment door. Sliding one hand from his coat pocket, he knocked twice—hard—on the door. Slipping his hand back into his coat, he turned his head casually from side to side, examining the length of the hallway. The cat continued to stare at him, its eyes glowing like headlamps.

Bolts turned. The door opened a crack, and Tressa Walker peered out. When she glimpsed Mickey standing on the other side of the door, all life seemed to drain from her face.

"Mickey . . ."

"How you been, Tressa? You alone?"

"Yes." The word was out of her mouth before she could avoid saying it. "What do you want?"

"Frankie-balls around?"

"I haven't seen him. What do you want?"

"Jimmy's got your money down in the car," he said. "It took us a while to get around to you." As part of their deal, Mickey had agreed to pay Tressa 5 percent on any counterfeit deal he worked with Esposito, seeing how she'd introduced them. However, as Mickey was prone to do when he knew he could get away with it, he hadn't fed her a dime.

Now, at the mention of money, some of the girl's anxiety was sloughed off. "Why didn't you just bring it up?"

"Didn't want Frankie to see it. Come down."

Greed has a tendency to impede judgment and blind the eyes to truth. Had Tressa Walker been a different person, she might have recognized the absurdity of Mickey's proposition. But having grown up in an abusive West Side household, having gotten involved with hard drugs and truculent older men at a very young age, Tressa Walker was *never* going to be a different person.

She grabbed her coat and stepped out into the hallway. "Not too long," she told Mickey. "My baby's asleep inside."

They moved down the stairwell quickly and out into the frigid courtyard beneath the winter moon. Snow covered the ground and reflected the moonlight. It was then, as they walked across the courtyard, that the preposterousness of the situation must have struck Tressa, for she paused briefly in mid-stride and went suddenly still. Turning, Mickey glared at her, his form hunched yet imposing in the darkness.

"What?" he said.

"Where . . ." She cleared her throat. "Where's Jimmy?"

"In the car," he answered, "just like I said. What's the matter? You want your money or not?"

And for the second time that evening, she forced herself to follow Mickey O'Shay.

Jimmy Kahn's Cadillac sat idling along Tenth Avenue, twirling snowflakes dancing in the headlight beams. Mickey moved slightly ahead as they walked and opened the back door of the Cadillac for Tressa.

She stood along the curb, watching the traffic pass along the street, unwilling to get into the car.

"Come on," Mickey said, "it's freezing out here."

He put a hand on her back and urged her into the back seat. It was the strength of his hand that broke her will and allowed her to climb into the Cadillac's back seat. Mickey climbed in after her, slamming the door.

Jimmy sat in the front by himself, smoking a cigarette and grasping the steering wheel. His dark eyes looked her over in the rearview mirror. Then he took the car out of park and spun the wheel, pulling into the traffic along Tenth Avenue.

"Where are we going?" she said, her voice suddenly trembling.

"Relax," Mickey told her, pulling a pack of Camels from his coat and shaking a stick into his mouth. He lit it with a frayed book of matches from the Black Box strip club. "Enjoy the sights."

She brought her knees up to her chest and leaned against the window, as far away from Mickey O'Shay as she could manage. Her face was frozen, expressionless, and wide-eyed. "Mickey . . ." she managed. Her voice sounded too dry, not her own.

"Tell us about Esposito," Mickey said. He took a long drag from his Camel and blew the smoke toward the Cadillac's ceiling. The entire car was filling with dense blue smoke.

A small moan escaped her throat.

"Who is he really?" Jimmy asked from the front seat, again eyeing her up in the rearview.

"I told you already," she said, leaning forward, her hands suddenly clenched together. "Everything I know, *you* know."

"You're lying," Mickey said. His voice was serene and mellow, like ice cream melting in the sun. "I'm so goddamn tired of listening to liars."

"We just want to hear the truth, Tressa," Jimmy said. "You bring this guy to us, and nobody's ever heard of him. We just wanna know who the hell he is."

"I told you!" she screamed, startled by the ferocity and terror in her voice. A single tear spilled down her right cheek, and she began to sob gently.

"Calm down," Jimmy told her. "Mickey, give her a cigarette—get her to calm down."

"Good idea," Mickey said. He leaned over to her, holding out his cigarette. "Try this. Maybe *then* you'll talk."

Like a striking snake, Mickey's hand shot out and grabbed Tressa's chin, pushing her face against the Cadillac's window. She screamed and tried to twist her head away. Struggling, her arms flailed hopelessly against Mickey as he tried to slide the cigarette into her mouth. He was laughing until one of her hands struck his bruised cheek. Howling, he slapped her across the face, gripped her jaw harder, then forced the burning end of the cigarette into her left nostril. She screamed and kicked, the back of her head knocking against the window, while Mickey held the cigarette in place. In his anger, he pinched her nose closed and heard the embers of the cigarette sizzle her flesh. With one final shake of her head, he pushed her back against the door and let go. The cigarette slipped from her nose as she sobbed and moaned. Mickey watched her with little interest as he slid another cigarette from the pack, lit it, inhaled.

"You wanna try this again, Tressa?" Jimmy said from the front seat. "You know something about this guy, you tell us now."

She cursed at him and began clawing at the door handle. Mickey hit her again in the face.

Jimmy pulled the Caddy down a narrow alley off Tenth Avenue, between clusters of blackened tenements. The front of the car nailed a group of tin trash cans, sending them scattering down the alleyway, and Jimmy Kahn cursed under his breath. A light went on in one of the tenement windows and Mickey stared at it, smoking his Camel down to the filter.

The car came to a jerking halt, and Jimmy pulled himself quickly from the vehicle. Tressa's door was open, and Jimmy dragged her out, one hand over her mouth. She still had plenty of fight left in her, and as Jimmy carried her around the front of the car, she kicked her legs and beat at Jimmy's arms with her fists.

Mickey climbed out of the car, grinning, and skulked down the alley.

"Fucking help me," Jimmy growled at him.

With some difficulty, Mickey grabbed Tressa's legs and slammed her ankles together. The girl's body went rigid with pain, her eyes rolling back in their sockets, all her energy suddenly drained.

Behind them, half hidden in the shadows at the rear of the tenement, a dark shape materialized and uttered something in a deep, inarticulate voice.

Jimmy barked something in return and then, with Mickey's help, swung Tressa around the side of the building. They carried her quickly through a small yard and up a flank of stone steps. The large figure stepped beneath the light of the porch, and Irish's features came into relief. Wrapped in a bright green windbreaker and a Coors Light mesh baseball hat, Irish flung open his door and waved the boys inside with one meaty hand.

"Come on, come on . . ."

Tressa administered another strong kick, freeing herself from

Mickey's grasp, and nearly clocked him in the face with her foot. Again, he grabbed her ankles and squeezed down on them, feeling the contours of her bones through her skin.

"Bitch," he growled. He had little patience with the uncooperative.

Inside, the lights seemed too bright and the strong smell of fresh coffee filled Irish's kitchen. The second Irish shut and locked his door, Jimmy and Mickey dropped Tressa on the kitchen floor. She hit hard, slamming her head against the tile, but wasted no time in trying to escape. Like a trapped animal, she spun onto her stomach and began scrambling on all fours toward the locked kitchen door. Jimmy lifted one shoe and placed it gently on the top of her head, impeding her progress. Grinning, Mickey just watched.

"Why don't you make some more goddamn noise?" Irish muttered, unzipping his windbreaker and tossing his Coors Light hat on the counter. There was a small transistor radio beside the sink. Irish turned it on, found a loud rock station, and cranked the volume. Turning to Jimmy, he pointed toward the living room. "Get her out of the kitchen."

Mickey bent and grabbed Tressa's legs, pulled her across the kitchen floor. She struggled to turn over on her side, and her shirt came up over her waist, exposing soft, white flesh. She clawed at the tiled floor like a cartoon character getting sucked up into a vacuum cleaner, and the sight made Mickey laugh.

Jimmy followed them into the living room. An armchair stood against one wall, its cushions stained with blood. It had been the chair Ray-Ray Selano had been sitting in the night Jimmy shot him. Now, Mickey managed to hoist Tressa off the floor and into the chair.

She immediately clung to it, the way cats will cling to the lip of a basin of water to avoid taking a bath. Her eyes were wide, her pupils practically nonexistent, and her entire body shook with fear.

Irish poked his head into the room. "You guys want some coffee?"

"Bring me a knife," Jimmy said.

"Don't start cuttin' her up," Irish told him. "This ain't no goddamn slaughterhouse, Jimmy."

Mickey lit another cigarette and leaned against the wall opposite Tressa Walker. He watched her with little appreciation. To him, this entire ordeal was a goddamn waste of time. It didn't matter to him what this bitch said about Esposito now—the bum was already in the middle of everything. Jimmy, on the other hand, had worries of his own. He liked to play everything out—another skill he'd learned from the Italians, Mickey supposed—and he despised operating without every single bit of information. He'd changed in the past year, Mickey understood. Jimmy had become more calculating, more industrial, more tedious. Mickey had no appreciation for tedium. There was nothing Mickey O'Shay hated more in the world than the slowing down of an operation. And for some reason, this guy Esposito was driving Jimmy crazy . . . which, in turn, was driving *Mickey* crazy. A year ago and Jimmy would not have bothered with shaking Tressa Walker down—they would have moved ahead on the deal with Esposito, and that would be that. If things came to blows, what would it have mattered? But the Italians had brainwashed his partner, had somehow instilled upon him the importance of doing things *heedfully,* and Mickey had no patience for such bullshit. All the deals they had worked together in the past, and Jimmy Kahn was finally starting to push his buttons.

Irish entered the room holding a six-inch carving knife by the handle. He handed it over to Jimmy without looking at him, his eyes glued to the squirming young girl in the bloodstained armchair.

"Who's she?"

"Frankie Deveneau's girl," Jimmy said, placing the knife on an end table. Its purpose was intimidation, and it seemed to serve that purpose well: the girl's eyes were drawn to the knife as if by magnetic force, and something deep inside her seemed to give. "She's the one who brought this Esposito to us."

"This Esposito smell funny?" Irish asked.

"Could be a snitch," Jimmy said, staring directly at Tressa. "Is that right?" he asked her, raising his voice a notch. "That fucker a snitch?"

"I'm done with this," Irish said, licking his lips and sauntering back into the kitchen. From over his shoulder, he called, "Remember—don't cut her, Jimmy."

"We won't need to do shit," Jimmy said, kneeling down beside the armchair, "as long as you answer our questions."

Tressa Walker no longer resembled the girl Mickey had picked up. Her face was red and blotchy, her eyes squinting into watery slits. Her teeth rattled in her head as if with feverish chills, and great tracks of sweat ran down her face. In her lap, she twisted her fingers together forcefully enough to crack the knuckles.

"Calm down," Jimmy told her. Then looking at Mickey, Jimmy said, "Calm her down."

"The fuck you want *me* to do?"

"Christ . . ." Jimmy stood and backed up against the wall. "Tressa . . . Tressa . . ." He must have repeated her name twenty times before her sobs subsided. Beside him, Mickey picked up the knife from the table and proceeded to scrape the filth from beneath his fingernails with the blade. Continuing, Jimmy said, "Where'd you meet John, Tressa?"

Her bleary red eyes darted from Jimmy to Mickey, then back to Jimmy again. In a quiet voice, she uttered, "Huh-high school."

"How'd you introduce him to Deveneau?"

"Uh . . ." She didn't seem to understand the question. She began to tremble harder, her fingernails digging into the chair's armrests.

"You brought him to Deveneau, right?" Jimmy said.

"Yes . . ."

"Where'd you meet him—where'd you meet John—before bringing him to Deveneau?"

"Brought him . . . to . . . Jeffrey Clay . . . first," she managed.

"Whatever," Jimmy barked. "Where the fuck did this guy John come from?"

She began crying again.

Hands on his hips, Jimmy turned away, rubbing his chin with one hand.

Mickey had had enough. Let Jimmy impress Angelo Gisondi and the rest of the Italians on his own time; this was utter bullshit. He crossed over to Tressa, who began squealing and tried to pull herself from the chair the second she realized she was in for some trouble. Mickey was on top of her quickly, though, pressing one knee into her hip and preventing her from moving. He grabbed her face as he'd done in the Cadillac, eliciting from the girl a hot shriek of terror.

Holding her firmly, he locked his eyes with hers. "Who is he?" Mickey whispered, pushing his face into hers. He could smell sour sweat rushing off her in waves. "Who is he, who is he, who is he?"

Behind him, Jimmy turned to watch. He'd folded his arms and was leaning against the far wall now, a look of frustrated anger on his face. Mickey glanced at him once, disgusted, then turned back to the girl.

Mickey slapped her across the face. Her head whipped to one side, her sweaty, matted hair brushing past Mickey's face.

"Who is he?" It had become a gruesome litany.

Another slap, whipping her head in the opposite direction. Too pained, too stunned, she was no longer making any sound.

"Tell us who he is," Jimmy said from against the wall.

The sound of Jimmy's voice broke a vessel of heat within Mickey's spine, and he could feel a boiling tension race through his entire body. Grabbing Tressa's left hand, Mickey hoisted her from the armchair and propelled her across the room. She sailed with the subordination of a rag doll onto the carpet, her fingers immediately clutching the rug, her shoulders hitched beneath the thin fabric of her coat.

"Come on!" Jimmy shouted at the girl, his shadow suddenly enormous across her supine body.

Mickey kicked her along the ribs, and she cried out and rolled onto her side. With her teeth clenched together, she made a sound like a rush of air leaking from a punctured car tire. He shouted at her, not realizing he was partially fueled by his frustration with Jimmy Kahn, and relented only when Tressa curled into a fetal ball and pushed herself against the wall.

"We'll keep this up all night if we have to," Jimmy promised her. "Tell us who he is. Is he a snitch? A cop? Is he the fucking Pope?"

"Better yet," said Mickey, "who are *you?* You a fucking snitch, Tressa? You a fucking snitch?"

She managed something inaudible.

Mickey bent and yanked Tressa up off the floor by her coat. Her legs were too weak to support her weight, and she slumped like a wet cloth in his arms. She managed to stand after a moment, her hair matted to her face, her breath coming in whimpers. Open-handed, Mickey cracked her across the face, and she stumbled backward against the wall. When she tried to run, he grabbed her by the back of her coat and dragged her back toward him. She struggled out of her coat and ran for the front door. In her panic, she struck the door with her face and chest, her hands grappling for the doorknob. But the door was locked, and she could go no further. Instead, she pressed her head against the knob, dropped to the floor, and continued to cry.

Mickey stalked over to her and grabbed her by the hair. She immediately rose to her feet. Like a caveman, he shook her by the hair.

Her right hand was swollen and looked broken; she clutched it to her chest, a trickle of blood running from one nostril, dotting her shirt. Tressa's knees buckled and she dropped to the floor again, leaving

Mickey standing above her clutching a fistful of sweaty hair.

Mickey stepped on her ankle. She moaned and squirmed along the carpet, articulating no words, her moans nonetheless pleading and pathetic.

Jimmy Kahn stepped beside Mickey, looking down at her body. "You better start thinking of the right thing to say," he told her, "before it's too late and you can't talk at all."

For a moment, she looked as if she were going to speak. One hand came out, her fingers grazing the material of Mickey's pants. She whispered something, her voice wet now with blood and trembling with fear. Mickey crouched, his right hand snaking around the back of her head and pressing his fingers into the soft flesh of her neck. With a jerk, he brought her face against his, almost cheek-to-cheek. Heat came off her in dreamy oscillations, and her hair was damp to the touch.

"What?" Mickey said, breathing into her face. Her entire body shook within the grasp of his right hand, quaking. She was like a newborn bird, hatched from the egg, blind and helpless and vulnerable. His heart began to race at the notion. "What? Tell me . . ."

There was blood smeared across her mouth. She pursed her lips wetly, blood running down the side of her face.

With all the power she could muster, she swung her fisted right hand around and slammed Mickey in his bruised, swollen cheek.

Grievous, agonizing pain blossomed like fireworks in the dark sky of his body, shooting from his face to the back of his head like a bolt of lightning. A moment later, his fingers closed on the flesh of her neck with such force that he could feel the blood coursing through her body. He hoisted her to her feet, and she refused to stand. Supporting her with one hand, he brought a fist to her face once, twice—repeatedly. There was no screaming—only the pummel of packed meat—and each retraction of his fist brought with it the crimson tendrils of fresh blood.

Jimmy's hoarse, angry voice came from directly behind him: "Mickey!"

With a heave, Mickey sent Tressa Walker across the room. For a moment, it seemed as though she would catch her footing . . . but then her legs gave out completely and she fell toward the wall, face first, and came crashing down against the radiator. Tumbled. Shook. Rolled and slammed against the carpet, unmoving.

The contrail of a bright red shooting star smeared the side of the radiator.

And the room was silent except for the strained respiration of two men.

Stepping onto the back porch for a breath of fresh air, Mickey shook his long hair down in front of his eyes and slipped his bloody hands into the pockets of his coat. Beside him, Irish stood smoking a cigar and leaning over the porch railing. His Coors Light cap was back on his head. From the back, his shoulders looked a good four feet wide. He'd been on the porch all the while.

Jimmy was there, too, beside Irish, hunched over the railing and smoking a cigarette. When Mickey stepped onto the porch, Jimmy shot a glance in his direction. Mickey folded his hands over the wrought iron railing. His hands looked like raw cuts of beef.

Without looking at him, Irish said, "You take care of that mess in there, Mickey?"

Lighting his own cigarette, Mickey met Jimmy's eyes. "She didn't know nothing," he said. It was his attempt at correcting the situation.

Jimmy sighed and exhaled a plume of smoke into the night. "Anybody see you go up to her apartment?"

"No," Mickey said. He hadn't seen a soul.

"Deveneau's gonna come sniffing around now," Jimmy said. Sucking the life from his cigarette, he turned so Mickey could make out his profile. In the poor light, he looked like a crude sculpture of himself. "You know that, right?"

"Fuck Deveneau," Mickey said.

"No," Jimmy said calmly, shaking his head. With one hand, he picked peeling flakes of paint from the railing and flicked them into the night. "I don't wanna have to watch my back for that asshole now."

"Not a problem," Mickey said, and blew a waft of smoke up into the sky. "We'll start the new year off good."

He'd never liked Francis Deveneau anyway.

Francis Deveneau and his good friend Bobby "Two-Tone" Sallance stood outside Deveneau's club smoking cigarettes, their foreheads glistening with sweat despite the temperature.

"You should do a ladies night," Bobby Two-Tone was saying, "like some of the clubs downtown. Free drinks and shit. Gets the girls to come down. Half the time it's mostly guys here, Frankie. A goddamn sausage fest. That ain't right."

"The hell you know about runnin' a business?"

"I'm just saying, Frankie," Bobby Two-Tone said. "Hippendorf's does it on Wednesday nights. Man, on Wednesdays, it like *wall-to-wall* skirts. And they lose no money 'cause all the guys bust their ass to get in and sniff around. Hit those fools with a twenty-dollar cover. Trust me, man, it's a goddamn brilliant idea."

"Sure," Deveneau said, uninterested. He happened to turn and glance at the traffic passing along the street, shivering against the cold, when he spotted the slow-moving Cadillac creeping along the curb. Uninterested, he watched the Caddy for a couple seconds before stomping on his cigarette and going back into the club. He thought nothing of the car—it was one of a million that passed in front of the club every night.

The thing about Manhattan nightclubs was that it took a catastrophe to keep people from coming. And to Deveneau's clientele, a shoot-out in the basement a month ago did not count as a catastrophe. Lucky for him.

He made his way through a crowd of dancers, slid by the bar, winked at Sandra behind the bar. One finger tapping at his waist, another finger flossing the smooth divot of skin beneath his nose, he crossed the dance floor and made his way down an unlit brick corridor. Here, the industrial pump of the dance music was absorbed in the walls. Before him, the hallway seemed to shift and sway. A couple necking near a pay phone hardly noticed as he bumped by and stumbled into the restroom.

A few guys were bent over one of the sinks. They'd taken down the mirror and laid it across the basin, and were doing lines of cocaine off it. Deveneau thought he recognized them, and he pointed a finger at one of them. The guy waved him over, clubbed him on the back with a meaty hand, and urged him to snort a line.

"Ahhhh . . ." He did, enthusiastically.

Turning, one hand fumbling with the zipper of his pants, he pushed himself against a urinal, his eyelids fluttering. The chatter of the men behind him swelled like a balloon in his head. There was a clatter, the squeal of a sneaker on the tile floor.

He muttered something in a singsong voice. No one responded.

When he turned around, two men stood behind him. It took him a second for his mind to adjust. A crooked smile broke across his face.

"Mickey . . . Jimmy . . ."

Jimmy Kahn lifted a gun and shot Francis Deveneau in the throat. Deveneau jerked backward against the wall and slumped to a half-crouch against the urine-splattered urinal. He held a hand to his throat, his eyes bugged, and blood squirted through his fingers in a torrent and washed down his shirt and pants, pooling on the filthy tile floor.

He opened his mouth to make a sound, but no sound came out. Only blood.

The whole world tilted and spun, and he saw Jimmy Kahn push the gun into his face. It looked enormous, hideous, fake . . .

Then—

Nothing.

☙

A light drizzle was falling as Jimmy pulled up outside Calliope Candy. The exhaust was kicking up white clouds that were quickly dispersed by the wind. Traffic zipped by in a blaze along Tenth Avenue.

Mickey slipped out of the car, his .25 Beretta wedged into the waistband of his jeans, his coat pulled tight around his body, and crossed over to the pay phone just outside the store. His heart was racing, his adrenaline pumping. There was a buzzing—a rattling—inside his head that reminded him of chattering teeth. Yet he was not cold; he was burning up.

Beneath the conic gleam of a lamppost's light, Mickey picked up the receiver to the pay phone, slipped in some change, and dialed a telephone number. Patting himself down, he found a nub of pencil and his Black Box matchbook in one pocket. He waited, the wind angry and biting all around him. He hardly felt it. Even his face, bruised and injured from the fight with Patty Nolan, did not bother him.

After a number of rings, Ashleigh Harris answered the phone.

"It's Mickey. You got Esposito's address for me?"

"You know it," Ashleigh said and gave Mickey the address, which he wrote down on the Black Box matchbook cover.

"He see you follow him?"

"No way," Ashleigh said. There was loud music on in the background.

"Sure?"

"Positive."

Mickey hung up and stared at Johnny Esposito's home address. For a moment, he lingered beneath the glow of the lamppost.

Then, with what looked very much like a smile on his face, he climbed back into Jimmy Kahn's Cadillac.

CHAPTER FORTY

"PHONE'S RINGING," KATIE WHISPERED.

"I know," he said. "I just don't want to get up."

"Up, up," she said, playfully yanking his hair.

He lifted his head from her shoulder and rolled onto his side of the bed. His left elbow went down on a box of Kleenex, crumpling it. "You want anything from the kitchen?" he said, moving past the foot of their bed and running one hand along the baby's crib before stepping out into the hallway.

"Orange juice," she called back, then blew her nose into a ball of tissues.

In the kitchen, he grabbed the phone receiver from the wall and pressed it to his ear. "Hello?"

"It's Kersh."

"What's wrong?" He knew immediately from the sound of Kersh's voice that there was trouble.

"Stay calm," Kersh said. "We just heard from one of the wire taps that Mickey's got your home address. They must have had somebody follow you home. The call was made, like, thirty seconds ago, John. I think they're heading your way."

He felt a sinking feeling in his stomach. The walls of the kitchen seemed to close in on him. "Holy shit, tell me you're joking."

"I'm on my way over to your place right now. I got backup on the way, too. They'll meet me there. We'll get this thing straightened out . . ."

He felt like a sleeping dog that had just been dumped from a moving car. The fact that he'd been so stupid, so easily bested by Mickey and Jimmy *to be followed home* . . . the notion made him crazy with anger.

"Wait. Take this address down," he said, and gave Kersh the address to his father's home on Eleventh Avenue. He was deliberately trying to keep his voice down, nearly whispering, so that Katie wouldn't hear. All of a sudden, the apartment felt preposterously small. "Don't bother coming here; we're getting out. I'm bringing Katie there—it's my father's house—and I want you there. I don't want her to be alone—"

"Alone?"

"Just go, Bill. I'll meet you there."

He hurried back into the bedroom, quickly grabbing a pair of pants from the closet.

"Where's my juice?" Katie murmured.

"Hon," he said, "you have to get up. That was work. I need to get you out of the house." He slipped his pants on and moved to the side of the bed, helping Katie up. He took one of her forearms, and it felt cold.

"John—"

"It sounds worse than it really is," he said. "Don't worry. We're just playing it safe. Get on shoes and a coat. I'll take you to Dad's house."

She went momentarily rigid at the foot of the bed. One hand gripped the crib's railing. "God, John—*what happened?"*

He smiled and somehow managed to summon a laugh. Rubbing the side of her face, he said, "Humor me. I'm just overreacting.

But let's move it."

"John . . ." She sounded very far away.

"Come on," he urged.

She covered his hand with her own, pressing his palm into the smoothness of her cheek. "You promise this is nothing?"

"I do," he said. "I promise. Now get dressed."

While she pulled on a pair of sweatpants and shoes, he hit the front windows and peered out through the curtains. Cars were parked up and down the street, and a few drove past the intersection. It was too soon—they wouldn't be able to get out here that fast.

"You almost ready?" he called to his wife.

"My shoes . . ." she said, shuffling into the front room. "I can't—"

"Don't come by the windows."

She didn't move, didn't say a word—just stood there with her coat draped over her nightshirt, the left side of her body illuminated by the dull orange light from the hallway. Unmoving and silent, she just stared at him. As if she were suddenly unsure of who he was and what he was doing . . .

"Come on," he said, leading her back out into the hallway toward the closet. "Your shoes . . . they're in here . . ."

He found them, bent down, and coaxed them onto her feet. She moved like a person comprised of cut wood and metal hinges. Looking down the hallway, he could see the kitchen table, the stove, the refrigerator—all those things spread out before him *in his home,* and how they seemed to pulse with life, with current, with vibration.

"Button your coat," he told Katie, then dashed down the hallway to the bedroom. Opening his dresser drawer, he slid his gun out and pushed it into the waistband of his jeans. He felt around for his undercover wallet and tossed that on the bed. Resting on the nightstand beside the bed were his real credentials, which he grabbed and stuffed in his pants pocket.

Back out in the hallway, Katie had not moved. She stood by the front door, her coat buttoned incorrectly and hanging lopsided from her shoulders, like a small child in the middle of some great and terrible commotion. And maybe she even was.

He unlocked the door, stepped out into the hallway, glanced around. It was dark and quiet. Reaching for his wife's hand, he led her onto the landing and shut and locked the door behind them. Still, Katie didn't say a word; she just moved as told, her mouth a slit beneath her nose, her eyes wide and dazed. He silently thanked God for her cooperation, for he did not know what he would have done had she gone into hysterics or refused, for whatever reason, to leave the apartment.

She was very pregnant and had some difficulty descending the stairs as quickly as he wanted. There, in the building's lobby, he peered through the diamond window on the door and out into the street. He could see the Camaro at the bottom of the walk, sandwiched between a blue van and a red Toyota Celica. He recognized both cars. And from where he stood, he could see no headlights moving down the street.

Behind him, the sound of a door creaking open broke the breathy silence, and he spun around with one hand over Katie's belly, his other hand whipping his gun from his pants and pointing it down the hallway.

Phyllis Gamberniece stood staring at them from the doorway of her apartment. Her hair in rollers, her enormous body confined to a purple terry cloth robe decorated with embroidered sunflowers, the woman seemed to freeze as if suddenly struck dead on the spot. Then, without a sound, she disappeared inside her apartment and slammed, then locked, the apartment door.

Beside him, Katie did not say a word. Yet her eyes had moved to his gun, which he quickly replaced in his waistband.

The walk from the stoop to the street was only about a dozen paces, but it seemed like an eternity. The Camaro—their refuge—

like a ship that had just left port, too far to jump to, too far to swim.

Then, like a miracle, they were there inside the car.

At first he'd been thankful for his wife's silence, but as they drove to his father's house, he grew worried by it. Glancing at her in the passenger seat, he was struck by how innocent and frightened she looked; struck even more by her silence, her fortitude. Yet . . . how much was bravery and how much was stunned and terrified silence?

"Katie? Babe?"

"I'm okay," she barely whispered. "Just drive."

He rubbed her left knee. She felt unyielding and cold even through her sweatpants. Like a corpse.

"I want you to listen to me, okay?" His tone was beyond placation, almost insulting. But he'd never done this before and did not know how to act, what to say, or the best thing to do. "Katie?"

"I'm listening." She kept her eyes focused on the street ahead, refusing to turn and look at him.

"You okay?"

"Yes." Irritation in her voice. The emotion—*any* emotion—was good to hear. At least she sounded alive.

"Bill Kersh is going to meet us at Dad's house. There'll be some other guys there, too. They'll stay with you so you're not alone, and then when I come back—"

"Back from where?" But she knew. "The apartment? You're dropping me off and going back to the apartment?"

And what could he say? She was not Bill Kersh—she would not be quelled by the reasoning that appeased a seasoned agent, would not care about what was important to his undercover role, did not care whether or not Mickey O'Shay and Jimmy Kahn went to prison or not. In fact, despite how much they consumed his life, Katie had never even heard of Mickey O'Shay and Jimmy Kahn, didn't know a goddamn thing about the vicious Irish hoodlums from Manhattan's West Side. She was saved from all that, protected from all that. Partially, anyway.

But not anymore, he thought, squeezing the Camaro's steering wheel tighter as he burned through the streets. *Not anymore. Because now it's come home to her, too.*

Home. *His* home.

Their home.

"I'm gonna take care of this," was all he could promise her. "Okay? I'm gonna take care of this."

Katie said nothing.

Kersh's car was already parked outside John's father's house when the Camaro pulled up. Leaving the Camaro running, John hopped out and hurried around to the other side to help Katie, but she wanted no assistance and managed to vacate the car on her own. At that moment, Agent Tommy Veccio swung around the street in an unmarked car and shuddered to a stop across the street.

Kersh moved quickly to John's side, his ample gut protruding over the waistband of his pants. His face was gray and pasty in the moonlight. He looked like death.

With an arm around his wife, John ushered her quickly up the stoop, Bill Kersh at his side. John could tell Kersh was busting with information but didn't want to explode in front of Katie.

Inside the house, Kersh radioed Veccio's car and brought him up to speed on the situation. Katie, her coat still on, wandered into the kitchen, flicked on the lights, and leaned against one wall. John hurried past her, pulling out a chair from the kitchen table and beckoning her to sit.

"I don't feel like sitting," she told him flatly.

"Katie . . ."

"I don't feel like sitting, John."

Kersh called his name from the foyer. He felt torn, ripped down the middle, with both halves of his body in disagreement as to which direction they should move. His wife looked lost, petrified, angry. Looking at her, he could feel a small twisting burn at the pit of his stomach, corkscrewing through his guts. Finally, he told Katie he'd be right back and then met Kersh in the foyer by the front windows.

"About an hour ago Francis Deveneau was gunned down in the bathroom of his club," Kersh said, his voice low. "There were no witnesses, but I got a strong feeling it was our guys. Meanwhile, I've been trying to reach Tressa Walker at home. Guess what?"

"No answer," John intoned. That sinking feeling he'd felt back at the apartment had returned, augmented a thousand times over.

In his head, Tressa Walker's voice filtered up through his brain like the vapors of a phantom: *They're asking questions about you. I can't give 'em answers for all their questions, John. I'm gettin' scared.*

And what had his answer been? Standing here now, he found he could not remember.

"They say anything over the phone about me being an agent?"

Kersh shook his head. His lips were pressed tightly together. "No. But that doesn't mean anything . . ."

"I'm going back to the apartment to see if they come," he said. "Stay here with my wife."

"I'll go with you, in case your cover is blown."

"No, no—stay with my wife. Keep Veccio on the street. I want my wife safe. I can't think otherwise." He pulled his wallet from his pocket and handed it over to Kersh. "We don't know what's going on," he said. "Not yet. This could all be unrelated. Let's play it out."

"So you're not home when they hit the place, *if* they hit the place—"

"Bill," he said, "I have to be there. They start trashing the place and find my real name on shit, find stuff out, then the case is dead and so is Tressa."

"And what if you're wrong?" Kersh said, gripping John's arm with one hand. "What if they already know you're an agent and they're coming to kill you?"

Breathing heavily, his hand tightening on John's arm, Kersh let his eyes bore into John's. Seconds ticked away—too many of them. John could feel the ground being torn out from under his feet.

They're asking questions about you.

Another few seconds crept by. Outside, through the sheer curtains over the windows, the headlights of another unmarked car pulled up outside in the street. He could hear doors slamming and the muted murmur of conversation far off in the distance.

And although Kersh's words made sense, he knew he could not allow it to end this way.

"Don't worry," he told Kersh. "Watch my wife."

CHAPTER FORTY-ONE

THERE WAS NOTHING UNUSUAL ALONG THE STREET outside his apartment building. He pulled the Camaro to the curb and jumped out, moving swiftly up the front stoop. It was cold, the snow on the ground confusing his perspective. Clouds of moisture rose from the sewers and were carried away by the wind. Every bit of movement caught his attention.

As he entered the building, he pulled his gun from his waistband, pushing himself along the wall. The hallway was dark and soundless. Slowly, he crept up the stairs to his apartment. He winced with each creak of the stairs, his breath coming in slow, labored waves. At the top of the risers, he could see that the apartment door was still closed. Relief swam over him. They hadn't come.

And maybe they're not coming at all, he considered.

But then he thought about Francis Deveneau and Tressa Walker . . .

At the top of the stairs, he tried the doorknob. It was still locked. More relief washed over him. He was beginning to calm down.

He would call his father's house and let Katie know everything was all right. He'd hated that blank expression on her face, hated the way she hardly spoke as they left the apartment. Back at his father's house, just before he'd left to come back home, he'd managed to get her to sit at the kitchen table. But she'd refused to take off her coat and shoes. He'd promised her everything was going to be fine, and he firmly believed that, but his words did little to allay her fears.

Sliding his key into the lock, he heard the bolt turn. He pushed the door open, his eyes wide and adjusting to the mixed lighting of the hallway. Only the hall light was on, casting shadows into the other rooms. If he'd been thinking, he would have turned on all the lights before he'd left. Still—there was no one here.

He pressed the door closed, locked it. Down the hallway, his shadow stretched the length of the black-and-white checkered floor. The palm of his right hand was moist and slick on the hilt of the gun; a roll of sweat trickled down his arm and soaked into the ribbed cuff of his jacket. He peered into the spare room off the hallway, running his free hand up the wall. It was cold; his breath came out in vaporous clouds. Yet his forehead was dimpled with beads of perspiration.

With the lights on, he winced and scanned the room. Nothing. The windows, too, were still locked. Moving against one window, he peeled the curtain away from the pane and scrutinized the dark streets. No movement.

At that moment, he was reminded of his father's disapproval when he'd joined the Secret Service. *A glorified cop with a college degree,* his father had said. *A young, married guy, and you want to run around the streets risking your life? For what, John? Why? Do something better for yourself.*

He entered the kitchen, going over to the telephone, his hand reaching out for the receiver. Then freezing.

There was a loud, metal clanging sound coming from the bedroom.

Also—*why was it so cold in here?*

He tightened his grip on the gun. At that moment, he was aware of the smoothness of the handle, the weight of the weapon, the indentations of the bolts and screws along the casing. He crept across the floor and paused before peering into the darkened bedroom. Yes, it was definitely cold. And that sound . . . that metal clanging sound . . .

With his gun held out in front of him, he turned around the doorway and stepped into the bedroom, his feet planted firmly in the carpet. The first thing he noticed was the moonlight reflected in the cheval glass on Katie's side of the bed. His eyes darted to the opposite wall and noticed that the window had been broken, the carpet beneath it littered with shards of glass. Outside, the loose fire escape ladder swung in the wind, banging against the side of the escape.

Son of a bitch—

Just as he went to turn, a great force slammed into his back, knocking him to the floor. He felt his gun spill from his hand and thump against the carpet. Propping himself up, he could feel the perpetrator's hands on his back, a knee to the lower part of his spine. Foul breath accosted his face. Lights came on, temporarily blinding him, and he was hit with something in the back of the head and yanked violently to his feet.

Mickey stood before him, a fistful of John's shirt in one hand, a large semiautomatic gun in the other. The muzzle of the gun was pressed against John's forehead. Mickey was breathing heavily, his teeth chattering, his eyes like two busted fog lamps.

Behind Mickey and against the wall stood Jimmy Kahn, one hand still on the light switch. He stood motionless, like a wax figure, his eyes locked on John's.

"The *fuck!*" he shouted, slapping Mickey's hand away from the collar of his shirt. His heart was jackhammering in his chest; the sound seemed to fill the room. He exhaled a shuddered gasp and felt the room tilt slightly beneath his feet. He took two steps back toward the bed, breathing heavily. Mickey's gun remained pointed at him. "What . . . the *fuck* . . . are . . ." His voice shook with anger—more anger than he had ever known.

"John," Jimmy began from across the room.

"Fuck you," he spat. "What kinda deal is this, bustin' me up?

And who the hell are you, breaking into my *house*—"

"Who the hell are *you?*" Mickey said. "Who the hell are *you,* Johnny?"

With his fists balled, his eyes boring into Mickey's, it was all John could do to not take a swing and kill the son of a bitch right here. Gun or no gun, he'd rip the bastard's face apart.

"Get that goddamn gun out of my face," he spat. His voice was steady, unafraid, teeming with torrid rage. He squeezed his fists so tightly that his fingernails cut crescents into the soft flesh of his palms. "Do it now."

Mickey's hand shook. "Don't be so tough," Mickey told him.

"You don't get that gun out of my goddamn face, nobody's walking out of this apartment tonight. You understand me?"

Mickey did not falter. The gun remained pointed at John's head. Against the wall, Jimmy took a few steps into the room, leaned over, and peered into the open closet. His boots left muddy footprints on the carpet. Casually, he turned and moved over to the dresser. He opened the top drawer and shifted through the clothes. Maneuvering the drawer from the dresser, he dumped its contents to the rug, kicked around balled socks and pairs of underwear with his foot.

"Don't be so tough," Mickey repeated. It was the voice of a robot, a machine, an unemotional foreign entity. Uninterested in his partner's work, Mickey had not taken his eyes off John. To emphasize how serious he was, he pressed the muzzle of the gun to John's temple. It felt cold and hot at the same time.

John didn't blink, didn't move. His right hand itched to knocked the gun away from his head and out of Mickey's hand.

"What do you want?" he said, watching as Jimmy moved around to Katie's side of the bed. Seeing him here in his bedroom hurt his mind. Jimmy and Mickey did not belong here. They were as out-of-place as two hyenas on the peak of an Antarctic iceberg.

Jimmy pulled back the bedspread and examined the sheets.

Bending down, he peered beneath the bed.

"What do you want?" he repeated. He could feel the muzzle of the gun twitching against his forehead. Mickey was shaking. But not from fear; from exhilaration.

We're all going to die tonight, he thought. *All three of us, right here in this room.*

Jimmy stood and noticed John's undercover wallet on the bed. He glanced in John's direction, then went to the wallet, picked it up. He dumped its contents out on the bed and shuffled through some of the miscellaneous business cards and matchbook covers. Jimmy examined the driver's license. Apparently convinced, he tossed it on the bed and moved around the baby crib. He peered over the railing.

"You got a kid?" Jimmy asked.

"What do you want?"

"You and me, we got a big deal coming up in two days, Johnny," Mickey said, taking a step back and lowering the gun to John's chest. "A lot of money involved. I just like to know who it is I'm dealin' with."

Jimmy slipped out into the hallway. A moment later, John heard the sound of kitchen drawers being emptied onto the floor. The cupboards next. A few dishes were busted. When Jimmy returned, he had one hand stuffed into his pants pocket, his other hand running through his hair.

To Mickey, Jimmy said, "This don't look like no undercover joint." Turning to John, he said, "Where's your wife and kid?"

"Her mother's place."

"Lucky for her," Mickey snickered.

Around them the walls were breathing—wavering in and out like plaster lungs. The carpet heaved; the lights faltered, blinked, sizzled in his mind. He was aware of every molecule in his body, was aware of the blood pumping through his veins and arteries.

Biting the inside of his cheek, Mickey took another step away from John. Behind him, Jimmy slumped against the wall, still running his fingers through his hair.

"Get on the bed," Mickey said for the last time.

Some cerebral autopilot managed to kick in and take over the controls. He felt his body move on its own accord . . .

If Mickey hadn't mentioned the million-dollar deal that was still set for two days from now, he would have never laid down on the bed. Instead, he would have knocked the gun from Mickey's hands and ripped out the son of a bitch's throat. Then he would have gone after Kahn, who would have most likely pulled his own gun and shot him dead on the spot.

He crept backward onto the bed.

"Lie down," Mickey said.

He eased himself down on his pillow. The entire room seemed incredibly small. The ceiling seemed to press against his face. He could hear his breath whistling through his throat.

"You look like you're in a coffin," Mickey said. "You sleep here?" Pointing the gun at the vacant pillow to John's left, Mickey said, "And I guess your wife sleeps here."

Mickey pulled the trigger and fired a shot into the pillow. John winced and felt the whole bed vibrate.

"And your kid over here," Mickey continued, pointing the gun at the crib and firing two more shots. One struck the mattress with a muted *whump!* while the other clipped the wooden railing, splintering it. "Get the point?" Mickey continued, leveling the gun back on him. "If you're a cop or a snitch, you're history. I don't care if you're the fucking commissioner. It won't matter."

"We'll see what kinda balls you have," Jimmy said, moving back into the hallway.

With the gun still pointed at John, Mickey slowly backed his way out of the room. A homicidal grin tore at his face, twisting and contorting his features. For one crazy moment, he looked like a Halloween mask with sunken pits for eyes and fangs for teeth.

"See you in two days," Mickey said, disappearing into the hallway. "And don't bother getting up. We'll let ourselves out."

Still feeling the vibration throughout the bed, John remained on the mattress, listening to Mickey and Jimmy's footfalls recede down the hall. He heard the bolts turn on the front door, the door itself squeak open, then slam shut, rattling the frame. Distantly, he could hear their footsteps on the risers in the lobby hallway, and their muffled laughter through the walls.

On the nightstand beside the bed, the alarm clock read 1:28 A.M. It was the first day of a new year.

JANUARY

CHAPTER FORTY-TWO

GET ON THE BED.

He could still hear Mickey O'Shay's words sounding in his head, racking his mind. And he could still see the clap of fire erupt from Mickey's gun, the first round slamming into Katie's pillow right beside his head. Then the second shot—into the crib of his unborn child.

Get on the bed.

Seated alone in the pit, his feet propped up on a second chair, John rubbed the side of his head with two fingers while his eyes stared blankly at the shelves of textbooks. Two nights since the events at his home, and his anger had dulled to a contemplative irritation, dispersed throughout his entire body with the malignancy of ingested poison. This morning, waking up in bed beside his wife at his father's house (it had been decided they would remain there until the West Side boys were apprehended), he'd felt as if his body had been filled with shards of hot, broken glass and jagged stones. Beside him lay the silent and unmoving shape of his wife. She'd been in a stupor since that night and refused to talk about it, refused to talk to *him.* That bothered him the most. He wished he could take all her worry and hurt and fear and carry that on his shoulders, too, along with his own. Katie didn't deserve any of this. And he hated himself for burdening her with it.

Yet there was no turning back from this thing now. He'd looked the beast in the eye—was the only man with a soul who had seen these animals up close and personal—and knew they needed to be stopped. It went beyond the job, beyond personal motivation. These guys were pure evil. And John knew he was the only man who could put an end to them.

For the past two days, Mickey O'Shay had been calling. John refused to answer the line. It was part of the undercover strategy but, in truth, the idea of talking to the son of a bitch sickened him. On the third day, after Mickey's persistence began to let up, John called *him.* Just hearing Mickey O'Shay's voice on the other end of the line was enough to get his blood boiling all over again.

"Where you been, John, I been trying—"

"Listen to me, you shithead. Dealing with you is the last thing I feel like doin' after that shit you pulled at my place."

Mickey snorted on the other end of the line.

"But I got a lotta guys waitin' on this deal and a reputation at stake," he continued. "We do it tonight. Then we're through. After tonight, I don't want to look at you again. You got me?"

Mickey sighed. "There's a park over on—"

"Fuck that. You meet me tonight at Nathan's in Coney Island. You're done calling the shots. And I want Kahn there for the deal. I don't trust you for shit. In fact, I don't care if you're there or not. No Kahn, no deal."

"Jimmy's—"

"He's there, or I walk."

A moment of silence passed over the line as Mickey considered the situation. In the end, he agreed and hung up the phone.

Following the call and a discussion with Bill Kersh, SAIC Brett Chominsky called John into his office. When he arrived, Kersh was already seated in one of the plush leather chairs before Chominsky's large desk. John felt himself hesitate in the doorway. Then he stepped inside and took his own seat.

"Mickey knows the money's gone," Chominsky said without pause. "We've verified that through the wire taps. The fact that this thing is still on now can only mean one thing."

"What's that?" he asked.

"Here," Chominsky said, pushing *play* on a tape recorder that rested on the edge of his desk. "Listen."

The tape came on in mid-conversation. It was a recording of a phone conversation between Mickey and Jimmy—John knew their voices immediately—and as they talked, Chominsky thumbed the volume knob louder.

"We do this thing tonight," Mickey was saying, "I'm gonna need you there. I ain't gonna do this on my own."

"I'll be there," he heard Jimmy say.

"All right," Mickey said. There was a tremulous quaver to his voice, and he sounded very much unlike himself. "This thing goes good, we made a score."

Chominsky clicked off the tape. Leaning back in his chair, he eyeballed John.

"They're meeting with you to rip you," Chominsky told him. "They don't have the counterfeit, and they're still talking about making a score. They're not dealing, John. They're planning on taking your money." The distraught tone of Brett Chominsky's voice also implied that he knew Mickey and Jimmy were planning on killing him, too.

"Not necessarily," John said. "They could have another stash somewhere that we don't know about."

"They don't talk about another stash," Kersh interjected. John could tell this thing was weighing heavily on him.

"That doesn't mean there isn't one," he said . . . although in reality, Chominsky and Kersh were probably right: Mickey and Jimmy were planning on killing him tonight and taking his money. Still, John was not obstructed by such thought. He felt smarter, quicker, *better* than Mickey O'Shay and Jimmy Kahn. And if he had to convince Chominsky and Kersh, then he'd convince them.

"John," Chominsky said, "we have to look at all the scenarios and figure on the worst. It's pretty evident this is probably a rip."

"You don't have to do this, John," Kersh added.

"Yes, I do."

"They're gonna *kill* you, John," Kersh said. "This thing got out of hand a long time ago. We should pull the plug." He turned to Brett Chominsky. "This thing isn't going to end well."

"They're not gonna do anything without seeing my money," John assured Kersh. "We set up a money car a few blocks away from Nathan's. I meet with them, ask to see the counterfeit, and whether they have it or not, I get conversation from Kahn. Then I take them to the money car. Once we get there, you bust 'em." Because he didn't like the looks Kersh and Chominsky were giving him, he added, "You heard the wire. Kahn's gonna be there. This is our chance to get him dirty in all this. Even if it's a rip, we'll have him on conspiracy. It's still our play."

"You think so," Bill said. "O'Shay's out of his mind. You have no idea what he might decide to do. A deal this big and the crap he pulled at your house, he's probably worried *you're* going to try and rip *him*. You don't show up with the money, he might freak and turn out your lights right on the sidewalk."

"He won't do that," he insisted.

"You don't know that . . ."

"He won't, Bill. I'm telling you. I've been around this guy enough to smell his moves. He's nuts, but he ain't gonna risk losing eighty grand." To his own ears, it sounded almost as if he were trying more to convince himself. Truth was, he didn't know *what* Mickey would do. The only thing he was certain of was his own refusal to let this thing go bad. He could handle it. "Trust me."

"Against my better judgment, John, I've *been* trusting you," Kersh said, "and that trust has gotten you up on a tenement roof with a gun pointed at your head and now, three nights ago, these animals break into your goddamn house. We've lost control of this."

He hadn't told anyone—especially Kersh and Katie—about how Mickey had held the gun to his face and made him lie on the bed, nor how Mickey had plugged his wife's pillow and the baby's crib. As far as Bill Kersh was concerned, Mickey and Jimmy showed up, asked a few questions, opened a few dresser drawers, and left. And as far as Katie was concerned, no one had ever shown up.

"I'm tired of trying to convince everybody," he said finally. Turning to Chominsky, he said, "I'm tired of this whole goddamn case. You wanna throw in the towel now after all I've been through? Is that what you want? Because I'm not ready to do that. You think I'm on some suicide trip, that I'm an asshole, but this is our only chance to get Kahn dirty." He glared at Bill Kersh. *"They're* not walking away, and I'll be goddamned if *we* are."

"Ultimately," Chominsky said, "it's up to you, John. If you're comfortable with this . . ."

"We can do this," he assured the SAIC.

"What about wearing a wire?" Kersh suggested.

"No way. They find that, I'm *really* a dead man. I'll take the transmitter."

"Transmitter's got limited range," Kersh interjected.

"I'm not wearing a wire. They pat me down, find a wire—"

"All right," Chominsky interrupted. "Brief the squad; get everybody ready. We'll meet again in two hours."

Now, some time later, he sat by himself in the pit, going over the details of the plan in his mind. It was quiet here, and the quiet bothered him. He'd asked Kersh once how he could stand such prolonged silence, and the older agent had simply replied, "Because I'm not afraid to listen to myself think." He wasn't afraid—he was convinced he'd be able to handle both Mickey and Jimmy—but there was still some gnawing at his gut, at the base of his brain. The pit's unbroken silence afforded him too much time to dwell on too many other things in his life—Katie and his father at the forefront. He pictured Bill Kersh as the type of man who had no trouble falling asleep at night—who, when his head hit the pillow and his eyes closed, was already halfway off to dreamland. He, himself, could not remember the last time he'd gotten a good night's sleep. Even now he felt wired, anxious to meet with the two West Side boys and put a lid on this thing.

Kersh returned with two Styrofoam cups of coffee. He set them on the table without saying a word, and eased his bulk onto one of the chairs that surrounded the table. On the tabletop, a detailed map of Coney Island lay before them. With grease pencils, Kersh had marked a number of street corners and intersections.

Looking at Kersh, John thought he could tell what the man was thinking. He was worried about tonight's bust, but was also undoubtedly thinking about the slumped form of Francis Deveneau that Dennis Glumly had discovered in the bathroom of Deveneau's club, his throat and part of his head blown apart. Also, after repeated unanswered calls to Tressa Walker's apartment, Kersh had gone there himself to check out the situation. No one had answered the door when he'd knocked, despite the sounds of the television through the walls. Flashing his badge to the superintendent, he'd been allowed access to Tressa's apartment. And the first thing he'd noticed upon entering had been that the television set was *not* on, and that the noise he had heard was coming from the bedroom, behind a closed door. It had been the crying of Tressa Walker's baby, abandoned and dirty and hungry and alone in the back of the apartment—and suddenly everything had seemed a whole lot worse.

"Okay," the older agent said now, sipping his coffee, "let's run through this again." He tapped the grease pencil against a scrawled star along Mermaid Avenue. "We'll have the money car here—the Camaro—and we'll have all four points covered by surveillance around it . . ." With the grease pencil, he drew four circles surrounding the star along Mermaid Avenue. "You bring Mickey and Jimmy to the money car, we got four teams ready to bust them." He dragged the pencil down the map and paused along Surf Avenue, which ran the length of the Coney Island bulwark. "Nathan's is . . . here," he said, pressing the pencil point to the map. "We should have two more cars out here to cover you."

"I think that's too many," John spoke up.

Kersh continued as if he hadn't spoken. "I'll be up here, on Surf and 15th Street. I'll have Veccio sit in the car, and I'll walk the strip so I can keep an eye on things. We'll have another car at one of the meters along Schweikens Walk. Mickey and Jimmy show up, you eyeball the counterfeit then take them right over to the money car. They don't have the counterfeit on them—and it's a lot, so they probably won't—you don't need to push the issue. Just take them to the car." He put the pencil down; it rolled along the length of the map and stopped before rolling off the edge of the table. Not looking at John, Kersh said, "They want you to go someplace with them, don't. Everybody's gonna be on edge here—especially them. Chances are, if they have the money it'll be in their car. Let them show it to you, then bring them right to the Camaro."

"Pretty simple," John said.

"Yeah, right." There was no inflection in Kersh's voice. "We should sit down with Chominsky again," Kersh said.

"Bill," he said, "I know you don't want to do this . . ."

Sighing, sipping his coffee, Kersh said, "John, you've got a very important decision to make tonight." Kersh would not look him in the face; he kept his eyes trained on the map of Coney Island. "You can handle this thing like a professional and do your job, or you can bury yourself in it and allow it to consume your entire life. I'm not your father, and I'm through trying to make you see things my way. You're your own man. Just understand that this deal—this money, these West Side animals—these things are not the ultimate. What's important," he continued, thumping a hand against his heart, "is what's waiting for you at home after all this is over." He waved a heavy hand carelessly across the map. "Not this shit."

He couldn't say anything to that. How could he make Bill Kersh understand that he *needed* to do this, *needed* to succeed, *needed* to get to the end of the long race he'd started back in November? That he wouldn't be able to look at himself in the mirror if he gave up on this thing? And oddly enough, his mind summoned the picture of his father in his fireman's garb—the picture that had been on the workbench in the garage when he was a little boy—and how tonight was just a piece of what would make him whole, what would make him complete, what would make him worthy. It was easy to give up and go home; it was difficult to fight things to the end . . . and even more difficult to emerge the victor. He wasn't out to win this case for Roger Biddleman or Brett Chominsky or Bill Kersh or anyone else. He was out there trying to win this thing for *himself.*

But he didn't know how to explain those things to Kersh. Instead, he stood and began rolling up the map of Coney Island into a tube. He worked quickly and did not look up to meet Kersh's eyes.

"Come on," he said after a moment. "Let's sit down with Chominsky before it gets too late."

The phone rang a number of times before his wife answered.

"It's me," he told her. "Just wanted to say I'm thinking about you. You doing okay?"

"I'm fine. Glad you called," she said. She sounded so small on the other end of the phone.

It felt good to hear her voice, though it sent a strong sense of impropriety running through him. He felt guilty, guilty for everything . . .

"It'll be over after tonight," he promised her now. "I know things have been crazy, but it'll bc different after tonight. I promise."

"Don't worry yourself thinking about me," she said. "I'm okay. I trust you, John. You take care of this thing, then come on home to me."

"I'll try not to be too late," he said, paused, then hung up the phone.

Outside, a strong wind shook the office windows.

CHAPTER FORTY-THREE

CONEY ISLAND PULSED LIKE A HEARTBEAT IN the night. The flashing lights of the bulwark illuminated a grand run of darkness and brought into impressive relief the mass of pedestrians along Surf Avenue. No weather was too cold, no hour too late, to keep people away. The boom of laughter was a constant melody. The shuffling of feet, the combined din of voices, the carnival music from the carousel, and the impatient growl and hum of impenetrable traffic along the avenue completed the soundtrack. Here, the aromas were both commonplace and unique: melted butter and popcorn, French fries and mustard, caramel and candy apples, hot sugar and the sharp roast of peanuts. And beyond, the caustic odor of the ocean and the noxious whiff of axle grease used to oil the amusement park rides.

John paused on the opposite side of Surf Avenue, staring across the street at the crowds of people and the panels of billboards that ran the length of the esplanade. The neon glitter of *Clam Bar* and *Sea Food* and *Delicatessen* converged in a blur of confused lights. The yellow and green Nathan's awnings dominated the walk, filthy and old and colorful like aged prostitutes. Along the sidewalk, the gantries bustled with dark-skinned laborers catering to large quantities of hungry people, even in the cold. And above and beyond the gantries and the billboards, the colored lights of Astroland dotted the darkness. The Wonder Wheel pulled sluggish rotations; the Cyclone clung black and silent to a dark winter sky. And all around, the elated cries and screams and shouts of young children, teenagers, and adults alike filled the night.

He'd parked the Camaro—the money car—on Mermaid Avenue, surrounded by four invisible units ready to strike once he led Mickey O'Shay and Jimmy Kahn to the car. In the cold he trudged down the street toward Surf Avenue. In his leather jacket he had his gun stashed, as well as the cigarette lighter transmitter. Now, as he hurried through the darkened streets, he zipped up his coat, slid his hands into his pockets, and moved quickly with his head down.

He felt inspired. The bones in his body seemed to hum with an electrical excitement. He felt alive. For a brief moment, his wife's voice reverberated in his head, but it was there and then gone, just as quickly as it had come. Everything was riding on tonight, and he did not want anything to clutter his mind.

He crossed Surf Avenue quickly, slipping through the spaces between car bumpers, and meshed with the crowd of people along the sidewalk. No one, from the lowliest bum to the wealthiest entrepreneur, was out of place in Coney Island. Limousines would pull up alongside dented pickups. Affluent businessmen and politicians brushed through mobs of the stricken and impoverished without a second glance. Young and old alike converged on every street corner. It was the only real attraction in the state of New York that catered just as much to the natives of the city as to the tourists.

A number of uniformed policemen stood in a cluster by a delicatessen embrasure, loud and boisterous in their conversation. He paused here, hands in his pockets, his hair hanging in his eyes. The smell of sugared cakes and candy and roasted peanuts accosted him. In the distance he could hear the roar of roller coasters mingling with the machinelike urgency of a passing El train.

To his consternation, he found himself now thinking of his father. As a child, John had come down here often with his father. And although he could not recall anything momentous about any of those day trips—at least, not at the moment—he could certainly remember subtle specifics: the cool summer breeze coming off the ocean and prickling the small hairs on his arms and neck; the calliope music, audible up and down the avenue; the puppet shows and stilt-walkers along the boardwalk; the heady perspiration stink of the Stillwell Avenue subway station. Standing here now, and despite those memories, he had difficulty comprehending that all of that had taken place within his own lifetime, and that he had actually been so young at one time.

Through the crowd, he made his way over to one of the Nathan's carrels and stood beneath a giant yellow sign that said, "This is the original NATHAN'S Famous Frankfurter & Soft Drink Stand."

Shivering against the cold, John perused the crowd. Beside him, a barker in an American flag top-hat was shouting at a group of teenagers. A large Hispanic man walked along the avenue carrying a small child in his arms, and bearing a stringy, pink slickness running the length of his back; the child had apparently gotten sick and vomited down the back of her father's coat without his noticing.

Through a parting in the crowd, John saw Bill Kersh move down the sidewalk, pushing the last bit of a Nathan's hot dog into his mouth and wiping his hands on his trousers. Though Kersh did not look straight in his direction, he knew the man was watching him even now. Bill Kersh had a certain voyeuristic, *vulturistic* quality about him.

Across the street, Kersh's sedan was parked. A second unit was somewhere behind him, parked along the macadam of Schweikens Walk. The walk itself was a narrow, paved road aligned on both sides by parking meters that led straight down to Riegelmann Boardwalk, which, in turn, overlooked the ocean.

A strong gust of wind preceded a small child's shout in the crowd . . .

Ahead of him, the crowd bisected and Mickey O'Shay pulled his way through. He was dressed in his usual garb: green canvas coat, unwashed khakis, scuffed black boots. His coat was zipped halfway, and John could make out the weave of thermal underwear underneath it.

Mickey kept his head down, hands in his pockets. His long hair was pulled out of his face in a ponytail. A loose strand hung over his right eye, streaming in the wind. With his shoulders slumped and his back hunched forward, he looked deceptively small. It was "Mickey's Walk," Mickey O'Shay's way of fading into the crowd.

And it took him a second or two to realize Mickey was *alone.*

Roughly three feet from him, Mickey brought his head up. His eyes were like two agate stones, clouded with a multitude of blues, and stunningly clear. Beneath them, dark grooves clung to his peaked flesh like a mask. The bruise on his cheek had dulled to a sour purple-green. His lips were cut into a single sliver, chapped and peeling from the cold.

Even now, after all that had happened, John was still struck by how passionate he felt about locking Mickey up. Seeing him now, he was only prevented from slamming the bastard in the face by the very real possibility that Mickey O'Shay had before him a lengthy prison sentence.

"Where's Kahn?"

"Back at the car with the money," Mickey said. He looked like a child on a school playground, shunned and ridiculed by the other children, his eyes busy on his shoes. It was difficult to see him as the guy from St. Patrick's Cathedral anymore; he was now the maniac from his apartment, the lunatic who'd pointed a gun at his head on a tenement roof. More than anything, he wanted to nail this son of a bitch . . .

"I feel like bustin' your head open," John said, eyeballing Mickey. "You pull any shit, I'm gonna open you right up on the street."

"No shit," Mickey said calmly enough.

"Then let's go," he said, anxious to move. "I'll follow you."

He was prepared for Mickey to insist he show his end first, but Mickey gave no argument. Instead, he simply turned around and began trudging through the crowd back in the direction from which he had come. John followed him, examining the faces of the people they passed, hoping to see that one of the faces belonged to Mickey's partner.

They crossed Surf Avenue, and the mob of people thinned out. A light rain began to fall, and John hurried along a little faster, but Mickey did not pick up the pace. He'd expected Mickey's ride to be parked along Surf Avenue, but Mickey continued up 15th Street without pause. John followed, eyeing the number of parked cars along the street, and remained very conscious of the slow-moving traffic at his back. Halfway to Mermaid Avenue, he realized he had one hand wrapped around the grip of his gun inside his jacket pocket. It had been an unconscious reaction, and he silently wondered just how long he'd been holding the gun.

"Where the hell did you park?" he asked, shivering against the soft rain.

"I shoulda grabbed a dog," Mickey muttered to himself, ignoring John's question.

They crossed onto Mermaid Avenue and turned left, keeping close to the strip of buildings along the avenue. In the rain, there were very few people out on foot, though the street itself was brimming with headlights and overanxious drivers. Just a few blocks over, the surveillance units were tucked away in the shadows, eyeballing the money car. If it wasn't for the thin fog that had started creeping up from the water and negotiating the alleyways, he might have even been able to see the car . . .

Mickey paused beside a parked Cadillac. The car's engine was running and blowing exhaust into the street. Someone shifted behind the wheel as they approached. Patting down his coat beside the car, Mickey hooked a cigarette from one pocket and tried to light it in the rain. He went through three matches before he succeeded. That was when the driver's side door opened, and Jimmy Kahn looked at John from over the car's roof. In the darkness, Jimmy looked like a cadaver.

"Jimmy," he said, perhaps sounding more surprised than he was.

"Esposito," Jimmy said. "You ready to do this?"

"I'm here, ain't I?" he said. "But I don't see the counterfeit."

Jimmy's face was only half visible beneath the glow of a street lamp. He didn't say anything. John shifted his eyes to Mickey, whose head was bent down at an angle, making his eyes invisible. They were like twin bookends—or like some hideous beast sliced down the middle to form two. The rain was coming down harder now, but no one seemed to notice.

For several beats, they remained standing in the rain without saying a word. Brooding, uninspired, Mickey sucked on his cigarette, the smoke enveloping his head before evaporating into the air. The rain continued to pelt down, and a sluggish mist crawled around their ankles. Along Mermaid Avenue, traffic appeared to slow almost to a stop.

Jimmy got back inside the Cadillac.

Turning to Mickey, John said, "Whoa, whoa—what's the deal? What's going on?"

"Come on," Mickey said, chucking his cigarette to the sidewalk and opening the Cadillac's passenger door. "Get in. We'll take you to the counterfeit."

"What are you talking about? It's not here?"

"We'll get it," Mickey said. He motioned for John to get into the Cadillac's passenger seat. Then Mickey stepped over to the back door, opened it, and climbed in.

Standing on the sidewalk in the rainy night by himself, John suddenly felt something was very wrong. It was an instinctual feeling . . . and one that he tried to talk himself out of. But he knew these guys wouldn't kill him without seeing his money first. It was his only anchor, his only safety line.

He slid into the passenger seat beside Jimmy Kahn and slammed the door.

Inside, the upholstery smelled vaguely of marijuana. It was dark, with the only interior lights coming from the dashboard. Still, his eyes managed to take in everything: the cracks in the leather seats; the overstuffed ashtrays in the door panels; the cracked dome light at the center of the ceiling. The windshield was beginning to defog as Jimmy worked the car's vents while checking his side mirror. There was a sharp buzzing sound to his right. One of the vents in the dashboard was vibrating in its plastic casing.

"Where are we going?" he asked.

"To get the money," Mickey replied from behind him. This close, John could smell Mickey's scent: camphor and chloride and sweat and dirt and smoke and booze . . .

"I told you not to fuck with me, Mickey."

"Relax."

Jimmy spun the wheel and pulled out onto Mermaid Avenue. Negotiating through traffic, they hit Stillwell Avenue and turned left, heading north. They drove for several minutes in silence, until John realized they were about to get onto the Belt Parkway, heading west.

"Belt Parkway," he said, mostly for the benefit of the surveillance teams listening over the broadcast . . . if they could still hear anything. "We going back to the city?"

"Take it easy," Mickey said. He stared at John, the intermittent sodium streetlights washing over his features as they drove. The shadows of raindrops speckled his face.

"What's going on?"

Mickey produced a gun and pointed it at him.

Standing a few booths down, Kersh had noticed Mickey moving through the crowd before John had seen him. Mickey was alone—that was the first thing Kersh noted. The second was that Mickey walked head down. Most people, if their partners hid among the mob, tended to walk with their heads up and their eyes on the crowd. Mickey's eyes were on the ground.

Through the earpiece he wore, Kersh could hear most of John and Mickey's conversation, though the music and commotion around them made it difficult. He hadn't expected the deal to go down right out in the open, yet he nonetheless suffered an uncomfortable feeling in the pit of his stomach when he saw that Mickey had not brought the counterfeit with him. Still . . . it was a big money deal. All parties were going to be careful.

With some distance between them, Kersh waited for John and Mickey to cross Surf Avenue before he hustled over to his sedan, which was parked at the corner of Surf and 15th Street. He climbed into the passenger seat. Tommy Veccio was behind the wheel.

"Follow them," Kersh said, and Tommy attempted to pull out into the street. "He gets too far, and we won't be in range for the transmitter."

The sedan jerked and Veccio glanced in his mirrors, muttering curses under his breath. Here, traffic was moving too slowly.

"Christ," Kersh sighed.

"They're on foot," Veccio said. "They won't get far." Squinting, Veccio examined the street signs, then stared at the quick-moving shapes of John Mavio and Mickey O'Shay. "He takin' him to the money car now?"

"I don't know," Kersh said, chewing on his lower lip, his eyes not leaving the two silhouetted men walking up the street. A light rain was falling on the windshield, and Kersh leaned over and switched on the wiper blades.

"What about Jimmy Kahn?" Veccio asked.

Kersh hadn't heard any mention of Kahn over the transmission and told Tommy Veccio so now.

"You hear anything else?" Veccio asked, watching Kersh fiddle with his earpiece.

"Just the cars," Kersh said. "I don't think they're talking."

At the intersection of 15th and Mermaid, Kersh spotted John standing outside a four-door Cadillac beneath a street lamp, Mickey to one side, another figure standing by the driver's side door.

"That's Jimmy Kahn," Kersh said, pointing through the windshield. He picked up Veccio's walkie-talkie and radioed the surveillance units farther down Mermaid. Speaking slowly and clearly, he relayed the visual to the other units.

"They're talking," Veccio said.

"I'm not picking it all up," Kersh said.

"Should we get in closer?"

"No," Kersh said. "I'm getting . . . bits and pieces . . ." He looked up sharply, squinting through the windshield. "Sounds like . . . they don't have the counterfeit with them . . ."

Across the intersection, Kersh watched as John got into the Cadillac.

Into the walkie-talkie, Kersh said, "John just got into the Caddy. They're pulling out. Looks like they're . . . They are—they're heading east down Mermaid in the Cadillac. They're going to pick up the counterfeit. All units stand by; we're tailing." To Veccio, he said, "Follow them, but not too close."

"With this traffic, I don't think it's gonna matter."

"Just don't lose them."

Cracking his window to let some air into the car, Tommy Veccio said, "Not a chance."

"Put your hands on the dashboard," Mickey said, the gun pointed at the back of John's head.

"You gotta be—"

"Do it now."

He took a deep breath and slowly moved his hands out in front of him, gripping the lip of the dashboard. The Cadillac jerked, shuddered, and someone blared their horn. Outside in the cold and rainy night, millions of people were living their own lives.

"You gonna fuckin' rip me?" he nearly whispered.

"Take it easy, Johnny," Mickey said again. His voice was soft and articulate, like a priest speaking in confidence during confession. "Relax. We're talking about a lot of money here. We just wanna make sure this thing goes down right. No funny shit."

With the gun still pointed at the back of John's head, Mickey leaned over the passenger seat and, with his free hand, began patting him down. He felt something in one of the pockets, slipped his hand inside, pulled out the cigarette lighter transmitter and a pack of cigarettes. Without interest, he tossed them to the car floor and continued to pat him down. When his hand struck John's gun, he hesitated, then dipped his hand into John's pocket and fished out the handgun. In the rearview mirror, John watched Mickey scrutinize the gun, turning it over in one hand, before slipping it into the pocket of his own coat.

"Lift up your shirt," Mickey said.

"You—"

"Lift-lift-lift-lift-lift," Mickey O'Shay uttered, his lower lip quivering, the gun stuttering in his hand. The glare of the highway lights caused Mickey's face to appear almost skeletal in the rearview mirror. Too often he'd looked unassuming, like the perfect choirboy, innocent and unimportant. Now, however, beneath the light of truth, all reality was made visible: before John stood a monster with hateful eyes, bleached and clammy skin, and stringy hair like the tendrils of a poisonous sea urchin. The gun he held was insignificant: it was the fire that burned deep in his eyes, resident in the man's soul for so many years now that all rationality and compassion and *calculation* had long since been destroyed. What remained was the bulk of a street animal whose mind had, over time, been hideously disfigured by the occupation of such psychotic epitomes. And there was an aura about him, even beneath the glow of the streetlight, that suggested some part of Mickey O'Shay wanted desperately to betray whatever plans he and his partner had and to kill John right here on the spot.

John lifted his shirt.

Mickey's hand, cold and sticky, slapped against his flesh, feeling for a wire, feeling for anything.

"Son of a bitch," Mickey muttered, his fingers like blunt pitons against John's ribs. "You're sweating like a bastard."

"You got a gun pointed at my head, asshole."

He couldn't take his eyes off Mickey's reflection in the rearview mirror. He was reminded of the night out on Mickey's roof, and the unshakable current of murderous content he could see—could *feel*—humming like a live wire through Mickey's body. And a similar feeling that had coursed through his body, as well. He was also reminded of the image that had been summoned from the depths of his own head that night—of tackling Mickey, their feet skidding against the flare of the roof and driving up dirt, both their bodies driven over the edge by the force of the tackle. The world would have spun around and around about them, ground and sky alternating, twelve stories down, eleven, ten, eight, five . . .

Beside him, the window had fogged up from his breath. He worked his fingers along the vinyl casing of the dashboard, his mouth suddenly parched and dry. With Mickey's voice still ringing in his ears, John felt his mind suddenly click into fast-forward: he saw a struggle in which he was overpowered and shot in the head by Mickey O'Shay; he saw Katie woken in the middle of the night by a crestfallen Bill Kersh who relayed the news; Katie weeping by his father's bedside; Katie in the delivery room, giving birth between mournful wails and sobs . . .

None of that will happen. I'll take them to the car, and they'll be grabbed.

"Where are we going?" he heard himself ask again. His own voice sounded very far away.

Beside him, Jimmy said, "We told you."

"To the money," Mickey added.

"Stay with them, Tommy," Kersh said. He was leaning forward in the passenger seat, one hand pressed to the dashboard, his eyes still squinted into slits. The traffic along Belt Parkway was heavy, and he didn't want to risk losing sight of the Cadillac. "Look—they're taking that exit."

"Where the hell are they going?" Veccio muttered. "Not back to the city . . ."

"No," Kersh mumbled, his eyes glued to the taillights of the Cadillac. Off the exit ramp, the sedan nearly bottomed out as it spilled out onto the street, and the smell of burnt tires filled the car.

The Cadillac made another turn and Veccio stayed with it, two cars behind. The rain was coming down harder now, blurring the glare from the headlights and streetlights across the windshield like an abstract painting.

"What street are we on?" Kersh said.

"Uh . . ."

"What are they doing all the way out here?" Kersh muttered. He picked up the walkie-talkie and radioed the units back on Mermaid Avenue. "They're still moving," he said. "Everyone sit tight. They have to come back your way to complete the deal. We're on them."

They sped by a row of shops, the multitude of lights washing over their faces and deceiving them as to the actual distance they were traveling behind the Cadillac. Up ahead, a traffic jam at an intersection filled the night with the incessant blast of car horns and the revving of disquieted engines. Kersh watched the Cadillac swerve around the mess of cars and jam itself up against a curb. The Cadillac paused for a moment, caught behind a line of other cars, then somehow managed to negotiate its way through the confusion. It hopped the curb and took off. A second car, provoked by the Cadillac's actions, attempted the same feat, but wound up getting stuck at an angle on the curb. Very quickly, the Cadillac's taillights started to ascend up the street and into the darkness.

"You gotta move this thing," Kersh said, keeping his voice calm.

"There's nowhere to go," Veccio said, sounding irritated at the whole situation. "Look at this asshole . . ."

Up ahead, Kersh continued to watch the taillights of the Cadillac dwindle into the night until they disappeared completely.

"Damn," he muttered, trying to keep his voice calm . . . while his fingernails cut into the dashboard.

It took them several minutes to work their way through the traffic jam at the intersection, and when they finally broke free, the Cadillac was nowhere in sight. Veccio pushed the sedan up the street, letting off the accelerator until the car slowed to a moderate speed.

"What now?" Veccio said.

"Drive up this street," Kersh suggested. "Maybe we'll see them."

"Damn . . ."

"It's all right," Kersh said. "John knows what he's doing. Looks like he was right, too—they must have a second stash down here somewhere."

"I don't like this," Veccio said.

"Turn down this street," Kersh said. "I think . . ." He froze, his eyes widening, his heart seeming to pause in his chest. The only sound was a small, ceaseless ticking in his left ear.

In a faint, miserable whisper, Bill Kersh said, "Holy shit . . ."

Looking out the window, his hands still gripping the console in front of him, John watched the lights of Brooklyn whiz by. The rain was steadily growing stronger. Outside, the night rumbled with the thunder, and a brief flash of lightning lit up the horizon.

The Cadillac was heading along the northbound lane of 65th Street.

He recognized the area, having grown up just a few blocks from here—the lights of the liquor store and the all-night convenience store at the end of the block, the unchanged string of houses on either side of the street. The Cadillac rolled up 65th Street impossibly slow, and every house was suddenly familiar as well—every street corner, every stoop, every lamppost, every crack in the pavement, and every fire hydrant. With the fluid momentum of the vehicle came the increasing discomfort of being in such familiar territory with these animals.

John knew the area, knew the people. Mickey and Jimmy's counterfeit could be stashed anywhere and with anyone. When John had been growing up, this particular area had been a burgeoning network of smalltime criminals. Over time, the network had become a thriving metropolis of gangsters, hit men, and thieves.

Jimmy Kahn's Cadillac bumped along the pavement and came

to a jerky halt at a traffic light. Theirs was the only car at the light. With his hands still on the console, John could feel the engine oscillating through the dashboard. Through the windshield, the glow of the car's headlights illuminated the shower of rain.

Glancing down toward Jimmy's lap, he could see the handle of a gun protruding from Jimmy's waistband.

Staring at the traffic light, he thought it would never turn green.

And then it did.

Behind him, one of the back doors swung open and Mickey sprang out into the night. The door slammed, causing John to jump, and he spun around to see Mickey through the passenger window hustling quickly across the empty street and disappearing into the blur of sodium lights along 65th Street.

"The hell—" John spun around in his seat as Jimmy jerked the Cadillac's steering wheel in a complete circle and slammed his foot down on the accelerator. The car leapt forward and peeled through the intersection, its rear tires fishtailing along the wet pavement. The headlight beams washed along the storefronts, and the pungent stink of exhaust fumes filled the car.

Confused, John turned and stared at Jimmy, who was racing back down 65th Street toward the parkway. The speedometer needle was steadily rising.

"What the fuck you doing?"

"Where the fuck's your money?" Jimmy said. "You tell me right now."

"Back at Nathan's. What *is* this? Where the hell's Mickey going?"

"Deal's off. We're taking your money. If you got a problem with that," Jimmy said, "you're dead. And so is your wife."

The words struck like a hammer. He was aware of a steady heat creeping up through his legs, spreading throughout his body, and coursing down the length of his arms. He could feel his body begin to tremble, to overload, and his ears went fuzzy, filled with cotton.

"Mickey don't hear from me in twenty minutes," Jimmy continued, "that means the deal's gone bad, and Mickey'll do some damage."

Around him, the world spun on its side.

"You and your wife don't gotta die over someone else's money."

Then something burst inside him. He sprung at Jimmy Kahn in a frantic, unthinking reflex, fingers clawing, arms flailing wildly. With all the force he could muster, John slammed the heels of his hands against Jimmy's face, tearing at his face, his eyes, felt the solidity of the man's flesh, the bone beneath, the texture and feel and temperature of the man's skin. The assault was unexpected, and Jimmy's head jerked to the left, spiderwebbing the window and leaving behind jagged streaks of blood and hair.

Jimmy's hands jerked the wheel, and the car lurched forward, swerving into oncoming traffic. The lights of the city seemed to spin all around them, distorted and made ridiculous by the rain-slicked windshield.

John grabbed two handfuls of Jimmy's hair and repeatedly slammed his head into the window until the glass finally shattered. Freezing rain and biting wind burst into the car. He could feel granules of glass pelt his face, wet with rain, freezing in the blinding wind. One of Jimmy's hands came off the steering wheel; he began clawing blindly at John's face.

Leaning over the seat, John slammed his own foot down on the accelerator. The car blasted through traffic. Letting up, John slammed the brakes. The car spun wildly, and Jimmy cracked his head against the front of the steering wheel.

John took one hand and grabbed Jimmy around the neck, squeezing until he could feel the lifeblood coursing through Jimmy's veins, then jerked the man's head forward, repeatedly slamming his face against the car's steering wheel. Jimmy uttered a strangled moan, coughed up a gout of blood across the dashboard and instrument panel, and shot a flailing hand upward, clawing blindly at the ceiling.

Before them the oncoming traffic split down the center, headlights cascading around them on either side in undulating streamers of light, horns blaring, tires screeching atop the wet pavement. He felt the tires catch, lose ground, spin ineffectually, then shoot the car forward like a missile. The lighted façades of innumerable storefronts were suddenly large and real all around them. There was a rattling crash, and the Cadillac hopped the curb on the opposite side of the street. A sound like a gunshot rang through the night as one of the front tires exploded, propelling the vehicle forward and to one side. The lights of a single storefront washed across the windshield in a dizzying blur—then brick—then street—then more lights.

There was a bone-crushing crash as the Cadillac advanced over the sidewalk and ran straight into the front of a pharmacy. The car was jarred to a sudden standstill while a shower of concrete and glass rained down upon it: large bricks and pieces of debris slammed the crumpled hood, windshield, and roof in a tumultuous concussion as a waft of white dust surrounded the vehicle.

The force of the crash sent both him and Jimmy against the dashboard, and he felt a sudden burst of pain flare up along his ribcage and upper thigh. His head jerked forward and rebounded off the dashboard, and a fantastic display of carnival colors blossomed beneath his eyelids. The driver's side door burst open, and he was hammered by freezing rain.

Pressing a clawed hand into Jimmy Kahn's face, John reached down and tore Jimmy's gun from his waistband, then scrambled up over Jimmy's body and out onto the sidewalk.

He started to run.

"Jesus!" Kersh shouted. "Tommy!"

Veccio spun the sedan's wheel and the car jumped lanes, sluicing through the wet street. "I see it. Jesus *Christ!*"

The sedan shuddered to a stop against the curb and a wall of people, bundled against the weather, stood like spooked cattle around the partially destroyed front of a pharmacy. Kersh already had his door open and one foot on the ground before Veccio could slam the sedan into park. Too many people, too much confusion. Kersh struggled through the crowd, scraping shoulders and elbows and knees, until he broke free to the inner circle of onlookers and stopped, his heart banging furiously against his chest.

The Cadillac they'd been tailing was here, driven front-first into the building. The car's hood was crumpled like an accordion, and steam and the smell of burnt rubber filled the air. The driver's side door flung open.

Kersh withdrew his gun and approached the vehicle.

Jimmy Kahn lay motionless behind the wheel, one leg slumped out onto the sidewalk, the left side of his body soaked in a cocktail of sleet and rain and blood. His face and scalp, too, were covered in blood and lacerated in a number of places. But he was still alive.

Veccio slammed through the crowd, his eyes bulging at the sight of the telescoped Cadillac. He wasted no time shooing the mob away, though they did not go willingly and remained standing in a semicircle around the perimeter of the scene. On the street, cars were slowing for a better look.

"John!" Kersh shouted, peering into the Cadillac. He could see no one else. "John!" Gun still leveled at Jimmy, he scanned the crowd for any sign of John. "Christ!"

Veccio appeared at Kersh's side and stared at Jimmy Kahn. "Where's John?" he asked Kersh.

And although he suddenly thought he knew, he did not say so to Tommy Veccio. Instead, he pulled his cell phone from his jacket and slammed it on the hood of the Cadillac. "Here. Get another car down here to take this son of a bitch."

"Where are you going?"

Coming down 65th Street, Kersh had recognized the area almost immediately . . .although the plausibility of his initial thought had then seemed inconceivable. He'd been a few blocks from here a couple of nights ago . . .

John's father's house . . .

"Where are you going?" Veccio shouted again.

Getting behind the wheel of his sedan, Bill Kersh did not answer.

The world a blur around him, John continued to run in the direction of his father's house. His body was racked with pain, his vision blurred from the crash, his head throbbing in a thousand different places. In his right hand, Jimmy's gun felt weightless. Time was lost to him now, indistinct and confused, and he had no concept of how much of a head start Mickey had on him. Up ahead was the Eleventh Avenue intersection, and he cocked his head back, closed his eyes, and pumped his arms and legs for all they were worth. The rain was coming down in thick, blinding sheets; it felt like cold, wet nails being driven into his body. His lungs burned, his breath hot and sour.

He turned onto Eleventh Avenue and nearly spilled to the ground to make the turn. The rain was coming down in torrents now, whipping him from every direction, and he threw himself forward and forced himself to charge down the street. In a hideous blur, the street appeared to tilt and waver before his eyes—and he saw, up ahead in the darkness, the lumbering, hunched shape of Mickey O'Shay moving down the sidewalk toward his father's house.

Mickey O'Shay.

He felt something rupture inside him. Somehow, his legs began moving faster. Mickey's shuffling form was suddenly close, very close . . .

A flashbulb image in his head: Mickey on the tenement roof, pointing the gun at him. Then Katie's voice over the phone—*I trust you, John.* The accumulation of Kersh's concerns suddenly tore through his mind like the tips of a million white-hot needles. In that instant he saw his father, dying in a starched white hospital bed, holding Katie's hand, their mouths moving but speaking no words—

Then he was on Mickey like a jungle cat, all pain and exhaustion wiped out by the adrenaline pump of his wrath.

Mickey turned around, startled, just as John cracked him across the face with Jimmy Kahn's gun. There was the give of Mickey's skin against his hand, the solidity of his skull, and then Mickey pinwheeled backward and lost his balance. He crashed to the sidewalk, the wind knocked from him, a large bloody gash across his left cheek.

Mickey had no time to recover.

Propelled by a confusion of rage, John was on top of Mickey a moment later, his teeth clenched, his arms swinging wildly. He grabbed the front of Mickey's long hair and continued to slam the back of his head against the concrete, blood and rainwater splashing up around him in icy sheets. Mickey didn't utter a sound. With his right hand, John brought the butt of Jimmy Kahn's gun down on Mickey's face, felt the give of Mickey's jaw, felt the rupture of his right cheekbone. A loud buzzing rattled through his head, and his eyes went funny, causing Mickey's image to double and triple before him. Rainwater and blood stung his eyes. A burning against his own face, down his neck: Mickey's fingernails digging into his flesh. Yet he did not relent; he was consumed by fury, driven by an unmitigated rage. Trapped heat inside his body, burning straight through to the surface of his flesh. It was as if a well of liquid madness had volcanoed from deep within him. Closefisted, John pummeled Mickey with his left hand. And each time he brought his fist down on Mickey's face, he felt that madness augment and multiply and grow—filling him with the divine ability to continue until forever.

I trust you, John. The way she'd looked when she'd told him she was pregnant, that they were going to be parents . . . the way she looked in her sleep, bundled—

Mickey swung an arm up, clipping John's chin, and quickly reached inside his green canvas coat for his own gun. In the blur of movement, he managed to hold the gun up—poised in the rainy night—then, with a stuttering hand, swung it—

John stumbled back, his mind reeling, his body strung like a taut wire about to snap.

He emptied Jimmy's gun into Mickey O'Shay's body.

He couldn't hear the sounds of the gunshots. He couldn't hear *anything.* In the cast of the moonlight, Mickey's eyes fluttered and his mouth coughed up a bubble of blood. His body, partially propped up off the ground, shook violently, then fell backward, splashing against the curb. Mickey's gun fell into the street. One leg twitched. He could see Mickey's chest rise once, twice—then stop.

The world continued to spin. Sounds began filtering into his head again, too sharp, too overbearing. Bursting, furious, he felt himself rise to his feet, only faintly aware of the empty click of Jimmy's gun in his right hand . . . only faintly aware that he was smashing his foot into the side of Mickey's ribs with feral brutality. He could single in on no specific thought or emotion, just merely felt them all course through him like charges of electrical current.

And then, as if he had run into a brick wall, he felt the world rush back to him. Pain exploded through his body, and his legs felt suddenly weak. He felt himself begin to tremble, hesitate, fluctuate—then crash down on top of Mickey's broken body.

Blood soaked the front of Mickey's canvas coat. Mickey's face, slack and openmouthed, stared sightlessly up at the rain. Tracks of blood, seemingly too bright, ran from his mouth.

Mickey O'Shay was dead.

Shaking, John thought he heard police sirens rushing up the street. Then the rush of a car engine, in the street and very close to him. Looking down, he saw he still held a clutch of Mickey's hair in his fisted left hand. To his right he could feel the looming presence of his father's house bearing down on him and, doubled over in the pouring rain, one leg in the rain-swollen gutter, he managed to turn his head in its direction.

One of the upstairs lights was on in the house. Katie's silhouette stood in the window, looking down at the street. Looking down at him . . .

Katie . . .

He'd brought it home to her. Like a common criminal, and after all he'd done to keep his two lives separate, he'd brought it home to her. The notion struck him like a sledgehammer to the chest, and he nearly collapsed under the weight of his own inescapable horror.

He did not hear Bill Kersh's voice behind him, did not hear the rush of sirens along 62nd Street, did not hear the downpour of rain all about him.

His eyes remained on his wife.

He wanted to go to her, but found he could no longer move.

CHAPTER FORTY-FOUR

HE AWOKE EARLY IN THE SOFT AMBIENT light of a new morning. Moving from the bedroom and into the hallway, the floor cold against his bare feet, John made his way into the kitchen and paused by the sink. Outside, the world was white with snow yet untouched by the toil of the day. The sky was gray and cloudless and absent of birds.

He found himself milling about the apartment for some time, doing nothing except thinking an occasional thought. Several times he deliberated just outside the bedroom door while his eyes moved across the tender terrain of his sleeping wife.

In the bathroom, he stood for several long minutes naked before the mirror above the sink. His skin looked too pink in the lighting. With disinterest, he looked up at the light fixture. He thought about how his wife had joked about installing a skylight. Thinking of that now, he managed to summon a half-smile. But the smile did not last long.

The shower water was cold, and he did not wait for it to warm up. He washed quickly and with a businesslike professionalism, hesitating only once to watch the water swirl and wash down the drain. For a few seconds he was hypnotized by it, soothed and unnerved by it at the same time. His head began to ache, and he pressed two fingers to the jutting brow bone above his right eye. It occurred to him then that he'd had the headache all morning. Only now had he really felt it.

It had been several weeks now since Tressa Walker's body had been discovered. Wrapped in a sheet and buried beneath busting trash bags, discarded soup cans, and folded cardboard boxes, she was found in an alley behind a barbershop in Hell's Kitchen. She'd been beaten to death.

Her daughter, Meghan, had been taken into the custody of child welfare and was quickly dispatched to Roosevelt Hospital to be treated for pneumonia.

He shut off the water and dried quickly, allowing his eyes time to linger on the fogged-up mirror.

A skylight would be nice, he thought. *I don't care what floor we're on—a skylight would be nice.*

Before leaving for the day, he stopped again in the doorway of his bedroom.

He felt hurt by how close she'd come to the whole thing. Yet throughout everything, she'd remained admirably strong—stronger than he had ever thought she *could* be—and he found that *he* was the one who had really been changed by the events of that night, that *he* was the one who had to move ahead and think past it. That night, looking out the window, she had seen everything. He hadn't known what to expect from her afterward, but she had surprised him by remaining very calm and understanding. Oddly enough, and for whatever reason, it was her sympathy that hurt him the most. This was his fault. All of it. He'd done this to her, and it weighed heavily inside him. And although she appeared sympathetic to the situation, seemingly unchanged after witnessing her husband's actions, he couldn't help but wonder what she thought of him now. Sometimes, he wondered if she thought of him with that same confused anxiety with which Tressa Walker had spoken of Mickey O'Shay and Jimmy Kahn.

He went to the hall closet. He automatically sifted through the coats for his leather jacket—then paused. There, wedged between his leather jacket and one of Katie's jackets, was his father's black wool coat. He pulled it out and stared at it for a moment, trying to remember how it had gotten here. He couldn't remember, but slipped it on nonetheless. The sleeves were too long, and it felt too tight in the shoulders.

His father had died alone in the hospital on the night he had chased Mickey O'Shay down and killed him in the street. And three days later, on a cold and overcast afternoon, the old man was buried in Greenwood Cemetery. He and Katie had remained by the grave for some time, whipped by the frozen, bitter wind, and daunted by both the simplicity and finality of life. As the wind picked up and the afternoon grew toward evening, he and Katie turned from the grave and moved back to the car. Neither of them said a word to each other.

Outside in the cold, he pulled his father's coat around his body, shivered against the wind, and moved down the stoop.

A light snow began to fall.

Agents had taken to stacking daily newspapers on Bill Kersh's desk whenever they contained some information pertaining to the counterfeit case. This was done partly in good humor and partly in silent veneration by those agents who had never, and would never, work an undercover case. And although Kersh appreciated both the humor and the veneration, he never read the papers.

"You're in early," John said, coming up behind Kersh and tapping the man lightly on the shoulder.

"Reports," Kersh said. "I think better in the morning, before anything important has time to happen. What are you doing here?

I thought Chominsky said to take some time off."

"I took time off. I don't need anymore. Anyway, I've got that meeting with Sullivan today."

Following Jimmy Kahn's arrest, the Secret Service had gone after as many of Kahn and Mickey's cohorts as they could round up. In most instances, no one said a word and there was no incriminating evidence against them to force them to talk. In other instances, there *was* evidence: Glenn Hanratty, known to most of the lowlifes in Hell's Kitchen as "Irish," was arrested based on fingerprints he'd left on the silencer boxes John had bought from Mickey. Following his arrest, Biddleman wasted no time issuing a warrant for Calliope Candy. When the back room was tossed, agents uncovered several more silencers, as well as the equipment used to make them. Also, packed inside a crate of Tootsie Pops was a large collection of handguns. NYPD was still checking ballistics, and probably would continue to do so for some time.

Sean Sullivan, the cutter who'd been paired up with John for the hit on Ricky Laughlin, was the only person they'd gotten a hold of who was half willing to cooperate. Sean was young and impressionable, and John actually felt there was a good chance the kid would go to the witness stand to testify.

"Horace Green," Kersh said.

John looked up from his desk, rubbing his hands together. He couldn't shake the numbness from them. A souvenir from his time on the frozen streets of Hell's Kitchen. "What?"

"Remember I said I recognized that name?" Kersh said. He tapped a finger against one of the printouts on his desk. "Telephone records from Charlie Lowenstein's house in Queens. Lowenstein's wife had made a few calls to a Horace Green. I'm going to pay her a visit this afternoon." Kersh frowned. "You okay?"

"Yeah. Sure."

"What about Katie?"

"She's doing all right," he said, uncertain whether that was even the truth.

Kersh's gaze lingered. "You let me know," he said after a moment, "if there's anything I can do."

John just nodded and turned away.

Clouds had appeared, and it started to snow lightly by midafternoon.

"You want something to drink?" he asked Sean Sullivan, sitting across from him at a diner booth in lower Manhattan. "Some coffee?"

Sean shook his head. The kid hadn't been sleeping properly, and the skin around his eyes was the color of rotten gums. He'd shown up just five minutes before, wrapped in a stiff ski jacket zipped to his chin. When he took it off, John could make out fresh bandages along Sean's arms through the sheer fabric of his shirt. He was cutting again.

"I want you to understand how important your testimony is, Sean," he continued. "Between you and me—we say the right things, Jimmy goes away for a very long time. And that means you don't have nothing to worry about."

"Yeah," Sean muttered, but he wasn't in genuine agreement. He had not yet agreed to testify at Jimmy Kahn's trial. However, John was confident the kid would do it if pushed in the right direction. Sean Sullivan just needed someone to hold his hand. Not to mention the Secret Service had a case against him, too. His refusal to testify would wind him up in prison.

"What we're gonna do," he said, "is get you out of the city when the trial starts, put you in a nice hotel room somewhere. We'll have an agent with you the whole time."

"This like that witness protection thing?"

"Kind of."

On the tabletop, Sean's hands shook. "Where's Jimmy now?" the kid asked.

"Jail," he said.

"I mean, like," Sean stammered, "he ain't gonna make bail or nothin'?"

"Not a chance, Sean."

Sean chewed at his lower lip. His eyes bounced nervously between John and the sticky tabletop. He cracked his knuckles, tapped one knee against the bottom of the table. "You think I can get one of those agents now? Like, to watch my apartment?"

With Mickey O'Shay dead and Jimmy Kahn behind bars, he could really see no reason. But to allay the kid's fears he said yes, that it could be done.

"And Jimmy—he won't know I'm doin' this, *if* I'm doin' this?"

"Not until the trial," he promised him.

He chewed his lower lip some more. Something in his eyes reminded John of Tressa Walker, and how frightened she'd been that night at McGinty's when she'd first started talking to him about Mickey O'Shay and Jimmy Kahn.

Then, after what seemed like a lifetime, Sean Sullivan said, "Okay. Yeah, I'll do it. I'll testify."

Since Mickey's death and Jimmy's arrest, Roger Biddleman was slowly becoming a prominent fixture around the New York field office. He walked the halls strapped in dark suits tight enough to work the creases out of his elbows, and moved with a lively expeditiousness that seemed more fitting for a runway model. Immediately after the case had broken, he'd commended John with a handshake and a pat on the back, saying the words prosecutors always said when they knew their number had come in—words that made them sound more like insightful modern art dealers than lawyers. He'd been a bit discontented that Mickey O'Shay had been killed, but he was not one to grieve over a loss. Instead, he focused on the path ahead. And as the days came and went, John was pleased to find that Roger Biddleman's interest in him, now that his work had been all but completed, was rapidly diminishing.

An interesting tidbit of information came from Bill Kersh's meeting with Ruby Lowenstein, Charlie Lowenstein's wife. Skinny and distressed, she had not taken long to admit to Kersh how strapped for cash she'd been ever since her husband had been locked away. Things had been too tight, she said, and she didn't deserve to suffer because her lousy husband had been tossed in jail. Some time before she'd made it a point to visit Lowenstein in prison and pester him about her situation. Finally, tired of his wife's badgering, he'd told her to contact a friend of his, a good Jewish guy from his old neighborhood, to pick up some old items of his and see what he could do. The items were the plates and negatives of the counterfeit hundreds. The good Jewish guy from his old neighborhood happened to be Horace Green.

So the connection was made: Green had taken the plates and negatives to try and sell as a favor to an old friend. . . but before he could, he ran into a little roadblock. The roadblock was two young Irish guys from Hell's Kitchen who would wind up hacking Green to pieces and stealing the plates and negatives.

As he was with everything, the ever-present Roger Biddleman was quick to tune in to Kersh's newfound information. He jotted notes and made phone calls and smiled wider and wider at the agents with each passing day. Along the way, he adopted the annoying habit of tapping a Bic pen against any available surface of the field office at any given time. He also started skipping lunch and, after just two weeks, trimmed down considerably.

For Roger Biddleman, life had never been better.

☘

To appease Sean Sullivan, the Secret Service agreed to put him up in a hotel room in Jersey until after the trial. Three times a day, agents would check in on him in alternating rotations. One gray, overcast Tuesday, Dennis Glumly arrived with Tommy Veccio at the hotel, hoping to get some more information from Sullivan about any other homicides he'd gotten wind of. Outside the hotel room door, Veccio knocked twice and shouted for Sullivan. The kid didn't answer.

"Maybe he's out?" Glumly suggested.

"He's supposed to stay here," Veccio said. He knocked again and called Sullivan's name. Still, no answer. He tried the knob. It was locked.

"Don't you have a key?" Glumly asked.

"No . . . Sullivan has always opened the door."

Both men exchanged a subtle look of discomfort. Several minutes later, an old Hindu woman shuffled down the corridor escorted by Dennis Glumly, and paused outside Sean Sullivan's door. She produced a ball of keys from her apron just as Glumly and Veccio unholstered their weapons. The old Hindu woman unlocked Sean Sullivan's hotel room door. It swung open, and she backed away.

Veccio stepped in first, followed by Glumly.

"Sean!" Glumly called. "Hey, Sullivan!" Scowling, turning to Veccio, who had crossed the room and was moving toward the closed bathroom door, he said, "If this goddamn kid split . . ."

Veccio pushed the bathroom door open. "Oh, for . . . Jesus Christ—"

Glumly hustled to Veccio's side while the old Hindu woman poked her head into the room.

The bathroom was humid, the mirror over the sink fogged, the taste of copper in the air.

Sean Sullivan lay naked in the bathtub, soaking in a few inches of lukewarm water stained pink. His eyes were open and glazed over, staring blindly at the tiled shower wall opposite him. His left arm lay draped over the side of the tub, split open from his wrist to the crook of his elbow. A pool of blood collected on the floor beneath his dripping fingertips. His right arm lay against his chest, also cut, bleeding against his pale flesh and into the tub.

Caught in the nest of his pubic hair like a netted fish was a straight razor, its blade shiny with blood.

CHAPTER FORTY-FIVE

THE NEWS CAME JUST BEFORE THE WEEKEND.

Roger Biddleman, standing before a glowing landscape of lower Manhattan, turned from the window as John and Kersh entered the office and smiled. He immediately went to both men and pumped their hands in a firm shake before slipping behind his desk and beckoning his guests to sit as well. The entire office conveyed the faint aromas of cedar and pipe smoke. Stacks of computer printouts sandwiched inside manila folders leaned against the side of Biddleman's desk.

"To begin with," Biddleman said as John and Kersh took their seats, "I just want to say how much I appreciate and admire the work you've both done on this case. Especially you, John. Mickey O'Shay was a lunatic. I can't even begin to imagine what it was like. It's unfortunate it ended the way it did though; I would have liked to have him stand trial. But," and his voice dropped an octave here, "the important thing is that you got him off the street."

John sensed a rising disquiet on the horizon. "Well," he said, "we have the Kahn trial."

Pressing his lips together, Biddleman rubbed two stiff fingers across his forehead, leaving behind white streaks in his skin. "Jimmy

Kahn's not going to trial," Biddleman said.

John's eyes swung in Kersh's direction, then back to Roger Biddleman. "What do you mean?"

Biddleman shifted uncomfortably behind his desk. All former amiability had been stricken from his face. "Kahn's attorney cut a deal with our office."

John felt like someone had just dropped a concrete block into his lap. "What are you talking about?"

In a toneless voice, Roger Biddleman said, "Kahn has been rising in the eyes of the Italians. He's tied in to the Gisondi crew over in Brooklyn. We're going to use Kahn to get to them."

"Oh, I don't believe this. You can't be serious. You're letting him walk?"

"No, not exactly," Biddleman said. "He'll plea to a conspiracy charge, do about a year or so. Then he gets to work for us. The time in prison will even enhance his reputation with the Italians."

He stared at Biddleman in disbelief. He felt numb. It took all his effort to pry his eyes away and face Bill Kersh. "You agree with this?" And without waiting for an answer, he turned quickly back to the attorney. "Chominsky knows about this?"

"I wanted to speak with both of you first," Biddleman said. Then, sensing John's rebellion, added, "But our decision is final."

"We have this guy nailed for over thirty years," he said, jabbing a finger at Biddleman, "and you're gonna let him plead to some shit-ass charge—"

"There are a lot of things involved here," Biddleman insisted. "This decision was not made hastily—"

"Why?" He stared at Biddleman with such intensity he could make out the fine web of veins that ran across the bulb of his nose. "What the hell's going on? This son of a bitch was your catch of the day and now, just like that, after all I went through, he's not important anymore? Help me make some sense of that . . ."

Biddleman folded his hands on his desk. His fingers pressed hard into his skin, turning the tips white. "This is a complicated business," Biddleman said matter-of-factly. "Targets change, priorities change. You did a great job. Without you, we would have never reached this point. It's the next step."

"So you're gonna let this animal back on the street just to catch some ninety-year-old Italian guy ten years from now? You've gotta be out of your mind! Our informant was killed, a witness commits suicide, I put my family in jeopardy—and for what?" He pushed himself out of his chair, his face red, his hands threatening to fist. "And you keep pushing and pushing!"

Kersh lifted a hand. "John . . ."

He spun on Kersh. "You're gonna sit here and listen to this?"

Kersh looked firm, impassive. "This isn't your personal crusade. You're wasting your time. I told you about this . . ."

"I'm not going for this," he said. "I'll go to the papers . . . be on every goddamn show." He leveled his gaze on Biddleman, who watched him from behind his desk with the eyes of someone completely detached. "You'll have to answer for this."

"You do that," Biddleman said simply, "and you're history. I'll have the FBI lock you up for obstruction."

He didn't want to be in here with Roger Biddleman a second longer. Just looking at the man, he was reminded of the months he spent on the streets and away from his family, while his father died and his wife sat home alone. "Where's your boss?" he barked at Biddleman. "Get him in here. I wanna talk to your goddamn boss."

Biddleman stood from behind his desk. Bulbs of perspiration dimpled his brow. His thin lips, too, were dotted with sweat, yet remained firmly pressed together. "You have to understand this is best for what we do. You know that, John. We work our way up the ladder. You did your part . . . and now we have to continue."

"How stupid is that? This is not just a normal case! I know how it works—but this guy's a maniac! You can't work with him."

"With O'Shay gone—" Biddleman interrupted.

"Mickey O'Shay was only half the problem! You've only cut out half the cancer! You let Kahn out, he'll *grow* another Mickey O'Shay! You know what this guy is like!" He could feel his anger boiling at the pit of his stomach. He took a deep breath, and it burned his throat. "I'm telling you right now—you're making a big goddamn mistake here."

"I hope not. But that's not your worry," Biddleman told him.

"I don't believe this . . ."

"John . . ." Kersh said beside him. He lifted himself from his chair. "I'm leaving. Let's go."

"You have nothing to say?" he said to Kersh.

"No," Kersh said. "Let's go."

"What's this?" Kersh said, stepping into the pit, his meaty arms folded about his chest. "I thought you hated coming down here . . ."

John looked up from the table. He had been sitting there smoking a cigarette, trying to cope with the information Roger Biddleman had dropped on him earlier that day. He felt so hollowed, gutted like a fish. Thinking about the case only managed to turn his stomach. In a way, it even embarrassed him, almost made him feel foolish and stupid.

"I can't believe this," he said to Kersh. "I just can't believe it. Sitting here, thinking over this shit. I screwed myself on this." He shook his head, blew smoke toward the ceiling. "Everybody made out on this but us."

Kersh bit his lower lip. "I don't think O'Shay made out too well," he said. "Or those other assholes we got that can't make a deal."

"You're a very practical man," he muttered.

"The truth is often a terrible weapon of aggression," Kersh intoned.

"So where do we go from here?"

"Don't know about you," Kersh said, "but I'm planning on going home and taking a nice hot shower, putting on a Charlie Parker record, eating some Frosted Flakes, and going to bed. I'm exhausted."

Shaking his head, John crushed out his cigarette. "I wish I could handle this thing like you."

"Eventually you will," Kersh said, speaking now as if the words were unimportant. "But for now, our part is over. Biddleman was right about *that,* anyway." His lips came together to form a smile. "But I know what you did, kid. And you impressed the hell out of me."

Offering Kersh a tired smile, John pushed away from the table and leaned back in his chair, rubbed his face with his hands. His eyes fell on his father's coat, slung over the back of one of the other chairs.

Kersh furrowed his brow and slowly unfolded his arms. "Ahhh," he finally muttered, turning to leave, "go home, John."

"Wait."

"What?"

"You knew," John said. Back at Biddleman's office when they'd gotten the news, Kersh had appeared disappointed . . . but not necessarily surprised, or even upset. "You knew this case was cursed from the start . . ."

Bill Kersh just shrugged. "Too many agendas, too many fingers in the pie. People lose sight of what the real deal is. I've seen it before. And it'll happen again." The older agent paused against the wall. "You never would have felt satisfaction on this case, John. You doomed yourself. You never would have gotten back what you put into it, and that was what I was trying to explain to you. But you didn't listen because you had *your* agenda." Kersh smiled without humor. He looked sloppy and tired and deep in thought. "Think about it."

Rubbing his eyes with his hands, he said, "Think about what?"

Kersh smiled wearily. "Learn to put your heart in what's important."

There was nothing he could say to that.

"Good night, John."

He watched Bill Kersh turn and walk away. From his seat at the table, he listened to the older agent's footfalls retreat down the hallway until he could hear them no longer.

Again, his eyes fell on his father's coat. It was folded messily over the back of a chair, half inside-out. He could see the inside pocket stitched into the lining . . . and could see something poking out from the pocket . . .

He leaned over and pulled the object out of the pocket. It was a thick white envelope with the raised Hallmark emblem on the back. Inside was a greeting card with a pair of cartoon mice propped against each other—an older mouse with glasses and a walking cane, a younger one with a propeller cap and a red balloon. He opened the card to find his father's shaky, concentrated printing inside. A number of words had been scratched out and rewritten, but he could read it all easily enough:

> Son,
>
> I have watched you grow from a wide-eyed little boy to a teenager, then finally to a man with a family of his own. I love you, Katie, and the new baby very much.
>
> I know I was hard on you growing up, and that it caused problems between us. But don't confuse my strictness with anything other than a father doing what he believed was best for his son. You were a good boy, John, and you've become a good man, a good husband, and soon you will be a good father, too. I love you, kiddo, and am proud of you and all that

you've accomplished. I couldn't have asked for a better son.

Thank you for a wonderful life.

Love,

Pop

"Christ, Pop." He felt a swell of emotions rise up inside him—anger, frustration, sadness—and he found himself deeply hurt by the loss of time and by the words he'd never had the chance to say to his father.

I love you, Pop.

Softly, he wept.

CHAPTER FORTY-SIX

He entered the darkened apartment in silence, pulling off his wet shoes and leaving them by the front door. In socks, he moved down the hallway and slipped off his father's coat, hanging it in the closet.

In the bedroom, he stood for several seconds beside the bed, listening to his wife sleep. Then, his body blue and pale under the moonlight streaming in from the bedroom window, he crept around to his side of the bed and sat down on the mattress, careful not to wake Katie.

She rolled over anyway. "Am I dreaming?" she whispered.

"It's me. I was trying to be quiet."

"You're real or a dream?"

He smiled. "I'm real."

"You had to work late again?"

"No," he said. "I stopped by Dad's house on my way home. I had to get something."

Leaning over, he set a framed photograph on the nightstand beside the bed. He could not see the picture in the darkness, but that didn't matter—he knew what it looked like from memory. His father stood, wearing his firefighter gear—strong, powerful, untouchable.

He peeled off his clothes and slipped beneath the covers beside his wife.

"I'm sorry," he said, and kissed the top of her head. She wrapped her arms around him. Warmed by the feel of her body, his hands no longer felt cold, no longer felt numb. "I'm just . . . I'm sorry . . ."

"For what?" Her faith had never wavered, her trust and belief never been in question. She'd been so much stronger than he'd ever imagined. In many, many ways, much stronger than he.

"Never mind," he said. "I'm taking some time off work for a while. I wanted to be here with you. I figured we could spend some time together, maybe have a baby."

She laughed quietly to herself, and he could feel her hot breath on his neck. "Speaking of babies," she said, "I thought of the perfect name."

"Yeah?"

"We'll name him John," she said, "after his father."

"And his grandfather," he said. Tracing a finger lightly across the contours of her face, he said, "You're sure this kid's gonna be a boy?"

"One hundred percent. Are you nervous?"

"About being a dad? I guess so. Maybe a little. I don't know."

"You'll do fine," she told him.

He pulled her closer in the darkness.

"The best that I can," he promised.

Don't miss the next exciting novel by
Ronald Damien Malfi from Medallion Press:

THE ASCENT

RONALD DAMIEN MALFI

**At the top of the world,
no one can hear you scream . . .**

Following the death of his ex-wife, Tim Overleigh gives up his lucrative career as a sculptor for the world of extreme sports, but after a caving accident nearly takes his life, he falls into a self-destructive downward spiral. Then he runs into an old friend, Andrew Trumbauer, who convinces Tim to join him and a team of men to climb the Godesh ridge in Nepal—a journey that will require crossing the Tibetan "beyul," or "hidden lands," to seek out the elusive Canyon of Souls.

But what begins as a journey steeped in Tibetan folklore and mysticism soon turns into an experiment in torment, destruction, and death, as the members of the team learn they are players in a game of personal revenge and may not escape the mountain alive.

ISBN# 978-160542067-7
Hardcover / Thriller
US $25.95 / CDN $28.95
SEPTEMBER 2010

FORTY-EIGHT X

THE LEMURIA PROJECT

BARRY POLLACK

A colonel with a shadowy past . . .

A military science experiment out of control . . .

The human race facing extinction . . .

On the tropical island of Diego Garcia in the middle of the Indian Ocean, the United States has gathered together its most talented geneticists to conduct top secret experiments. Their goal—to create a revolutionary new warrior. A warrior so strong, so valiant, so expendable that the age of "casualties of war" would become only a sad and distant memory. And so the Lemuria Project is brought to life.

Haunted by a dark and dangerous past, Colonel Link McGraw is the officer chosen to train these new "soldiers." He understands the rules of engagement and agrees to serve his country, reestablish his professional reputation, and secure his freedom in the process. As a trained and commissioned officer in the United States Armed Forces, McGraw knows what constitutes the perfect soldier. It's simple: Follow orders without question.

When Egyptian beauty Fala al Shodaha and Israeli Joshua Lantz, scientists in their own right, stumble across the top secret project, they are determined to uncover its true nature and pursue their quest to Diego Garcia. Tensions mount as Lantz and McGraw clash over the project—and vie for the affection of the lovely Fala. When they discover they aren't the only ones on the island competing for her attention, shocking truths are revealed.

Is it too late to save themselves—and the entire human race—from almost certain annihilation?

ISBN# 978-193475502-0
Hardcover / Thriller
US $24.95 / CDN $27.95
DECEMBER 2009

M
edallion
PRESS

M
Medallion
PRESS

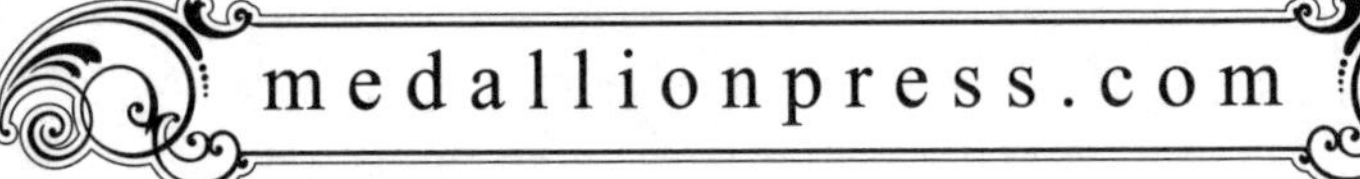
medallionpress.com